SAVING JACE

A FADA NOVEL

REBECCA RIVARD

WILD HEARTS PRESS

Saving Jace: A Fada Novel, Book 4

The Fada Shapeshifter Series

Wild Hearts Press~P.O. Box 628/Havre de Grace, MD 21078

Publisher's Note: This book is a work of fiction. The names, characters, places, and incidents are products of the author's imagination, or have been used fictitiously and are not to be construed as real. Any resemblance to actual persons living or dead, locales, or events is entirely coincidental.

Cover art and design by Laura Gordon/The Book Cover Machine

Editing by Katherine Teel

Saving Jace/ Rebecca Rivard. — 1st ed.

ISBN 978-0-9985826-5-8

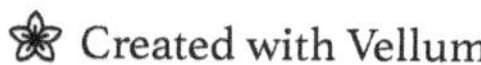 Created with Vellum

PROLOGUE

OF GODS AND SHAPESHIFTERS

They say Dionysus is a wild, untamed god, beautiful in the way of all gods. He loves wine and women, and his rites are dark, tempting, addictive. It was Dionysus and his followers, both fae and human, who created the first fada during his infamous bacchanals. By some mysterious magic, the fada were shapeshifters, a mix of fae, human and animal genes—and a touch of the god himself.

The first fada lived in the Mediterranean Sea, water shifters who could change to dolphins, seals, otters, even sharks and other fish. They were dark, ruthless, and as untamed as the god who'd first given them life. From the Mediterranean, they spread throughout the world's rivers and seas.

Centuries passed, and then one day, a tiny clan of Arab fae from North Africa's Fertile Crescent got together and created the earth fada, shifters who could change to land-based animals like cougars or bears or deer. Dionysus found it amusing to provide the spark of life to this new creation. The North African fae gifted the quartz and its special energy to earth fada alone. But like most fae gifts, it came with an edge—with the right incantation, a fae can control an earth fada through his or her quartz.

Fortunately, that knowledge is known to only a few North African fae.

When an earth fada reaches a certain age, he or she is taught the secret of the quartz. They vow to guard the secret with their lives. Because if the fae ever learned the earth shifters can be controlled through their quartz, they're doomed.

1

THIRTEEN YEARS EARLIER: THE DARKTIME

ace Jones slogged through a cold December rain to his den on Baltimore's west side. He was dog-tired after a rough two-month assignment in South America. All he wanted was a shower and a six-pack.

His best friend Adric was pacing the street in front of Jace's den. "Takira had her cub."

Jace's exhaustion fled. That was bad. His sister wasn't due for at least another month. He'd hated like hell to leave her, but you didn't say no to your alpha. "She's okay? It's too early—"

"She's fine, and the cub is, too. I just came from their den."

Jace raced down the stairs to his den, Adric behind him, and tossed his backpack on a chair. "Your uncle Leron? He's expecting me to report."

Leron was the Baltimore alpha. An abusive, out-of-control alpha who didn't deserve the title. Sending Jace out of the country when his sister was heavily pregnant was typical behavior for the bastard—keep families and friends apart.

Adric's face hardened. He was Jace's age—barely in his twenties—but the past few years had left him with an old man's eyes. "Leave him to me."

"Thanks, man." Jace stopped just long enough for a shower and then rushed across town.

He'd missed the clan's winter solstice celebration. It was early Christmas morning. The streets were empty except for a few hard-eyed humans for whom December twenty-fifth was just another day.

Takira's mate let him into their tiny apartment. Silver was a half-blood fae, beautiful in the way of all his people. Right now his stunning face was drawn. He looked as exhausted as Jace.

"How is she?" Jace demanded.

"Fine. Tired, but fine."

Takira was in bed, a tiny bundle in her arms. She looked weak and way too thin for a mother who'd just given birth, her skin an ashy brown, but she smiled proudly up at Jace.

"She has her father's chin." She touched the infant's sharp chin. "And his pointed ears." She grinned at her mate.

Silver's spare features softened. "She's got a lot of her mom in her, too—and I thank the gods for that."

Jace kissed his sister's cheek and stroked a finger over the cub's soft black curls. "She's beautiful."

"Do you want to hold her?"

He gulped. It had been years since he'd held a baby. He and Takira were earth fada. Their Baltimore clan had been decimated by a bloody civil war. The two of them had lost both their parents by the time they were in their teens.

The Darktime. That was what the clan called the bloody civil war that Leron Savonett had sparked when he'd set out to become alpha no matter what the cost—and the gods knew, the cost had been tremendous, year after year of killing and dirty deeds.

Things had become so bad it was all they could do to survive. Food was scarce, which meant the few cubs that had been born were sickly or died.

His lungs clenched as he stared down at the infant.

Takira kissed her tiny nose. "Meet Uncle Jace, sweetie."

"Hello, love." He lifted the child from his sister's arms. "She's so light," he murmured. "Can't weigh much more than a feather."

Takira chuckled weakly. "She's a newborn, idiot."

"Mm," he said, all his focus on the precious bundle in the crook of his arm. He pressed a kiss to her soft forehead. Her scent was milky-sweet, not a whiff of the graveyard stench that emanated from most night fae. He detected a hint of silver and iron, though—silver from her fae blood, iron from the human.

My niece. I'm an uncle.

It struck him like a punch to a gut.

The cub gazed unseeingly up at him with wide, catlike eyes. Then she gave an adorable little stretch like the unfurling of a flower before settling back into the tightly curled position of a newborn. Jace swallowed hard—and just like that, his heart was hers.

"Her name is Merry," Takira said. "Because it's Christmas— and it's a happy name." As followers of the old gods, the fada celebrated the winter solstice, but their Jamaican mom had made a big deal of Christmas, too.

"It's perfect," he said. "She's perfect."

"I just wish Mama could've seen her." A tear leaked from the corner of Takira's eye.

Jace's chest squeezed. "She would've loved her, and Dad would've, too." Their father had been a mix of Cherokee and Scottish, with a deep, fierce love of family that he'd passed on to his two offspring.

"Yeah." Takira smiled through her tears.

Silver was hovering protectively nearby. He touched Takira's shoulder. Their eyes met, and Jace guessed he was sending reassurance through the mate bond. Takira rubbed her cheek against Silver's palm.

Merry's tiny brow furrowed, and Jace rubbed a finger over it. "Don't worry, little one. I've got you safe."

"Thank you," said Silver.

Jace gave Merry a last kiss and handed her to her father. Night fae were stunning, with pale skin and black hair. Silver might be half-human, but he looked all night fae—mesmerizing as a glittering cobra. Jace could barely tolerate being in the same room with him; the man made his skin crawl. Night fae were the energy suckers of the fae world. They fed on dark thoughts and emotions.

How the hell had Takira fallen in love with the man, and worse, taken him as her mate?

But Silver's expression was tender as he looked down at his new daughter.

Takira moved restlessly. "You can't tell the alpha. He thinks I lost the baby last month. Promise you won't tell."

"The alpha doesn't know?" Jace pulled a chair up next to the bed. "How the fuck did you manage that?"

Takira flicked a glance at Merry, then lifted her chin. "I lied."

"The hell you did. With a cub inside you?" He scowled. Fada couldn't lie, not without making themselves violently ill. And since she was pregnant, the cub would've been affected as well.

"I had to." His sister's expression was fierce. "It was the only way to save her."

"She was sick as a dog after," Silver interjected. "That's why she's so thin—for two weeks, she could barely keep food down. But she had no choice. Your friend Adric told us that Savonett was going to force Takira to abort the baby. He doesn't want the clan to be saddled with a fae bastard." His mouth twisted.

Anger flared in Jace. "When you were seven months along?"

At his sister's nod, he snarled. "Someone needs to put that S.O.B. down."

It was Leron Savonett's fault their parents were dead, too. Oh, he hadn't killed them directly—just sent their mom to almost certain death in an overseas skirmish, and then dragged their dad into clan politics. Leron was a vile, power-hungry excuse for an alpha.

"She's a fada," Takira said. "I know it. We all have a few drops of fae in us, just like we all have some human. But she's going to be able to shift."

"How do you know?"

His sister touched her quartz. "I can feel her drawing on my energy already."

He nodded.

"We're going to hide her," Takira said. "Only you, Adric, and Marjani"—she named Adric's sister—"will know about her. For now, Marjani's covering for me—Leron thinks I'm still in Florida on a mission. I'll go back to work in a few weeks."

"Maybe you should just run," Jace said, but even as he spoke, he knew it was hopeless. The alpha was too powerful—and fada trackers were the best in the world.

"He'll hunt us down," she returned. "You know he will. The best thing is to hide in plain sight."

Jace nodded. "I'll back you up any way I can. And you know Adric will."

"I know." Takira grabbed his hand. "Promise me something. If anything happens, you'll keep her safe."

"Of course," he replied. "You don't even have to ask. You know I'd die for her."

"Say the words." Her gaze searched his desperately.

He clasped her hand between his. "You have my vow. I will keep your daughter safe no matter what it takes."

And between the five of them—Takira, Silver, Adric, Marjani and Jace—they were able to keep Merry a secret for four years.

And then one bleak January day, Jace had stopped by his sister's apartment to find it had been trashed. The small family was gone.

Jace, Adric and Marjani had torn Baltimore apart looking for them—and then extended their search up and down the East Coast. But Jace never saw Takira or Silver alive again.

2

THE PRESENT DAY

*E*vie almost didn't see him.

It was after eleven, and she was walking home from a late shift at the restaurant. Thunder rumbled and raindrops splattered onto the asphalt. She raced the last few yards down the alley and into her tiny backyard. The lavender her mom had planted was about to bloom. The purple spikes trembled in the rising wind, their sharp scent mixing with the coming storm.

Suddenly, every hair on her nape lifted. She froze and glanced around. The yard was dark save for the light cast by a single bulb over her back door.

There. A man huddled by the stoop, his eyes an unearthly green glow in the gloom. His breath shuddered in, and the chunk of quartz hanging from a cord around his neck caught the light.

Earth fada. With those glowing eyes and the quartz, he had to be.

Without taking her gaze from him, Evie scrabbled in the garden for something she could use as a weapon. The fada were shapeshifters: hard, dangerous creatures who rarely interacted with humans. An earth fada lurking outside her door could only mean trouble.

Her fingers closed on a rock. She came back to her feet and raised it threateningly. "Get the hell out of here."

The man gazed back at her, unblinking. Then his lips curved. The bastard was *laughing* at her.

Anger shivered through Evie. Anger, and fear. Her younger brother Kyler was in the house—at least, he was supposed to be. She had to get this man—this fada—out of here.

"Did you hear me?" Her fingers tightened on the rock. "I want you gone. *Now.*"

His eyes closed. The small smile faded, and he rested his head against the concrete foundation. "Can't."

"What do you mean, you can't?"

She inhaled sharply as he slid sideways, boneless as a ragdoll. *Was it a trick?*

Several seconds ticked past. The man didn't move.

She took a step forward. That's when she smelled the blood, sharp, metallic.

Fuck. She darted a glance around her. She lived in a rowhouse, with three houses to one side of her and six to the other. Usually you couldn't walk two yards without a neighbor popping out to see what was up. Where was nosy Mrs. Linney when you needed her? Or Kyler, for that matter?

"Hey." She nudged the shifter's shin with her toe. "You all right?"

When he didn't move, she dashed up the steps to the back door and yelled for her brother. "Kyler?" She pounded on the door. "Open up! It's me, Evie."

No answer.

She set her jaw. Would it kill him to be where he was supposed to be for once? She dropped the rock and dug in her backpack for her keys, her eyes on the motionless earth fada.

Her fingers closed on the keys. She shoved the house key in the lock and pushed open the door. The kitchen was empty but the light was on. She dropped her backpack on the nearest chair.

Her brother sauntered into the room, tall and thin and full of sixteen-year-old attitude until he saw her face. "Evie? What's the matter?"

"Outside." She jerked her chin at the back door. "A shifter. He's hurt—bleeding."

"Seriously?" Kyler pushed past her and vaulted over the railing to the injured man.

Evie was right behind. "Hurry. I have a bad feeling about this."

Somehow, she *knew* she had to get the shifter inside—and soon—or he was dead. The fada were the killers of the magical world—assassins and mercenaries. If this man was injured, someone dangerous was after him.

Kyler slid his hands under the fada's shoulders and head. "Grab his legs."

She hurried to obey. The rain was pouring down now, drenching all three of them.

"Ready?" Kyler asked.

"Yep."

"One, two, up," he said, and they lifted him.

Evie staggered, struggling to keep her end up. "Damn, he's heavy."

"Here, let me." Kyler moved his hands lower on the shifter's back, taking more of the weight.

Together the two of them maneuvered the limp body up the stairs and into the kitchen.

Her brother raised a dark brow. "Where should we put him?"

"The floor, I guess."

They set him down on their sad excuse of a vinyl floor. Evie swiped the rainwater from her face and peered down at the unconscious man. His face and shoulders were wet, but the dark stain spreading across his T-shirt wasn't from the rain.

While Kyler locked the door, Evie scrubbed her hands in the kitchen sink and squatted down for a closer look.

Despite her worry, she couldn't help noticing how good-looking he was. A lean, powerful build. Warm brown skin. High, broad cheekbones and thick black lashes spiked with water drops. But then, the fada had a few drops of fae blood, and with it a touch of the fae's beauty.

She eased up his T-shirt and sucked in a breath. He had a deep slash across half his lower abdomen, and there was another small but deeper wound right above it.

"Damn," said Kyler. "Somebody cut him good."

She nodded grimly. "Get me something to clean it with. Hot water, but not too hot."

Kyler nodded and filled a bowl with warm water. Meanwhile, Evie found a couple of clean kitchen towels, and then knelt next to the fada and dabbed at the blood. From what she knew about first-aid, the wounds weren't life-threatening. Neither was spurting blood, which meant the knife or whatever had cut him hadn't hit an artery. And the blood seemed to be clotting.

The biggest danger was probably infection, and hopefully he'd be out of here before she had to worry about that.

She wrung out the cloth and dabbed at the gashes again. She'd heard somewhere that whiskey disinfected a wound, but only thing she had in the house was a six-pack of beer.

"Do you think we should pour some beer on it?" she asked Kyler. "You know, to kill the germs?"

"*No.*" The earth fada's eyes opened. The intense green had faded to hazel. "Use...my quartz."

Evie didn't know much about shifters, but everyone knew earth fada had a special connection with their quartz. This man's looked like a run-of-the-mill rock to her, but what did she know?

She reached for the pendant.

"*No.*" He grabbed it himself. "Don't touch. Only...me."

"Okay." She jerked her hand away. "Take it easy. I'm just trying to help."

The fada's fingers toyed with the quartz, and it started to glow the same green as his eyes had. His lips moved, and the blood stopped seeping. His wounds seemed to close a bit, too.

"Wow," said Kyler.

The fada's head dropped back onto the vinyl. "Can't."

He released the pendant. The quartz lost its glow and turned back into a plain, smoky gray with a touch of purple. Pretty, but nothing out of the ordinary.

She swallowed. "So what can I do?"

His eyes shut. "Nothing."

She sat back on her haunches. "Look, you are *not* going to die in my kitchen. You got that?"

He just grunted.

Kyler dropped onto the floor on the other side of the shifter. They met each other's eyes over his body.

"Maybe I should call an ambulance," she said.

"What good would that do? Fada use their own healers, and I'm not sure a human doctor could help anyway."

"They could clean it out and stitch him up."

Outside the storm boomed. Wind whipped through the trees and rain drummed against the kitchen windows. A crash of thunder shook the house. She and Kyler stared at each other but neither moved to take out their phones.

Her shoulders slumped. It had been a long day. First, she'd gone to her biology class at the community college and then she'd rushed home to work her waitress shift. Now she was exhausted, out of ideas.

Hopelessness rolled over her. "He's going to die," she said dully. "And take us along with him."

Kyler's throat worked. "There's nothing we can do."

The earth fada roused himself to growl, "Fucking fae. He's messing with your minds—you have to fight it."

"What do you mean?" Evie asked.

The fada's hand was on his quartz again. The muscles of his neck strained with effort. The glow infused it again.

"Touch me," he gritted.

"Touch you?" she repeated. *What was the point?*

"*Now*. Anywhere."

She and Kyler glanced at each other and then Evie shrugged. "All right."

She took the earth fada's hand while Kyler touched him on the shoulder. Nothing happened.

Evie blew out a breath. Why bother? She was so tired, and soaked from the rain. Maybe she should just lie down…

Then something odd happened. The hand touching the earth fada warmed. She frowned down at it. The heat moved up her arm to her shoulder, and then she and Kyler were enfolded in its warmth.

Her brother's mouth dropped open. "What the fuck?"

"Night fae," the fada rasped. "Don't…talk. He—hear you."

Evie's stomach did a complete flip. "A night fae? That's who's after you?"

She'd only seen one night fae in her entire twenty-six years, but one had been enough. He'd been coming out of an after-hours club in downtown Baltimore, tall and loose-limbed with black hair and pale skin. She'd stopped and stared. He was rock-star sexy in his tight black shirt and leather pants.

Then he'd turned and caught her looking—and smiled, a cold show of teeth. Darkness washed over her, powerful, seductive. When she'd shuddered, his smile had only increased.

Evie had sprinted out of the alley, his mocking laugh echoing in her ears.

The earth fada gave a terse nod. "Afraid so."

Evie shut her eyes. *What had she done?*

For the most part, the fae kept to themselves, considering humans as somehow less—which was fine with her. You did *not* want to attract the attention of a fae. You especially didn't want to attract the attention of a night fae.

She looked at her white-faced brother, the brother she'd promised her mom to protect, and stifled a moan.

The rain eased. They all heard the crunch of gravel.

The night fae was right outside.

Evie grabbed the fada's hand with both of hers and prayed. Hard.

3

———————

Why the hell had Jace stopped for a drink at a Grace Harbor bar?

Grace Harbor wasn't his town. It was right on the edge of Rock Run river fada territory, and normally a Baltimore earth fada wouldn't be welcome this close. But he'd been visiting the quartz mine his clan was excavating just north of Grace Harbor, so when a couple of Rock Run men had invited Jace and the other miners out for a beer, he'd figured why not? It wasn't like he had anyone to go home to.

It was Thursday night and a popular local band was playing, so the bar was crowded. Some of the fada males had hit on the human women, but Jace made it a practice to stay far away from humans—especially females. He'd drunk a couple of beers, watched a few innings of the baseball game playing soundlessly on the TV behind the bar, and then called it a night.

Outside, night had fallen, but the air was still warm from the June sun. Jace headed out the back door to the parking lot and his motorcycle.

The night fae had been waiting in the narrow opening between the bar and the building next door: tall and pale and humming with a dark excitement. Night fae liked to toy with their victims—a scared, panicky victim was catnip to a creature who fed on negative energy. First, he'd attacked Jace energy-wise with invisible tentacles that slid over his skin, seeking to entwine him in a net made of all his darkest moments: *fear...death... loss...betrayal...*

To fight back, Jace had been forced to draw on his quartz's energy. For a good ten minutes, they'd been locked in a silent battle in the shadows.

Sweat beaded Jace's forehead. His quartz's song was faint, and fading fast. The night fae had smiled, sensing that his foe was almost out of energy. He darted forward and slashed a knife across Jace's belly.

It was like taking a red-hot poker in the gut. Jace grunted and doubled over. The night fae came at him again with the knife, going for a deep, killing blow. The knife slid into Jace's stomach below his navel. But his attacker had made one mistake —he'd let himself get within reach of a man whose animal was a jaguar.

Jace twisted away. His claws shot out. He whirled around and struck at the night fae, ripping out his throat. The man gurgled and staggered back until he hit the side of the bar. He slid down the wall and slumped to the ground, dead.

Jace crouched on the asphalt, breathing hard. The pain was excruciating. He drew in a breath, and the blade's scent confirmed it. The bastard had stabbed him with an iron knife.

Iron was poison for a fae. The only way the night fae had been able to handle the knife was to wear leather gloves, and even then, he would've only been able to wield it for a short time.

Iron didn't affect the fada like it did a pureblood fae, but the blade had nicked a small artery, sending the poison directly into his bloodstream. Already his vision was hazing over.

Jace had dragged himself to his feet.

Take it...out.

He'd grabbed the hilt with both hands, set his teeth, and jerked the knife out.

From far away, he'd heard himself groan. The fucking thing hurt even worse coming out than it had going in. He let it fall to the ground and used the last bit of energy in his quartz to heal the nicked artery. The spurting blood slowed to a trickle.

He looked around with blurred vision.

Must...get out of here.

He shook his head and forced himself to focus. The night fae was sprawled at his feet. He could still see his mocking smile as he thrust the knife into Jace's belly.

The man wasn't smiling now.

Thunder grumbled in the distance. Jace's skin prickled. He glanced around but the parking lot appeared empty. That didn't mean another night fae wasn't nearby—or about to teleport in.

There was no way he could ride a motorcycle right now. He grabbed a bandana from his pocket, pressed it to his abdomen and hurried around the corner of the nearest building. The movement sent a dizzying jolt of pain through him.

He leaned against a loading dock, his breath sawing in and out. He grasped his quartz, drawing what energy he could from the vibrating crystals. The quartz warmed in his hand. Given time, it would refill with energy, but time was something he didn't have.

From the parking lot came the sound of two men speaking in hushed tones. He stilled, his heart rate ratcheting up. He couldn't tell if they were night fae, but his skin was still tingling, so he forced himself to move.

He limped around a chain-link fence and zigzagged through a couple more blocks, trying to throw off any trackers. He was fading fast when he slipped between two buildings and ended up on a dark, quiet street. At some point, he'd lost the blood-soaked bandana, but maybe that was a good thing—if he was being tracked, it would draw the tracker's attention, give Jace time to escape.

He'd left Grace Harbor's small business district. To his left was a hair salon and across the street there was a post office, but on his side, there was a long row of attached Formstone houses.

Two doors down, a plump gray-haired human sat on a concrete stoop, cigarette in hand. She glanced at him and did a double take.

His lips peeled back to show his canines, and he snarled lowly, his animal rising at the sign of a threat.

"Easy now." The woman came to her feet and backed up. "Tim?" she called through the screen door. "You there?"

Jace didn't wait to meet Tim. He hurried at an awkward, lurching pace down the sidewalk. Thunder crashed and he scented the rain close behind. That was good—it would wash away the blood, hide his scent.

There was a break about halfway down the row of houses. He darted into it and found himself on a narrow asphalt path that led to an alley behind the houses.

Fuck. He was almost back where he'd started, the bar just a hundred yards to the left. He cursed under his breath and headed the opposite way. He was staggering now, the sole streetlight hurting his eyes. A few doors from the end of the alley, his legs gave out.

Hide. Dark. Den.

But his den was thirty-some miles south in Baltimore. He crawled into the nearest backyard, instinctively seeking a shadowed corner, and collapsed against the concrete steps.

He was lightheaded from the iron burning in his blood. He took a few short, ragged breaths and then tested his quartz. The tiny crystals were nearly depleted. Instead of humming their customary song, they were barely vibrating. Too weak for him to draw on its energy to heal himself. Too weak even to signal for help.

Jace leaned his forehead against the side of the steps and waited to die. If the iron didn't kill him outright, the night fae would find him.

A woman appeared out of the dark. Dreamlike, he wondered if an angel had descended to save him from the night fae. An edgy blond angel in jeans and a black muscle tee.

Then she threatened him with a rock and he jolted awake. *Fucking wonderful.* She was going to bash his head in. A female, and human at that.

His mouth twisted wryly—and then he passed out. The next thing he knew, he was on the kitchen floor blinking up at a fluorescent light.

He tensed. There were two humans now—the pretty blonde and a lanky teenager with short brown hair and suspicious eyes.

He had to get out of here. He tried to roll over, but the blonde was doing something to his stomach. He got ready to fight before he realized she was cleaning his wounds. But that wouldn't be enough, not against iron. He tried to use his quartz, but he was too weak, the crystals still barely vibrating.

He let his head drop back to the floor. An earth fada's quartz was almost a living thing. With rare exceptions, his crystals' song had always been with him ever since he'd bonded with his own personal quartz as a cub. To have the song fail now was hard, like watching a family member do a slow fade into death.

And there was nothing to stop the iron burning a path through his veins, poisoning him slowly and inexorably.

His gaze fixed on the woman. She was striking, a study in contrasts—warm brown eyes topped by dark, definite eyebrows; high cheekbones in a narrow, intelligent face. Her mouth moved. She was scolding Jace, telling him he'd better not die in her kitchen.

Inside he chuckled—if he were himself, he could take her out with a single swipe of his claws. But she had spirit. He liked that —it reminded him of Takira.

He inhaled, testing the humans' scents. They were tense and afraid, but they seemed to want to help. And his cat liked the blonde's smell. It relaxed a bit, easing them both. When the female touched Jace's stomach, the cat damn near purred.

That was strange.

Then every fine hair on his body stood on end. All the sass went out of the blonde. Even her hard-eyed brother drooped.

Night fae. Hell. Jace had brought trouble straight to these people's door.

"Think," he managed to say. The woman leaned closer to hear. "Happy thoughts."

He used the last ounce of energy in the crystal to protect them and then passed out again.

"Happy thoughts?" Evie repeated. "Yeah right." She met Kyler's eyes and said, "Better do what he says."

The door knob rattled and she froze. She darted a glance at the deadbolt. But somehow either she or Kyler had remembered to lock it in the rush to get the injured man inside. Fortunately, the door was solid wood and the shade was down on the back window so he couldn't see into the kitchen.

Because she *knew* it was a man. She could almost picture him on the top step—tall, dark and coldly determined, sending feelers out.

A night fae.

She stilled, her breath shallow—as if she could fool the fae when she knew he could sense them somehow. But the earth fada was helping to shield them. The sense of dread lessened, but her mind was a complete blank.

Across the unconscious man's body, Kyler had his eyes screwed shut. Her wannabe badass looked scared to death, his face pale, his lips pressed tight.

Her heart clenched. That frightened, vulnerable expression took her back seven years to when Kyler's dad had died and all they'd had left was their mother.

Their mom had tried her best, but those first few months, she walked around like a zombie. Evie's dad had left before Evie was two, but Kyler's dad had been an anchor for all of them. His sudden heart attack was just too unfair. Meanwhile, the money was slowly running out. Her mom's part-time job and food stamps only stretched so far.

Kyler had tried to act tough, but one night their mom had snapped and thrown them outside, telling them not to come back until bedtime.

Kyler had slipped his hand into Evie's. "What are we going to do?" he'd asked in a small voice.

Evie had taken a deep breath. "Why don't we walk to the playground?" Fortunately, it was summer, and there was another hour of light. She and Kyler rode every piece of equipment on the playground at least three times, and by the time they went home, their mother had calmed down and let them back in without any fuss.

The rattling stilled. But the fae was right outside. Evie didn't know how she knew, but she would've bet her pitifully small bank balance on it.

Happy thoughts, Evie. Happy thoughts.

Kyler's tenth birthday. Yeah, that had been a good day. Things were better by then. Their mom had a job as a server at an upscale restaurant and Evie was working at a pizza place after school and on weekends. They were living paycheck to paycheck, but at least they had food in the house.

She and her mom had pooled their money to buy Kyler the latest video game console and a couple of games. Evie had baked Kyler's favorite cake—chocolate banana, but hey, he'd asked. Now she tried to visualize his expression as he blew out the candles and then tore open his packages.

He'd learned not to expect much. That made his grin when he'd seen the console all the more special. His face lit up brighter than the ten candles on his cake. "This is the best birthday ever!"

Evie smiled at the memory, even as she squeezed the fada's hand a little more tightly.

More footsteps...but they were moving away.

Evie expelled a breath as the ominous presence receded. She *felt* the night fae moving down the alley, testing other doors.

She stiffened. There had to be blood on the back steps. Had the fae seen it, or had the rain washed it away in time?

Happy thoughts, damn it. Don't think about it—not now.

Things went completely quiet—and then, whatever was shielding them abruptly failed.

She glanced down to see the earth fada was unconscious again. The ominous feeling increased. Evie's spine iced. The night fae was coming back.

She and Kyler exchanged a look.

"Don't stop," she mouthed. "Happy thoughts." She set a finger on either side of her mouth and mimed a smile.

His lips twitched. "If you could see what you look like..."

She made a face at him, and then they both smiled. Weakly, but it worked. The ominous feeling slid past her.

She made another face at Kyler, and he caught on and made one back. They took turns making silly faces at each other. A chuckle escaped Evie, and she froze until she realized the best thing was to make the night fae believe they didn't know he was out there.

Kyler made a monkey face at her, and she returned, "Yo mama."

He chuckled.

And the night fae was gone.

Evie let out a shaky breath. "Better wait another couple of minutes," she said in a low voice.

"Yeah." Kyler looked down at the unconscious man. "What are we going to do with—"

"Hell if I know. What's he doing in Grace Harbor anyway? This is Rock Run territory."

The local fada were shifters who changed to water animals like dolphins or sharks. The nearest earth fada clan was thirty-five miles away in Baltimore.

"We can't just throw him out," Kyler said. "The night fae could come back."

"I know." Evie pinched the bridge of her nose. Their narrow rowhouse consisted of two floors, with the first floor taken up by the kitchen, living room and a tiny half bath. The upstairs consisted of two bedrooms and a full bathroom, but they couldn't carry an unconscious man up a flight of steps to one of the bedrooms. "I guess we'd better move him onto the couch."

"Sounds like a plan." Kyler rose to his feet.

It took them a few minutes to work out the best way to transport the injured man to the living room, but finally Kyler had the idea of putting him on a sheet. They each took an end, Evie at his head this time.

"One, two, up," her brother said.

This time Evie was ready for his weight. She braced herself, bent her knees and lifted her end of the sheet—and she still staggered. But she gritted her teeth and said, "Got him."

They maneuvered him past the kitchen table, Evie walking backward. She turned into the living room and almost knocked the man's head against the wall.

"Almost there." Kyler strained to take more of the weight.

The couch was just another few feet, backed up to the wall that divided the living room from the kitchen and the hall.

"Just lift him a little higher," Kyler said. "He's sagging in the middle."

Evie gripped the sheet and obeyed. "Good grief," she muttered as they eased him onto the couch. "What does he have, concrete for bones?" The man had a lean, powerful build. He didn't look like he should be so heavy.

The man lay sprawled where he'd landed, his breath shallow and one foot dangling off the couch. Evie lifted his head and slid a small pillow beneath it while Kyler pulled off his sneakers. He wasn't wearing any socks. Kyler arranged his legs so that his foot wasn't dangling off the couch anymore.

Evie folded up the hem of the fada's T-shirt and sucked in a breath. The cuts on his stomach had turned an angry, puffy red.

Her brother gave a low whistle. "That doesn't look good."

"Can a wound get infected that fast?"

"I have no idea," he returned, "but their biology isn't like ours."

She frowned. "I thought they healed faster than us. Plus, he did something with that crystal to heal it. He shouldn't be getting worse."

The earth fada moaned.

Evie laid a hand on his forehead. His skin felt clammy. "Shh. You're okay."

A pulse at the side of his neck jumped erratically. She set two fingers on it. "It feels really fast," she said to Kyler. "Is that normal?"

He moved a shoulder. "Fuck if I know."

The earth fada's eyes popped open. They were a bright, feverish green again. "Salt."

"Salt? Are you thirsty?"

Kyler stood up. "I'll get him some water."

"Yes." The fada moistened his lips. "But...iron—poison. Need salt. Clean." He indicated his stomach.

"You want me to clean it out with salt?"

He gave a short nod. "Salt. And warm water."

Kyler returned with a glass of water. Evie took it and lifted the fada's head enough so that he could drink. His eyes closed but he greedily gulped the water down.

She handed the glass back to her brother and helped the fada resettle his head on the pillow. He lay there, eyes closed, breathing shallowly. His light brown skin had an unhealthy yellowish tinge to it. Evie narrowed her eyes. Were those red streaks moving from the wounds out across his belly?

"What was he saying about the salt?" Kyler asked.

"He said clean it out with salt and warm water."

The fada's eyes opened. "One part salt, four parts water," he said in a clear voice. "And now. Or I...die."

4

———————

Jace could guess who was behind the attempt to kill him—Lord Tyrus. Nothing else made sense.

Tyrus was the son and heir of the night fae prince himself—and Silver's half-brother. When Tyrus learned that Silver had mated and had a daughter, he'd put out a contract on the entire small family to ensure his father had only one heir —himself. The assassins had gotten first Takira, then Silver, but a Rock Run fada had saved Merry.

Prince Langdon, Tyrus's father, didn't want it known that he'd spawned a mixed-blood granddaughter, but after he'd learned Tyrus was hunting Merry, he'd protected her with a special ward that would kill any night fae who tried to harm her, even Tyrus.

Thank the gods Merry was safe at the Rock Run base. She didn't live with Jace. He'd lost track of her for several years, and when he'd finally found her again, she'd been adopted by two Rock Run fada. As far as Merry was concerned, they were her parents now. Jace hadn't had the heart to take her away from them.

The pretty blonde frowned down at Jace, and his mind spun away from Merry.

The pain in his belly was a raging fire now. The small amount of healing he'd been able to do before seemed to have been reversed while he was unconscious, another sign of iron poisoning.

"Salt and warm water?" The blonde's low, practical voice came from down a long dark tunnel.

All he could do was tell her what to do and hope it worked. Because if not, Jace would die, and probably the two humans as well. He'd somehow eluded Tyrus's henchman, but the night fae lord was smart—and brutal. He'd track Jace down, and snuff these two like flies.

Fortunately, his rescuers followed directions. The boy returned with a pitcher filled with the salt solution. The woman knelt on the floor next to the couch and then, to Jace's surprise, touched his cheek.

He squinted in her direction and her face swam into view, pinched with concern. "I'm Evie, by the way, and this is my brother Kyler." She indicated the skinny dark-haired teenager.

Her fingers were cool—or was it because he was so hot? He moistened dry lips and then croaked his name. "Jace."

"Nice to meet you, Jace."

His lips twitched despite himself. It was so human, introducing herself at a time like this...but sweet.

Her fingers brushed his forehead and he tensed, anticipating what was to come.

"Try to relax," the woman—Evie—murmured.

She smelled like fresh soap; she must have washed her hands again. He could've told her there was no need. The iron would kill any germs, and if not, the salt solution would do the rest. That was, if the iron didn't kill him first.

"Relax," Evie repeated, and to please her, he smoothed out his forehead.

"Okay." She wet a clean rag with the salt solution and dabbed at the wounds. "I'm going to clean this out for you."

"No," he said, and she stopped and looked at him, her brow furrowed. "Pour it into the cut," he said. "You have to...rinse it out. Poison." He rolled onto his side and dug his fingers into the couch, knowing what was to come.

"Okay," she said. "Take it easy."

He drew a slow breath, but there was no way he could relax. "Just do it," he said between clenched teeth.

Her brother handed her a folded bath towel. She tucked it under Jace's stomach to catch the overflow, and then set her fingers on either side of the lower cut and gently pulled it open. "You pour," she told Kyler.

"Good," Jace said. "That's good. Clean it out."

The kid tipped the pitcher and salt solution poured into the wound.

Jace's whole body bowed in pain. God's cat, it was like getting stabbed all over again. He tightened his jaw and rode it out. Because screaming, especially in front of two humans, would be the final humiliation.

And then, mercifully, he passed out.

When he came to, Evie was stroking his forehead. "There, there," she said in a motherly voice at odds with her edgy appearance. "It's all over now."

He stared at her through slit lids. "Thanks," he managed to say.

She looked down at his stomach. "Did it work?"

He frowned, checking inwardly. The fire in his blood had subsided to a simmer. "Think so."

"Can we do anything else?"

"Water."

"Just plain water?"

He gave a single nod.

She removed her hand from his forehead and he grabbed for her, latching onto the hem of her shirt. "Not you. Him." He jerked his chin at the teenager.

Her dark brows lifted. "You want me to stay?"

He nodded again. He knew he was being unreasonable, but both cat and man wanted her to remain close.

"Okay." She took his hand. "Kyler will get you the water, then."

His fingers folded on hers. "Thanks," he whispered.

When the water came, she put an arm beneath his shoulders to support him while he drank greedily. It was ice cold and wonderful.

He finished the glass, and she laid his head back down on the cushion and pressed a wet rag to his forehead. He closed his eyes in relief at the coolness. How did she know exactly what he needed?

The storm had slowed to a drizzle. From far away, he heard Evie tell her brother to go outside and make sure there wasn't any blood. Smart woman.

"The rain must have washed it away," Kyler replied.

"Get the hose out and wash it down anyway."

"'Kay." He heard Kyler's footsteps move into the kitchen.

Evie touched Jace's arm. He pried opened his eyes to see her holding another glass of water. "You need liquids—you're burning up. Unless that's your normal body temperature?"

He shook his head. "Water...good."

"That's what I thought." Again, she slid an arm beneath his shoulders and held the glass to his lips.

After drinking his fill, he rested his head against her shoulder and let his eyes close again. She'd changed into a dry T-shirt—gray with a purple star in center. She stilled and then to his satisfaction, remained where she was. She was a sturdy little thing—the arm around him had a lean strength—but the spot between her shoulder and her breast was soft and comforting. He inhaled deeply, filling his nostrils with her sweet, womanly scent.

His breath sighed out. Tomorrow he'd be embarrassed at how

weak he was acting, but right now, he didn't fucking care. Because he needed this.

"Do you want any more?" The glass nudged his lips.

When he shook his head, she lowered him carefully to the pillow. His cat whined, but both of them were too weak to do anything about it.

Evie came to her feet. He watched through slit lids as she stretched. The hem of her T-shirt rode up to reveal a tan strip of skin above her waistband.

She glanced down and caught him looking, and her eyes flickered. She unhurriedly brought her arms down and straightened the shirt.

"I'm going to see how Kyler's doing. You'll be all right for a few minutes, won't you?"

He nodded. His cat wasn't happy, but the man told the cat to suck it up.

She touched his shoulder. "Try to rest. I'll be back as soon as I can."

He listened as her footsteps moved down the hall to the kitchen.

He drew a slow breath. With Evie out of the room, the effects of the iron seemed worse. He touched his abdomen. The salt had neutralized the iron so that it wasn't still feeding into his bloodstream, but he felt like he'd been run over by a frigging semi.

He'd live, as his soldier mom used to say, but he was in for a rough night while his body worked to eliminate the small amount of iron that had entered his bloodstream. The best thing was to sleep, and let his body's natural healing abilities take over. That would also give his quartz time to reenergize so he could call for help.

He trusted that Evie and her brother would do their best to keep him safe—and trust didn't come easily to Jace. Even so, he instinctively sized up his surroundings, noting the exits.

The living room ran the length of this side of the narrow

house. He was on the single couch, which backed up against an inside wall. The two windows behind him faced the alley, their blinds closed. An air conditioner hummed in one window, which was good, even though his animal preferred fresh air. Closed windows meant that he couldn't be scented from the outside. Fae didn't have any better sense of smell than a human, but they could be working with a fada.

On the other side of the living room, two more windows looked onto a narrow front porch. If he lifted his head, he could see the front door to the left of the windows. The room itself only had a few pieces of furniture. Other than the couch, there was an easy chair, a sturdy oak coffee table, and a bookcase filled with books, DVDs and other knickknacks, and crowned with a large green fern.

Evie returned. She sat on the edge of the couch, careful not to bump him. "Is there anyone we should call?"

Jace considered that. He shared a den in Baltimore with a handful of other unmated men. They were friends, but they didn't keep tabs on one another. He wouldn't be missed until tomorrow morning at the earliest.

Adric was alpha of the Baltimore clan now. He'd be pissed off when he found out Jace was hurt and hadn't tried to contact him, but the night fae clearly didn't know where Jace had gone to ground. In fact, calling for help might lead the bastards straight to this house.

"No," he told Evie.

"Not even your mate?"

"No mate," he said firmly, and then wondered why he'd told her. As a fada, he couldn't tell a lie without making himself violently ill, but that didn't mean he had to answer the human's questions.

"That's good."

He watched, fascinated, as she pinkened. His clan was mostly brown-skinned. He didn't know anyone could blush that easily.

"I mean," she added, "no one will be worrying about you then."

"No," he agreed. "No one will worry." And for a moment that seemed so fucking sad. He tightened his jaw. Hell, in another minute he was going to be tearing up like a girl. "I'll leave in the morning." By then he should be well enough to slip away without anyone being the wiser.

"Okay, sure." Her relief was clear, but she hurried to add, "If you feel up to it, I mean."

"I'll leave," he repeated grimly.

Evie took out her phone. "You mind if I play some music?"

"Go right ahead."

She tapped the screen and set the phone on the coffee table. Music filled the room, a soothing mix of nature sounds, flutes and drums that sounded like something he'd heard coming out of a yoga studio in downtown Baltimore.

His lids drifted shut.

"Go to sleep," Evie said. "You're safe. Kyler didn't see anyone outside."

He nodded. No sense explaining that a night fae could blend into the shadows even better than a fada. Because the night fae was gone for now—Jace's skin would've been crawling if he were near. The assassins' orders would've been to get in and out quickly, standard operating procedure.

Besides, the remaining night fae—because he suspected there had been three altogether—had to remove their fallen comrade before he was found by a human, or worse, by one of the local fada. The Rock Run alpha would be furious to find a night fae in his territory—dead or alive.

Evie grabbed a laptop and sat in the easy chair at the foot of the couch. She folded her legs tailor-style and frowned at the screen.

Jace studied her profile through half-open eyes. She was... fascinating. Thin but sturdy, with clearly defined muscles on her upper arms. Her platinum hair was cut short as a man's and she had those strong dark brows, but her cheek had a soft curve that could only belong to a woman. She wasn't wearing any makeup, but her earlobe was pierced by a delicate gold hoop from which dangled a silver disc.

Evie touched the screen, scrolling through a document.

"What are you doing?" he asked.

"Writing a paper for my biology class." She started typing. "It's due next week."

"You're in school, then." He swallowed a touch of envy. No one in his clan had been to a human college, but it wasn't unheard of. As a teenager, Jace had already been studying the clan's quartz technology, and he'd have loved to major in physics and IT at one of the local universities.

But the clan had been in the midst of the Darktime, the bloody internal war that had come to a head in his late teens. He'd been too busy surviving to even think of going to college.

"Yeah. I just started back, but I'm going to be an LPN." She slanted him a grin. "I just thought of something—you're my first patient. You *can't* die on me. That would be too effing wrong."

He stared, entranced, at the dimple that winked to life in her right cheek. Just as quickly, it was gone. He wanted to keep watching her, but his eyelids drooped.

Outside, rain was falling again, a soothing patter against the windows.

"I'll do my best," he muttered and slid into sleep.

EVIE GLANCED at the sleeping shifter. His color looked a little better now, and he seemed to be breathing normally.

Relieved, she turned her attention back to her paper. When you worked two jobs and went to school, you learned to focus whenever you could snatch the time. In fifteen minutes, she had the first couple pages written.

Kyler returned to report that he'd washed down the whole area behind the house, even the alley as far as the hose could reach. "Of course, Mrs. Linney came outside and asked what I was doing washing the steps in the rain." He flopped down on the floor and took a gulp from a can of soda.

Evie shut her laptop. "You didn't tell her—"

"Yeah, right." Kyler gave her the kind of look only a teenager could give. "She'd broadcast it to the entire frigging block. I told her I spilled my soda and you'd be pissed off if I left it until morning. Ants, you know. And then it started raining harder again, so I probably didn't need to bother."

Evie gave him a thumbs-up. "Quick thinking, squirt."

"I hate it when you call me that," he grumbled, but she could tell he was pleased at the compliment.

Jace muttered something and both their gazes shot to him. He sighed and moved his head against the pillow before curling up on his right side.

Kyler lowered his voice. "What are we going to do with him?"

"Hell if I know. He says he'll leave in the morning."

"Good. The dude's trouble. I mean, what the fuck do the night fae want with him?"

"Who knows? But it doesn't matter. Tomorrow he'll go back to Baltimore or wherever he came from, and we can forget he was ever here." Her heart pinched at that, which was crazy. Shifters didn't mix with humans, except for the occasional hookup—and hookups weren't her thing.

Kyler glanced at the curled-up fada. "Wonder what his animal is?"

"A cat."

"He told you?"

"No." But she'd bet a night's worth of tips she was right. "Look at how he moves. And his body—that's a cat's body if I ever saw one."

Kyler glanced at Jace's long, powerful body and shrugged. "If you say so." He took another slug of soda. "It's kind of cool having a shifter in the house—especially a Baltimore shifter. I've never seen one up close before."

"Me either. I wonder why he was in Grace Harbor?"

They contemplated the sleeping man for another minute, and then Kyler finished his soda and rose to his feet.

"Are you going out?"

"I was thinking about it, yeah." He paced to the front windows and twitched aside a curtain to peer out at the dark street.

Evie took a moment to choose her words. Kyler was so easy to set off these days.

"Do you think you should? That night fae could still be out there."

He glanced over his shoulder. "Why would he care about me? But I guess I should stay here in case he comes back. I don't want you here by yourself."

Evie blinked. Was this the brother who just that morning had growled that Evie wasn't his frickin' mom and he didn't have to answer to her if he didn't want to? But all she said was, "Thanks."

Kyler returned to her side of the living room. He sat down with his back against a wall, phone in hand.

She frowned. "You're not going to tell anyone about Jace, are you?"

"No, Evie," he said with exaggerated patience. "I'm just letting Ben and the other guys know what's up." Ben lived three doors down from them and was Kyler's best friend. He sent a flurry of texts, and then settled into play one of his online games.

Evie glanced again at Jace. He looked okay, so she went back to her paper. By eleven o'clock she had a rough draft done. She shut the laptop and rubbed her forehead.

Kyler had gone to the kitchen to make popcorn. He returned with two large bowls and handed her one.

She accepted it with a grateful smile. "Thanks. All I had time for tonight was a sandwich."

"Thought you might be hungry." Her brother popped a handful of popcorn into his mouth. "I'm going upstairs," he said as he crunched his way through it. "Shout if you need me—or if you want me to sit with him."

"I will. And Kyler?" He halted in the doorway to look over his shoulder. "Thank you. For helping tonight, and for staying in with me."

His narrow face split in a grin. "Hey, it was an adventure. I only wish I could tell Ben. But don't worry, I won't."

"I think that's best. Maybe in a few weeks, but for now, we'd better keep this between us and him." She jerked her head at the sleeping man.

With Kyler in his bedroom, she went upstairs to brush her teeth and grab a sheet and pillow from the hall closet. She told her brother not to stay up too late and then went back downstairs, where she shut off all the lights except the one in the hall and curled up again on the easy chair.

She had fallen into a light doze when something made her open her eyes. Jace was staring at her, his irises glowing that odd feral-green again. Her skin prickled. She glanced around the room for a weapon.

Then his breath sighed out and she reminded herself he couldn't hurt anyone right now.

She rose to her feet. "You okay? Would you like some water?"

"Yeah." He swiped his tongue over his lips. "I'm so damn thirsty. And I need to take a piss."

"Water first." She hurried into the kitchen and returned with a large glass, which he drained in a couple of gulps and then handed back to her.

"Can you walk?" She glanced at him doubtfully as she set the glass on the coffee table. "I can get Kyler. He's upstairs."

He eased his legs over the side of the couch. "I can do it." He set his feet on the floor and used the coffee table to push himself to standing.

He only took a couple of steps before he winced and grasped his belly. "I could use some help here," he said ruefully.

She was already moving the coffee table out of the way. "Put your arm on my shoulders," she said as she slid an arm around his waist.

Together, they shuffled into the hall and turned right toward the bathroom. Fortunately, it was only a few steps further. Evie flipped on the light and helped him inside.

Jace gripped the sink and dragged in a breath, head down. He was flushed, his temples beaded with sweat.

She bit her lip. "Will you—I mean, do you need any help?"

"I'm okay," he muttered.

"Okay, good." She backed toward the door. "I'll be in the hall if you need me."

"I won't. But thanks."

She shut the door and walked a few feet down the hall to wait. The toilet flushed and then she heard water running, followed by a long silence.

She rapped on the bathroom door. "Everything all right?"

"Yeah." The door opened and he limped out. "Just moving a little slow."

He'd washed the sweat from his face, but what made her blink was that he'd taken his shirt off. Her gaze went to a hard chest covered by wiry black hair, and then she jerked it back to his face.

The look he gave her made her cheeks heat. The man might be injured, but that considering expression told her he was recovering fast. They stared at each other. A heartbeat passed, then another, and then he indicated the shirt balled in his hand.

"It was bloody. Where do you want it?"

She swallowed. "Just drop it next to the sink and I'll take care of it."

He nodded and tossed it into the bathroom.

She hesitated and then reminded herself she was a nurse. Well, almost, anyway. "I'll help you back to the couch," she said in her most professional voice and slid an arm around his back.

He shook his head. "You don't look strong enough to hold up a kitten," he said, but let her take some of his weight.

Jesus, the man was all muscle. Beneath her hand, his waist was taut, the skin hot from his fever. She tried not to notice how good he smelled—warm, sweaty male.

Down, girl.

Sure, the man was sexy in a dark, dangerous way, but he was hurt, for God's sake. And even if he wasn't, he was a fada—and a Baltimore earth fada at that. Everyone knew they were a murderous clan. She was surprised any of them were still left alive.

The last thing she wanted was to have anything to do with a Baltimore shifter.

No, she'd make sure Mr. Jace No-Last-Name left as soon as he was able, and then pray she never saw him again.

Back in the living room, Jace sank down on the couch. He closed his eyes and bent forward at the waist, his breath ragged. It was clear he was hurting.

Evie turned on the lamp next to the easy chair. "You're hot. I'll turn up the air conditioner." With that done, she shoved her hands into her back pockets, feeling helpless. "Are you hungry? I can make you some chicken soup. Or—"

"I don't think I can eat anything right now," he said without opening his eyes.

"Yeah, right." She flushed, recalling he'd taken a knife in the belly. "Maybe something that digests easily? I have popsicles."

Her mom had given them popsicles whenever she or Kyler were sick.

"A popsicle." His hard mouth edged up. "Okay, sure."

"Be right back." She hurried to the kitchen and returned with an orange popsicle. It would put more liquids in him, and maybe the sugar would give him some extra energy.

While he ate the popsicle, she rinsed his T-shirt out in the bathroom sink and hung it up to dry before getting a popsicle for herself. When she came back, he was reclined on the couch, still sucking the popsicle. A cat's paw was tattooed in black and gold on his upper left arm. He saw her looking and his face shuttered, so she didn't ask, just curled up on the easy chair again.

The cuts on his abdomen were still an angry red, but they were starting to close. "I think you're healing," she said.

He nodded. "It's going to be a rough night, but this helps." He indicated the popsicle. "Feels like my fucking belly's on fire."

"I wish I could do more."

"You did good. I just need to rest now, give it time to heal."

She wrapped her arms around her legs. "What happened, anyway?"

"Some bastard night fae stuck a knife in me."

"The one that was outside?"

"No. The guy who stabbed me is dead."

She gulped. "Oh."

He regarded her from beneath thick lashes, as if expecting her to cringe from him. But she knew that sometimes, you don't have a choice.

Jace's eyes closed. Silence fell while they sucked on their popsicles.

"Iron," she said. "It was an iron knife? That's why you're feverish?"

He nodded. "You know what iron does to a fae?"

"Sure." Everyone knew that iron was a fae's Achilles' heel.

They couldn't even stand it against their bare skin. "It's like poison for them. But you're a fada, aren't you?"

"Yeah. But we have some fae in us. Iron doesn't affect the fada as bad, but it's still poison to us. And the knife was probably cold-forged—formed into a blade at room temperature. That makes a difference."

"Salt neutralizes the iron?"

"Yeah, but don't ask me how. It just does."

She opened her mouth to ask why the night fae had stabbed him, and then closed it again. It was better she didn't know.

"That's right," he said, seemingly reading her mind. "The less you know, the better." He slid down on the couch until he was prone again. "I'll be all right, now. You can go to bed."

She shook her head. "I'm staying right here in case you need me."

His brow lifted—and then he smiled. A quick but real smile that lit an answering warmth inside her. "You don't have to," he said, "but thanks." And with that, he curled up on his right side, closed his eyes and fell back asleep.

She finished her popsicle, and then set a pitcher of ice water on the coffee table within easy reach of her patient before curling up on the chair again.

She was too wide awake now to sleep, so she took out her phone and checked her messages, and then downloaded a book to read, but her gaze kept flicking to Jace. He was a beautiful man: big shoulders, six-pack abs and long, strong legs. And inked—besides the cat's paw, an intricately rendered tat of a snarling black jungle cat stretched across most of his upper back.

Kyler came downstairs in a pair of gym shorts and she jerked her gaze back to her phone.

"You sure you're all right?" he asked.

"I'm fine."

He yawned and scratched his stomach. "Okay, but holler if you need me. I'm all grown up—you need me, you call for me."

He frowned down on her, and for a second, she was reminded of his father, even though Aaron had been shorter and square-faced, while Kyler had a narrow, sharp-boned face. But those dark eyes and the frown were all Aaron, who had been just the same when it came to protecting his family.

"I will." She crossed her heart. "Promise."

"G'night, then." Kyler gave another big yawn and went upstairs to bed.

Evie shut off the light and snuggled up on the chair again.

Kyler had made her proud tonight. All spring, he'd argued with her about every little decision. Some nights he'd slammed out of the house and then not come home until after midnight. She didn't know what she was going to do with him when school let out next week. He'd tried to find a job, but so far, no luck.

But tonight, he'd really come through. His dad would've been pleased. She smiled. She'd have to remember to tell Kyler that in the morning.

She glanced at her sleeping guest one last time. His face had gone slack, his lashes dark crescents against his cheeks. Curled up on the couch like that, it was hard to believe he was as dangerous as people said.

Her eyes drifted closed and she fell asleep.

Two hours later she jerked awake to see Jace thrashing about on the couch.

"No," he muttered. "Mary—" He bolted upright.

She fumbled for the switch on the lamp next to the chair. It came on and he hissed, an angry cat-sound.

She narrowed her eyes against the sudden light, trying to see him. "Jace? You all right?"

He ignored her to chug water from the pitcher she'd left on the table and then fumbled with the zipper of his pants.

She rose to her feet. "Jace? What are you doing?"

His gaze swung to her and she took a step back. His eyes were that strange bright green again. His growl raised fine hairs all over her body.

"Okay." She raised a palm. "Take it easy."

He snarled and dragged off the pants. Bright bits of color danced over his skin—and then a huge black panther was crouched on her couch.

5

———

$\mathcal{J}$ ace was hot. So effing hot.

He groaned and thrashed on the couch. His belly was burning. But the heat seemed to have spread everywhere.

He turned onto his side and then onto his back again.

"No...Merry—"

He dragged a hand over his face—and was thrown back seven years into his worst nightmare. Adric had finally tracked Merry and Silver to their latest address. It had been over a year since Jace had last seen any of Takira's family. His sister had turned up dead, and Merry's fifth birthday had come and gone while she was on the run with Silver.

The call from Adric came just after midnight. Jace rushed to the site—only to find a burned-out house. The bitter scent of ashes and death filled the air.

Adric had been waiting in the shadows. His throat worked. "I'm sorry, bro."

Jace had backed away, shaking his head. "No. No. There must be some mistake."

"No mistake. I tracked them both here." Adric's eyes were

bronze holes in his face. "It burned down last night. The neighbors said no one got out alive."

"Leron," Jace had rasped. "I'll kill him. I'll fucking tear him to pieces." He'd turned to stride off, but Adric's hand clamped on his arm.

Jace tried to shake him off. "Let. Me. Go."

"No. I won't stand by and watch you commit suicide."

Jace's mouth had twisted. "What the fuck do I have to live for?"

His friend blew out a breath. "I can't answer that for you, but I do know I need your help to take Leron down. And we will. We're close, Jace. But if you go after him now, you could blow it all to hell."

"You ask too damn much."

"I know," his friend returned quietly. "But it's not for me. It's for the clan."

Jace had stared at the house's charred remains, the desire for revenge raging through his veins. He'd fisted his hands, dropped back his head and roared his fury at the moon. The local dogs had joined in, an eerie, mournful howl.

When he'd turned back to Adric, he knew his eyes blazed a feral green. "Fine," he bit out. "But promise me he'll die. No mercy."

"No mercy," Adric had agreed.

Now Jace writhed on the couch, his soul as dark and bitter as that burned shell of a house that he'd believed had contained his niece's remains.

An unfamiliar scent recalled him to the present—a female. *It's only a dream.*

With an effort, he forced his eyes open and looked wildly around until he recalled he was in some human's home in Grace Harbor.

Evie. He grabbed onto her name like a drowning man would a life preserver.

She'd left a pitcher of water on the table. He fumbled for it and, without bothering to pour the water into a glass, drank deeply. His cat was to the fore now. It wrinkled its nose at the chemical taste of the water. But it was cool and wet. The burning eased, but he was still too hot.

He had to shift; he'd heal faster in his cat form. He sat up and reached for his zipper.

The female was staring at him, eyes wide. He hesitated. He distantly recalled that he hadn't shifted already because he didn't want to frighten her. Humans tended to get edgy around a 250-pound black jaguar.

His cat rubbed at his skin, frantic to get out. He could feel his eyes had gone night-glow, signaling his animal was in control.

The woman backed up and his chest rumbled. *Didn't she know he wouldn't hurt her?*

The hell with it. He dragged off his pants and let the shift take him—and almost didn't make it. Energy danced over his skin, and for a few frightening seconds he thought he'd get stuck between man and cat and die, his organs unable to adjust to a half-shifted state.

His quartz. A quick check told him it had recharged to about forty percent. He drew deep, pulling energy from the slowly vibrating crystals, and completed the shift. He lay on his side, weak and trembling. So much for his big, scary cat.

But the woman took another step back. The cat instinctively leapt off the couch to stop her. She froze and babbled something, and he scented fear, sharp and acrid.

No. He nudged her hand. *It's all right.*

She sucked in a breath.

He rumbled low in his chest but held still.

"Okay," she said in a strangled voice. "Okay. I'm the good guy, all right? The one who's trying to help you."

He huffed a breath and waited, his head against the back of her hand.

At last she understood. Her hand turned and she stroked his head.

Ah... He pushed back against her hand, rubbing his scent onto the skin. Then he got his head between her hand and hip and that was even better.

He breathed in her spicy feminine aroma and rubbed his head against her hip, taking her scent on him and marking her with his. His chest was rumbling again.

"Are you *purring*?" She let out a high, nervous laugh. But to his satisfaction, she relaxed.

He pushed her hip, herding her toward the couch.

"You want me on the couch?"

He gave her another nudge.

"Okay, but you must be thirsty. Why don't we get you some more water first?"

That seemed like a good idea, so he followed her to the kitchen and watched as she filled a large bowl with water and set it on the floor. When he lapped it up, she gave him some more.

Then he went to the back door and waited. He needed to keep voiding the iron in his system.

This time she guessed immediately what he wanted and unlocked the door. He paused on the small concrete landing to test the air. He could smell his own blood, but just a trace—the kid had done a thorough job. There were other scents—a dog, a nearby car engine that had only recently been turned off—but he couldn't pick up the noxious, graveyard odor of a night fae.

He padded down the stairs, pissed on a patch of grass next to the driveway, and then came back up to where Evie had waited in the doorway to let him in.

Back in the living room, Evie got the sheet from the easy chair and sat on the couch. He figured she wouldn't want him on the couch with her, so he lay down on the floor beside it. The jaguar wanted to stay close for two reasons; it liked how she smelled, and it feared the night fae would come back—or even another shifter who scented Jace's weakness. This way, Jace would be between Evie and any danger.

Evie curled up, her head on the pillow he'd been using. He could see her watching him in the darkness, and then she sat up and patted the cushion on the other end. "That floor's got to be hard."

He didn't need a second invitation. He heaved himself onto the couch, circled once and then settled on the cushions near her feet with a contented sigh.

Evie lay back down. He could tell from her breath that she was awake, and he felt a twinge of guilt at waking her. Well, tomorrow he'd be gone and her life could get back to normal.

But he'd been right to shift. The fever had broken, and even though the shift had drained more energy from his quartz, he could hear the tiny crystals humming a healing song. The quartz had recovered enough energy to aid in his healing now, although he was still shaken from the nightmare.

Merry's fine, he reminded himself. *She's safe at Rock Run.*

But if he died, what would happen to her? Sure, Rui and Valeria do Mar—the Rock Run couple who'd adopted Merry— had given her the family Jace couldn't, but they were river fada, not earth fada. Someday Merry would probably want to return to the Baltimore clan, to be with her own people, and Jace wanted to be there to ease her way. Not everyone in the clan would welcome a mixed-blood with open arms.

And only another earth fada could teach Merry the secrets of her quartz. Yes, Adric would instruct her if Jace died, but by tradition, it was Jace's right as her only living family.

Evie nudged him with her knee. "It's all right," she murmured. "Go back to sleep."

He edged closer and waited until her breath smoothed out and she relaxed into sleep again. Then he laid his head on her thigh. Even through the blanket and her jeans, he could smell her. Summer and lavender.

He inhaled deeply, imprinting her scent on his mind.

SOMEONE WAS at the back door. *Rat-a-tat-tat. Rat-a-tat-tat.*

Evie jolted upright, because it was barely dawn, and there was no good reason for someone to be knocking on her door so early.

Jace-the-panther was already off the couch and disappearing around the corner into the hall. She hurried after him into the kitchen to find him with his nose to the door.

She crept up next to him. He stepped back and indicated with a twitch of his head that she should open the door. Just to be sure, she whispered, "You know who it is?"

For answer, he nudged her hand in the direction of the doorknob.

"Okay," she muttered. She slid the bolt to the left and cracked open the door.

A lean, good-looking man stared back at her. The tips of his spiked black hair were bleached blond, and he had a gold stud in one earlobe. She couldn't see a chunk of quartz, but he had a tell-tale lump beneath his T-shirt. A frisson of warning tightened the back of her neck as he looked her over with cool bronze eyes.

But his words were polite enough. "Peace to you and yours," he said in the traditional fae/fada greeting. "Sorry to bother you this early, but I believe you have one of my men here." His gaze flicked to Jace, who had edged the door wider so he was standing beside her.

Evie kept a firm grip on the doorknob, her every instinct screaming not to let this stranger inside. "Peace," she returned. "And you are?"

"Adric. Jace's alpha."

"Lord Adric." Her fingers clenched on the doorknob. Even in the human world, the Baltimore alpha's reputation was known. People said he'd killed his own uncle and driven his cousins out of the clan. In Baltimore, he had as much power as the mayor, and even the gangs left him alone.

The alpha inclined his head.

Jace leaned into her. Not pressuring her, just reminding her he was there.

She glanced down and he rumbled in reassurance. It was clear he wanted her to let his alpha inside. Moreover, the longer she left Adric standing there, the more likely one of her neighbors was to see him, which would only complicate things.

Besides, the alpha could've easily pushed his way in. The fact that he hadn't was a good sign.

She forced her fingers to release the doorknob. "Why don't you come in?"

"Thank you." He didn't seem to hurry, but he was past her almost before she knew it.

She shut the door behind him, but didn't bother bolting it—because what was the point?

Adric crouched next to Jace, a hand on his shoulder. "You okay, bro?"

Jace nuzzled the alpha's hand.

"You're hurt?"

While Jace rumbled what Evie took to be a yes, she scrutinized Adric. Like Jace, he was all muscle in jeans and a camo-print T-shirt that strained over his shoulders. Average height, but with a powerful build that reminded her of the ex-Army ranger in her biology class. But what struck her was how young he was. From what she'd heard, she'd have expected the Baltimore alpha to be older, in his mid-forties at least. Sure, the fada lived much longer than humans, and so aged more slowly, but this man didn't look much older than Evie herself.

Adric glanced up at her with those odd metallic eyes. World-weary eyes. Eyes that had seen too much, too soon, and suddenly Evie didn't have trouble believing the stories. This was a man who'd killed, more than once.

But however dangerous the alpha was, his concern for his injured friend was clear. He rose to his feet. "Can you shift?" he asked Jace.

Evie raised a brow. So the fada couldn't always change forms? Last night, Jace had made it look easy, but then she'd never seen anyone shift before.

Jace-the-panther twitched a soft black ear.

Adric bent to look at Jace's quartz. "Better not," he agreed.

Evie would've loved to know what the man could learn from the quartz, but whatever it was, he wasn't sharing.

Adric turned to her. "I know he's hurt. I followed the trail to your house. I have a man cleaning it away, so no one else can follow it."

"There was a storm, and we hosed down what we could."

The Baltimore alpha nodded. "I know. But he dripped blood all the way down the block. Thank the gods the storm came when it did. If whoever was tracking him had picked up his trail—" He shook his head. "What happened, anyway?"

"It was a night fae."

The alpha tensed—an almost imperceptible tightening of his neck and shoulders. "You're sure? It wasn't a fada?"

"No. The night fae followed Jace here, but he didn't seem to know which house Jace was in. Jace protected us somehow."

"Good. You don't want to know what a night fae can do to you."

"I can guess." Evie rubbed her arms, remembering the darkness that had slithered out of the night. "He stabbed Jace with an iron knife."

"Iron?" Adric shook his head. "No wonder his quartz is so drained."

Evie nodded. A glance at the clock above the stove told her it was a little after seven. "Look, why don't you sit down and I'll make some coffee. That's if you drink coffee?"

Jace snorted.

The alpha's mouth quirked. "I would fucking kill for a cup of coffee. I've been out most of the night tracking him. When we didn't find a trace of him in Baltimore, we came up here."

He took a seat while Evie started a pot brewing. She tried to act normal, but it was unnerving having a creature who was basically a human cat seated at her kitchen table.

Jace-the-panther had settled on the floor next to the table and was watching her as well. She filled a bowl of water and set it next to him. She and Adric watched as he greedily lapped it up.

"We did what we could," she told the alpha. "He wouldn't let me call for help."

"We?"

"My brother and me."

"Ah." He waved a hand. "Relax, love. I'm not here to cause trouble—I just want to take him back home. All I know is one of my men was hurt and you helped him."

She nodded but remained near the coffeepot as the water heated and started dripping through. She did *not* want to sit at the table with Adric, and if worse came to worst, she could always use the hot coffee to protect herself.

Kyler's footsteps sounded in the hallway above.

Evie briefly closed her eyes. She didn't care what she'd promised last night—she didn't want her brother involved in this. But it was too late now.

Adric rose to his feet with a feline grace as her brother entered the kitchen, barefoot and clad only in a tank top and loose gym shorts.

Kyler's eyes bugged at the sight of Adric and the big black cat. "What the hell's going on?"

Evie inserted herself between Kyler and Adric. "This is Lord Adric," she told him. "The Baltimore alpha."

Kyler's mouth dropped open. "No shit."

"Good to meet you." Adric stuck out his hand as Evie hurried to introduce them.

"This is my brother, Kyler. He helped me with Jace last night."

Her brother pumped the alpha's hand. "Wow. It's an honor to meet you, my-my lord."

"Call me Adric."

"Okay, sure." Kyler glanced down at Jace, who had risen to his feet again. "And that's Jace? He's a...panther?"

"Yeah," Evie said.

"Actually, he's a jaguar," Adric said. "A black jaguar. You can see the spots if you look close."

"Wow," Kyler said again.

A lean, furry body brushed Evie's hip. Jace had moved closer. It was almost as if he were protecting her.

Adric's brow raised. A look passed between the two fada, but all the alpha said was, "I'd still like to hear what happened last night."

"Yes, of course," she said. "Please, sit down."

While Adric sat back down and Kyler got himself a tall glass of milk, Evie set milk and sugar on the table and handed Adric a mug of coffee before pouring another for herself. She and Kyler took seats at the table across from Adric, while Jace lay on the floor near her feet, his gaze on his alpha.

Adric dumped a hefty amount of milk into his coffee and then drained the cup in a couple of gulps. Evie went to refill his cup, but he rose to his feet. "I've got it."

She and Kyler exchanged a look. It was just so surreal—the notorious Baltimore alpha making himself at home in their kitchen.

Adric sat down and leaned back in his chair, one hand wrapped around the mug, seemingly at ease. But his eyes were watchful.

Evie cupped her own mug and tried to imitate his calm.

"So," he prompted, "a night fae, huh? And where do you come into it?"

"I found him—Jace—outside. I didn't know he was hurt until he passed out."

"He passed out?" Adric scowled at Jace. "How the hell did the asshole get close enough to hurt you that bad?"

Jace's growl was low and vicious. Evie blinked, but Adric just shook his head.

"Go on," he told her, and she explained what had happened after she'd found Jace on her doorstep, with occasional interjections from Kyler.

"I don't think the knife went in too deep," she finished, "but he was getting worse until we cleaned the cut out with salt water. Thank God he was able to tell us what to do."

"You say he shifted in the middle of the night?" Adric glanced at Jace.

His eyes were closed, his big black head resting on his paws, but his ears twitched.

"Yes," Evie confirmed. "I think his fever spiked. He was restless and moving around, and the next thing I knew, he'd changed to a jaguar."

Adric shook his head. "You should've had her call me," he told Jace.

The big cat huffed in disagreement.

"Stubborn ass," his alpha returned. He looked at Evie. "He hasn't shifted since?"

"No. But he seems better—he's definitely moving easier this morning."

"Right. Okay, let's talk about the night fae. Did he get a look at you?"

"No," Evie said. "He was right outside the door, but he couldn't see us. The window blind was down."

"So he didn't see you, and he doesn't know for sure Jace was here?"

"No on both counts."

"That's good. And night fae can't scent any better than a

human, so I know he didn't follow Jace's trail here. He was trolling the neighborhood, seeing what he could find."

"But I could swear he could somehow feel us on the other side of the door."

"He could." Adric took another gulp of coffee. "Night fae get off on dark energy—fear, anger, pain. He could sense you all right, but he couldn't be sure one of you was Jace. And from what you said, Jace used his quartz to tamp down your energy. The only way to hide from a night fae is to sit quietly and slow your breath and heartbeat."

"And think happy thoughts," Evie said.

"Is that what Jace told you?" The corner of Adric's mouth twitched. "I suppose it didn't hurt—but if Jace hadn't been here, all the happy thoughts in the world wouldn't have helped you. He was trying to keep you from panicking."

Evie exchanged a glance with her brother. *What if Jace hadn't recovered enough to protect them?*

She felt another rush of last night's dark fear. This time it was mixed with anger. That the night fae had dared mess with their minds...

Adric's calm, businesslike tone recalled her to the kitchen. "Sounds like you're safe enough. We'll make sure there's nothing to trace Jace to you or your house." He finished his coffee and came to his feet, and Evie and Kyler rose with him. "And now, I believe we'll be on our way." He came around the table and held out his hand to her. "I owe you, Evie Morningstar."

She stiffened. How the hell did he know her last name? In fact, now that she thought about it, she hadn't told him her first name either.

"No worries," he said with a hint of amusement. "I just wanted to know what I was walking into."

"Of course," Evie replied faintly as she shook his hand. His fingers were warm and strong—perfectly normal, in fact. It was easy to forget he was one of the most dangerous men in America.

"You don't owe us anything. We couldn't let him bleed out on our doorstep, could we?"

"Some humans would've." Adric was turning toward the door when he drew a deep inhale and swung back around. "What the fuck? You're fae?"

Evie took a step back. Kyler put an arm out to steady her.

"What are you talking about?"

"I smell silver." He leaned closer and took another breath. "It's you, not your brother."

Jace had gotten off the floor and was growling lowly. One side of his mouth peeled back to reveal a sharp white canine.

"You're a fae," Adric said. "It's faint, so maybe you're a mixed-blood, but I know a goddamn fae when I smell one. What clan? And I want the truth, woman."

6

____

Fae.

Jace snarled, low and savage. He was operating at a primal level, his animal close to the surface while he was healing.

To his jaguar, the fae were the enemy. They'd tried to kill him last night. They'd been behind Takira's death, and they'd almost killed his only niece.

His lip peeled back. Now he could taste as well as smell Evie's scent, allowing him to separate the different notes. She definitely had some fae in her: he detected a hint of silver. The only reason he hadn't noticed before was that his own body had been emitting a metallic odor as it rid itself of the iron in his system.

Evie paled but held her ground.

That gave his animal pause. The cat shook its head, confused.

"What clan?" Adric asked again. His voice was softer now. Menacing.

"Look," she said, "I'm not fae, okay? Do you think if I were a fae I'd be living like this?" Her gesture encompassed her shabby surroundings. "And why does it matter anyway?"

"It matters," Adric returned grimly.

Neither Jace nor his cat liked the alpha's tone. He had to shift. The energy drain on his quartz was still considerable, but he needed to be able to speak.

He focused inward, drawing deeply on the tiny crystals. Normally, he had the strength to change forms with ease, and he enjoyed the buzz of energy it brought. But today, the energy was weak—more a prickle than a buzz. It increased and he almost had it, and then it faded.

"Jace," Adric said, "are you sure—"

Jace barely heard him. He sucked in a breath and tried harder.

And then his friend was beside him, adding his quartz's energy to Jace's, and the prickle strengthened to something close to normal. Through sheer force of will, he wrenched himself back to man, and then immediately doubled over, gulping oxygen.

Evie's eyes narrowed. "Get out of my house," she said, low and mean. "Both of you."

"As soon as I get some answers," Adric replied.

Jace came upright. The man was in charge again, and things didn't add up. "Leave it, Ric."

The alpha stiffened, but Jace was a lieutenant, directly below Adric in the hierarchy. More than that, he was an old friend. Adric was wrong, and he needed to hear it.

"She had nothing to do with this," Jace said. "It was pure chance I ended up at her house. And when the night fae came, she and the boy could've told him I was in here with them. Instead, they were nearly caught. There's no way she was working with him."

He turned to Evie. She had an angry flush on her cheeks, but that was better than seeing her pale with fear.

"I'm sorry about this," he told her. "As you can see, we don't like the fae."

"Don't fucking trust them, either," Adric muttered.

She blew out a breath. "I am *not* fae, damn it."

"No?"

But her scent held the freshness of truth. Whatever she was, she believed what she was saying. Adric scented it too, because he relaxed.

And at least she wasn't night fae—she didn't have that grave-yard stench. So she was sun fae or ice fae. Still an enemy, but not the dark hunters the night fae were.

Adric backed off. "If you would just get Jace's clothes, we'll be on our way."

Evie's gaze flicked at Jace. "Fine," she said coldly, and jerked her head at her brother. "Kyler—"

"No—you go. I'll stay here with the two of them."

She opened her mouth to argue, then glanced at the teenager's tight jaw and said, "All right."

While Evie went into the living room, Jace and Adric stood quietly, hands open and relaxed to show Kyler they meant no harm. It was funny, really. Like the kid had a prayer of a chance against two shifters—but Jace respected that Kyler had stepped up to protect his sister, and he could tell that Adric did, too.

The alpha examined the lanky teen. "How old are you, anyway?"

Kyler balled his fists. "Sixteen. Why?"

"No reason."

Jace slid Adric a look. What was he up to? But his friend just stood there, his sharp gaze taking in first the pugnacious teen, and then moving around the kitchen, noting the scuffed and peeling vinyl floor, the cheap plastic blinds on the window and the fact that the table and chairs were clearly secondhand.

Like Evie said, if she were a fae, would she live like this? Even the most down-on-their-luck fae usually had something to sell— a ward or a spell, or a Gift that was valued in the human world. Her fae blood really must be just a trace, probably less than most fada.

Evie reentered the kitchen and thrust Jace's pants and shoes at him. "Here."

He took the pants and pulled them on, leaving the top button undone in deference to his still-healing wounds. To put on the running shoes, he had to sit on a chair, because there was no way he could bend over to lace them, and he was damned if he'd ask anyone for help. He shoved his feet into the unlaced shoes and stood back up.

Evie shot a glance at his bare chest and then met his eyes. She pinked up and pressed her lips together.

So he hadn't imagined her interest last night. He'd been too hurt to do anything about it then, but he'd had a mind to come back when he felt better. For this woman, he would have made an exception to his rule about human females.

Now that was blown to hell. She just wanted him and Adric out of here, and frankly, he'd think twice—make that three times—before getting involved with a mixed-blood, especially one who didn't even know what strain of fae ran in her veins.

But as he took in her set face, regret twanged through him, a single harsh note. Just once, he would've liked to touch those soft cheeks of hers, smooth a finger over those strong dark brows. Taste her pretty lips.

Adric had his wallet out. "I'd like to give you something for your trouble." He held out a handful of bills to Evie.

Jace tensed. "No," he started to say, but it was too late.

Evie's eyes flashed. "Get out—now. Both of you." She pointed to the back door.

"Okay, okay," Adric said. "Just trying to show our appreciation."

"I don't need your appreciation," she gritted. "I did it because I'm a fucking nice person, got it?"

"Got it," Adric said mildly. Jace could tell he was trying not to laugh. He tucked the money back into his wallet and glanced at his quartz. "Luc's here."

Jace held out a hand to Evie. She hesitated, jaw tight, but took it.

"Thank you." He squeezed her hand. "And you, too, Kyler. I won't forget this."

"Fine." The kid shook his hand and then jerked his chin at the door. "Now get out." He moved closer to his sister so they stood shoulder to shoulder, their expressions hard.

But beneath the anger there was fear, and that made Jace's heart twist. Because he'd stood like that with his sister, too—more than once.

With a last nod to the two siblings, he followed his friend out the door.

7

Outside the sun was rising over the alley. The storm last night had cleared the air. It promised to be a bright, cloudless day, the kind that made Jace itch to run free as his cat, far away from humans and buildings and roads.

Luc was waiting in a jeep. Luc was another lieutenant, although unlike Adric and Jace, he was a wolf, with his animal's narrow, hard-boned face and amber eyes. When Adric's cougar uncle had been alpha, he'd appointed only other cats to top positions. But Adric was too shrewd for that. If a man was good, he was good—didn't matter what his animal was. In fact, out of his four lieutenants, two—Luc and another man, Zuri—were wolves. And the fourth was a female, Adric's sister Marjani.

Jace approved. The clan was the stronger for it. Diversity at the top meant everyone was represented when Adric met with his lieutenants. What they lacked were older, wiser heads. All five of them including Adric were younger than thirty-five turns of the sun, but that was because most of the elders had died during the Darktime.

Adric rode shotgun with Luc, while Jace eased himself into the backseat. He leaned against the door and stretched out his legs, trying to get comfortable. That last shift had been a bitch, and now his body, especially his injured abdomen, was protesting.

"Damn," Adric said as Luc put the jeep in drive. "Woman's a wildcat, isn't she?"

"Leave it," Jace said. "She's part fae, remember?"

"Sure, dude." Adric shot him a look. "She's not for you, you know."

"You think I don't know that?"

"All I know is there was something going on in there. Your cat was protecting her—from me."

Jace closed his eyes. "She saved my life. I owed her. End of story." And it wasn't a lie—it just wasn't the whole truth.

"What the hell happened, anyway?" Luc asked as he pulled out of the alley.

"Night fae," Jace replied without opening his eyes. "Son of a bitch stabbed me with an iron knife."

Luc snarled. "Tell me he's dead."

"He is."

"What the fuck were you doing in Grace Harbor?" Adric asked. "I thought you were in Rising Sun, examining that new vein of quartz."

Jace opened his eyes. It was clear the alpha wasn't going to let him rest until he answered a few questions.

"I went to Rising Sun first." On a normal day, Jace wouldn't have been at the mine; he was the clan's chief tech, not a miner. But the miners had found a new vein of high-grade quartz and he'd wanted to see it for himself. "By the way, those crystals just might work in the clan's smartphones."

Every fada had a Gift, and Jace's was to work with the tiny crystals in quartz. He'd designed a quartz smartphone that had promising applications, but they were still working out the bugs.

"No shit?"

"Yeah. We'll have to run some tests, but it looks promising. I asked the miners to send some to the Factory for testing."

"That's good news." Adric permitted himself a rare smile.

Jace nodded. "Anyway, after work, I went out for a drink with a few of the guys. Some of the Rock Run men were there, too. Tiago do Rio invited us."

That got Adric's attention. Tiago was the youngest brother of the Rock Run alpha and a high-ranking member of the clan in his own right.

"Do Rio, hmm? Think Rock Run had anything to do with it?"

"Why the fuck would they help a night fae?"

"Because Tiago's big brother Dion would love to stop our mining. He hates having us on his mate's territory." Lord Dion wasn't just the Rock Run alpha, he was mated to Cleia, the sun fae queen.

"And he's not happy about us mining so close to Rock Run, either," Luc added. "They may have figured out that you're the guy who developed the smartphone technology."

Jace considered that, but it didn't compute. "I don't like him any better than you, but if Dion wanted me dead, he wouldn't hire a fae. He'd do it himself."

"True," said Adric. "And we signed a contract with the Rising Sun fae. If Dion doesn't honor it, his mate would have his balls on a platter."

Luc snorted and Jace grinned. "She would." Dion might be a big, dominant man but Queen Cleia was one of the most powerful fae in the world.

"Which leaves us with Lord Prick." It was their code name for Tyrus.

"That's my guess."

A muscle ticked in Adric's jaw. "God's cat, I'd like to take him out. But the prince would wipe the floor with us if he found out we killed his only living son."

Jace nodded. They'd discussed this before, and the answer

was always the same. It wasn't fucking worth it. The only consolation was knowing it was a stalemate. They couldn't take out Tyrus, but the reverse was also true. Prince Langdon had kept his son in check for the past six years—although Tyrus had apparently slipped the leash.

Thankfully, Merry was protected by Langdon himself. The night fae prince had woven a protection ward deep into the crystals of her quartz. If anyone—fae or not—tried to hurt her, they would die. Instantly.

"The bastard will go too far one of these days," Luc muttered. "And then, he's dead."

Adric growled in agreement.

Luc took the I-95 ramp south toward Baltimore. They bumped over something in the road and Jace tensed against a jolt of pain.

"Sorry, bro." Luc eased the car onto the interstate. "Couldn't avoid it."

"Hang in there," Adric added. "We'll have you home in less than an hour."

Jace nodded, tight-lipped. "I need you to do something for me—call my niece. Rui and Valeria should know what happened."

"Of course." Adric tapped his quartz. "Merry? How are you, love?"

"Uncle Ric!"

Jace's mouth curved at her excited response. In the days after they'd first found Merry with the Rock Run fada, she'd been terrified of Adric, especially after he'd tried to steal her back from the couple she thought of as her parents. But the alpha had a soft spot for cubs, and it hadn't taken long before she adored him like all the clan's young.

"Don't be worried," Adric said, "but Uncle Jace got hurt. He's going to be okay, though."

"Uncle Jace?" The brightness went out of her voice, which

made Jace want to kill the night fae assassin all over again. "He's okay? You're sure?"

"Absolutely. He's here with me right now."

"Why didn't he call me then?"

"Because he's using all his energy to heal."

"Oh. That's good, then. Can I talk to him? Please?"

"Of course." Adric removed his quartz and held it over the seat so Jace could speak into it.

He leaned forward. "Yo, Merry. I'm okay, like Uncle Ric said. I won't be able to see you tomorrow, though. But I'll come and see you in a couple of days."

"Promise?"

"Promise."

"Okay, then." Her relief came through the quartz. "I hope you feel better soon."

He smiled even though she couldn't see him. "I feel better just talking to you. Now, is your dad around?"

"Yeah, we just had breakfast."

"Tell him Uncle Ric wants to talk to him. And Merry? Love you."

"Love you too."

Jace sat back. His belly was throbbing, which meant he was healing, but he'd had enough talk. He leaned his head against the seat and listened as Adric told Rui do Mar about the night fae attack.

Rui was also Dion's second-in-command. He understood immediately that Merry could be in danger. Wards could be broken. Yes, it would be suicide to kill Merry, but that didn't mean Tyrus wouldn't send someone after her. If the assassin died, Tyrus would chalk it up to collateral damage.

"Thanks for the heads-up," Rui told Adric. "I'll let the alpha know. We'll keep her safe."

"I know. That's the only reason she's still with you."

"Try and take her," Rui retorted, "and you won't live the week."

Adric ignored that to say, "We'll keep you informed."

"You do that."

"And do Mar?"

"What?"

"Give Rosana my love." He tapped the phone, cutting off the other man's growl.

Jace's mouth twitched. Rosana was the youngest do Rio, a sultry black-haired beauty about twenty-two turns of the sun. Adric singled her out every chance he got: dancing with her at the sun fae's big midsummer celebration each year, bringing her small gifts.

And Rosana encouraged him.

It drove the Rock Run men insane, especially Tiago and Dion. Jace didn't know what Rosana's game was, but Adric did it to tweak the older alpha.

Adric and Luc fell into a low-voiced conversation. Strategizing. Jace tried to listen, but his eyes closed, and all he heard was the healing hum of his quartz.

The next thing he knew, Luc said, "We're here."

Jace sat up. They'd arrived in Baltimore. Adric hopped out and opened Jace's door, holding out his hand. Jace took it, because frankly, he needed the help.

The clan lived in small dens scattered around the city. Most of them lived underground, with a house on the surface as camouflage. Some of the dens were connected by underground tunnels, although not Jace's.

After his parents died, the brick house on his lot had fallen into disrepair, but Jace had fixed it up and rented it out to a single mom and her kids. The mom was grateful to have a landlord who kept things in good repair, and in return, she ignored the odd hours he and his den mates kept—and the big cats, wolves and bears that could be seen in the backyard from time to time.

Adric slid an arm around Jace's waist. When Jace tried to shrug him off, he growled, "Let me help, you idiot."

"Asshole," Jace returned, but gratefully accepted the alpha's strength as he limped around back to where his den entrance was concealed in a small shed protected by a *look-away* spell.

Suha, the clan's head healer, was waiting in her usual colorful tunic and capris. A slender, black-haired woman whose animal was a deer, she had a doe's soft brown eyes and calm ways, except where it came to her patients. Then the woman could out-hardass Adric.

She greeted Jace with a careful hug and a kiss on each of his cheeks, then set her hands on her hips. "Don't you know better than to mess with a night fae?"

"He messed with me, babe. And I'm the one who's still walking around."

She rolled her eyes. "Inside with you."

Adric touched his quartz and murmured the words that dissolved the *look-away* spell. The den was two flights down. Jace could no longer keep up the pretense that he wasn't in pain. He shuffled down the stairs, gripping the rail like a lifeline. Adric stayed on his other side, taking as much of his weight as he could.

By the time they reached the bottom, sweat had beaded on Jace's forehead. He leaned against the stone wall as Adric opened the door to his den and then helped him into the small foyer.

Jace's parents had carved the den out of the bedrock long before he was born. Both of them had been soldiers, but his dad had been an engineer at heart. In his downtime, he'd built this big, solid home for his mate, their two cubs, and assorted other members of the clan. Even in the Darktime, everyone knew they always had a bed at the Jones' den.

He limped into the living room, a large, comfortable space with exposed stone walls and furniture that dated to his parents' time. The floor was covered with worn throw rugs and large pillows for their animals to curl up on, and the mantelpiece held a collection of quartz that his soldier mom had brought back from her tours overseas. Other than replacing the pillows, the only thing Jace had added was the big screen TV on the wall. He'd had to rig up a solar-powered electricity system, but it was worth it.

Now the only thing that greeted him was Tigger, a testy orange tomcat who'd moved in last year and never left. That was strange. Jace glanced around, nostrils flared, testing the air for his den mates' scents. With four men besides himself calling the den home, it was rarely empty.

"Everyone is out looking for you," Adric said. "They should be back soon—I sent word we found you. But I had people searching in a fifty-mile radius."

He grunted. "Call out the effing cavalry, why don't you?"

"Shut up and get into bed."

Suha had gone down the hall to Jace's bedroom. She didn't have to ask where it was. She'd patched up his wounds more than once.

With Adric's help, he hobbled after her and lowered himself onto the edge of the mattress. Damn, he'd swear these cuts had been seared into his gut by Hades himself. This morning he'd thought they were almost healed, but now they felt worse than ever.

Suha placed a small, blunt-fingered hand on his shoulder. "Lie down before you fall down."

He gritted his teeth and obeyed. But it was good to be home in his own bed. His muscles softened.

Suha scanned the wound with her quartz as he stared at the ceiling. His dad had left the stone walls bare in here, too. The stone was dotted with mica, giving the dark gray rock a pretty shimmer. He could almost hear the walls humming.

"Not bad," Suha murmured. "They're healing, especially the shallow one, but deep inside, they're still open. And you're spiking a high fever."

Her voice seemed to come from far away. He dragged his gaze back to her face.

A fever. That's why he felt so odd, as if he were floating above the bed. He dug his fingers into the sheets to ground himself.

Adric got a chair from the kitchen for Suha and set it next to the bed. "The humans cleaned the cuts out with salt water," he told her.

"Within a half hour," Jace added.

"Thank the gods for that." Suha frowned at her quartz. "But the iron had already spread into your blood. That's why you still feel—"

"Like shit," Jace finished for her. "But I'll heal."

"With help." She fixed him with a stern look. "Now relax and breathe."

Jace scowled. "I don't need your energy. Save it..." He trailed off as he lost his train of thought.

"I'll be the judge of that," the healer returned. "Close your eyes and breathe. Picture your body filling with healing energy...a warm, golden light."

"I'll help." Adric moved to Jace's other side, but Suha shook her head.

"I know you're strong, but you're burnt from being out searching all night. Save your energy for yourself. I've got this."

Adric nodded but remained where he was. He gave Jace's shoulder a squeeze. "You heard the woman. Close your eyes and let her do her stuff."

He obediently closed his eyes and focused on the warmth in his belly. At first it seared, the unhealthy fire of last night, but even worse. He went hot, then cold. The humming of the walls grew louder, became an irritating buzz that made him want to clamp his hands to his ears.

He moved his legs restively. "Hot."

"I know." Suha murmured something to Adric and a minute

later he returned with a damp cloth. Suha placed it on his forehead, and Jace gave a hiss of relief.

The burning changed, became a pleasant glow that infused his wounds with healing energy. The buzzing in his head receded as his own quartz's crystals hummed louder in response, until his whole body was vibrating with an unearthly music that was both sound and magic.

He drew a deep breath and released it, and let himself float in the soothing sea of energy.

Time passed. Ten minutes, then another ten.

Adric touched Jace's shoulder, ignoring Suha's directive to add his energy to the mix.

Jace slit his eyes. His friend squeezed Jace's shoulder, his normally sculpted, arrogant face soft with concern.

Suha shook her head at Adric, but allowed him to braid his energy through hers. They all knew that he couldn't remain idle when any of his people were hurting. The vibrations swelled to an ocean of sound, peaceful and yet energizing.

More time passed as the energy ebbed and flowed, washing the pain away. His eyelids grew too heavy to lift.

"There," Suha said. "That should do it. You're going to have a couple of scars, but that can't be helped." She touched his cheek. "How do you feel?"

He forced his lids to open. Suha's pretty oval face hovered above him, her large doe-eyes narrowed with concentration.

"Great," he murmured. "Sleepy, but great. Thank you."

"Good. I want you to stay in bed for a few days, got it?"

He nodded.

"He'll be fine," Suha said to Adric.

He briefly closed his eyes, and Jace realized how worried he'd been. "Thank you," he told the healer.

"You'll stay with him?"

"Only until his den mates arrive, and then I have to get home to Marjani. But I'll check back later."

"How is she?"

Adric shrugged. A year ago last spring, Marjani had been kidnapped and raped by a den of feral water fada. All the ferals were dead, and Marjani's body was healed, but it was going to take a long time before her mind was whole again. It clawed at all of them, but Adric had taken it extra hard—because how do you get over your sister being hurt like that?

Jace knew the answer: you didn't. It was always part of you. The regrets, the what-ifs, the fucking helplessness. Because if you'd only known your sister was in danger...

"About the same," Adric said at last.

Suha pressed her lips together. "I'll come by to see her later."

"Thank you." The alpha's face was naked with the love and hurt he felt for his sister. "I thought she was getting better, but she hasn't been outside in over a week. I can't—" He spread his hands.

Jace roused himself to say, "Tell her...I need a visitor."

"That's not a bad idea," Suha said. "Tomorrow, maybe." She squeezed Jace's hand. "You be good now, you hear? When I say stay in bed, I mean it. You don't want a relapse."

"Yes, ma'am."

A slim black brow winged up. "And don't think I don't know when someone's being evasive. Say the words."

He scowled, but she simply gazed back until he muttered, "All right. I'll stay in bed. For the rest of the day."

He caught Adric's smirk and scowled at him as well, but his friend returned, "Listen to the healer, Jace. I need you at full strength to help get the bastard that did this. Now, are you hungry?"

And Jace realized he was. Starving, in fact.

"Just liquids today," Suha said. "Broth, a yogurt smoothie. We don't want to stress his digestive system yet." She gave them both a kiss and let herself out.

With her gone, Jace took a nap while Adric went out to a

diner to pick up some food. Yogurt wasn't his usual fare, but it was about all he could handle right now. At least it was strawberry. He sipped the smoothie and watched enviously as Adric wolfed down his own two ham-and-egg sandwiches in rapid succession.

Jace's den mates returned. They wandered in and out of the room to see how he was doing. Sam, a burly redhead whose animal was a Bengal tiger, was first. He was followed by Beau, a slow-moving, slow-talking bear, and Horace, a cougar who was one of the clan's best trackers. They stood over Jace, shaking their heads and needling him about being caught off-guard by a fae until Adric told them to get the hell out and let him rest.

The last to arrive was Zuri, who'd been directing the cleanup in Grace Harbor. A fellow lieutenant, Zuri was a tall, dark and charismatic wolf who pretty much had to beat women off with a stick. Along with Adric, he was Jace's closest friend.

Zuri got a second chair from the kitchen and set it next to the bed. "Everything's calm." He propped his long legs on the foot of the mattress. "I followed Jace's trail myself from the bar to the human's house, and I couldn't scent a thing."

"And the woman and her brother?" asked Adric.

"I have Kara watching the house." Zuri named a young female who had recently arrived from their sister clan in Jamaica. "She's good at blending in with humans. Even if they see her, they won't know she's one of us."

"Excellent," Adric replied.

Jace nodded, relieved. He'd been going to ask that Adric see to Evie's protection. "The woman—Evie—she's good people. I'd hate to see her and her brother get hurt because they stuck their necks out for me."

Adric and Zuri exchanged a look.

"You don't usually go for human women," said Zuri.

He growled. "Who the fuck says I'm going for her?"

His friend raised his hands, palm out. "Nobody."

Adric snorted and got to his feet. "Look, I have to go. I could use a shower—bad—and I told Marjani I'd bring her some breakfast." He lifted the takeout bag. "She doesn't remember to eat sometimes. Feel better, okay?"

He squeezed Jace's shoulder and with a nod to Zuri, left.

Zuri stayed another few minutes and then started yawning until Jace told him to go to bed, he'd be fine. The other men were either in bed or in the living room watching TV.

Jace looked at Tigger, who had stretched out between his open legs. "Looks like it's just the two of us."

Tigger yawned and kneaded the sheet, narrowly missing Jace's balls with his claws, and then settled his head on his paws. A minute later he was snoring.

8

―――――

"And don't come back." Evie slammed the deadbolt shut behind the two fada.

Kyler was studying her as if she had two heads.

"Damn it," she snapped, "I am *not* fae."

"Part fae." He leaned in to sniff her. "You smell human to me."

"Very funny." She shoved him away, but he just chuckled. "Of course, I do. If I were fae, wouldn't I know it?"

"Maybe. But one thing we do know—if you have fae blood and I don't, then it's not Mom."

She scraped both hands through her hair. "Drop it, Kyler."

"So it's Fane."

She heaved a sigh. "And God knows where he is."

Her dad wasn't the type to leave a forwarding address—if he even had an address to leave. Fane Morningstar came and went as the spirit moved him, and Lord knew, that wasn't often; she could count on her fingers the number of times she'd seen him in the past ten years.

It wasn't that she didn't like her dad. Everyone liked him. He was tall and blond, with a laidback way of moving and talking as if time moved slower for him somehow. He always had a smile for you, and she'd never once heard him raise his voice.

If her mom asked difficult questions, like how long he was staying this time, the man just...disappeared. Evie had learned early not to count on Fane. You just enjoyed him while he was around, and then did your best to forget him when he left.

"If anyone has fae blood, it's Fane," Kyler said. "There's that picture we found. You know, after Mom died."

"Yeah." Evie set her jaw and started tidying the kitchen, picking up the bowl and coffee cups and setting them in the sink.

They'd found the photo tucked in a cigar box along with other mementos. In it, Fane had an arm slung around their mom's shoulders, and they were both grinning at the camera. It had to have been taken over twenty-five years ago.

The last time they'd seen Fane, he'd looked exactly the same, right down to his wide grin and unlined face.

"What are you going to do?" Kyler asked.

"Make pancakes." She took a box of pancake mix from the cupboard.

Her brother blew out a breath. "About this fae thing."

"Nothing." She measured a cup of the mix into a bowl, added milk and broke an egg on top of it. "Even if it's true, what does it matter?" she asked as she stirred the batter. "It's not going to change anything. If I do have some fae in me, it's probably something like one-hundredth. It's not like I can work magic or anything."

Kyler placed his hands on his narrow hips and shook his head. "My sister, a fae."

She pointed her fork at him. "This is between you and me, got it? You tell anyone, and you're toast."

He grinned and raised his hands. "Okay, okay. Don't shoot me with a fae ball, sis."

"Very funny. I mean it, Kyler Ferris." She gave the batter a vicious stir. "Just get the plates out, will you?"

"Hey, don't be so touchy. At least you have a dad to visit you. I don't really even remember mine. I probably wouldn't know him if I passed him on the street."

Evie bit her lip. She ached to hug her brother, but she knew from experience he'd shrug her off. Their eyes met.

"You'd know him."

"Yeah, sure." Kyler opened the cupboard and took out two plates.

AFTER BREAKFAST, Kyler went to school and Evie finished cleaning up. She double-bagged Jace's bloody T-shirt and, then, recalling what a good sense of smell the fada had, threw it into a dumpster on the next block. Meanwhile, she washed and dried the sheet he'd used.

In a short while, there was no trace that Jace had spent the night on her couch. She'd almost believe she'd dreamed the whole thing, except she didn't have that good of an imagination.

How was he doing? She bit her lip. He was the kind of man who'd do too much, too soon.

Not my business, she told herself. He had his friends to take care of him now. The best thing was to forget they'd ever met.

Her mind turned to what Adric had said about her being part fae. He'd seemed so certain.

If only there was some way to get hold of her dad. But the last time she'd seen him was two years ago, right before her mom died. She wasn't even sure how he'd heard her mom was sick, but he'd arrived in time to say goodbye. Her mom had been alert enough to smile at him, and Evie would always be grateful for that.

Fane had stayed through the death and, to Evie's surprise, had even taken charge of the arrangements, including paying for the memorial service and cremation. On the third night he'd said,

"You seem like you're doing okay, Evie love," and the next morning he was gone, leaving only a glittering stone on her night table...which turned out to be a diamond worth close to ten thousand dollars.

Trust her dad to give her a gift that caused even more trouble. She'd been afraid a jeweler would ask awkward questions, so she'd pawned it instead. But the pawn shop had given her five thousand for it, and she had to admit the cash had helped.

Evie shook her head and took out her laptop. She had homework to do.

That afternoon she ate an early dinner with Kyler, and then headed to the Wine Bar, an upscale restaurant on the water where she was a server. Grace Harbor was a small, historic city bordered on two sides by water—the Susquehanna River to the north, and the Chesapeake Bay to the east. This time of year, the streets were filled with boaters and weekenders. It was Friday evening, and the restaurant was packed.

She should've been too busy to think, but Jace kept popping into her head at odd times. That curious smile as he'd been hurt and bleeding next to her stoop. His broad shoulders and cat-like grace. The way his eyes changed from hazel to green...

"Excuse me." The man at the table before her spoke. "Miss? Is that our food?"

Evie blinked. She was standing in the middle of the restaurant, a plate in each hand. "Sorry about that," she said with a smile, and slid the plates in front of the man and his date.

He closed his mouth on whatever he'd been about to say and gave her a brief smile back. She smiled at the woman he was with as well, because it was low class—and bad for tips—to flirt with a guy in front of his date. "Can I get you anything else?"

"No, we're fine." They each waved a hand, eager to assure her there was no problem. She'd always had a gift for soothing people's feathers, making them smile. It was why she was such a good waitress.

But was there more to it than that? Her mom had said Evie's way with people came from Fane.

Damn it, she was *not* going to think about it. Fae or not, what did it matter? It wasn't like she could do anything useful, like change straw into gold. Now that would be a real Gift.

She got off work a little after eleven. She'd taken her car this time, because after last night, she was wary about walking home after dark. Now she came out of the restaurant to find a light rain falling.

Hell. She hadn't brought an umbrella. She grabbed her keys and her backpack and hurried through the lot to where she'd parked her ancient blue compact under a street light—just in case.

At least it was a warm rain. Evie swiped the water from her face and started the car. The ignition sputtered and went dead. The car had been her mother's, and it had grown cranky with age. It especially didn't like wet weather.

"C'mon, hon." She crossed her fingers and tried again, and this time the engine ground to life.

The half-mile drive home took less than five minutes. She drove slowly along the wet streets. The black iron lampposts cast a warm yellow glow. Grace Harbor had once been a working-man's town, with crabbers, fishermen and a herring cannery, but these days, it had a funky, small-town vibe with mom-and-pop stores sharing space with art galleries, antique shops and upscale restaurants like the Wine Bar.

She passed a couple of her neighbors out for a stroll, umbrellas lifted. It was hard to believe that just last night a man had almost died right in her backyard.

She parked her car on the concrete pad behind the house, took a thorough look around, and then sprinted up the steps to her back door.

Kyler wasn't home yet, but there was nothing unusual about that. His curfew on the weekends was midnight, and he usually came home the last possible second. That wouldn't have both-ered her, but the last few weeks he'd started pushing the curfew—coming home at twelve-thirty or one and daring her to object.

Tonight was one of those nights. She started texting him five minutes after midnight.

At least he replied, telling her not to worry.

Too late, she replied. *I'm worried and I want you home. NOW.*

She could see he'd viewed the text, but he didn't reply. She sat on the easy chair, fuming, as she finished her paper. Because she *was* worried about him, especially after last night. What if that night fae came back? Her whole body went cold, just thinking about it.

It was almost one o'clock before Kyler sauntered in the front door, red-eyed and smelling of pot. He flopped on the couch and regarded her through slit eyes.

"Go ahead. Tell me what a bad boy I am."

She clenched her jaw so hard her teeth hurt. "You're only sixteen, Kyler. Too young to be out after midnight, and too damn young to be smoking weed."

"Go to hell, Evie." He rested his arm over his eyes. "You're not my mom."

Her stomach sucked in. For a few seconds, she was blinded by hurt and anger.

"No," she said as calmly as she could, "but I'm responsible for you until you're eighteen. If you get arrested, it's on my watch."

"Don't worry about it. I'll tell them it's me, not you."

"You think I care about that? I care about you, asshat. And I promised Mom I'd take care of you, damn it."

He raised up on his elbows to glare at her. "Fuck your prom-ise. If taking care of me is so hard, then forget it. Mom never should've asked—"

"Oh, for Chrissake." She rubbed the bridge of her nose. "I didn't mean it like that. You know I didn't."

"Yeah, sure."

"But I mean it, Kyler. From now on, you'd better be home at midnight, or I swear I'll—" She halted because she didn't have anything to threaten him with, and they both knew it.

Kyler levered himself off the couch. "Okay, okay," he grumbled. "Don't get your panties in a twist."

She watched as he stalked out of the living room, his thin body rigid, his T-shirt a little too small. He'd grown six inches this year so that she was barely able to keep him in clothes.

She blew out a breath and rested her head on the back of the chair.

What am I going to do with him this summer?

9

———

ace spent most of Saturday in bed.

Tigger kept him company. Jace wasn't sure who'd first let the tomcat in, but within a week he had the run of the place. He'd adopted Jace, wisely zeroing in on the alpha of the small den. Jace had christened him Tigger, just to yank Sam's chain, because Tigger was basically a mini-Sam—an orange tiger-in-miniature.

Jace did sleep for a couple of hours. When he woke up, Zuri brought him some beef broth. They talked a little, and then Zuri left to run some errands. With the coast clear, Tigger jumped on Jace's bed and settled against his leg. A short while later he was purring.

Touched, Jace stroked the cat's fur. Tigger didn't usually share anyone's bed, preferring a perch on the living room couch where he could survey both the kitchen and the front door. He was clearly offering support to an injured den mate.

The afternoon passed slowly. Jace took another short nap. When he awoke, his head was clear for the first time in twenty-four hours. He stared at the ceiling, stroking Tigger and thinking.

Frigging woman. Because he couldn't get the tough little human out of his mind.

He knew damn well she needed help. It couldn't be easy, raising a kid who wasn't much younger than her.

Jace knew something about that himself. Yeah, Takira had been older than him, not younger, but only by two years. During the Darktime, the alpha—Adric's uncle Leron—had separated families as punishment or simply to keep them from conspiring against him. Jace's own mom had been sent on a military mission to South America that had kept her away for a year. While she was gone, his peace-loving, half Native American dad had been killed in a bloody spate of fighting.

By the time Jace was fifteen, he and Takira had been on their own save for the small pack they'd formed with Adric, Marjani, and some of the other young members of their clan. At fifteen, Jace was already bigger and stronger than his sister, so he'd been her protector as much as she was his.

And then Takira had fallen for Silver, a half-fae, half-human who turned out to be Prince Langdon's illegitimate son. Langdon had kept Silver a secret—the night fae frowned on mating with anyone but another pureblood—but somehow Tyrus, his only other living son, had found out. Maybe even from Adric's bastard of an uncle.

Remembering, Jace's fingers tightened in Tigger's fur. The cat hissed and Jace released him. Tigger shot him an outraged glare and then stalked off, stiff-legged, to the foot of the mattress before lying down again.

The Darktime. It had been like a virus attacking the clan, a killing fever that swept through the ranks, sucking in even good men and women until no one knew who to trust. Darkness and hatred had ruled.

But the day Jace had heard that Takira had been raped and murdered had been the day he'd truly understood darkness. A familiar acridness coated the back of his tongue. If only he'd known that Tyrus had targeted Takira and her small family...

Jace had been with Adric, planning a strike against Leron Savonett. That small, well-planned attack had turned the tide, eventually leading to the battle that finally took down the vicious alpha. Jace had rushed to Takira's den with the news that she no longer had to hide Merry. But they were gone. The next he'd heard, Takira was dead, and Silver had taken his daughter and gone into hiding.

He dragged a hand over his face. What the hell made him think he could help Evie and Kyler? Better he stayed away. If Tyrus was stalking Jace, he was a danger to them.

He threw off the sheet, earning another irritated hiss from Tigger, but Jace was going to go insane if he spent any more time staring at the ceiling.

He limped into the living room and sprawled on the couch. One by one his den mates woke up from their naps and joined him, taking seats on the chairs or the large pillows strewn on the floor.

When Adric returned it was after six o'clock, and the four of them were eating Chinese take-out—soup for Jace—and watching the Orioles. When Adric entered, everyone except Jace rose to their feet. They hugged and nuzzled each other—their animals needing the touch—and then Adric took Sam's seat on the couch next to Jace.

Sam didn't even blink. Adric was the alpha, but more, he'd earned their loyalty a hundred times over. The man would die for them, and nearly had.

Adric looked Jace over with a professional eye. He wasn't a healer, but like all of them, he'd done his share of field medic work. "Should you be out of bed?"

Jace growled. "Don't start."

"It's your funeral," he said, helping himself to a plate of ginger garlic chicken. He watched the last two innings of the baseball game with the rest of them, and then jerked his chin at the other men. "I need to talk to Jace and Zuri."

The room cleared immediately. Adric spun a chair around so its back was facing Jace, and sat down, arms draped over the back, while Zuri took a seat on the opposite end of the couch.

Adric scrutinized Jace. "You sure you're all right?"

His nape tightened. "Why?" He set his empty soup bowl on the coffee table. "What is it?"

"I've been thinking. That night fae was waiting for you, right?"

"Far as I could tell."

"So, d'you think it was Lord Prick?"

"I didn't see him," Jace said, "but who else could it be? The man was right outside Evie and Kyler's door. We could feel him out there, trying to sense where I was. I protected the three of us the best I could, and then I passed out. Somehow she held him off. Hell, maybe thinking happy thoughts worked."

"Could be the fae in her. If I had to choose, I'd say she was sun fae, and if there's one thing the sun fae are good at, it's being happy."

Jace nodded slowly. Sun fae were rich, sexy, hedonistic—the fae world's version of a Hollywood elite. Evie might not have the wealth, but she had a sun fae's magnetism. Hell, even with a knife wound to the gut, he'd wanted to fuck her.

"But if it was his royal prickness," Adric continued, "then why? He targeted you for a reason."

"Merry," Jace said, tightlipped. "He can't get at her because she's too well protected. That ward of her grandfather's keeps the night fae away from her, and Rock Run has adopted her into their clan. You'd have to be touched in the head to fuck with Rui do Mar." The river fada who was Merry's adopted father was also Rock Run's most feared assassin. "No." Jace shook his head. "The only way the night fae can strike at her is through me."

"Merry, yeah—but why you? Sure, you're her uncle, but it's

Silver's line he's worried about. And if he really wanted to hurt Merry, he'd go after Rui and Valeria."

"True." Jace rubbed his forehead. "But then why?"

Adric was out of his chair and pacing. He could never sit still for long.

"Think about it, Jace. You're the key to my whole strategy for getting the clan back on its feet. You're the one who knows the quartz technology inside out. Yeah, we've got others who can do some of what you do, but no one has a grasp of all the pieces like you do. If you die, the project could be set back years—and who knows what would happen in the meantime?"

"Hell." Jace met Adric's eyes. "You think someone's trying to sabotage the project."

"I do."

Zuri's brow creased. "But why would the night fae care?"

Adric and Jace spoke as one. "Because he's not working alone."

10

____

$\mathcal{M}$onday morning, Jace woke up feeling almost like his old self.

Suha had returned on Sunday to nag him to take it easy. He nodded and obeyed, because the healer knew her stuff—and he did need the rest. Suha's healing combined with the energy from his own recharged quartz to speed things along.

Zuri had brought Jace's bike home, so just after dawn, he slipped out of the den, Tigger on his heels. Somehow Suha got wind of it, though—he'd swear the woman was part Seer—and he found her waiting in the backyard.

The healer set her hands on her hips. "Where d'you think you're going?"

Tigger perked up—he had a crush on Suha. He butted her calf, marking her with his scent.

She ignored the lovesick tabby to glare at Jace. "I haven't cleared you to work, Jones."

_Uh-oh._ She'd used his last name. Not a good sign.

He attempted a winning smile. "I'm fine. See?" He lifted his T-shirt to show her. The cuts had healed, but as she'd predicted, they'd left behind two raised red scars. Normally fada healed quickly and cleanly, but not when iron was involved. Jace would bear the night fae's marks the rest of his life.

"I'll be the judge of that." Suha removed her crystal and ran it over his belly. "Not bad," she conceded. "But you nearly died, Jace. Iron poisoning is no joke, and you suffered some internal damage. I want you to take it easy this week."

"I am taking it easy. I'm only going to the Factory to test some of the new quartz. Those new smartphones are losing their charge too quickly."

The Factory was the name Adric had given their combination test lab and manufacturing plant. Right now, it was just a big room in a building they'd rescued from the wrecking ball, but Ric liked to think big.

Suha nodded. The clan had been informed about the basics of what they were doing—produce quartz smartphones to Jace's design, and then sell them to the other earth fada clans.

"So?" she returned. "They can survive a few days without you."

"But I can't. If I stay in another day, I'll be climbing the walls. Even Tigger is sick of me." He nodded at the tomcat, who'd tired of trying to gain Suha's attention and was investigating an interesting smell near the fence. "Please?"

The healer cast her gaze skyward. "Don't blame me if you have a relapse."

"I won't." Jace planted a kiss on her cheek. "Relapse, that is."

And they both knew Suha would come running if he did.

THE FACTORY WAS ONLY about a mile away in a blighted section of West Baltimore. The building had once been a grocery store, and the sign outside still read Allen's Stop-and-Shop because that was as good a camouflage as any. After they'd cleared out the display shelves and cash registers, they'd been left with one large room for the tables, computers, and equipment used to manufacture the smartphones, and a storage room in the back.

Jace felt a familiar pride as he entered the Factory. This was his baby; Adric had given him free rein to set up shop, directing the small crew to not just manufacture smartphones for the clan, but to refine and improve the technology. The beauty of quartz was that it produced a strong current when fed by an earth fada's natural energy. It was also strong and waterproof.

Adric was even considering selling the phones to water fada, whose biology tended to short out regular electronic devices, although none of them were sure they wanted to put such a tool in their rivals' hands. They'd have to work out the energy issues, too. Water fada didn't require quartz for life energy like the earth fada did, but on the other hand, they couldn't work with the crystals from an early age like Jace's people could.

And after that, who knew? If Adric could work out a deal with a human communications company—and figure out a way for humans to operate the quartz—the sky was the limit. They might one day sell the phones to select humans as well. The military would love a waterproof phone that could hold a charge for several weeks. Right now, though, you had to have at least a few drops of fae blood to operate a smartphone.

But there was one big problem; the technology burned the quartz up. It wasn't reusable like an earth fada's own quartz, and low-grade quartz didn't work at all. The clan desperately needed a new supply of high-grade quartz like the vein they'd located on the border of Rising Sun Fae territory.

Resolving all the issues would take years, but Jace was up for it. During the Darktime he'd used his Gift with crystals to design weapons. It was a pure joy to use his Gift in a positive way.

Now he took a deep, satisfied inhale, breathing in the familiar scents—the sandiness of ground quartz, the oil they used to reduce dust, the metallic odor of machinery. A couple of people were already at work—an engineer known as Frog for some damn reason, and a pretty, dark-haired tech named Dina. They glanced over their shoulders and did a simultaneous double take.

"Jace?" Dina came to her feet. "Shouldn't you be in bed?"

"Suha gave me the green light."

Dina inhaled, testing his statement for truth, and then shrugged. "Okay, great. I have an idea as to why the energy is getting sucked out so fast." A cougar who'd inherited her mom's Italian coloring—and brains—Dina was even more single-minded than him.

He pulled up a chair and the three of them hashed out her idea. A couple of other men came in a few hours later, and they all traded ideas before breaking off to test them.

They were eating take-out pizza at their work stations around one o'clock when Adric walked in. Jace removed his goggles and rose to his feet. "Hey, Ric. What's up?"

"Meeting. Zuri and Luc are on their way." Adric helped himself to a slice of pizza. "What the fuck?" He frowned at the broccoli and spinach.

"Dina thinks we need more greens," Jace said.

"We're cats, not cows," Adric muttered. But he took a large bite and then smiled at Dina. "Actually, that's not bad." He took another bite.

Dina beamed. Like all the unmated women, she perked up around the alpha, even though everyone knew Adric wasn't ready to take a mate. Not that the man was deprived. He had his pick of the clan's women, who were happy to hook up with the alpha even for a night.

A minute later, first Zuri and then Luc entered, following their practice of arriving separately at meetings for security reasons. Adric gulped down his pizza and jerked his head in the direction of their underground war room.

Dina, Frog and the rest of the Factory crew looked curious, but they knew better than to ask questions. Adric shared information on a need-to-know basis, having learned the hard way that the less people knew about your business, the better. Sometimes it even saved your life.

Zuri and Luc grabbed some pizza and the four of them headed for the storage room. There, Adric opened a trap door and they all passed through a ward set to allow only Adric and his lieutenants through before climbing down a ladder.

The war room had been carved by Adric and a couple trusted stoneworkers from the bedrock beneath the Factory. Adric was a Gifted tracker—he hired himself out to the fae for outrageous sums—but what he really liked to do was work with stone. He could make a rock practically sing with joy as he used a combination of chiseling and magic to transform it into art.

A thin vein of white quartz twisted through the rock walls. The quartz had been magically engineered to soundproof the room. Combined with the ward, it even allowed them to speak a fae's name freely without attracting his or her attention.

They seated themselves around the large table Adric had carved from a single large rock. Like Camelot's famous table, it was round. This way, Adric said, each of them could see everyone else—and everyone's ideas had equal weight.

Adric spoke to Jace first. "I hear you're cleared for work, just nothing too strenuous."

Jace scowled. "Suha snitched on me."

"Of course. You're not going out on this one, bro. But I wanted your input." He looked around the table, addressing all three of them. "On Saturday night Zuri went back to the bar in Grace Harbor where Jace was attacked. He asked some questions, but no one knew anything."

Jace nodded. No surprise there. "The assassin 'ported in. I don't know about the other two, but they must have blended in somehow or I'd have seen them myself."

"They probably used a glamour," Adric said. "Made themselves look like someone else—someone who fit in. Maybe even a river fada."

"But a glamour only fools the eyes—not the nose."

The alpha shrugged. "So they didn't get too close. You weren't going to scent them across a crowded bar." He looked at Zuri. "Tell him what you found out."

"I didn't discover a damn thing inside the bar," the tall, dark wolf said, "but I thought I'd sniff around the parking lot, see if I could pick up anything. That's where I ran into Rui do Mar, who was having a look around himself. I figured we should coordinate our efforts. Grace Harbor is their town, not ours."

"Do Mar knows Tyrus's scent," Adric inserted. "You know what he did to the prick after he tried to kidnap Merry."

"Tracked him to his lair in France," Jace said, "and beat the shit out of him. Almost killed the bastard."

Officially, Rock Run remained quiet about the attack on Tyrus, because if it became known that Dion's second-in-command was the man who roughed up his son, Langdon would've been forced to act. This way, the prince could pretend nothing happened—and Tyrus wasn't going to broadcast that a fada had overcome him so easily.

"Anyway," Zuri said, "Do Mar was pissed as hell that a night fae dared attack a fada practically in Rock Run's backyard. He promised to let Dion know, and then we went over the parking lot with a fine-toothed comb. Not only does do Mar have Tyrus's scent memorized, the man's animal is a shark. He can detect a few particles of blood in a fucking ocean."

Jace nodded impatiently. None of this was news to him. "And? He picked up Tyrus's scent?"

"Yep. Do Mar was sure—said he'd never forget it. And he recognized the scent of the man you killed, too. Tyrus's chief enforcer."

Jace was on his feet. "That sonofabitch." He spun to look at Adric. "I'm going after him."

"No fucking way."

Jace slapped his palms on the granite table. "Damn it, Ric.

You're my alpha, but this is my family. Don't ask me to choose between the two."

Adric's snarl made Jace's spine tighten. The other two men moved uneasily.

"Sit. Down."

Jace's claws pricked out, but he grabbed onto his patience and obeyed.

"First," the alpha held up a finger, "you're in no condition to take on a toddler, let alone a fae. Second," he held up another finger, "if we do this, we have to be smart about it. You're a smart man. Use that brain of yours."

Zuri murmured agreement, while Luc looked on, his wolf-gold eyes watchful, but Jace knew he'd be a hundred percent behind whatever Adric decided.

"Fine," Jace spat out. Adric might be right, but Jace was sick unto death of Tyrus targeting his family. "But this time, he's dead. The man's not going to rest until every last Jones is wiped off the face of the earth."

"If it's you he's targeting," Adric returned. "I'm not as sure as you are. Is it you he wants, or would any of my lieutenants have done?"

"Does it matter?" Zuri asked. "Either way, I vote we put the man out of his misery." His lips peeled in a show of canines.

"I intend to," the alpha returned. "When he tried to kill Merry six years ago, I had no choice but to let Rock Run go after him. We weren't strong enough."

They all nodded. At that point, Adric had only been alpha for a few months and the clan was still reeling from the Darktime.

"But things are different now." Adric's smile was deadly, his cougar a shadow on his face. "We're a hell of a lot stronger than we were six years ago. If Tyrus wants a fight, he's going to get a fight. I'll bring it right to his fucking lair."

They all rumbled agreement.

"But we have to be careful," Zuri said. "If Prince Langdon finds out, we're all dead."

"Agreed." Adric looked at Jace. "Thoughts?"

His mind was already ticking along: analyzing, examining patterns. "We find out everything we can about Tyrus. Where he lives, who he hangs out with, what he fucking eats for breakfast. Then we figure the best way to take him out so that it doesn't rebound on us."

"My thoughts exactly," said Adric. "I don't care if it takes a month or two. In fact, that might be good. He's a fae. He'll think we're too stupid—or afraid—to come after him."

Zuri fingered his quartz. "The night fae compound is in Virginia, but Tyrus spends most of his time at his lair in France. We'll have to catch him outside. The night fae guard their lairs with triple wards."

"So we catch him outside," said Jace. "Drag him into the noonday sun and keep him there until his fucking skin fries."

"First, we need more intel," Adric said, "including exactly where his lair is."

"Do Mar will tell us," Jace said. "He has as much skin in this game as we do."

"Good." Adric looked around the table. "Well? You in?"

They nodded as one. "Fuck yeah," Luc said.

"You're elected, then," Adric told him.

Jace made a sound of dissent, and Adric slashed him a look. "We need you here to work on the smartphones."

"They'll keep for a few weeks."

"Do you really want to be out of the country if he sends someone after Merry? We're not even a hundred percent sure he's in France."

Jace blew out a breath. Adric was right; he'd rather stay close for now. "Fine," he said, even though his animal was scraping against his insides, coldly eager to go hunting.

Adric turned back to Luc. "Take Nash with you."

"Nash Savonett?" Luc lifted a shaggy black brow. "You sure?" Nash was Leron's youngest son.

Adric nodded. "He's shaping up to be an excellent tracker, and he's earned it. It's been six years, and he's proved his loyalty to me. It's time we gave him a chance to work his way up the hierarchy."

"What about Kane?" Jace asked. "He's not going to be happy if you pass him over for his younger brother."

"Then he can prove himself the way his brother has. He works hard, but he plays both sides. I don't trust him with a covert job like this."

Zuri cleared his throat. "There's one more thing. You were right, Jace—you heard a third man that night you were attacked. Do Mar doesn't know who it is, but he had the scent of an earth fada."

11

$\mathcal{A}$dric loped across the broken-down Westside neighborhood he called home. A third of the houses were boarded up or turned into squats for junkies. But there were families here too—a tricycle was overturned on a small, neatly-kept lawn, and two women sat on a stoop, a toddler between them.

A man with a gangster tat on his neck strutted down the sidewalk, all broad shoulders and attitude. Then he got a closer look and continued past, eyes down. Adric was the most dangerous predator around, and everyone knew it.

Adric rented the house above his den to a pair of baby-faced drug dealers barely out of their teens. The older one leaned against the porch rail, arms crossed, a cigarillo hanging out of his mouth.

"Wassup, bro."

Adric jerked his chin. The drug dealers were camouflage—no one would guess the Baltimore alpha lived here—but he was thinking it was time he cleaned up the neighborhood like Jace had.

The teenager's flat brown eyes tracked him as he headed

around the house. He pulled up the trap door concealed beneath the back porch and loped down the two flights of stairs to his den. As he entered the living room, the motion triggered the quartz wall sconces he'd installed when he and Marjani had first moved in.

The den had belonged to a family who had been completely wiped out in the Darktime, but Adric didn't think about that. Not anymore. It was his home now, the first since his parents had died and he and Marjani had been sent to live with their uncle. Leron's den had never felt like home.

The wall sconces cast a warm amber light over his sister, curled up on a rug in front of the fireplace. She was in her cougar form again. She'd turned on the fake fire—also quartz-powered —and was gazing into it, eyes slit. The flickering firelight turned her pelt a soft gold, but it couldn't conceal her weight loss or that her fur was patchy with ill health.

Adric blew out a breath. Sometimes an entire day went by without his sister taking her human form.

"Did you eat today?"

Her head lifted, turned. Cool blue eyes examined him as if he were an annoying insect.

He clenched his hands, feeling helpless. "You have to eat, Jani."

She tilted her head, considering that.

His claws pricked his palms, his cat wanting to slash something. He drew a slow breath and retracted them.

"You can't go on like this. You didn't go out the whole weekend. Jace asked for you. He almost died, you know. Would it have killed you to pay him a visit?"

That got through to her. She'd always liked Jace. Her furry gold brow knit, and she yowled a question.

"He's fine," Adric replied. "He was back at work today."

She set her head back on her paws. Discussion closed.

He let out a growl of frustration. Marjani was one step away from becoming feral, lost in her animal—and forever lost to him. Because he'd have to put her down if she became truly wild. He couldn't have a feral cougar with her intelligence roaming Baltimore.

He fingered his quartz, tempted. He was one of the rare fada with two Gifts. He was a tracker, one of the best in the world. But he had another, secret Gift—the ability to hypnotize others with his quartz.

Marjani was one of the few people who knew about his second Gift. He could hypnotize her, compel her to forget what had happened last year. But she'd made him promise that he wouldn't.

"No," she'd snarled when he'd suggested it. "This is me. My life. I need to deal with it. You can't make everything better, Ric—not this time."

For Marjani, he'd break a sworn vow, even if the backlash killed him. But she was the one who'd extracted the vow, and that was what stopped him.

He dropped onto the rug. It was a plush orange shag like something from the sixties, one of his few indulgences. He'd installed it as much for Marjani as for himself—a reward for the times they'd shivered all night in some boarded-up house, or crouched in the chilly rain because Leron had ordered them to stand watch.

He sat cross-legged and stared into the fire. The fake flames danced, bright flickers of warmth. Even in the summer, their cats craved heat.

"I need you, Jani. I need all four of my lieutenants. There's something I'm not seeing. Lord Prick was behind Jace's attack, but it looks like he might've been working with one of us."

He swallowed something acrid. He'd done some terrible things to end the Darktime, including assassinating his own uncle rather than challenge him to a duel for alpha. But he hadn't been able to risk losing. Leron had been out of control, and Adric was the only one strong enough to take him. It was either kill Leron, or see everyone he loved die.

When he'd first taken over as alpha, he'd cleaned up the last pockets of resistance and declared the Darktime over. Most of their elders were dead, and the ones that weren't either swore allegiance to Adric—or were executed. That should've been the end of it. He'd turned his attention to rebuilding his ragged, war-torn clan, believing he had the full support of his remaining clanmates.

But six years later, he was still fighting an underground conflict that he suspected had been instigated by his own cousin, Corban Savonett. Marjani's attack had been carried out by some rogue river fada—but the rogues had been working with some of Adric's own people.

Corban had never accepted Adric as alpha. He believed that as Leron's oldest son, he should've been made alpha after his death, but the fada didn't work like that. An alpha had to earn the title. And strength wasn't enough; an alpha needed his people's respect, too.

Corban had challenged Adric anyway, and lost. But even though Adric had made his cousin a high-ranking sentry, a position just under his four lieutenants, Corban hadn't given up. Instead, the bastard had struck at Adric's weak spot—Marjani. His sister was strong—a hard-ass soldier—but they'd drugged her and smashed her quartz so she couldn't fight back.

Adric's fingers curled. If he'd had any proof that Corban was behind it, he'd have slit the bastard's throat, but his cousin was too smart to get caught. He hid behind others, and every single one of them had either died or killed themselves before Adric could question them.

He gazed broodingly at Marjani's silent form. He questioned his decision to let Corban go every day. Every single fucking day.

But—"I couldn't execute Corban without proof," he told her. "I swore when I became alpha things would be different." Plus,

Corban and his brothers were still a power in the clan. Adric had been afraid that if he pushed too hard, he'd set off another clan war.

So instead, he'd sent Corban out of the country on a job for the ice fae, after first forcing his cousin to swear he wouldn't come back until the job was complete. Corban was to capture a rogue ice fae and return her to her king for justice. Corban would be lucky to come back alive, and they both knew it. A powerful ice fae could literally freeze you where you stood. They fed on the energy of motion, meaning they could stop your heart, your lungs...or simply lock your muscles in place until you died of starvation.

Marjani's head swung toward Adric. His breath hitched. She was listening.

He hurried back into speech. "If only we knew what the fuck happened to Corban. But he's gone missing. I can't even raise him through his quartz. He could be dead—but I don't think so."

And why wasn't the ice fae king more concerned? Sindre had listened to Adric's explanation with an inscrutable expression and then said, "The agreement is void, then."

Adric had inclined his head, relieved Sindre wasn't demanding he send another man out on what amounted to a suicide mission. But it was damned odd. Sindre was an old, cold fae, and the fae had a thing about honoring a contract. The king should've been out for blood, but instead he'd given up with barely a protest.

Marjani rose to her feet, gave herself a shake and padded out of the room.

"Jani?" he asked, but she didn't acknowledge him. Disappointed, he scrubbed a hand over his face. He was so damned tired.

But a short while later, she returned, a woman once again. She paused a few feet away and gazed down at him with shadowed eyes. She'd put on gray shorts and a T-shirt. Once, she'd worn bright, colorful clothes like Suha. And just the other day, he'd come home to find she'd given herself a buzz-cut.

But she was up, and the eyes gazing down at him were the rich brown of her human form. For now, that was enough.

She stuck her hands into the back pockets of her shorts. He'd thought she was too thin as a cougar, but this was shocking. Her arms and legs were bony brown sticks.

His breath whistled in. He rose to his feet, trying to conceal his dismay.

Marjani didn't seem to notice. When she spoke, her voice was rusty from disuse. "Tell me what you know."

12

———

*M*onday evening found Jace on his way up to Grace Harbor. Suha would bitch that he was doing too much, but Merry was worried about him, and if Jace could ease that by visiting her, then he would.

He reached the Grace Harbor exit and tried not to think about Evie. But his jaguar was more basic. It perked up, flexing its claws and vibrated its throat in an instinctive mating vocalization. A picture of Evie formed in his mind—shiny blond cap of hair, big dark eyes and that tight muscle tee cupping small but perfect breasts.

"Yeah, yeah," Jace muttered. "But we're here to see Merry, remember?"

The cat settled. The cub came first. But after...

Jace headed west until he reached the narrow dirt road that led to Rock Run. Two minutes after he crossed the line into Rock Run's territory, two large men on motorcycles appeared on the next hill. They zoomed down the incline toward him, leaving a cloud of dust in their wake.

Jace stopped his bike at the top of the hill. He was in a lush old-growth forest, the Susquehanna River visible over the treetops to the north. The big river undulated in the late afternoon sun, a wide ribbon of bronze and gold. To his left, Rock Run Creek snaked through the greenery on its way to the Susquehanna.

The Rock Run men skidded to a stop a few yards way: Tiago do Rio and Chico Nobrega. The alpha had sent his own brother, and Nobrega was Tiago's best friend and a Rock Run sentry.

"Peace to you and yours." Jace raised a hand in greeting. "I came to see my niece."

"Peace," Tiago returned. "But this isn't your scheduled day." Both men were dark, good-looking Latinos, but Tiago was a younger copy of his brother Dion—big, broad and arrogant with a mane of black hair tied back with a leather thong and blue eyes so light they appeared almost silver.

"Do Mar knows why I couldn't come on Saturday," Jace returned.

And if Rui do Mar knew, then Dion knew, which meant Tiago was giving him a hard time for the hell of it. Jace's jaw tightened, but he kept his posture relaxed, nonthreatening. He'd put up with worse to see Merry.

Tiago's gaze raked over Jace. "I hear you ran into some trouble the other night."

"I did. You wouldn't happen to know anything about it, would you?"

It was Tiago's turn to tighten his jaw. "Is that what you think?"

Jace shook his head, because this wasn't worth a pissing contest. And if Rui was correct, an earth fada was to blame, possibly one from Jace's own clan. He was still reeling over that piece of information.

He gave Tiago the same response he'd given Adric. "If you wanted to take me out, you'd do it yourself, not hire a fae."

Nobrega's eyes creased with amusement. "He's got a point, Ti."

Tiago's tension eased. His mouth quirked. "If you think I'd

dare harm a hair on that pretty head of yours, you don't know your niece. She'd have my effing balls. Come on, then." He turned his bike and roared off toward the base.

"Pretty head?" Jace muttered. But he followed at a matching pace.

Nobrega fell in behind, hemming Jace between the two of them. A not-so veiled threat.

They were deep in the forest now, passing through huge old oaks, beeches, sycamores and maples. The path narrowed until they were nearly brushing the vegetation on either side: lush fiddlehead ferns, tiny pawpaw trees, a stand of mountain laurel. Jace had never seen the inside of the Rock Run base—Dion had drawn the line at that. Instead, he met Merry in the woods at the edge of the river fada's territory. It suited them both. Sometimes they ran as their jaguars; sometimes they walked as humans.

Tiago stopped near an ancient tulip poplar with a double trunk that twisted its way through the leafy green canopy, one trunk mirroring the other in a slow, ponderous dance. Jace pulled up next to him. "Thanks for the escort," he drawled as he set his bike's kickstand.

Tiago gave him a thumbs-up. "Anytime."

Merry was waiting in a clearing with Rui do Mar. She was thirteen-and-a-half now, all arms and legs in shorts and a tank top in her new favorite color—lipstick red. It was obvious she was a quarter fae; she had the sharp chin and pointed ears. But she had Takira's hazel eyes and crinkly black curls, and sometimes she did something that was so like her mom that it took Jace's breath away.

Merry spotted Jace and her face lit up. She sprang across the clearing, graceful as a leggy young deer, while her adoptive father followed at a slower pace.

Jace enfolded her in his arms. "Hey, baby."

"I was so worried about you, Uncle Jace." She hugged him back and pressed her face into his chest.

He ran his hand over her head. Her cheeks were wet when she lifted her face.

"Yo, none of that." He looked helplessly at her dad.

Do Mar was a large man with shoulders the width of a door and the cold eyes of his shark. Jace was never going to warm up to him, but the man would stop a bullet for Merry. The Rock Run second stared back with his usual stony expression, but a muscle jumped in his jaw.

"I told her you probably used up one of your nine lives," he said, "but that means you still have a couple left."

Merry rolled her eyes at her dad. But the joke worked, because she stopped crying.

Jace reached around her to clasp the other man's hand. "Thanks for letting me see her."

Do Mar tugged one of Merry's curls. "She asked," he said simply and then added, "I'm going to stick around today. Just in case."

The two of them exchanged a look over her head. The first year, either Rui or Valeria had always been there when Jace visited, but over time, they'd trusted him to be alone with Merry. That trust hadn't been easy for them, and Jace appreciated it. But he didn't fault Rui for sticking close today. Hell, if the shoe were on the other foot, he'd do the same.

Merry gave a last sniff. Jace swiped the backs of his fingers down her cheek. "I'm hard to kill, you know that."

Her slim dark brows snapped together. "No, you aren't. You almost died. I felt it—here." She touched her neck, where a shard of his own quartz hung next to hers. Six years ago, he'd broken off the piece to save her life at a time she'd been dangerously weak, and she'd kept it even after she'd found her own.

"But I didn't. Now give me a smile." He slung his arm around her narrow shoulders.

She crinkled her nose at him and then giggled when he waggled his brows at her. They started walking, following a path along the creek. Do Mar trailed at a distance, allowing them privacy but keeping them in sight.

"School's out," Merry said, "so I went fishing with Mama Ria this morning. I used my jaguar to scare the bass into her net."

"Poor bass."

"She says she catches twice as much fish when I come along."

"I'll bet she does." He squeezed her shoulders.

This. This was what he wanted for Merry—a safe, happy life with people who loved her. It tore him up that he couldn't give it to her himself. Cubs were everything to the fada, and he was her only living relative.

For two long years, he'd thought Merry was dead—and then she'd turned up at Rock Run. At first, he'd have done anything to bring her home. When Valeria and Rui had refused to give her back, he and Adric had tried to kidnap her back. But in the end, Jace hadn't been able to go through with it. Merry barely remembered him. Valeria and Rui were her parents now.

Adric hadn't wanted to leave Merry with the river fada. The clan needed their children; they'd lost so many in the Darktime. But he'd allowed Jace to make the final decision, and Jace had left her with Rock Run, even though it had gutted him to do it.

It had been the right thing to do. She had a whole family now —Rui and Valeria had had two more children since adopting Merry—and the powerful Rock Run Clan behind her. All Jace could offer her was a den with five males and a place in a dirt-poor clan that might never fully accept a mixed-blood, whatever Adric might say.

Merry wrapped a wiry arm around his waist and rested her head on his shoulder. "I've been practicing with my quartz."

"Good girl. You can show me what you learned next time."

She nodded. She understood that the lessons between them were private. When she was younger, she'd run to Valeria with every new skill she mastered. Some things were instinctive, like soaking up energy from vibration of the crystals. But there were tricks to using the energy—how to focus it to heal yourself, or turn it outward to make a shield—and for those, she was sworn to secrecy.

When she turned sixteen, he'd teach her the final, dangerous secret, but Adric had to be present for that.

Merry slanted him a grin. "Do you know how to tell a smallmouth bass from a largemouth?"

"Uh—count their teeth?"

She bumped her hip against his. "No, silly."

And she proceeded to give him a lesson about something called a maxillary, a large flap on a bass's upper jaw, which apparently extended further on the largemouth than the smallmouth. There was something in there about vertical and lateral stripes, too—Jace didn't catch which belonged to which. He was just enjoying being with his niece.

He stayed an hour, and then reluctantly took his leave.

Do Mar sent Merry into the base. The two of them watched as she trotted off.

The air snagged in Jace's chest. He made himself say the words, because do Mar deserved to hear them. "You're doing a good job with her. Her mother—Takira—would've been so damn proud."

"My mate deserves the credit. Without her..." Do Mar grimaced. "I was in a dark place, that first year after I brought Merry home. I don't know what would've happened to her if not for Valeria."

Jace nodded. He didn't know the details, but he'd heard do Mar had gone into a bad place for a while where his best friend was a wine bottle. Jace didn't judge; he'd been tempted a few times himself.

"I know, and I've thanked Valeria, too. But you're Merry's dad, a good one."

Do Mar slanted him a fierce glance. "I love her like she's my own daughter."

"I know. I should've thanked you before this."

"No thanks necessary. She is my joy." The other man swallowed hard. "I want you to know she's been under close observation. She will not be outside our wards without at least two guards as protection. So even if her grandfather's ward fails, she is safe. This, I promise you."

"That's good to know." It sucked, to know that his niece was safer at Rock Run than with him in Baltimore, but he'd made his peace with it. "You'll keep me informed if anything changes?"

"Of course."

After that, Jace should've gone back to Baltimore. He was tired and his wounds were starting to protest all the running around he was doing, but both he and his jaguar needed to make sure Evie was okay.

So Jace joined the sentry assigned to guard Evie and her brother. Suha was going to bite his head off, but if she had her way, he'd still be in bed.

The sentry reported that everything was quiet. "The woman went out for groceries—I heard her telling her brother—and the kid's at the high school shooting hoops with his friends." He jerked his chin in the direction of the schoolyard on the next block.

"I'll look around anyway." Jace took a stroll through town to satisfy himself there was no hint of the night fae or the mysterious earth fada. Everything seemed quiet, but he still wasn't satisfied. Grace Harbor might not be big, but it had a population of over ten thousand—plenty big enough for a man to hide in. If something happened to Evie or her brother, he'd never forgive himself.

He waited with the sentry in the shadow of the warehouse across the alley until Evie pulled up in a rusty blue car. His chest rumbled in a purr, his jaguar happy just to be near her.

He watched as she gathered her groceries and headed up the back steps. She paused on the stoop to glance around, and his whole body snapped alert. Both man and cat wanted to go closer...to talk with her, fill his nostrils with her scent. Find out if her skin was as soft as it looked.

But it was best he stayed away. The Darktime had left him scarred, bitter. He'd lost too many people—his parents, his sister, good friends. Even his niece was being raised by another man. And he'd killed—because he'd had no choice. Those grim years were a part of him, however much he wanted to forget them.

He liked women, enjoyed the release of sex, but other than that, he walked alone—and he could count the number of people he trusted on one hand.

No, Evie wasn't for him. He'd guard her, make sure he hadn't accidentally dragged her into whatever had sparked the attack on him. Nothing more.

Because on top of everything else, he didn't do humans, and he especially didn't do humans who were part fae.

The sentry sent him a curious look and Jace forced himself to turn away. He faded further back into the shadows. He waited until Kyler was safely home, and then headed back to Baltimore.

But the next night he was back.

13

$\mathcal{E}$vie stopped her car on the pad behind her house and turned off the ignition. The ancient compact shuddered and then went ominously silent. She muttered something dark. The car wasn't long for this world. Somehow she'd have to find the cash for a new one.

It was Saturday night, nine days since she'd found Jace bleeding in her backyard. Not for the first time, she wondered how he was doing—and then scowled and told herself he was fine, and probably back doing whatever it was he did.

She grabbed her backpack and got out of the car. The house was dark except for the light she'd left on over the back door. Kyler must still be at Ben's house. At least she hoped that was where he was, because he hadn't bothered to check in with her—again. He'd been pushing her all week, "forgetting" to check in and then coming home way after his curfew.

"School's almost out," he'd said. "All we're doing is taking finals, and I'm allowed to go in late."

"You'd do better on your tests if you had a good night sleep."

"Relax," he returned in a tone that had Evie tightening her

jaw. "I've got practically a four-point average." And he did, so what could she say?

Now she glanced at her phone—it was after midnight. He should be home, damn it. And he hadn't left a message either.

She sighed and slung her backpack over one shoulder, flipping her keys so that the tips stuck out between her knuckles. If someone attacked her, she was going to be ready.

Evie was almost at the steps when her nape tingled in an eerie repeat of last Thursday. *Someone was watching her.* She gripped her keys and glanced around.

Across the alley, a pair of luminous green eyes stared at her, unblinking, from the shadows.

Her heart kicked into a gallop. "Jace? Is that you?"

Please let it be him.

He stepped forward. She blew out a breath. It *was* Jace.

He crossed the alley in a few long, loose strides. An atavistic tremor went down her spine. This was the real Jace—and he was nothing like the injured, feverish victim of last week.

No, this man was dark. Powerful. Raw-boned. A panther in a T-shirt and jeans.

She squared her shoulders and lifted her chin, because damn it, she'd saved the man's life. She refused to let him spook her.

He stopped a few feet away. "Hello, Evie."

He was bigger than she remembered, but then, last week he'd been hunched over nursing his injuries. Now she realized he was a good half foot taller than her with the lean, hard build of a soldier. Another shiver went down her spine—but this one had nothing to do with fear.

She swallowed. "You're better?" She glanced at his stomach, although the wounds were covered by the shirt.

"Suha thinks I should still be in bed, but yeah, I'm much better."

"Suha?" Evie felt a pinch of jealousy, which she immediately stomped on. Why should she be jealous? She barely knew the man.

"Our head healer. She knows her stuff, but she's one tough mother, you know?"

Evie pictured an older, somewhat overprotective woman and smothered a smile. "Seriously? You let her boss you?"

"Better than listening to her nagging. She's so calm and reasonable—and she makes you feel like a shit if you don't take her advice. But we're lucky to have her. We lost our last healer in the Dark—" He halted.

Evie flashed on those stories about the murderous Baltimore shifters and glanced away, somehow sure she didn't want to know.

"Anyway," Jace said, "I came to see how you are."

"Me?" Her eyes narrowed as she recalled how he'd acted when Adric had accused her of being part fae. The man had *growled* at her. "Aren't you afraid I'll bewitch you or something?"

"No." Shame flashed across his face. "I'm sorry about that. You helped me, and you didn't deserve that in return."

She shrugged. "I would've done the same for anyone." And he *had* stood up for her with Adric. From what she knew about the fada, the alpha was king, so that meant something.

He stepped closer, a slow, graceful ripple of his muscles. "Would you? Have done the same for anyone?"

Her mouth dried. "Yes."

Their gazes snagged and Jace smiled—not with his lips, but with his eyes. The corners creased in a way that made her stomach flip. "You have a good heart."

She smoothed her hands down her pants, painfully aware that she was still dressed in her server uniform—straight black slacks and a white button-up shirt. And she probably smelled funky; it had been a busy night at the restaurant.

He fiddled with the hoop in her left earlobe. "But you should be more careful, living alone with only a young kid like your brother."

"I've known most of the neighbors for years. We look out for each other."

"Yeah? That's good. I'm glad you have someone, at least."

As if on cue, Mrs. Linney's stoop light went on three houses down and she stepped out her back door dressed in flip flops and an outsized neon-green nightgown. Jace immediately stepped back from Evie and tucked the quartz pendant out of sight beneath his T-shirt.

Mrs. Linney lit a cigarette and peered at them over the top of cat's-eye glasses. "'Evening, hon. You're out late."

"I just got off work."

"Ah..." The older woman blew a perfect smoke ring and then narrowed her eyes at Jace. "Don't I know you from somewhere?"

Evie concealed a grin. Not much happened on their block that Mrs. Linney didn't know about.

"No, ma'am," he responded. "I don't believe so."

"This is a friend of mine," Evie said. "Jace—" She realized she didn't know his last name.

"Jones." He nodded politely to the older woman. "Good to meet you."

Evie glanced from him to her neighbor's curious face and made up her mind. "We were just on our way inside," she told Mrs. Linney. "Tell Mr. Linney I said hi."

She grabbed her backpack and headed up the steps, Jace following. Inside, she flipped on the kitchen light and shot him a rueful smile. "That's our version of a neighborhood watch. I swear the woman never sleeps."

"I don't mind. For all she knew, I was some strange man looking for trouble."

"I do feel safer knowing she's keeping an eye on things." Evie opened the refrigerator. "Want a beer? Or I have ice tea if you'd rather."

"Beer, please."

She got out two cans and handed him one. He glanced curiously around the kitchen while she took a sip of her beer. It was ice-cold, just what she needed. She leaned against the counter and let out a breath, tired to her very toes.

Jace frowned. "You work too hard."

She moved a shoulder. "It's the weekend. I run my ass off but I make a ton of tips."

"When will you graduate from nursing school?"

"In two or three years. I just started."

He shook his head. "It's too much."

"Maybe, but it's worth it." She set the can on the counter. "Why are you here, Jace? I thought you lived in Baltimore."

"I do, but I come up pretty often. My niece lives near here, and the clan is mining across the river."

"Mining what?" she asked curiously.

"Quartz. This whole area sits on a thick vein of quartz. That's why radios and cell phones sometimes can't get a signal—the quartz blocks it."

"But what do you do with quartz other than wear it around your neck?"

"We make things with it." He took a gulp of beer, clearly done with the subject. "Anyway, I wanted to let you know we had someone watching you and Kyler all week, and there's been no sign of the night fae."

"You had someone watching us?" She frowned, not sure how she felt about that.

"Just as a precaution. You don't know the night fae."

She recalled the cold, malevolent presence that had come to her door and decided to be grateful. "I have to admit, that guy creeped me out. In fact, that's why I drove to work—normally I just walk or ride my bike."

His brows knit. "At midnight?"

"It's a small town."

"Your brother should pick you up at night."

"What would he do against a night fae?"

"Nothing. But there are human predators, too."

She rubbed her nape. "Look, I'm careful."

Jace pressed his lips together but let it go. "Well, you don't have to worry. He must know I'm back in Baltimore."

"You know who it was?"

"Yeah, but it's better if you don't know. Besides, saying a fae's name aloud can draw their attention."

"Right." Evie recalled hearing that somewhere, although with the fae you never knew what was real and what was myth.

Jace finished his beer and set it in the kitchen sink. "How long have you lived in Grace Harbor?"

"Since I was eight. My mom and dad bought this house." Or rather her dad had—right before he left for good.

"But it's just you and your brother?"

"Yeah. Mom passed a couple of years ago, and who knows where my dad is?"

His eyes flickered. "I'm sorry about your mom. That's too young."

Evie swallowed. "Yeah." That's what she thought, too; your mom wasn't supposed to die before you were out of your twenties. "It is."

"So your dad's the one who's part fae?"

"I guess. If I'm part fae, it must've come from him."

She'd had a week to get used to the idea. She supposed it could be true. Fane was tall and blond like the local sun fae—and gorgeous, even if he was her dad. He could be a mixed-blood. Her mom had never really gotten over him, although she'd made a good life with Kyler's dad.

And Fane had a way of knowing things, like that her mom was on her deathbed.

"I'm sure it's just a trace," she added. "I mean look at me—no magic, no Gift."

Jace prowled closer. "You're beautiful like the fae."

Evie's pulse sped up, but she rolled her eyes. "Yeah, right." He was the one who was beautiful—a spare male beauty with high cheekbones and a firm, knowing mouth, his eyes a brilliant mix of gold and green and brown framed by those impossibly thick lashes.

"And your brother—Kyler?" he asked, just as if he weren't standing so close. "He hasn't seen or heard anything?"

"Not that he told me. He's at a friend's house right now—but you already know that."

He shrugged but didn't deny it. "I was standing guard outside the restaurant most of the night, but yeah, I checked in on Kyler a few times."

Those beautiful eyes were fixed on her mouth, making her lips tingle. She had the curious feeling they were having two conversations, one aloud, one silent.

"So there's no one else out there?"

"Just me tonight. We're pulling off the guard after this."

"Thank you."

Another silence. "So we're alone," he murmured.

"Yeah." She crossed her arms. "Should I be scared?"

His brows drew together. "Never. I'd never hurt you, Evie."

His scent filled her head. Warm and masculine. A bit spicy. Already she recognized it; she could be in a pitch-black room and she'd know it was Jace.

"Because I helped you."

"You know that's not the only reason." He was just two feet from her now.

Desire fluttered in her belly. Her fingers flexed on her arms. She itched to pull him closer. To run her lips over the golden-brown skin of his throat...taste him.

His nostrils flared. She had the uncomfortable feeling he could scent her reaction to him. But damn, it had been a long time. She didn't have time for a relationship, and she didn't do casual, especially with Kyler at such a tricky age.

She uncrossed her arms and gripped the counter behind her. *What had he said?* "Don't be scared." She gave a jerky nod. "Got it."

They stared at each other, and abruptly, the silent conversation became audible.

Jace's throat worked, the sound loud in the sudden hush.

Her heart pounded in her ears. She drew a jagged breath.

He stepped closer. Slowly, carefully, he framed her face with his palms. "I want to kiss you."

She set her hands on his chest. "Not yet."

"No?" His mouth brushed her cheek.

She shook her head. "I need to know one thing."

"What?" His warm lips moved to the side of her neck. His body radiated warmth. An answering heat slid through her, a slow, hot river that pooled in her belly.

"Who's Mary?"

The muscles under her hands went rigid. He pulled back. "How do you know about her?"

"You said her name—twice. When you were hurt."

"Oh." He relaxed. "My niece. Her name's M-E-R-R-Y like in Christmas. There's no one else, if that's what you're asking." Those warm lips were against her ear now. "Only you. I can't stop thinking about you. It's like you're under my fucking skin."

"I know—I mean, I can't stop thinking about you either." Her eyes drifted shut as his tongue traced the outer edge of her ear. "I'm busy," she said. "I don't have time—"

"I know." His teeth closed on her earlobe, and something dark and delicious flashed down her spine. "And I don't...you're a human—and a fae."

She stiffened, and then shrugged. Because how could she be insulted? She didn't want to get involved with him either, did she? "Yeah. Me and you...we don't—"

"Mix." He sucked at the turn of her shoulder.

She opened and closed her mouth—and stopped thinking.

His mouth moved up her neck, leaving rivulets of pleasure in its wake. Her head fell back. From far away, she heard herself moan.

"You're so soft," he said against the vulnerable underside of her throat. He rubbed his cheek against her and the rasp of his stubble was so damn erotic. She slid her hands up to his shoulders.

He stepped closer, his cock hard and powerful against her belly. Her leg bent of its own accord so that she could hitch herself up against him. That was better—now she could feel him right against her sex.

He slid his arms around her and fit his mouth to hers. His lips were warm and dry and tasted of beer and mint. He licked at the seam of her mouth, but when she opened to him, he didn't move his tongue inside, just lapped at the edges. Tiny tastes interspersed with little bites. Quick bursts of pleasure that had her digging her fingers into his shoulders.

"Jace."

"Mm?" His tongue moved inside, played with hers.

She sucked on it and he groaned. One hand came to her nape, holding her in place while the other gripped her ass, pulling her tight against him.

The kiss went on and on. The playful sensuality turned urgent. A pulse beat between Evie's thighs—there, where he was pressed, big and hard, the zipper of his jeans rasping over the seam of her pants.

He raised his head and they both dragged in a breath.

Evie pushed against his chest. "I—we have to stop. Kyler…"

Jace's lungs heaved. His heart slammed hard and fast beneath her palms. He nodded, his gaze on her mouth.

"He's going to be home any minute."

"Okay." He brushed his lips over hers and stepped back. He

picked up her beer and offered it to her. As she took a gulp, he said, "We're going to finish that someday," with a little half-smile.

Something about that silky self-confidence made her womb clench. But hey, if it weren't for Kyler, Jace would be taking her up against the counter right now.

"Maybe," she returned. Now that he was a few feet away, common sense had returned, cool, pragmatic. Sometimes she hated how damn sensible she was.

She tilted her head. "Why *are* you here, Jace? Not for this." She waved a hand between the two of them.

"Don't be so sure about that." His gaze raked up and down her body. "But I did have another reason. Suha says the reason I healed so fast was because of you and your brother. If you wouldn't have flushed the iron out of the cuts so fast, I'd be dead. We take those things seriously. I owe you my life."

Her jaw tightened. She did *not* like where this was going. "No, you don't. Not the way I think you mean it. Like I told you guys last week, I would've done the same for anyone."

His face set. "Yes, I do." She went to say something and he raised a hand. "Let me explain. Here, I brought you this so you can contact me." He fished a quartz from his pocket and held it out to her.

She eyed it without touching it. It was a clear rose pink, flat on one side and a conglomerate of crystals on the other side. "A quartz? But what good is that to me?"

"It's a kind of a smartphone. If you need me for anything, you just tap it."

"A smartphone? But it's just a rock—a chunk of quartz."

"It's quartz engineered to be a phone. You tap here." He touched a small depression on the flat side and an orange light glowed on in the center. "Then just talk into it. It's set to contact me directly."

He tapped the depression again and the light turned off.

"How does it work?"

He moved a shoulder. "A mix of engineering and magic. It doesn't work for humans, but with your fae blood, you should be able to operate it. Try it and see." He offered it to her again.

When she still didn't take it, he took her hand and pressed the phone into her palm. "Please, Evie. We want to help you, me and Adric both. He—we—would've said something last week, but we wanted to give you a chance to cool down."

She pressed her lips together. "I don't need help."

"I thought you'd say that. But you don't have to use it, just keep it on you."

She stared down at the quartz in her palm. It was warmer than she'd expected.

"Try it," he urged. "Just once, so I know you understand how it works. You never have to use it again—but please, keep it with you at all times."

She blew out a breath. "If it will make you happy..." She touched the depression and the orange light came on.

"Speak into it." He tapped his own quartz.

She brought it to her mouth. "Earth to Jace," she said, and then jolted when her voice came out of his pendant.

"That's all you have to do," he said.

She shrugged and put the quartz into her back pocket. "Fine. But don't expect me to use it."

"I thought you'd say that, but you're wrong. You need help. You're trying to do everything yourself, and that's hard. I bet you're working two jobs and going to school."

"One and a half. And it's not forever."

"And your brother—where is he, anyway? Shouldn't he be home by now?"

She stiffened. "That's none of your business," she said evenly.

Jace expelled a breath. "Hell, I'm no good at this. But I want to help, Evie."

"I appreciate that, but it's not necessary."

"I had a sister," he told her. "Older than me, but just by a couple of years."

"*Had* a sister?"

He nodded, jaw rigid. "She was around your age when she died."

"I'm sorry. That sucks." The anger left her as quickly as it had come. She couldn't imagine life without Kyler. "So this is because I remind you of your sister?"

He huffed a laugh. "Hell no. Well, maybe. You may be a human, but you're tough. Nobody pushed Takira around—and she would've done anything for me, just like you and Kyler." He scraped a hand over his short black hair. "But I'm not looking for sympathy. I'm just telling you why I'd like to help."

"Thank you, but we're fine. Really."

"All right. But if you change your mind, I mean it—I'd like to help you, Evie."

She could've sworn she saw a flicker of pain in his eyes, but why would he care if she accepted his help? He was only there to repay a debt because apparently, his sense of honor demanded it.

He turned toward the door. "I'd better be going. Thanks for the beer."

"No problem." She chewed her lip. "Jace?"

Ask him, you chicken. Ask if he wants to see you again. Because her body was still humming, and she was afraid that when he left this time, it would be forever.

He swung back toward her. "What?"

The back door slammed open and Kyler burst inside. The two of them leapt away from each other.

"Evie?" He turned on Jace. "You *are* hitting on my sister. I didn't believe him."

Jace's head whipped around. "Believe who?"

"That guy outside. The one from your clan."

"My clan? I'm here alone." He turned to Evie, suddenly all soldier. "Use the phone. It will go to my quartz, but if I don't answer, it will route to Adric next. Tell him to get up here. Stat. And you, Kyler"—he stabbed a finger at her brother—"lock the door and don't open it for anyone but me or Adric."

Her brother's mouth dropped open. "What the fuck's going on?"

"That's what I'm going to find out. But I need you to stay in here with your sister. Can you do that?"

Kyler looked from him to Evie and then jerked his chin. "Yep."

"Good man." Jace clapped Kyler on the back.

To Evie he said, "You'll call Adric?"

"Yeah." She showed him the quartz phone already in her hand. Behind her, Kyler grabbed the baseball bat they kept in the pantry.

"Lock the door," Jace repeated, "but if someone breaks in, swing first. Your only chance is to take them by surprise."

Kyler tightened his grip on the bat. "I'm on it."

And then Jace was out the door.

14

_____

$\mathcal{J}$ace hadn't meant to let Evie see him. He'd been there every night this week, blending into the shadows, and she'd never even suspected. But tonight, he'd known his eyes had gone night-glow in the dim light. He could've lowered his lids when she'd turned toward him.

Instead, he'd stared back. His heart had given a jubilant thump, his animal thrilled that she'd sensed him when she hadn't the night before or the night before that. And before he knew it, he was crossing the alley to her.

Talking to Evie, having a beer in her homey little kitchen, was a balm to a man who'd been raised on war and bloodshed. He'd reveled in the unaccustomed sense of peace, like lying in the grass on a summer day and watching the clouds drift by. And kissing her was even better. He could get addicted to this woman: her spicy mouth, that sexy dimple, the taut body that was a perfect fit for his...

Then Kyler burst in and jolted Jace out of his pleasant haze. Because he'd come up here alone, and if a man from the clan was outside without his knowledge, it meant trouble anyway you looked at it.

Now he halted on the stoop, scanning the area with his night vision. Behind him, he heard Kyler shoot home the deadbolt.

Good man.

The other fada had disappeared. So he didn't want to be seen. Jace's skin prickled.

A scrape of gravel. He narrowed his eyes. There—across the alley, right where he'd been standing.

The shadows near the wooden fence coalesced, became a large animal. A shaggy black wolf.

No. It couldn't be.

The wolf darted around the corner and disappeared.

Jace threw off his clothes and shifted to jaguar. As his animal, he could run faster and his senses were more acute, but he lost precious seconds in the shift. He shot out of the yard and around the corner in the wolf's wake. Tracking it in a sea of small-town scents wasn't easy, but he caught a wild, distinctive scent to the left and turned in that direction.

Two houses down, a dog's indignant yapping changed to a terrified whine. Jace swerved in its direction and bounded over a chain link fence. The dog was pressed against the back door of a small white house. At the sight of Jace's 250-pound jaguar, it whimpered and then peeled back its lips in a last, pitiful defense.

Jace ignored it to soar over the fence on the opposite side, hot on the wolf's trail.

He still couldn't quite believe it was Corban Savonett. The man was supposed to be dead. But Jace had known that scent since he was a cub.

When last heard from, Adric's cousin had been in the Himalayas tracking a rogue ice fae female—and then he'd disappeared, his quartz winking out along with him.

But it made sense. Corban was a sly S.O.B. If he couldn't beat Adric in a fair fight, it was just like him to try and take out his lieutenants.

Jace pounded after the huge black wolf. His jaguar was fast, but he hadn't regained his full strength yet. He began to flag, but then something odd happened—Corban slowed down, too.

The fur rose on Jace's nape. *Too easy.* With Corban's head start, he should've been able to easily shake Jace off.

Trap!

He swerved just as another earth fada appeared beside Corban, a cougar Jace didn't know. The two of them turned as one and charged Jace.

He went airborne, bounding sideways over a white picket fence. He was in a backyard with a wood playset. He ran up the slide and along the top bar and then launched himself onto the garage roof, hoping to confuse Corban. Wolves relied heavily on their sense of smell, especially at night.

Corban and the cougar raced into the yard, but Jace was already soaring off the other side of the garage. He hit the asphalt at a full run.

He considered his options. His main priority was Evie and Kyler, but even if he led Corban and his henchman away from their house, Corban knew where they lived. And Corban wouldn't give a damn about collateral damage, especially two humans.

Jace would have to stand and fight.

He headed for Susquehanna River and the small park that would be empty at this time of night. Thank the gods he knew Grace Harbor from his visits with Merry. For the first couple of years, this had been the only place the Rock Run fada had allowed the two of them to meet. Neutral territory, but close to the base.

Now Jace knew the perfect place to take a stand.

He reached the park and sprinted toward a stream that fed into the Susquehanna, Corban and the cougar right behind. He ran onto a footbridge that spanned the stream and whipped around to face them. The bridge was too narrow for them to both attack him. They'd have to take him on one at a time.

They skidded to a halt a few yards away. Two sets of gold eyes gazed at him. All three of them were panting hard.

He caught a good whiff of the cougar's scent and mentally raised a brow. A female—interesting. But then, Corban never seemed to have trouble attracting women, although why any female would align herself with a prick like Adric's cousin was a mystery to Jace.

Corban snarled a warning. *Surrender—or die.*

Jace curled his lip. Like the wolf would let him leave alive anyway. *Go fuck yourself.*

Corban gathered his muscles and leapt. Jace rose to meet him and they collided with a crash that would've broken the bones of any creature who wasn't a fada.

And damn, it hurt. Jace's breath left his lungs. Pain ripped through his almost-healed knife wounds. Suha wasn't going to be happy.

Then he stopped thinking and went for Corban's jugular. The wolf jerked right, but Jace got a mouthful of fur and blood.

Corban went for Jace's throat, silent and deadly. Meanwhile, the cougar had somehow slipped past Jace and was snapping at his hind legs.

Two against one wasn't fair, but then Corban had always fought dirty, even back when they'd been cubs and he was several years older and nearly twice Jace's weight.

But Jace wasn't a cub anymore—and he'd learned some dirty tricks of his own.

He slashed at the cougar's face with a hind leg, claws extended. She yelped and jumped back. Jace dodged Corban as he lunged a second time for Jace's throat. He slid past the wolf and then turned and sank his teeth into Corban's hind leg.

His jaguar's long, curved canines were powerful enough to pierce a skull. He sliced through muscle above the hock and crunched against bone.

The wolf's furious snarl split the night. He struck wildly at Jace, biting whatever he could reach—Jace's face, his shoulder.

Jace released Corban's leg to go for a killing bite to the neck, only to have the cougar leap on his back. Sharp canines sliced into his nape. He ignored the pain to slam her against the bridge's metal railing. She released his nape and fell to the wooden planks, unconscious.

Jace turned toward Corban, but the coward was racing off as fast as he could on three legs. Jace looked after him, chest heaving, itching to chase him down but knowing it wasn't worth it. From the amount of blood he'd left behind, Corban wouldn't try anything else tonight.

Meanwhile, Jace had Evie and Kyler to protect, and on top of that, he was bleeding from several places himself.

He hissed a cat's version of a curse after the wolf's retreating figure and turned to the cougar. Adric would want to question her.

Shifting back to man, he tapped his quartz. The alpha answered immediately; Evie must have gotten through to him. "On my way," he said over the muted roar of a motorcycle.

"We've got a situation here." Jace explained what had happened.

When he got to Corban, the alpha snarled. "I *knew* the bastard wasn't dead—that would be too fucking simple. I want to talk to that female. I don't care how you do it, but make sure she doesn't leave."

"That's what I thought. But your cousin—what if he goes after Evie and her brother? He knows I was there."

Jace didn't have to spell it out. They both knew Corban wouldn't give a damn if innocents got hurt, especially humans.

"Fuck. What the hell were you doing there, anyway? No, don't answer that. You can explain when I get there."

"I'll meet you at Evie's house. I'll bring the cougar with me."

"I'll be there in twenty minutes." Adric ended the connection.

The cougar's eyelids fluttered. Jace knelt on the bridge to check her for injuries. Other than a gash on her head, she was all right. In fact, his injuries were worse.

He wrapped his hand around her quartz; lightly, but she felt it all right. She tensed and opened her eyes, her upper lip twitching in an attempt at a snarl.

"Shift," he ordered. "Now."

She growled weakly.

"Maybe I'm not being clear. You don't have a choice." He tightened his grip on her pendant.

She jerked in pain. Deep within, he sensed its panicked vibrations, echoing its wearer's terror. You didn't touch anyone's quartz without their permission, and even then, only a close relation or a lover could wrap a hand around it without causing a deep, visceral discomfort.

He was being a bastard, but he didn't fucking care. The fada who'd kidnapped Marjani had smashed her quartz to bits. This woman might not have been part of that, but she'd attacked Jace for no reason other than Corban's say-so. Worse, she was a threat to Evie and Kyler.

The cougar whimpered. He let up on the pressure but kept the quartz in his palm. "*Shift.*"

Deep within, a single point of silver glowed to life, then another and another. Jace added a small portion of his energy to hers. He was the stronger, but his quartz was still being drained of energy to heal him, both from his earlier iron poisoning and now the cuts Corban and this female had inflicted during the fight. He'd give her an energy boost, but she could drain her own damn quartz to shift.

Silver and blue and purple sparkles spread over the cougar's fur, and then a naked woman was curled up on the bridge, chest heaving, her hair a wild tangle around her shoulders.

Jace released her quartz and grabbed her arm. "Don't even think about running. Understand?"

She growled, but nodded. He rose to his feet, bringing her with him.

She was tall and curvy. Jace took in her body with clinical detachment; shifters were used to seeing each other in their skins. He was more concerned about getting a naked woman back to Evie's without some asshat human calling the cops.

The woman touched the side of her head. "Hurts."

She was telling the truth, and yet he sensed the lie beneath. She wasn't as injured as she was pretending.

He hardened his jaw. "What's your name?"

She pressed her lips together. Names had power in their world.

He jerked her close and slid a finger over her quartz.

Her eyes flashed angrily. She knocked his hand away and wrapped her own fingers around the quartz, protecting it. "Nika," she gritted.

"That's better." He took a firm hold of her upper arm. "Let's go."

Their mad dash through Grace Harbor had taken the form of a large circle. They'd ended up just a few blocks from Evie's house.

Jace hurried the woman through the night, keeping an eye out for both the cops and Corban, although Jace was pretty sure the wolf would have to go to ground. Even with the help of his quartz, that leg of his was going to take a few days to heal.

They reached Evie's house without incident. Jace marched his captive up the steps and tapped on the back door with his free hand. "Evie? It's me, Jace."

She did a double take when she saw him standing there naked, bloodied, and with a tall, curvy, and very naked female. "What the—"

"I'll explain—just let me in, please."

She hesitated another few seconds and then stepped back. "Come in."

"Thanks." Jace strong-armed his captive into the kitchen. "Do you have any rope?"

Evie started to nod, then her eyes widened. "You want to tie her up?"

"She attacked me, Evie. I promise I won't hurt her—I just want to keep her quiet until Adric arrives."

The shift had healed both his and Nika's superficial cuts, but he was still bleeding from the claw marks on his face, shoulder, and thigh, and Nika's face had a deep gash from the blow he'd struck with his hind claws. Evie's gaze flicked to the blood on Jace's face to Nika's, and then she opened the door to the pantry.

"I think I have something in here..."

While he was gone, she'd changed into a purple tank top and loose gray shorts that stopped halfway down her thighs, exposing a length of strong, shapely legs. He eyed her calves as she rummaged in the pantry for rope and silently wished Nika back beneath whatever rock she'd crawled out from under.

"Is there anything I can do?" Kyler asked. To the kid's credit, after one quick look at Nika, he'd kept his eyes on her face.

Jace nodded. "Get her a towel or something to cover up with."

"Right." The teenager jogged upstairs and returned a minute later with a large beach towel and a pair of gym shorts for Jace.

Jace wrapped the towel around Nika and pulled out a chair. He twirled it to face him. "Sit."

While she obeyed, he dragged on the shorts. His own clothes were still outside where he'd dropped them, but he wasn't going to open the door until Adric got here. He didn't think Corban would try anything until his leg healed, but he wasn't going to take any chances with Evie and Kyler.

He snagged a paper towel. "Give me your quartz," he ordered Nika.

Her claws slid out. "And if I say no?"

He locked gazes with her. He couldn't risk Nika changing to her cougar. With her teeth and claws, she could do serious damage to a human within seconds. "You don't want to play games with me."

She snarled but gave in, conceding Jace the silent contest. As he'd suspected, he was several degrees dominant to her. She scowled and dragged off the quartz, setting it on the towel. He wrapped it carefully and stowed it in his pocket.

Nika wound the beach towel more tightly around herself and slumped in the chair.

Good. She wasn't going to try anything without her quartz. She wouldn't even attempt to escape. An earth fada could survive without a quartz, but no one would do it willingly. It was like having a vise around your chest. You couldn't breathe as well, you had less energy. You could make do with another quartz, but finding the perfect match, a quartz that resonated with you on a magical level, could take weeks.

Jace leaned against the counter and examined his captive. She had red hair and unusually pale skin for an earth fada.

She stared back impassively. "You have sent for Lord Adric?" It was the longest sentence she'd said yet. For the first time, he realized she had a foreign accent—Russian or some other Slavic country. Where the hell had Corban found her, anyway?

"Yeah." Jace glanced at the kitchen clock. "He should be here any minute."

Fear etched her face.

"I see you've heard of him."

"Of course." She smoothed her expression, but he scented her rising dread. "He is well known."

Jace nodded. Earth fada weren't as prolific as the water fada; there were only a dozen clans scattered around the world. The Baltimore clan had come to Maryland about fifty years ago by way of Jamaica and the Persian Gulf. Adric might be the youngest alpha, but his reputation as a ruthless S.O.B. had quickly spread.

"You entered Adric's territory," Jace said, "and attacked one of his own people. I'd say you were asking to meet him."

She moved a shoulder, her gaze on the floor.

"And Nika?" He leaned closer. "Everything you've heard about him is true."

She remained silent but a fine tremor went down her spine. He grinned evilly and came upright to find Kyler eyeing him with a mixture of horror and respect. He winked at the lanky kid over the top of Nika's head.

Evie exited the pantry with a ball of clothesline. "Will this work?"

"Perfect." Jace took it and turned to Nika. "Put your hands behind the chair."

The cougar bit her lip. "Please. There is no need. I will not run—I swear it."

Jace inhaled. She had the scent of truth. Beside him, Evie tensed and he caught a whiff of fear.

A spike of anger lanced through him—not at Evie, but at Corban and the life he, Jace, led. He knew damn well any headway he'd made with Evie tonight had evaporated the minute he dragged a naked and injured woman into her kitchen. His stomach hollowed.

And things were about to get worse, because he was going to have to convince her to leave town. Corban Savonett was a cold-hearted bastard and Jace's scent was all over Evie. If Corban couldn't take down Jace, he'd go after her next. Grace Harbor was no longer safe for her or Kyler.

Evie dragged a hand over her cropped blond hair. "I know she attacked you, but she's hurt."

Jace swore under his breath but dropped the clothesline on the table. "All right," he told Nika. "But one false move and I'll smash your quartz into a hundred pieces. Are we clear?"

Her throat worked. She dropped her head so that her tangled red hair hid her face and gave a jerky nod. "Yes." She touched the bump on her head. "Hurts."

Jace didn't trust her worth a damn, but the pitiful-me act worked with Evie. "Can I give her a glass of water?"

He sighed in defeat. "Sure. Why not?"

While Evie got Nika water, Kyler handed her an ice pack for her head. Jace hooked his foot around the bottom rung of the nearest chair and dragged it in front of Nika. He dropped onto the seat and crossed his arms. Not speaking, just making it clear she wasn't moving an inch without his say-so.

Nika pressed the ice pack to her head and stared down at the floor. At least she was smart enough not to challenge him directly.

Evie touched his shoulder. "Jace?"

"What?" he rapped out without taking his gaze from his prisoner.

"You're hurt."

"I'll live." But now the adrenaline had worn off, he was feeling every single one of the bites and cuts Corban and Nika had torn out of his hide. Shifting had caused most of them to scab over, but a gash on his thigh was oozing blood. The worst was his abdomen, where it felt like the deeper of the knife wounds had torn open again.

"This is getting to be a bad habit." Evie's tone was dry. "You bleeding in my kitchen."

He barked out a laugh and glanced up in time to see her lopsided grin. The hollow feeling eased. "Clean it up then," he grumbled. But his cat twitched its tail in delight.

Evie dampened a clean washcloth and used it to dab at the cuts on his face and shoulder. When she got to the gash on his thigh, she sucked in a breath.

"Just clean it," he said. "I can heal it."

"Sure you can."

When she was finished, he ran his quartz over his thigh. The wound tingled and started closing up. The knife wound was trickier, but he sent a burst of energy into it and hoped it would hold until Suha could work her magic.

Nika watched, the ice pack to her head.

Evie sent him a look from where she was washing her hands in the sink. He could practically hear her urging him to help the injured woman as well. With a sigh, he rose to his feet and ran his quartz over the gashes on Nika's face and head. Just a few quick pulses, but it would ease her pain as well as speed up her healing. Without her quartz, her ability to heal herself was even worse than the average human's, since all her energy was now being directed to merely staying alive.

Kyler took a seat on the other side of the table, while Evie remained standing. The kid raised a shaggy brown brow. "So we're waiting for Lord Adric?"

"Yeah. Tell me," Jace said, "what did that guy say to you, anyway? The one who was outside?"

Kyler glanced at his sister.

She cocked a hip against the counter. "Tell him, Kyler."

"He said that you were just fucking with Evie. That you eat little girls like her for breakfast."

15

———

Evie rubbed her hands over her arms. Kyler had told her the whole thing while they waited for Jace to return. If it wasn't so serious, she would've laughed.

She rolled her eyes. "I know you guys are shifters, but does he have to go all Big Bad Wolf? Besides, you're a cat."

Jace's mouth twitched. Score a point for Evie. She had a feeling Jace didn't smile much. She liked that she could make him laugh, if only inside.

Then he replied, "Actually, he *is* a wolf," and she gulped.

Because she'd only been joking to hide her fear, and now it was creepy. How long had the other man been outside? And what if he'd gone after Kyler?

Her brother folded his arms. "Fuck this wolf-and-cat thing. Is it true?"

"*Kyler*," she hissed, but Jace calmly met his eyes.

"What happens between me and your sister is our business. But I would never hurt her. He was just trying to pull your chain."

"So where's the wolf-man now?"

"I don't know." Jace jerked his head at the woman wrapped in the towel. "We'll talk when the alpha gets here."

Evie nodded. The woman hadn't moved from her slumped position, but of course, she could hear every word. Evie didn't know exactly what had happened, but it was clear the woman and the missing man had attacked Jace. That was why she'd let Jace back in her house, and allowed him to hold the woman until his alpha arrived—but that was as far as it went.

What the hell was going on? Evie fingered the quartz in her pocket. She'd been so damn worried. Each minute with Jace gone had seemed like an eternity. She'd hated that the only thing she could do was to call Adric and then wait for him to drive the fifty minutes up from Baltimore.

Jace trained his gaze on his prisoner. He appeared relaxed, long legs stretched before him and an elbow resting on the chair back, but it was the coiled energy of an animal prepared to spring.

The woman slid a look at Evie. Her pale blue eyes were flat. Not angry or cold, just flat, as if Evie were too insignificant to worry about.

Evie wasn't sure if that was good or bad. "Well," she said, "I don't know about the rest of you, but I'm hungry." She'd been too busy to grab more than a snack tonight.

Kyler brightened. "Works for me."

She rolled her eyes. "Why aren't I surprised?"

"Hey, I'm a growing boy."

But the tension in the room dropped several notches.

Evie got out sandwich fixings and went to work. A few minutes later, she had four thick tuna sandwiches topped with slabs of melted cheddar. Jace inhaled appreciatively as she handed him a plate. "Tuna. Great."

"I figured you'd like it."

"Why?"

She smirked. "You're a cat, aren't you?"

His mouth twitched again. "A jaguar, not a house cat."

"Here." She handed him a plate for the red-headed woman,

who was eyeing Jace's sandwich hungrily. "I made one for her, too."

He shook his head, but passed it on to her. When the Baltimore alpha arrived, he found the four of them eating tuna melts.

Evie opened the door at Jace's request and Adric strode in as if he owned the place. He nodded hello to Evie and Kyler and then eyed the woman, who straightened up and set her plate on the table behind her.

"This is her?"

"Yep." Jace rose to his feet. "Name's Nika."

A small woman with a shaved head slipped in after Adric, Jace's clothes under her arm, and Adric jerked his chin in her direction without taking his eyes off Nika. "This is one of my lieutenants," he said.

The newcomer set the clothes on an empty chair and stuck out a hand. "Marjani. I'm also his sister—and you must be Evie."

"That's me." Evie shook her hand. Marjani was a female version of Adric—a lithe cat of a woman with smooth butterscotch skin, large dark eyes and a perfect oval face. But her body was scarecrow-thin and her eyes had hollows beneath them so that Evie wondered if she'd been sick.

"You're the humans who saved Jace's life." Marjani looked from Evie to Kyler. "Thank you. He's like a brother to me."

Evie moved a shoulder. "We didn't do much."

Marjani touched Evie's arm, and then moved to where Adric and Jace were staring down at Nika. The redhead moistened her lips and kept her gaze on the alpha. Adric and Marjani stepped closer, and Nika shrank into herself.

Evie's stomach tightened. She could almost see the teeth and claws come out, two predators homing in on their prey. She swallowed and glanced at Jace, who had stepped back, allowing Adric to take over. He gave a slight shake of his head, and she forced herself to remain silent. This was between the fada.

"So. Nika." Adric set a hand on the back of her chair. "You're new around here, aren't you?"

She jerked her head in assent.

"I thought so. But we're going to get to know each other, won't we, love?"

Nika's throat worked. Her gaze darted from him to Marjani and then back to the floor.

"She's not from around here," Jace said. "I think she's from Russia or Eastern Europe."

"And you say she was with Corban?"

"Yeah."

Adric shook his head. "You're bullet bait to him," he told her. "Someone he can throw at me to save his own ass."

She raised her chin. "He says you lie. That you can do it without harming yourself."

"Do you scent a lie?"

Her nostrils flared. Then she shook her head. "No," she admitted. "But maybe I would not."

"Corban is the one who plays with the truth. And the man's a fucking coward, too. Look how he left you behind to take the heat."

Nika pressed her lips together.

"You know the rules," Adric said. "You come into my territory without permission, you're mine. I could slit your throat right here and no one would say a word."

Kyler moved uneasily, but Adric sliced him a look, and he kept his mouth shut.

Nika merely nodded. "As you say."

The alpha turned toward Evie. "Can I trouble you for some clothes for Nika here?"

"Yes, of course." She hurried from the room. The redhead was several sizes larger than her, but she found an oversized T-shirt and a pair of yoga pants that she thought would work. When she returned to the kitchen, Jace had taken the opportunity to get dressed in his own clothes as well.

Nika shed her towel and pulled on the shirt and pants, unconcerned with her audience. Evie elbowed Kyler, who had his gaze locked on the woman's full breasts. He reddened and dropped his eyes.

Adric was holding the paper towel with Nika's quartz. Her eyes went to it, but she didn't say anything. The alpha unwrapped it without touching it. He cocked his head, and Evie had the odd impression he was listening to it. He gave a nod and then wrapped it up again before tucking it into his pocket.

"We'll take care of her," he told Jace. "You two"—he nodded at Evie and Kyler—"go with Jace."

The two men exchanged a look.

"What do you mean?" Evie asked.

"Jace will explain. But my cousin is a coldhearted S.O.B. If he thinks he can hurt me through you, he will."

She passed a hand over her face. None of this made sense. "Why would hurting me hurt you?"

"Jace is one of my top men—a lieutenant. And it's clear he's interested in you, or else he wouldn't have been here."

Jace was a lieutenant? But it fit; he had that air of calm, confident power.

"Come on." Jace set a hand on her back. "We can talk upstairs. You too, Kyler."

As they moved into the hall, Adric said to Nika, "I'll ask you one time. Where's Corban?"

Silence.

Evie glanced back to see the alpha dangling his quartz in front of Nika's face. Then Jace moved to block her sight and hustled her toward the stairs.

She dug in her heels. Yes, Nika had helped attack Jace, but Evie couldn't help feeling a little sorry for her. "What's he going to do?" she demanded.

He propelled her forward. "Don't worry," he said in an undertone. "He won't hurt her. She'll tell him what he needs to know."

"But—"

"Upstairs. The less she knows, the better."

Evie nodded and led the way to the front bedroom—her mom's. Evie still didn't think of it as hers. The walls were still the same deep plum her mom had chosen, and she had her mom's colorful orange, blue, and purple Boho quilt on the bed. Even the sturdy fruitwood dresser had been passed down through her mom's family. The only furniture Evie had added was an inexpensive table which held her printer and a stack of books and papers.

Jace closed the door and turned to face her and Kyler. "I'd like you to come to Baltimore with me for a few days—hide in my den until we track down Corban."

"But why? What's going on?"

He scraped a hand over his short black hair. "We're not sure," he admitted. "But we're afraid Corban is behind the attack on me last week, which means he's working with the night fae. And that's twice now my trail has led right to your door. Until we know what's happening, you're not safe here."

Evie sank down on her bed. "This is insane. I have work. And Kyler—"

"Is out of school for the summer," her brother inserted. "Maybe we should listen to the man."

"You want to go?" An hour ago, he'd been ready to punch Jace out, and now he was all for leaving with him.

He moved a shoulder. "You didn't see this Corban. I did. He's one scary motherfucker."

Jace crouched before Evie, his hands on the mattress on either side of her. The claw marks on his face were healing rapidly, but they'd come dangerously close to his eye. "I'm sorry, Evie. Corban knows I was with you, and he scented you on me.

He doesn't play by the rules—and he likes to hurt women. Do you want to take a chance he won't come back?"

She grimaced. "No, of course not."

"It's Saturday night," Kyler said. "You don't have to be at work until Monday evening. We could go for a couple of days at least."

Evie stared at the marks on Jace's face and went cold as she realized that both Corban and Nika must have been out there, watching Kyler come home from Ben's. They could've grabbed him, torn him to pieces...and she'd never have known why.

"Please," Jace said. "I promise, you can leave whenever you want. But this house is too hard to protect. He could come at you from either side." He jerked his chin at the windows overlooking the street. "Even climb in through the windows. Climbing up here would be nothing for a fada."

Evie glanced at Kyler and made up her mind. "All right."

Because she trusted Jace. If he'd wanted, he could've hurt her and Kyler ten times over by now; but instead, he'd been outside the house, guarding them. He'd lost sleep to make sure they were okay, and damn it, she was touched. Yeah, she was tough, independent—and proud of it—but she wasn't stupid enough to think she could take on a fada. If Jace believed they were in danger, then they probably were.

"Thank you," Jace said as if she were doing him a favor and not the other way around. He stood up. "I'll wait in the hall while you pack. Make sure you bring enough for a few nights."

Kyler followed Jace into the hall. "I can send my friend Ben a text, right? Tell him we're going to be in Baltimore with friends?"

"Sure. Just don't give him any details."

Evie took out her own phone. She'd taken the biology final last Tuesday, and her summer class didn't start for another week. The only people she needed to contact were her bosses at the restaurant and the coffee shop. She'd been so busy the last few years that she'd lost touch with her friends from high school. Her only uncle lived in Canada, and she hadn't seen him since her mom's funeral. Evie could disappear for a month and no one would notice except Kyler and her boss and maybe Mrs. Linney.

Lord, that was sad.

It was rare for her to have a Sunday off, so she'd been planning to surprise Kyler with a trip to the beach two hours away in Delaware. But Monday she was due to work the evening shift at the restaurant and then Tuesday morning at the coffee shop. She texted her boss at the restaurant saying she might not make it in on Monday, but decided not to contact the coffee shop yet. Surely they'd be back home by Tuesday—because she really couldn't afford to lose more than a day or two of work.

She pocketed her phone and went to her dresser.

16

———

*A*dric removed his quartz pendant and pulled up a chair in front of Nika.

She squared her shoulders and set her hands on her thighs. "What are you going to do?"

Her voice was calm although he knew she was afraid. Interesting. She'd been giving a good imitation of a completely cowed submissive, someone low on the dominance scale, but a fada that low would be trembling with the effort of fighting an alpha.

"You know where my cousin is," he murmured. "Tell me, love."

He swung his pendant in front of her face. Back and forth, slow and steady.

Nika moistened her lips. Her gaze flicked to the pendant and her right hand fisted.

She wanted his quartz, even though it wouldn't do her any good—the tiny crystals within were aligned to his unique frequency, vibrating with him on a primal level. But with her quartz removed, her body would be craving the magical energy it was being deprived of.

He focused on his quartz. Deep within, the heart flared a fiery mix of bronze and blue that even he found mesmerizing. He dragged his gaze away and back to Nika's face.

Back and forth.

"Tell me," he said again. "Where's Corban?"

On Nika's other side, Marjani was careful to keep her gaze on the woman's face, not the glowing quartz. At least something good had come out of this. It was the most animated he'd seen his sister in months. But then, she had even more reason to hate Corban than he did.

Back and forth.

Nika followed the movement with her eyes. The flickers in the quartz were mirrored in her pupils, twin blue flames in the black.

"Talk to me, Nika. All I want is information. Tell me what I want to know and I'll let you live."

Her mouth compressed, but her gaze remained on the swinging quartz.

In the Darktime, he would've forced the information from her and then smashed her quartz before dumping her on the streets of Baltimore—if he didn't just slit her throat. Nika might not be the meek mouse she was pretending to be, but she was no match for a man of his strength.

But the Darktime was over, and he had little taste for hurting a woman, even one working with Corban. Of course, raiding her mind for information against her will wasn't much better. But the clan came first.

His first question was simple. Get her to answer one question, and the next one was easier. "Where did you meet Corban?"

Her jaw clenched tight. Dislike and fear came off her in waves, a bitter, unpleasant scent. He didn't think all that fear was for him, either. No, she was afraid of Corban, too.

Back and forth.

He repeated the question. "Where did you meet Corban?"

When she still didn't answer, he drew deeply on his Gift. Hypnotism: his dirty little secret. Most earth fada could hypnotize others if given enough time and opportunity, but he could do it so quickly and thoroughly that it was akin to compulsion. He was sure other people suspected, but only his top people knew for sure, because if his Gift ever became general knowledge, he could lose the clan's trust. How could his clanmates know what was true and what he'd planted in their minds?

Panic flared within Nika. He kept up the dark, steady pressure —and felt the moment her will collapsed in on itself.

Something deep inside her howled in fury, but her mouth opened. "In Iceland." The words were slow, a little blurred.

Adric raised a brow. Iceland was the ice fae's home territory.

"What were you doing in Iceland?"

"My alpha, he sent me to the ice fae."

"Why?"

She shrugged, her gaze on the moving quartz. He drew more energy from it. The flickers coalesced into a vivid cobalt fire.

"Tell me, Nika."

"I am to work for them. The ice fae, they pay the clan good money."

"And Corban? Why was he in Iceland?"

"He works for them too."

"Who? Who is he working for?"

She swallowed and then whispered, "The king."

Adric considered that. He hadn't heard from Corban since he'd disappeared soon after leaving for the Himalayas to track Sindre's rogue female. For the first three months, Adric had kept tabs on his cousin; as alpha, his quartz was linked to everyone in the clan. But then the link had been abruptly cut. As far as everyone knew Corban had died, but Adric suspected he'd smashed his own quartz so that he could go into hiding.

It had been left to Adric to explain to King Sindre why the

Baltimore fada hadn't completed the job they'd been hired to do. The ice fae king was a tall, striking man with long blond hair and the ice-gray eyes of a predator. He'd been waiting at the entrance to Adric's den. A clear message: the king could find him anytime, anywhere.

Adric had apologized and offered to send another tracker, but Sindre had simply scrutinized him with those frosty eyes. Adric's hand had gone to his quartz. Ice fae fed on the energy of motion. A powerful fae like Sindre could suck the energy out of your very molecules. The only way to resist was to shield yourself—either with iron, or by putting up an energy barrier.

"Very well," the king said at last. "I'll find the woman myself. It seems she is too clever for even a fada tracker."

Now Adric realized his cousin must have struck a deal with Sindre. He narrowed his eyes at Nika. "Where is Corban now?"

"He ran away."

"Yes, but where is he staying?"

"Nowhere. We flew in last week. By now he's already gone." Nika surfaced enough to shoot Adric a triumphant look. "You must travel to Iceland to find him."

Adric swore under his breath.

"Sounds like him," Marjani muttered. "Strike and run."

Adric shook his head. He tried to get more information from Nika, but she didn't know much else. She did tell him which flight they'd been booked on, but Corban wasn't stupid—he'd take another flight under a different name. Adric would send a man to check the airport anyway, but he knew it was a waste of time.

Like hell, he'd chase Corban to Iceland. That was exactly what his cousin wanted. Adric's fingers tightened on his quartz.

Nika twitched and he focused on her again. He was going to have to bring her out of the trance soon. His own energy was being drained at a rapid rate, and if he pushed Nika any harder, he risked damaging her brain.

But first, he had another question. "What about the night fae? Why are they working with Corban?"

"The night fae?" But her eyes flickered.

"*Tell me.*" He threw everything he had into extracting that last bit of information, but he'd lost her. She'd thrown up a barrier he couldn't penetrate.

"I do not know."

It might be the truth—and it might not. Because "I don't know" could mean anything, or nothing.

He ground his teeth. "Then who?"

But she'd regained control of her mind. She closed her mouth and refused to say anything else.

The last thing he did was erase Nika's memory of how he'd hypnotized her. She'd remember that she'd given him information, but blame herself for being weak.

Sometimes Adric was an even bigger bastard than his cousin.

Nika's breath sighed out. Her chin fell to her chest as she slid into a deep sleep. He grabbed her shoulders to keep her from falling off the chair.

"Let's get out of here," he told Marjani.

"What about her?" She jerked her chin at the sleeping woman. "You're not bringing her back to Baltimore, are you?"

"No fucking way." Nika was hiding something, and he was damned if he'd bring her into their den, or anywhere near the clan, for that matter. "We'll leave her on Rock Run territory. Let them deal with her."

Dion wouldn't hurt Nika for no reason, but he *would* keep her captive while he tried to figure out why Adric had left her on his land.

Marjani's brows shot up. "I like it. And her quartz?"

"You hang onto it." Adric handed the pendant to Marjani and lifted Nika in his arms. His scent would be all over her. The river fada would know he'd left her there deliberately—what they wouldn't know was why.

They'd driven up in one of the clan's jeeps. After he laid Nika on the back seat, his sister took the wheel while he put in a call to a high-ranking sentry, directing the woman to send some men to the Baltimore airport on the off-chance they could catch Corban.

Next he contacted Zuri and brought him up to date. "Corban still has friends in the clan," he said. "If he's hurt bad enough, there's a chance he'll go to ground in one of their dens. Start with his old den. I want someone we trust to visit every single one of the bastard's friends. He's gone too far this time. He knows damn well an attack on Jace is an attack on me. I want him, Zuri."

"If he's in Baltimore," the lieutenant replied grimly, "I'll find him."

His last call was to Bryah, a tough young sentry itching to prove herself. He'd left her and another sentry searching Grace Harbor for Corban while he was occupied with Nika and Jace. "Find anything?" he asked.

"Only some traces of blood, sir. We followed his scent as far as the bay and then we lost him. We ran along the shore for half a mile in each direction but there was no trace of him. We criss-crossed the town after that. I can tell you he was up here for a day, maybe two. He could be hiding somewhere, but my guess is he left by boat."

"Unless he was 'ported out," Adric muttered. His fingers tight-ened around his quartz. He'd swear Corban had the DNA of a fucking weasel, the way he wriggled out of tight spots.

"You think he's working with a fae?"

"It's a possibility."

"I didn't pick up a fae's scent."

Adric nodded. That was useful intel, although not conclusive. "You did good," he told Bryah. "Go back to Baltimore. Zuri could use you in the search down there."

Marjani drove west along the Susquehanna River. Rock Run owned several thousand prime acres along the shore, including the mouth of Rock Run Creek. The river fada's underground base followed the creek; its actual location was a closely kept secret. Adric had gotten inside once, but the sun fae had wiped his memory of the details, and he'd never been able to get past the wards again.

Adric felt the familiar clench of possessiveness. God's cat, he wanted Rock Run's territory for the clan. It had everything—forests for their cats and wolves and bears and deer to run free in. Fresh water to swim and fish in. An underground base that was perfect for a growing clan.

Once, he'd plotted to take Rock Run's territory, but he'd set that plan aside. Rock Run had three times the people, and now that Dion had mated with the sun fae queen, it would be suicide to go up against them. Queen Cleia could literally incinerate a man where he stood. No, his clan was going to make the money they needed from selling the new quartz technology, and then they'd buy their own chunk of prime forestland.

And Jace Jones was crucial to that plan. He was the brains behind the smartphone project. Kill Jace, and the clan could kiss their plans for new territory goodbye—and Corban knew that as well as Adric.

They reached Rock Run's border. The road narrowed to a strip of asphalt and gravel. To their left the terrain was thick with trees; to the right, the Susquehanna rushed by just yards away, the rising moon casting a shimmering gold trail on its wide black waters.

"Here?" asked Marjani.

When he nodded, she stopped the jeep. Nika was still unconscious. Adric set her in the grass beside the road.

Marjani followed with Nika's quartz. "She's stronger than she's pretending," she said as she unwrapped it. "You know we have to do it."

"Fine." He dragged a hand over his spiked-up hair. "Do it then."

His sister's eyes flashed the chilly sapphire of her cougar. She found a heavy rock, set the quartz on the road and smashed it into several jagged pieces.

Nika jerked and slipped further into unconsciousness.

The quartz shards sparkled like dim stars, still sharing energy with Nika. Scooping them up, Marjani walked onto the narrow beach and tossed them into the river. The last piece, she placed on Nika's chest where she'd be sure to find it.

"She'll be all right," Marjani said, as if he were arguing. "That's more than Corban allowed me."

The sparkling pieces were carried rapidly downriver. One by one, they winked out of sight as they sank beneath the water.

A dolphin's fin appeared upriver. A Rock Run sentry coming to investigate.

"Let's get out of here," Adric said, and they jogged back to the jeep.

But he glanced over his shoulder as the dolphin shifted—and felt the shock clear to his bones. It was Rosana do Rio, the only sister of the Rock Run alpha—and the woman he'd wanted for six long years.

"I'll be right there."

"Damn it, Ric," Marjani growled, but he was already moving down the road.

Rosana strode onto the beach. It was too dark to see her clearly, but her image was emblazoned on his brain: a heart-shaped face, a cloud of wavy black hair, and eyes the rich blue of the ocean. Her irises turned a bright, night-glow silver, and their gazes locked.

His heart thundered in his ears. He stopped a yard away. "It's been a while." A year, in fact.

They'd danced at Tiago's mate ball. She'd melted into him for that single dance, and he'd murmured in her ear, trying to entice her to come to him later. But when the dance ended, she'd pulled out of his arms, saying, "I can't do this," and walked rapidly away.

Now he hungrily took in her naked body. She was a man's wet

dream—slick from her swim, with high breasts and sleek thighs. Her hair tumbled in damp ringlets over her shoulders and beneath his heated gaze, her nipples beaded. But she kept her chin level and met him look for look, a proud and arrogant do Rio to her very toes.

But she wanted him. He gave a slow, deliberate inhale, letting her know he scented her need.

She glanced from him to Nika. "You're on our territory." Her voice was naturally husky. The woman could read a fucking menu and sound sexy.

"I brought you a gift."

"A gift?" A delicate black eyebrow winged up.

He indicated Nika. "She attacked one of my men in Grace Harbor. I figured your brother might want to question her."

"Grace Harbor isn't our territory."

He shrugged. "Close enough." Which she knew as well as him.

Upstream, another dolphin was making a beeline for them. Adric stepped closer, fingered a wet black ringlet. "I have to go."

He prided himself on his control. He'd never have made alpha without it. But then Rosana moistened her full lower lip and his control broke with an almost audible snap. With a growl, he speared his fingers into her hair and dragged her up against him.

She went stick straight—and then she gripped his shoulders and opened her mouth. Adric sank into her. There was no other word for it. He went deep and mindless. One hand tangled in her hair while the other smoothed over her firm ass, urged her up against his aching cock. His tongue sought hers and they tasted each other. One slow, sweet kiss.

His heart slammed against his rib cage. His head swam with her scent—fresh water and green grass layered over something that was all woman...a fragrance that could only be Rosana do Rio.

A furious snarl sounded from the river. A young, hard-driving *tenente* named Davi rose from the water, his gaze lethal.

Adric raised his head and resolutely set Rosana from him.

Behind him, Marjani had backed up the jeep. She shoved open the passenger-side door. "Get in, you ass."

He ignored her to touch Rosana's cheek. One last stroke of her downy skin.

Her throat worked. She captured his hand—and set it firmly against his chest. "Goodbye, Lord Adric."

"Rosana—" He was close to begging...and he'd never begged a woman in his life.

Davi strode toward them. "What the fuck's going on?"

"It's all right." Rosana slapped a palm on the *tenente*'s chest. "Go," she told Adric.

His cougar gnashed its teeth at seeing her touch another man. But Marjani was right. Rosana do Rio wasn't for him—and not just because he was alpha of an earth fada clan and she was a river fada. No, there were other, darker reasons he couldn't allow himself to take Rosana.

With a mocking salute to Davi, he hopped into the jeep. The Rock Run man growled and started toward them, but Marjani slammed her foot on the gas pedal and they sped off in a hail of gravel.

His sister shook her head. "God's cat, Ric. You have to get over this obsession with her."

"I don't want her." It was a lie, and his stomach lurched in response. "Not for more than a fuck," he amended.

Marjani snorted and he scowled at her. They drove in silence until she reached the main road. Then her eyes creased with amusement. "Dion's going to go insane trying to figure out why we left Nika here."

It wasn't a smile, but it was the closest she'd come in a long while. Adric blew out a breath—and wrenched his mind away from the sexy Rock Run female.

"And then he'll give up," he said, "and have his mate 'port her back to Iceland or wherever the hell she's from."

"Either way, she'll be taken care of. Smart."

"Exactly." Adric smirked and tapped his quartz. "Zuri? Any news?"

17

"So," Kyler said, "are you going to sleep with him?"

"Jesus." Evie's fingers tightened on the steering wheel. "You're my brother, not my dad."

"You're all I have."

Her heart pinched. "Ditto, squirt."

"I just want you to be careful."

"I will. But I like him. I really like him." She slanted him a look. "Would it be so bad?"

"Nah, he seems like an okay dude. A hardass, but not like that guy I talked to—Corban. He was cold right to the bone. That guy would slit your throat and smile the whole time."

A chill inched up Evie's spine. Right then and there, she decided to stay with Jace as long as necessary. She and Kyler were in over their heads. They couldn't even go to the cops; the fada policed themselves. Yeah, there were rules—the fada weren't supposed to mess in human affairs. There was even a human-fada treaty between the US and the American fada. But everyone knew that in reality, the fada did whatever they damned well pleased. The authorities turned a blind eye to everything but the most blatant violations of the treaty.

"Jace and Adric will get Corban," Kyler said. "You'll see."

"I know." She didn't doubt that for a second.

"And it's okay with me." He waved a hand. "If you two...you know."

She compressed her lips, trying not to laugh. "Thanks."

"Like I said, he's an okay dude. But that doesn't mean you're more to him than a piece of ass." And with that brotherly warning, he put his ear buds in and leaned back in the car seat.

JACE PULLED his bike into the shed. As he eased his injured leg over the seat, he stifled a groan. Damn thigh had stiffened up during the hour ride south. But what worried him was the way his knife wounds were burning. He slid a hand under his shirt and grimaced when he touched blood. Just a few drops, but he'd definitely ripped something open.

Behind him, Evie's car wheezed to a stop and let out a couple of explosive pops. He made a mental note to have Sam go over her car. He was the clan's best mechanic; the engine would be purring by the time he was through with it. It was the least they could do after dragging her into what was shaping up to be a clan war.

Besides, Jace *wanted* to help her. The woman carried too much weight on those tough little shoulders. As a fada, he never understood why the humans didn't rally around their single parents—female or male, raising a cub alone was a damn hard job. Evie wouldn't accept his money, but he figured she wouldn't say no to Sam tuning up her car, especially after she saw that nothing made the tiger happier than to be elbow-deep in an engine.

Evie and Kyler exited their car, backpacks in hand. As they walked toward the shed, they glanced around, taking in the freshly painted house and the neat, fenced-in backyard.

"I'll show you around in the morning," Jace said. He was proud of his block. He'd worked hard to make it safe for his human neighbors. The rats had been chased off, and he made sure that the landlords kept the houses up to code. In return, when a house fell vacant, he helped the landlord find a responsible tenant. Adric might tolerate drug dealers on his block, but not Jace.

It had paid off. The yards were well kept and blooming with flowers, and a group of elders had started a community garden on a vacant lot. The woman who rented his house had tubs filled with tomatoes and zucchini on the front porch, and as soon as morning came, the street would ring with the shouts of children unafraid to play outside.

"I'd like that," Evie said.

He walked toward them, intending to take her backpack, and then winced as his leg protested. Evie hurried up and slid an arm around his waist.

"You're hurt."

He grunted, but set an arm on her shoulders. If she wanted to plaster that sweet little body against his, he was all for it.

"Where's your den?" Kyler asked.

"Here." Jace touched his quartz and murmured the words that dissolved the *look-away* spell.

"Wowzer." The teenager's jaw slackened as the stairs appeared. "That's frickin' cool."

"Your den is underground?" Evie peered down the two flights.

"Yeah."

He'd never taken a human into his den. Ever.

And his cat was calmly satisfied. As far as it was concerned, everything had worked out just as it should. Except that Evie was in danger. The cat didn't like that, but that was all the more reason to keep her close. And her brother, too, because the cub was essential to Evie's happiness—and besides, the cat liked him.

"Sick." That was Kyler. "Ben would never believe this."

Evie's scent was wary, but interested too.

"What's the matter?" Jace asked her.

"It's so...dark."

Ah. He'd forgotten she didn't have a cat's night vision. And maybe she was a little cautious about entering a fada's den?

He led the way down the stairs, leaving the two siblings to follow or not as they wished—and then held his breath, not sure what he'd do if Evie changed her mind. Because both man and cat wanted her here, had a deep, primal need to protect her.

He glanced over his shoulder. "There are quartz lights built into the walls. Our motion will turn them on." The lights glowed on as he spoke—tiny blue and silver crystals set into the dark gray stone in irregular patterns.

"They're beautiful," Evie breathed, and started down the stairs after him.

He sent her a smile. "Thanks. They were my mom's idea."

Evie trailed her fingers down the wall. "They're like stars in the night sky."

"That's what Mom said."

When they reached the bottom, he touched his quartz to the lock in the heavy oak door. It swung open and he ushered his two guests through the small foyer into the living room. They looked around curiously, taking in the exposed stone walls, the quartz wall sconces and the colorful pillows scattered on the floor.

Evie fingered a beautiful rose quartz that his mom had brought back from Brazil, and then peeked into the spacious kitchen. "Wow, this is a big place."

"My dad built it." He watched as Kyler wandered into the kitchen and then back out again. "Five bedrooms, because he and my mom were always bringing someone home."

Her mouth curved. "They sound like nice people."

"They were." He felt the familiar tug of grief that his parents had died so young. Fada normally lived for hundreds of years, but his mom and dad hadn't even reached their seventies.

Were. Her dark eyes met his in shared compassion. "But you don't live here alone, do you?"

He shook his head. "I have four den mates, although right now Luc is out of the country. And there's Tigger—thinks he runs the show."

On cue, the tabby leapt off the back of the couch and strolled over to sniff Evie. Introductions over, he butted her leg, completely ignoring Kyler.

"A cat?" Evie broke into a smile and to Jace's disgust, crouched down to coo over Tigger. The damn housecat got all the attention. But he had to admit, Tigger had his uses, because when Evie stood back up, her wariness was completely gone. It was hard to be suspicious of a guy with a fat tabby for a pet.

"Let me show you the security system." He and Sam had installed it themselves. It ran on crystal power, and was keyed to each of his den mates' individual quartzes, as well as Adric's. "We can work it with our quartz," he said, "but you just have to key in this code." He showed them the sequence on the touchpad next to the door and then made sure they both had it memorized.

"That will keep out a fae?" Evie asked.

"We worked iron into the lock. We have to be careful not to touch the lock itself, and I guess you should, too, since you have some fae in you. Kyler, it shouldn't affect you at all. Between this and the *look-away* spell, nobody can get in here without my permission."

She touched his arm, her face solemn. "Thank you."

"You're safe," he added. "The night fae aren't interested in you, and I'm not leaving you or Kyler alone for a minute until we find Corban. He'll have to go through me to get to you."

"Where are your roommates?" Kyler asked.

Jace inhaled, checking for scents. "Beau's in bed—he's a bear and likes his sleep—and the other two are out. Adric has them sweeping the city for Corban."

The teenager stifled a yawn and nodded.

"The bedrooms are through here." Jace led the way into the hall, where the five bedrooms were arranged in a semi-circle around the living room and kitchen. "We have two bathrooms, one at either end of the hall." He pointed them out. "Kyler can take the extra bed in Beau's room. Don't worry about bothering him, he's used to it. And Evie, you can have my room. I'll sleep on the couch."

"Your friends won't mind?"

"It's my den. But no, they don't mind. They're used to it—we have packmates staying over all the time."

He ushered Kyler into Beau's room. A single fae light winked on, enough to show the huge lump curled up on the bed. His animal was a brown bear, and even as a human he was huge.

Beau cracked open an eye. "A human?" Bears had an even better sense of smell than cats.

"Yeah. Name's Kyler. He and his sister need a place to stay."

"Help yourself, bro." Beau waved a massive hand at the spare bed.

"Thanks." Kyler set his backpack at the foot of the bed.

Jace left them to it and opened the door to his own room. His dad had left the walls uncovered. Three fae lights glowed to life, casting a soft yellow hue over the worked gray stone.

It was a plain, masculine room, save for the colorful Native American rug at the foot of the bed; the room of a man who lived alone. Other than the large oak bed, the only furniture was a chair and a nightstand with another of the large chunks of quartz his mother had brought back from her tours overseas. This one had come from Morocco, where his mom still had a few relatives, her family having migrated from North Africa to Jamaica several centuries ago. It was a piece of art—an oblong tower of white calcite encrusted in places with silver crystals and a darker gray mineral running through the center.

"I thought it would be damp," Evie said, "like a cave. But it's warm. And I love the rug."

"My great-grandma wove the rug. Dad was part Cherokee."

"It's beautiful." Evie crouched to trace a finger over the red, green and black pattern.

"Our cats don't like the cold, so we have heating coils set in the floor. Actually, the wolves don't either. The bears don't give a shit, but they're in the minority."

She gave a gurgle of laughter and rose back to her feet. "I can't imagine anyone telling Beau what to do."

"You don't. But like I said, he doesn't care. It takes a lot to rile Beau."

"I like him already." The fae lights drifted toward her and her eyes widened. "Are those what I think they are?"

"Fae lights? Yeah. I did a sun fae a favor and she gifted them to me."

She stretched a hand toward one of the glowing balls, and to Jace's surprise, it floated down and slid over her palm as if welcoming her.

"I can feel it." She turned awed eyes on him. "It's warm and a little tingly."

"Tap it, and it will shut off."

She obeyed and the light winked out.

"You can leave it on while you're sleeping if you want—it will sense how much light you need and power down."

"Wow." She tapped the light a second time, and it glowed back on and wafted its way toward the ceiling.

"You can put your stuff in there." He indicated the closet. "Feel free to take a shower if you want."

She nodded. "I really appreciate this. I hate to put you out—"

Her gaze went to the large unmade bed in the center of the room. It was a tangle of sheets and the red print bedspread he'd bought because it didn't show dirt. He hadn't expected to be bringing anyone home.

She glanced at him and he just knew her mind had gone the

same place as his: the two of them nestled in the sheets, bodies joined.

Not tonight.

He'd brought her here to protect her, not fuck her. You didn't take advantage of a woman like that. And his knife wound—the deeper one—was throbbing.

But he could almost taste her nipples in his mouth, feel her fingers digging into his shoulders, her body moving with his.

She dragged a hand over her hair, ruffling the short blond strands.

"I'll be fine," he said.

"What?" Her pupils were big and dark, the irises a rich brown shot with gold.

"Sleeping in the living room. I can change to my jaguar and curl up on a cushion."

She stepped close and his lungs seized. She touched his cheek. "Your jaguar is beautiful. I'd like to see him again sometime."

His animal preened. The cat loved to be admired.

Jace smoothed down her ruffled hair. It was silky soft, like a kitten's fur. "You will." It was a promise, even if she didn't know it.

He brushed his mouth over hers. Their lips clung, and then he stepped back. "I'll help you make the bed."

She touched her mouth. "All right."

He grabbed a spare set of sheets from the closet, and together, they stripped off the old sheets and put on the new ones. And damn if that wasn't almost as intimate as touching her. His cock was painfully hard.

He balled up the dirty sheets and tossed them into the closet. "If you need anything, I'll be in the living room."

She nodded her thanks, and he closed the few feet between them. "Good night," he said, and swayed closer. Not to kiss her again. He just wanted one last whiff.

But she turned her head and their mouths met, and then she was in his arms.

Heat flashed up his spine. Fuck his injured belly, and to hell with what was right or wrong.

They twined around each other. It was as if the two hours between their last kiss and this one had never been. They picked up right where they'd left off: his tongue in her mouth, his hand on her ass. She pressed herself against his aching groin, making sexy little moans that vibrated through him like a tuning fork.

He wrenched his mouth from hers and dragged in a breath. "I didn't bring you here for this."

"I know, but—" She set her lips to his throat and sucked. Heated sparks danced over his skin. "It's okay. I want this—I want you. But you're hurt."

"Not that hurt. And Suha's going to stop by. I'll be okay by the time she leaves."

"Yeah?" She nibbled his ear, and his eyes slit with pleasure.

He nudged her chin up, gave her a last, deep kiss and then resolutely set her from him. "Later. I'll come back after your brother's in bed."

"All right." Her lips were moist and reddened from his kiss.

His gaze fixed on her mouth, his mind painting a lurid picture of those moist lips on him. He almost grabbed her again, but instead he reached blindly for the doorknob. "Later," he repeated.

Her dimple flashed. "Sure."

She took her backpack and set it on the bed to unpack it. The three fae lights floated down to circle her head like a faerie crown.

His brow creased. Fae lights sensed when the user needed them, but these three acted as if Evie was some kind of a lodestone.

He'd never seen a fae light do that, even around another fae.

～

EVIE SHOOK OUT HER CLOTHES—A couple of T-shirts, a sleepshirt, and a pair of cargo pants—and hung them on hooks in the closet. The underwear could stay in the backpack, which reminded her that she still had on the plain black panties and white sports bra she'd worn to work that night. She hadn't planned on anyone else seeing them.

Not that Jace seemed to care; she had a feeling he was just fine with bare skin.

She did a little happy dance. This was really happening—her and Jace. Even it if was just for a couple of nights, she intended to squeeze every last ounce of enjoyment out of it.

She headed for the bathroom to wash up. The fae lights trailed after her, casting a warm glow over everything.

The bathroom was jaw-dropping—two sinks, a walk-in shower carved from speckled gray stone, and a black jacuzzi taking up one corner. Plain white towels were stacked on a small table, and the shelves were scattered with razors, shaving soap and other masculine paraphernalia.

Back in the living room, she found Jace and Kyler had been joined by a large man with curly cinnamon hair and pale gold eyes. The fae lights had trailed her down the hall. They spread out across the room as Jace turned to smile at her.

"There you are. I want you to meet Sam."

The big redhead held out a blunt-fingered hand. "A pleasure."

Evie's hand was swallowed in his. His grip was firm, but it was clear he was holding his enormous strength in check. "Thank you."

"I was telling Sam what happened tonight," Jace said.

The other man nodded. "Adric already sent word to me and some of the other soldiers. We're searching Baltimore for that bastard cousin of his. I just wanted to make sure you have things under control."

"We're fine," Jace replied. "Beau's in his room, and I have Kyler here as backup."

Her brother straightened his shoulders and gave a short, unsmiling nod as Jace's quartz buzzed.

"It's Suha," Jace said.

"I was just on my way out," said Sam. "I'll let her in." With a nod to Evie and Kyler, he headed for the door.

Jace limped to the couch and sat down, his injured leg stretched out on the cushions. "I'd better sit down, or she'll yell at me."

Evie suppressed a smile. She was looking forward to meeting the woman who could make a badass like Jace scramble to please her. Then Suha entered and Evie's eyes widened. This was no motherly healer—in fact, she didn't look any older than Evie—and she was pretty, with a dancer's grace. Her flirty yellow summer dress made Evie feel like a bag lady in her tank top and sweat shorts.

"You must be Evie." The healer gave her a warm smile. "Nice to meet you. And you too, Kyler." Tigger gave an imperious meow and bumped her shin. "Yeah, yeah, I see you." She scratched the tabby behind the ears and he rumbled with pleasure.

Kyler stuck out his hand. "Hello. I'm Kyler." He winced. "Right. You know that."

Evie met Jace's eyes and tried not to laugh, but Suha just smiled and shook his hand. "Peace to you and yours."

"Peace." He gazed down on her, a silly grin on his narrow face.

The moment stretched until Suha gave her hand a tug. Kyler's cheeks reddened and he released it like it was a hot coal.

The healer gave him a wink, like the two of them were in on a joke, and Kyler's embarrassment faded. Right then, Evie decided she liked her.

"So." Suha turned to Jace. "I hear you had a run in with Corban and tore something open inside. I suppose you had to chase him down yourself."

"There was no one else."

Suha rolled her eyes. "Let me have a look."

"Should we leave?" Evie asked.

"That's up to Jace."

Jace leaned back on the cushions. "It's fine with me if you stay."

Evie and Kyler helped move the coffee table so Suha could pull up a chair next to Jace. Evie sat on the other end of the couch while Kyler sprawled on a nearby chair, his long, knobby-kneed legs stretched out before him.

Suha removed her quartz and lifted the hem of Jace's shirt. His knife wounds were seeping blood.

Evie bit her lip. "He wasn't bleeding a couple of hours ago."

Suha muttered something that sounded like "stubborn ass" and ran her quartz over his abdomen. The stone began to glow with warm, healing colors—pink, yellow, peach.

Jace's eyes closed. He was quiet, but fine lines of pain radiated from around his mouth.

Evie stroked his ankle, wishing there were more she could do to help. His breath sighed out and Suha gave her an approving nod, so she kept doing it.

Suha moved to the gash on Jace's thigh. It had scabbed up, but it was still nasty looking. The healer ran her quartz up and down it, and then went to his nape, where she clucked at the puncture wounds. "An inch to the right, and you'd have been paralyzed for life."

Evie gulped and met Kyler's eyes, but Jace just shrugged.

Suha moved back to Jace's abdomen. Several minutes passed. Evie scooted closer and took Jace's hand. His lips curved, although his eyes remained shut.

Kyler got up to wander around the room, examining the TV and the colorful chunks of quartz on the mantelpiece. He crouched down to examine the fireplace. Instead of logs, there were several large amber-and-brown chunks on the firebox floor.

Tigger strolled past him and the teenager held out a hand.

The cat ignored it with a lordly disdain, continuing past to the kitchen. A moment later, they heard the crunch of kibble.

Kyler sat down with his back against the wall and took out his phone. He swore under his breath. "I can't get a signal."

"It's the quartz," Jace said without opening his eyes. "There's a streak of it in the bedrock. It messes with the signal."

"Can I charge it?"

"Sure. I rigged up an outlet for the TV. There's one in the kitchen, too."

"That's lit. At least I can play games." Kyler got a cord to charge the phone, and then sat down in the chair again, eyes half-shut. It was past two o'clock, and he'd been up early to apply for a job at a local pizza place.

Evie opened her mouth to tell him to go to bed, and then closed it. He'd only snap at her, and it wasn't like they had anywhere to be in the morning.

Suha continued working on Jace, moving from his thigh to his stomach to his nape. A trio of fae lights drifted down to circle Evie's head. She felt that curious tingle of energy, and the hand holding Jace's warmed.

She blinked, and looked again. The gash on his thigh was visibly healing like a fast-motion video.

When it was just a thin red line, Suha shot Evie a look, her brow furrowed, and then sat back. "There," she told Jace. "You can run a frickin' marathon if you want. But for God's sake, can you go a couple of weeks without letting someone take a chunk out of you?"

He propped his elbows on the couch and winked at her. "You're the best."

"Yeah, yeah." But she grinned back at him before turning to Evie. "And you—you're part fae."

She shrugged. "That's what they say."

"But no one told me you're a healer."

18

A healer? Evie frowned. "Because I'm not. Am I?"

Suha fingered her quartz. "I drew on your energy to heal Jace, and I can only do that with some of the stronger members of the clan—or another healer."

Evie shook her head. "I wish it were true, but when my mom had cancer, I tried to heal her. I put my hands on her and prayed she'd get well. I even tried sending healing energy into her—you know, like faith healers do. But it didn't work."

But damn, wouldn't that be something? She'd wanted to be a doctor or a nurse as far back as she could remember. When her mom got sick, Evie had found out everything she could about the treatments, gone to every appointment. Maybe if she knew enough, she could fix her—but it hadn't worked.

And in the end, all she'd been able to do was hold her mom's hand and promise she'd take care of Kyler.

"I'm so sorry." Suha touched her hand. "But even a trained healer can't save everyone. And it's possible you hadn't come into your Gift yet. With fada, it can happen anywhere from the time we become teenagers to our late twenties."

Evie's gaze slid to Jace. He was looking at her with an unreadable expression.

"I—" She scrubbed her hands over her face. Her brain felt sluggish, too tired to take in one more shock.

Jace jerked his chin at Kyler. "She needs to eat. Get her something from the kitchen—apples, peanut butter. Suha too—a healer burns through energy fast."

"I'm on it." He rose to his feet and headed for the kitchen.

Suha indicated the glowing orbs hovering around Evie. "The fae lights are drawn to you. Trust me, they're not like that for just anyone."

Evie swallowed. "They aren't?"

"No. The only time they get that close to me is when I'm healing someone and about to run out of juice."

"Huh." She glanced at the lights. "Still, even if I have some fae blood, it's probably just a few drops."

Suha shook her head. "If you have a fae Gift, it's probably more than a few drops."

Kyler returned with a plate of sliced apples, a jar of peanut butter, spoons and four sandwich plates, and set everything on the coffee table.

"Eat." Jace scooped some peanut butter onto a slice of apple, set it on a plate and handed it to Evie, while Suha helped herself.

Evie realized she was hungry—starving, in fact. She downed the slice and helped herself to another. "But how can I heal people without a quartz?" she asked Suha.

"Fae healers use their hands. You probably felt your palm heating when you were touching Jace."

She nodded slowly. "I did. But that doesn't mean I healed him."

"You helped."

She rubbed her forehead. "If you say so."

"Look," Suha said, "you're tired. Why don't I come back tomorrow and we can talk some more?"

"Thanks—I'd like that."

Suha ate another couple apple slices and came to her feet. "I'm off then."

"Not by yourself." Jace made to stand up. "I'll walk you home. Corban would love to get his hands on our healer."

Suha raised a brow. "He has to catch me first. Besides, you're the one he wants, not me. Beau can take me."

"On my way," a deep voice rumbled and Beau shambled in. The man was *big*, with wiry black hair and shoulders as wide as a door, but he had a sweet smile. Jace sank back onto the couch as the bear-man slung a massive arm around Suha's shoulders. "How's my girl?" he asked her.

"Good." She slid an arm around his waist and raised her face for his kiss.

Kyler's face fell, but he smiled manfully. "Nice meeting you, Suha."

"You, too," she said with a kind smile.

"Don't wait up," Beau said as the two of them headed out. "I'll crash at Suha's place tonight."

Kyler let out a gusty sigh, and then helped himself to some more food. Not much interfered with his appetite. "If you're a healer," he said to Evie between bites, "you didn't get that from Fane."

"Fane's your dad?" Jace asked. "So you know who he is."

"Sure, but he never said he was fae."

"But he never seems to get older," Kyler said. "And he's tall and blond and looks like a fucking model."

"Sounds fae to me," Jace said.

"He couldn't help our mom," Kyler added. "I mean, the dude's a flake, but he wouldn't have just let her die—not if he could've healed her."

"He loved her in his way. He's just...Fane." Evie moved a shoulder. "He comes and goes as he pleases."

"He's your dad," Jace growled. "The man should've helped you out."

"He did. After Mom passed, he gave me a diamond worth thousands of dollars."

Kyler snorted. "Only Fane would give you a diamond instead of cash."

"It saved our butts," she shot back.

Jace shook his head. "That's just like a fae. Throw some fucking glitter at a problem and hope it goes away."

"That's Fane." And it was true, but it hurt to hear it from Jace, because if the fada were right, she was fae, too. And besides, she loved her dad—she'd just learned not to count on him.

She blew out a breath and decided to think about it in the morning. "I'm for bed." She crossed the room to drop a kiss on Kyler's cheek. "Night, squirt. You should go to bed too. It's late."

He gave a big yawn and for once, didn't argue. "'Kay. See you in the morning." He gathered the empty plates and carried them into the kitchen.

"'Night, Jace." Evie gave him a smile that she hoped didn't look as forced as it felt. Jace had closed down. Apparently, the fact that she might have more than few drops of fae was a game changer for him. "Thanks for everything."

"Don't thank me." He rose to his feet. "It's my fault you got dragged into this." They stared at each other across the coffee table, and then he said, "Have a good sleep."

Her heart sank. So he wasn't coming. "You, too." She turned blindly toward the bedrooms.

JACE SAT on the living room couch as Evie and Kyler got ready for the night and then retired to their separate bedrooms.

Adric called to check on him and to report that they were still looking for Corban. "According to Zuri," he said, "the bastard never got on the plane. It was to Costa Rica, by the way."

"Who the fuck does he know in Costa Rica?"

"Hell if I know. But he's been gone for over a year. Maybe he met someone, or maybe it's someone he knew from the Darktime—one of my uncle's contacts. Leron used to send him on secret missions. But then again, maybe he just wanted to hide in the fucking rain forest. Anyway, I've got every tracker in the clan out looking for him. If he's still in Baltimore, we'll find him."

"Good. And Ric? When you question him, I want to be there."

"You got it. But meanwhile, you're the best protection Evie's got."

"That's the only reason I'm not out there with you right now."

Adric ended the call and Jace glanced toward his bedroom. Evie was probably in bed now—his bed. Jace's cat was awake and swishing its tail.

The woman. She waits. Go to her.

Jace remained stubbornly on the couch.

Why *had* he let Evie see him tonight? As he'd crossed the alley, he told himself that all he wanted was to make sure she was okay. His clan wasn't rich. Hell, they were hanging on by their fingernails, with every spare penny going toward rebuilding the homes and businesses that had been destroyed during the Darktime. Anything left over was invested in this new venture with the smartphones.

But Jace had some cash set aside. He could help Evie if she wasn't so stubborn about not taking his money.

He sure as hell hadn't planned to kiss her. But she'd looked so damn brave, clutching her keys like she had a prayer of chance against a man who had six inches and sixty pounds on her. And holy singing crystals, that had been some hot kiss. He'd been seconds away from stripping off her clothes and taking her right there in the kitchen.

But what the fuck was he thinking? She was a human and a

fae, and he had a policy about not mixing with other races. Look where it had gotten Takira.

The wall sconces sensed the lack of motion and dimmed, but Jace barely noticed. He was recalling how happy his sister had been with Silver.

"So he's part night fae," she'd said. "He's not his genetics any more than we are. Who knows how much fae we have in us? You have a powerful Gift yourself. Does that mean you have more fae than me?"

"But a night fae," he'd growled. "Mate with anyone but one of them."

"Oh, Jace." His sister's dark eyes were knowing and a little sad. "You don't choose your mate—you just *know*. He's the one. And he's a good man. If you'd just meet him, you'd see."

"Is this what we've been fighting for all these years? For the right to mate with a fucking fae?"

"He's half fae." She'd lifted her chin. "And I thought we were fighting for the right to live our lives however we choose—instead of as Leron's pawns."

"You're right." Shame had tightened Jace's stomach. "Forget I said that. Go with your Silver."

"You'll come to our mating ceremony?"

He'd crossed the room in two strides and wrapped her in a hard hug. "Try and keep me away."

His sister was thin. Food had been scarce for a long time. Her stomach shouldn't have bumped against his.

He'd stepped back and ran a hand down her tunic. "You're—"

"A baby." A smile split her face. "We're having a baby. Can you believe it?" There hadn't been a cub born to the clan for three years.

Now grief swamped him. He dropped his head into his hands. If only he could go back and unsay those words to Takira. Because what had happened hadn't been either her fault or

Silver's. All she'd tried to do was make a family with her mate and daughter.

It had been Leron and Tyrus who'd smashed his sister's happiness like a fragile glass.

Jace heaved himself off the couch. *Fuck this.* Takira wouldn't say he was honoring her by staying away from Evie.

She'd say Jace was being an ass.

19

———————

$\mathcal{A}$s Evie exited the bathroom, she heard Jace in the living room on his quartz phone.

She said goodnight to Kyler and then went into Jace's bedroom. The fae lights brushed over her as if saying hello, and then spread themselves across the ceiling before dimming to a soft glow—which was pretty effing awesome when you thought about it. Maybe Jace would let her take one home.

She left the door slightly ajar and changed into a striped cotton sleepshirt. Jace came down the hall and she tensed in anticipation, but he went into the bathroom and a short while later the shower came on.

She set the quartz phone he'd given her on the night table next to a pretty chunk of amethyst and sat cross-legged on the bed. Waiting for Jace—who probably wasn't going to come.

She combed her fingers through her damp hair. *What was so bad about being part fae?* Sure, the fae could be selfish, unpredictable creatures—look at Fane. But Evie wasn't like that, and if Jace couldn't see that, then to hell with him. She scowled in the direction of the bathroom.

A fae light brushed against her chest, right over her heart. She felt as if she'd been hugged.

She gave a wry smile. "You're trying to make me feel better. Thanks."

The fae light pulsed a bright yellow, and then dimmed again. Evie held up a finger, and another light—this one a soft pink—floated down to balance on her fingertip.

She stilled, afraid to breathe. It weighed no more than a soap bubble, a globe of miniscule stars. But unlike stars, the tiny points of light were in constant motion, turning in hypnotic spirals so that she had the unsettling sensation of falling endlessly into the center. The colors changed, the pink changing to a shimmering copper and gold and then back again.

The shower turned off. She dragged her gaze from the fae light and it wafted back to the ceiling.

She smoothed the sleepshirt down over her thighs and looked at the door. Several minutes crawled past, but still no Jace.

She blew out a breath. He wasn't coming, and she was tired. Time to go to bed. She gave her pillow a few hard punches and went to lie down.

A tap sounded on the door. Her heart leapt. "Come in."

Jace slipped into the room along with a few more fae lights and closed the door behind him. He'd changed into a white ribbed tank and brown shorts that hung low on his hips. His short black hair was damp from the shower, and stubble shadowed his jaw. He leaned against the door and stared at her—all hard muscles and honey-dark skin.

God, the man was beautiful. She moistened her lips. "Hello."

"So," he said, "you have more than a few drops of fae."

She lifted her chin. "So what? If I'm fae, then I'm one of the good ones, right? Being a healer is a good thing—like Suha."

He took a step toward her, then another. Lithe, catlike steps that made her heart slam against her rib cage. He was a predator, a man who literally had teeth and claws, but she trusted him with her life—and more, with Kyler's life. And when her heart sped up, it wasn't because she was afraid.

He stopped beside the bed. His gaze raked down her body, dark...hungry. Heat curled through her belly.

"Later," he murmured. "We'll talk about it later."

"Fine with me." She held out a hand. His fingers closed around hers, but instead of joining her in the bed, he drew her to her feet.

"You're not too tired?" He caressed her upper arms, and even that slight touch sent sensation jolting through her.

She pressed a kiss to the hollow of his throat. He smelled of soap and warm, spicy male. "Not anymore."

His pulse pounded beneath her lips. "God's cat, I want you— since the minute I first saw you." He gave a short laugh. "Even when I thought you were going to bash my head in with that damn rock."

Her mouth curved. "Really?"

"Yeah. I thought I was dying and you were a fucking angel. But what about you?" He leaned back so he could meet her eyes. "I'm an animal, Evie. The jaguar's part of me. Can you handle that? Because if not, tell me to get the hell out of here."

She fisted a hand in his tank. "Jace?"

"Yeah?"

"Shut up and kiss me."

He blinked, and then his cheek creased in a smile. "Yes, ma'am."

Powerful arms enfolded her. His mouth came to hers in a slow, bone-melting kiss. First, warm lips slid over hers. Then he teased the seam of her mouth with his tongue. When she opened to him, he slid his tongue inside, tasting her in leisurely sweeps that had heat licking through her.

She moaned and rose onto the balls of her feet to get closer. Big hands gripped her hips, urging her up against his erection.

He dragged up the hem of the sleepshirt and then stilled as he palmed her ass.

"No panties?"

She ran her lips over the stubbled edge of his jaw. "I never wear panties to bed."

He squeezed her bottom, his mouth a wicked curve. "I like how you think, woman." A long finger delved between her cheeks, stroking into her cleft from behind.

He touched her clit from below and pleasure stabbed through her. She tightened her grip on his shoulders and rested her forehead against his chest while he played with her—sliding his finger into her, stroking over her most sensitive flesh. Her arousal ratcheted up, became an aching need.

She wriggled against his hand. "*Jace.*"

"Mm?" He brought his hand to his mouth and sucked her cream from his finger, his gaze locked on hers.

She shook her head. "I—"

"I know." He traced his lips over each of her eyebrows. "I know." And somehow, she felt that he did. They were in this together, each of them helpless against the other.

He took her mouth in another hard kiss. His tongue swept between her lips, demanding a response. Heat curled through her belly and lower, between her thighs. A pulse beat deep in her core. She sucked his tongue deeper and twined a leg around his hip, pressing her bare flesh against him.

He groaned low in his throat and ground himself against her. Electricity danced up and down her spine: hot, bright pricks that stoked her desire even higher. His hands moved to her breasts, now pinching her nipples, now caressing them.

He dragged his mouth from hers and regarded her from beneath thick black lashes. A flush painted his broad cheekbones, and the hazel of his irises was spiked a brilliant jade.

She curved a hand around his cheek. "That green in your eyes—"

"That's my cat."

"That's what I thought. When you're a jaguar, your eyes are green."

"The jag wants you too." His voice was guttural, and she knew both cat and man were present at this moment. His lids lowered, and he studied her warily, as if expecting her to change her mind and send him away.

She stroked his neck, his shoulders. "I'm not afraid of your cat. He's beautiful."

His jaguar had fascinated her from the first night. After Jace and Adric had left, she'd googled black panthers and found out that they could be either jaguars or leopards. A black panther still had the jaguar or leopard markings, but they were hidden by the extra black pigment. Even when Adric had first accused her of being fae and the jaguar had snarled at her, she'd still found the cat gorgeous in a savage, primal way. But even then, Jace's cat had seemed to want to protect her—he'd put himself between her and his alpha, and she guessed that for a shifter, that was a huge deal.

"He thinks you're beautiful, too. And sexy as hell." Jace angled his head against her palm, inviting her to stroke him more deeply. She obliged, combing her fingers through the short strands of hair on his nape.

"I was afraid you wouldn't come to me," she confessed.

Teeth scraped over her throat, sending dizzying waves of delight through her. Her fingers dug into his shoulders.

"I couldn't stay away."

"I'm glad."

He bent her over one strong arm and sucked at the base of her neck. She made a sound of sheer pleasure. "Jace..."

"Mm?" he said against her throat.

She set her lips against his ear and whispered, "Take me to bed."

His muscles locked. His nostrils flared, as if drawing her scent to his very heart—and then he snapped into action, scooping her up and setting her on the mattress. She scooted back against the pillows and watched as he dragged off his tank top.

He crawled onto the bed, part cat, part man—and in one smooth move, had her on her back, his thighs straddling hers, his hands on either side of her head.

He had a soldier's body, hard and roped with muscle. Her breath sucked in at the sight of all that smooth male flesh. She smoothed her hands down his chest. "You are one fine man."

"Yeah?" He nuzzled her neck.

"Oh, yeah." She trailed her fingers over his ridged abdomen. The muscles twitched under her hands, and she smiled inwardly. She loved that she affected him as much as he did her.

She came to the scars on his belly and frowned. "I'm sorry you got hurt again." She traced a finger over the longer, shallow mark.

He moved a big shoulder. "I've been hurt worse. I'm just sorry I dragged you into all this shit."

She nodded. And yet a part of her whispered that it wasn't all bad. Because if Jace hadn't come to her door, she wouldn't have ended up here with the sexiest guy she'd ever met pressing her to the mattress.

Jace tugged at the hem of her sleepshirt. She lifted her upper body, and he pulled it over her head and dropped it on the floor.

He sat back on his heels, taking her in as if she was the most delicious treat. Her nerves tingled. It was like he was touching her with his eyes, searing her with his gaze.

When she reached for him, he shook his head. "Let me touch you."

"All right." She set her hands back on the mattress and waited to see what he would do.

He started by feathering his fingers over her rib cage—light, delicate touches that sent a quiver over her skin. Next, he moved to her breasts, cupping them in his large hands.

"Beautiful," he breathed as he brushed his thumbs over her nipples.

She smiled up at him. She was average and she knew it—nothing special. But Jace made her feel like a freaking sex goddess.

Her nipples puckered and his eyes darkened. "Fuck, you're hot." He pinched them, and she sucked in a breath as pleasure shot from her breasts to her womb.

She traced her fingers up and down his wrists. He was strong, with those hard, heavy bones she'd noticed right from the first. His forearms were corded, the backs of his wrists covered with fine black hairs.

She slid her hand up his arm to the tattoo on his upper arm. The cat's paw itself was black, with touches of gold fire at the claw tips. She outlined it with her finger. "This is something to do with your cat?"

He grunted, and something about the way his face tightened told her he didn't want to talk about it. Then he swooped down to nip at her throat and everything else flew out of her head.

His fingers went to work again on her breasts, stroking and pinching until she was writhing on the bed. He bent down and sucked each nipple until they were both a wet, rosy pink.

She dug her heels into the mattress and tried to lift her hips toward him, but her legs were closed, her thighs pinned between his. She pushed at his chest, but he took her hands and pressed them to the mattress on either side of her head.

She moaned. "Please, Jace."

"Please what?" His lips moved against hers, soft and warm. "Do you want me to kiss you?" He teased the seam of her lips with his tongue.

"Yes." She lifted her head and tried to deepen the kiss, but he just gave her a quick peck before sitting back again.

"Maybe you want me to touch you here..." His fingers moved

down her abdomen, leaving tiny flames in their wake, driving her to madness.

"Yes," she rasped.

"I like to take things slow." His voice was warm and a little rough. It stroked over her nerve endings like coarse silk. "That's okay, isn't it?"

Her head moved from side to side against the pillows. "Yes. No. God, Jace."

He chuckled, and then—finally, blessedly—he moved so that his knees were between hers. She gave a whimper of relief and bent her knees, opening to him. He slid a finger over her curls, and she lifted her pelvis, straining toward his touch. His finger slid lower, brushing over her most sensitive flesh so that she clenched her jaw at the pleasure of it.

He played with her, sliding his finger in and out of her, teasing her clit, until she was wound so tight, a single touch would've set her off, and then he lifted his hand.

"*Jace.*"

"Hm?" He brushed his fingers over her again.

She narrowed her eyes. "Stop teasing."

He nipped her ear. "You do know that I'm a cat?"

"So?"

"We like to play."

She gasped as he touched her again. "Oh," was all she could say as he slid two long fingers into her and then out again.

He nuzzled her collarbone. "You know you like it."

She angled her head so that he could kiss her throat. "If I say yes, are you going to tease me more?"

"Yeah." He nipped her skin. "But remember, I can scent a lie."

She raised her hands in mock surrender. "Then yes. Do your worst."

"Oh, angel." His breath rasped in. "I'm going to make you scream."

He brought his hands back to her face and lowered his body

onto hers, keeping himself propped on his forearms. His legs came between hers and she automatically widened her thighs. He was still wearing his shorts. His hips settled against hers, his cock hard and thick against her through the thin layer of material separating them.

"So soft." He cupped the base of her skull in one big hand and nuzzled her cheek. "Everything about you is soft. Your hair, your lips. Your skin." He moved his mouth to her ear, sucking the hoop with the silver disc into his mouth, tonguing and nipping the sensitive lobe. "Soft. But strong where it counts."

"Mm." She wrapped her hands around his shoulders, exploring the round, hard muscles. His quartz lay between them, smooth and warm against her breast bone. It felt almost alive, like a bird's egg.

Jace lifted his head. The pendant hung from his chest, the smoky gray and purple infused with a faint green glow.

"May I?" She reached for his quartz but didn't touch it, recalling how he'd recoiled the night he'd been stabbed.

He shook his head. "It hurts if anyone but a close relative touches it...or my mate, if I ever take one."

"But it doesn't hurt when it rests on my chest?" she asked, and ignored how her heart constricted at the thought of his someday taking a mate.

"No. And don't ask me to explain why—it's not logical. Magic has its own rules."

"Why is it glowing?"

"Is it?"

He looked down, frowning, and then shrugged. "Thing has a mind of its own. Now, where was I? Oh, yeah—I was talking about how soft you are. Here and here." He pressed a hot kiss to each of her nipples, and then licked the undersides. "And here."

Her legs writhed beneath his. She reached down and tried to push off his shorts.

His hand went to his waistband. "You want these off?"

When she nodded, he murmured agreeably and got out of bed to remove them. He grabbed a handful of condoms from the nightstand drawer and dropped them on the table next to the amethyst before crawling back on top of her.

She touched his chest. "Jace?"

"Mm?" He smoothed a hand down her belly.

"I should tell you it's been a while."

His thumb brushed over her clit. A quick, light touch that made her muscles tense. "I'm honored then."

"You should be." Her mouth quirked. "I don't take my clothes off for just anyone."

He stilled and stared down at her, eyes shuttered. "I am."

But she sensed his withdrawal. So this was just sex. She kept her smile—but inside, her stomach twisted, even as she told herself that was all she wanted, too.

He lowered his mouth to hers and she kissed him back hard, wrapping her hand around his nape. He met her kiss for kiss, sweeping his tongue into her mouth. Tasting her. Teasing her.

She felt hot, unbearably aroused. Her hips moved restively against his, and she sucked his tongue deeper.

His groan vibrated deep inside her belly.

When he lifted his head, they were both sucking in oxygen. They stared at each other without speaking, and then Jace pressed a kiss to her collarbone.

"Your skin is like strawberries and cream," he rasped. "And fuck, I want to eat you."

He didn't wait for her response, just headed down her body. When he reached her mound, he pressed her thighs apart. "Beautiful."

She pressed her palms on the mattress, her thighs rigid in anticipation.

He pressed an open-mouthed kiss to her clit. Sensation zinged up her spine, tightened her nipples. He feathered his lips over her needy sex, licking and teasing her until she thought she'd go mad—and then he swiped his tongue up her moist center.

"Oh, God," she said on a moan. "No....no."

"No, what?" he asked against her pussy.

Her head moved back and forth on the sheets. "I mean yes."

"Yes to this?" His tongue slipped over her, circling her clit. Light, sure touches that had every muscle in her body constricting.

She threaded her fingers through his hair. It was almost dry now, the strands silky thick. "Yes."

"Or maybe you like this better?" He opened her with his thumbs and dipped his tongue inside her.

Her core contracted. She muttered something incoherent.

"Can't make up your mind?"

She shook her head, unable to form words. She only knew that she wanted more, so that was what she said: "More—please."

He gave a throaty chuckle against her inner thigh. "I like a woman who begs." He rewarded her with more licking and sucking.

The tiny flames danced up and down her body, gathered at her center.

He nibbled at her belly. "I'm waiting, Evie."

Heat spiked through her. There was something so sexy about the way he said it, low and firm. Her hands fisted in the sheets. "Please, Jace. Please. Kiss me. Suck me."

He murmured something rough and dark. He slid a long finger into her and at the same time, set his lips to her tender, aching flesh—and sucked. Hard.

Electricity arced through her. Her hips bucked and he pushed her back down onto the bed. She dug her fingers into the mattress and whimpered his name. Her thighs tightened on his arms, and then she pressed up against him.

"That's it," he murmured, stroking a finger into her wet opening. "Come for me, pretty Evie."

She cried out one more *please*, and then the fire at her center exploded in a series of rapid, molten bursts.

Jace gave a last, voluptuous lick to her pussy. She lay on the mattress, too pleasured to move, and watched as he fitted a condom on himself.

He came back over her body. She was still feeling the aftershocks. He worked his way up her body, kissing her as he moved: her stomach, her nipples, the sensitive indentation of her throat.

He settled between her thighs. His tip nudged her center, blunt and so good. She raised her hips to take him in and he thrust into her in a leisurely glide.

She moaned as her body stretched to accommodate him. It was too much. It wasn't enough. And then she was completely filled.

"Yes," she said hoarsely. "Just like that."

He buried his face in her neck. "You're so tight," he gritted against her skin. "So fucking hot."

He pulled out and thrust in again. Every nerve ending in her body shuddered with wonder. She dug her heels into his ass. "More."

He lifted his head and gazed down at her, his eyes a gorgeous swirl of green and gold and brown. His canines looked sharper, as if he were truly half cat at this moment.

Her jaguar man.

"More of this?" he asked in guttural tones, and thrust back in —hard.

"Yes." Her breath sawed in. "Please, yes."

She gripped his head and kissed him. He kissed her back, and then took her hands and, threading his fingers through hers, pinned them on either side of her head, holding her in place while he continued moving in and out of her. Slow, deep strokes that she felt clear to the base of her spine.

It was erotic, sensual. Perfect.

And then slow wasn't enough, and she canted her hips toward him, tightening delicate inner muscles around his thrusting cock.

"Holy fuck," he muttered, and they moved together, fast and hard. "That's it. Take it, Evie."

He released her hands. "With me," he said. "I want you with me." One arm wrapped around her shoulders while the other cupped her hip so he could thrust into her at a new angle.

Oh. My. God.

Pleasure and pain fused into one glorious burst of sensation. She heard herself cry out, and then she shot over the edge. He pumped into her a few more times, and then groaned out her name and followed her.

JACE RESTED his face in the turn of Evie's neck, lungs heaving. He felt as if he'd been run over by a steamroller like a cartoon coyote —but what a way to die.

He inhaled deeply, steeping himself in her summery scent— fresh, sexy, and all Evie.

Her breath huffed out, a warm puff against his temple, and he gave her a last kiss on the lips before rolling onto his back. He curved an arm around her, tucking her close to his side. She murmured something and set a hand on his waist. A minute later, she went lax with sleep.

Poor baby was exhausted. A wave of protectiveness washed over him.

It's just sex, he told himself. *She doesn't want more, and neither do you if you're smart.*

Then he dragged in a breath. Because who the hell was he kidding? His cat was already acting possessive and the man was halfway in love with her.

Still, Evie wasn't his mate. He didn't feel the mate bond—not even a hint. Not that he was sure what it felt like, but everyone said you just *knew*. And yet...the cat was so content in her presence. He'd never felt that around any woman—fada, human, or fae.

The fae lights had drifted closer to Evie. There were six of them in the bedroom now. The woman was a fucking light magnet. They hovered near, tinting her face with a warm glow. Her dimple flashed in her sleep.

He recalled how she'd looked when he'd come into the room —impossibly beautiful, her hair the color of sunlight, her eyes a deep topaz beneath her dark brows.

He smoothed a thumb down her cheek. How had he fooled himself into believing she had only a few drops of fae? The woman practically glowed, just like the rest of her kin.

But she wasn't just fae, she was human, too. A mixed-blood, just like Silver.

"Fada don't mix with other humans or fae." Leron had pounded that into all of them, until Jace had believed it. "Humans are weak, easy to break, and the fae would sell out their own mothers for a handful of jewels. And you'll have cubs who can't take an animal form."

Jace had shuddered. The cat was part of him, clear to his soul. Being without it would be like cutting out a vital, irreplaceable piece.

That had clinched it for him. He was pretty sure he'd muttered that to Adric, when he'd given his friend the news about Takira's mating. "Her cub probably won't even be able to shift."

Gods, he'd been so fucking self-righteous.

And Leron had been wrong because Merry *could* shift. She was a beautiful black jaguar, just like him.

He tucked Evie closer and stared at the ceiling as one by one, the fae lights winked out until the room went dark.

20

———————

*E*vie came awake in slow increments. She was curled on her side, a big arm draped over her waist.

Jace. Her lips curved.

No covers except a sheet tangled around her legs, but he was spooned around her, and his body generated plenty of heat.

She was pleasantly sore in places that hadn't seen any action in way too long. She might even have a couple of slight bruises where he'd gripped her hip at the end, but who cared when she felt so good? She curled her fingers around his hand where it rested on her stomach and opened her eyes.

Without windows, there was no way to tell the time, but she guessed it was close to morning. Above her, the fae lights glowed on, painting the room with the muted colors of dawn—rose, a soft yellow, a pale sky-blue.

"Nice trick," she murmured.

Lips tickled her nape. "Who're you talking to?"

Her cheeks heated. "No one."

The arm on her waist tightened. "The fae lights?"

"Yeah," she admitted. "They seem almost alive. I thought about morning and they came on."

"It's you. They're somewhat self-directed, but I've never seen them as responsive as they are to you."

"Really? Huh." She stretched out a hand on the mattress. A shining ball the color of sunlight slid over her palm, sending a tingle up her arm. "So why does that bother you?"

He released her waist and rolled onto his back. "It doesn't."

"No? It sure seemed like it did last night."

"It's like we said in your kitchen—we don't mix. Fada, humans, fae—" He moved a hand.

"Wow." She sat up and swung her legs off the bed. "So I have two strikes against me. Maybe I'd better just leave."

"No—wait." He grabbed her wrist. "Don't be mad."

She pinned him with a look. "Let. Me. Go."

He released her and sat up. "Just listen—please? I'm sorry. But you said yourself that we don't mix."

She had. And she'd be wise to remember it.

She sank down on the edge of the mattress. "What?"

"I told you about my niece Merry. Her mom—my sister—was killed by some of our own people. But the night fae helped." He blew out a breath. "Because she had a baby girl who was a quarter fae. I know you're not a night fae, but the baby was part human, too, and it caused problems for Takira in the clan. Things were so bad then, anyway—people went a little crazy. After Takira died, a night fae went after her mate and the cub. Merry was the only one who survived."

"Oh, Jace." She closed her eyes. "I'm so sorry."

He jerked his head in acknowledgment. "Merry has to hide from the night fae. They have a thing about keeping their blood-lines pure. She'd be dead now if not for the Rock Run fada."

"Oh, God." Evie's heart squeezed. She could only imagine how she'd feel if it were Kyler.

"It was almost nine years ago, but—" He looked away.

She touched his thigh. "You still miss her. Your sister."

"Every fucking day. You asked about the tat." He indicated the cat's paw on his shoulder. "It's in honor of Takira. Her jaguar was gold and black."

She swallowed, and then scooted closer. Just touching him—thigh to thigh with her shoulder against his.

He slanted her a look. She'd thought he had a hard face, but now she knew him better, she saw there was something soulful about it, too—as if the hardness were a mask he wore to hide whatever was beneath.

He's sad. Underneath, he's sad and lonely. Evie didn't know how she knew. She just did. He was still grieving—for his sister, his parents.

"If both her parents are dead, why doesn't your niece live here?"

"When things went south, Takira took her family and disappeared. Merry was just four years old and she had to go into fucking hiding. And Takira"—his breath rasped in—"I never saw her again."

"I'm so sorry." She threaded her fingers through his.

"Anyway, after Takira was killed, Merry's dad took her and ran, but the assassins found him, too. Merry was about five by then. Somehow she ended up in Grace Harbor with the Rock Run fada." He shook his head. "I thought she died with her father. By the time we found her again, two years had passed and she thought of the woman who'd adopted her as her mom. I..." His throat worked. "I couldn't take her away."

Evie nodded. She understood, even agreed—but her heart hurt for him. To be forced to make such a choice...

"It's for the best," he said. "She's got a family—a mom and a dad and a little sister and brother. And I get to see her every week or so. At least I know she's alive, and happy."

His hand clenched around hers. She brought it to her mouth and kissed it, heart hurting for him. "How old is she?"

"Thirteen. She's frickin' smart, too—and even prettier than her mom." His voice rang with pride. "Her animal is a jaguar, like all the Joneses. And she's all black like me—another black panther."

"She sounds awesome."

"She is." He didn't speak for a while, and she was about to say something when he grated, "For two years, I thought she was dead. *Two fucking years.*"

"Oh, Jace." She hesitated, and then did what came instinctively—took him into her arms.

"Takira should've come to me, damn it. Why didn't she come to me?" His voice was a harsh whisper against her neck. "Why did she run like that? She had to know I'd help her, no questions asked."

"I don't know." She stroked his nape, heart breaking for him. "But if things were as bad as you say, maybe she thought it was better you didn't know."

He pulled away and stared down at his hands. "Or she just didn't trust me."

"Oh, Jace. Why would you say that?"

He lifted his head, his expression bleak. "Because I told her straight out not to mate with Silver."

"Oh." She swallowed hard. "I see."

"I was a fucking ass. But I came around. I could see how much she loved Silver, and he would've done anything for her. And when I found out she was having Merry, I was so happy for her. She was such a cute cub—still is. So when Takira disappeared like that with no warning, what was I supposed to think?"

"Maybe she was protecting you. If you didn't know where she was, you couldn't be forced to tell anyone."

His eyes flashed cat-green. "I wouldn't have given her up to anyone."

"Not even your alpha?"

"No." His fingers curled on his thighs. "Fuck. Maybe. It's hard for a fada to say no to his alpha. And our alpha then was the mother of all bastards. He might've dragged it out of me—I was younger then, not much older than Kyler."

"That has to be it. It's the only reason that makes sense. She didn't hide Merry from you—you knew her up until she was four. If your sister ran without telling you, it was to protect all of you, not because she didn't trust you."

He scrubbed a hand over his face. "Maybe you're right. I guess I'll never know." He pulled her toward him. "I want you, Evie. Come back to bed—please?"

That please arrowed straight to her heart. She cupped his face. The kiss they shared was soft, special. She knew he wouldn't want pity, but she ached for him. "All right. Just give me a minute." She pulled on her sleepshirt and headed to the bathroom.

When she returned, the room was awash with early morning light. Looking up, she realized that the ceiling had slits reaching all the way to the surface. An air circulation system was running as well, but the slits let in sunlight and additional fresh air.

Jace had used the other bathroom, but he'd beat her back to the room and was reclined against the headboard, an arm behind his head. Even at rest, his biceps bulged. His stomach was ridged, the scars thin pink lines that somehow made him even sexier. Nearly hidden beneath black chest hair were flat brown nipples, and lower down, his cock nestled in another patch of dark hair. It was already at half-mast, but as she watched, it lengthened into a full erection.

She swallowed, her mouth literally watering.

His hazel eyes gleamed in the dawn light. "Come here." He beckoned with one hand.

She pulled off the sleepshirt and climbed on top of him. His thighs were large and hairy between hers, his penis a hard stalk between their bellies. She set her hands on his shoulders and gave him a long kiss. Pouring all the understanding in her heart into him.

Because sometimes sex was just sex, and sometimes it was more—a way to share your deepest self with someone. To say, *You're not alone.*

The kiss transformed, went from compassionate to heated.

She raised her head and looked down at him through lowered lids.

Jace's mouth quirked. The sadness in his eyes had retreated, replaced by something hot and a little wicked. He rocked his hips, his meaning clear.

She began to move, sliding up and down on his erection, not taking him inside, just teasing them both as the underside rubbed against her pussy.

Jace's fingers tightened on her hips but he allowed her to take the lead. When she stopped, he cupped her breasts, pinching the nipples into sensitized points before reaching between their bodies to swirl his thumb over her swollen little nub. Unhurried, tantalizing strokes.

She closed her eyes and let him tease her. Tiny shocks reverberated up and down her spine, and her inner thighs tightened as she began the slow spiral to climax.

But she didn't want to hurry things, so she moved his hand away and leaned forward to rub her lips over his. He tasted of mint and morning. She gave him a leisurely kiss and then started to move down his body.

He went to roll her onto her back but she stopped him with a hand on his chest. "Stay there. I want to taste you."

His indrawn breath was all the answer she needed. She moved down his hard, flat stomach and circled his erection with her fingers. He was long and thick and a little sticky from her juices.

She lapped at him. Delicate licks that made his thighs go rock-hard.

"Fuck, you look hot," he said, and slipped a hand around her nape. "Take me, Evie," he said in a stern voice that made her insides melt. "Now."

She tightened her grip on him and obeyed. He tasted dark, salty.

She glanced up to see him watching her with smoky eyes. She smiled and sucked him deep into the pocket of her cheek.

"Yes," he said between gritted teeth. He tightened his grip on her nape, guiding her to please him. She continued working her mouth up and down him, loving that she could excite him like this. When she got tired, she scraped her teeth lightly over the cap, and his groan told her how much he liked it.

She palmed his balls. They were cool and tight. She rolled the sacs between her fingers.

He let her suck him a few more times, and then stopped her, saying, "I want to be inside you."

"Mm." She licked him one more time—a leisurely slide of her tongue up and down his heavily veined erection that had him muttering a curse.

When she lifted her head, he reached for her. "Give me a kiss."

She straddled him again and fitted her mouth to his. He framed her face with his hands and stroked his tongue over hers, firm and self-assured. A man preparing to take his woman.

He kissed her until she was panting for breath and squirming against him, and then he lifted her away from him. She gave a groan of protest and his mouth quirked.

"Easy, angel. You'll get what you want." He flipped her onto her stomach and smacked her bottom. "Raise your hips."

JACE WATCHED as Evie obediently propped herself on her forearms, her pretty round ass lifted to him. She was all smooth pale curves. Her scent filled his head, tart with arousal.

He'd never told anyone the whole story about him and Takira, and it had left him churned up inside. Scraped raw—but with the promise of peace. Maybe not today, but someday soon.

Now he just wanted to forget. Seeing Evie in such a graceful, submissive posture triggered the dominant male animal in him.

Lust punched through him. He wanted to fuck her long and hard, hear her make those sexy little moans that went straight to his dick.

He wanted to fuck her soft and slow, until she was begging to come—and then he wanted to make her scream.

He covered her body with his and speared his fingers in her short platinum locks. His cock was hard enough to drive spikes. It nudged against her ass, but he ignored it to nibble at her nape.

She made a sound of pleasure and arched her back, pushing that heart-shape bottom up against his erection.

His heart smacked against his ribcage. Every muscle in his body strained to take her.

He grabbed a condom and rolled it on, even while his animal grumbled at putting anything between him and that lush pink perfection. He probably didn't have to. Fada didn't spread diseases to humans and vice versa, and it was rare that a fada impregnated a female who wasn't his mate. But it could happen, and he didn't want to take the choice from her.

Evie's breath shuddered in. She glanced over her shoulder at him, her pupils so dilated her eyes appeared almost black.

He placed himself at her center and thrust home. Her body clenched around his, tight and hot.

Yes. Fuck, yes.

He withdrew almost to the tip and thrust in again. Taking her slow and hard and perfect.

She made a high, needy sound and he curved his body over hers, scraping his teeth over her nape, tonguing the turn of her shoulder.

She gasped his name. "Please. I need..."

He took one of her hands and brought it to her clit. It was slippery and swollen with arousal. "Touch yourself."

She rubbed herself, shuddered.

He cupped her chin, drawing her head back so her spine arched.

"Harder," he told her. "Make yourself wet for me."

She shook her head, and he knew it was more that she was dazed than that she was saying no, but he nipped her shoulder anyway. "Evie." He put all the force of his dominance in his tone. Fada males liked to master their women in bed, and his animal craved this. But he would've backed off if he couldn't tell it was exciting her as much as him.

At his tone, she squeezed around him like a hot fist, and he nearly came out of his skin. *Holy Mother Goddess.*

He felt her fingers move beneath his as she began playing with herself in earnest.

He dragged in a breath, his muscles shaking with the need to drive into her harder. "That's it." He set both hands on her hips as he rocked slowly out of her and then back in. "Touch yourself. Just like that. Make yourself come."

He couldn't see her touching herself, but he could picture it. The visual filled his head with a dark heat.

Lost in pleasure, he didn't even question why it was so important that she submit to him. He just pumped in and out, teeth gritted at how good it felt.

His quartz brushed over her back, and that felt good, too. Somewhere in the back of his mind he thought, *That's fucking odd.* Because even a casual touch of his quartz by the wrong person could send a shock of pain through him. But as he'd told Evie, magic had its own logic.

Just before he came, his quartz heated against his chest. He glanced down to see that the smoky gray and purple was shot through with emerald.

And suddenly, he just *knew*. She was his mate.

Damn, he was an idiot.

He growled in helpless surrender—and then thrust into her, hard and deep until he touched her womb.

She moaned and twisted under him, saying his name over and over, and then changing to *please please please*.

And in the end, she screamed.

21

———

Jace tucked Evie close to his side and stared at the ceiling. What the hell was he going to do?

He could deal with her being a mixed-blood. He felt a stab of shame that he'd taken Leron's twisted prejudices as his own. If nothing else, he'd seen with Merry that a fada who was one-quarter fae and one-quarter human could still shift—and be the best niece a man could possibly ask for. If Takira were here, she would've slapped him upside the head.

Leron was dead, and it was time to bury his prejudices along with him.

Not that this was a done deal—the female always had the right to refuse a mating. But Evie wanted him, was maybe even a little in love with him. Hell, just the fact that she'd had sex with him was proof. He'd known she wasn't the type to sleep around even before her confession that it had been a while.

But would she want a fada for a mate? Because the prejudice wasn't all on his side. It was a huge step from taking a fada as a lover to joining his clan, and as his mate, she wouldn't have a choice. He was too important to the Baltimore fada, and besides, he didn't want to live as a solitary.

And yet how could he walk away now? Might as well ask him to rip out his heart.

Court her, said the cat and conjured up a hazy scene with candlelight and wine and Evie in a skimpy red nightgown.

His lips quirked. But hell, yes—wine, flowers, chocolate... whatever it took. And a job for that brother of hers, because the two of them were a package deal. Jace wanted to ease her burdens, let her focus on what she really wanted to do, which was become a healer. His mate was strong in a way both man and cat approved, but that didn't mean she couldn't use a helping hand.

He pressed a kiss to her mussed blond head, and with a fatalistic shrug, accepted that this was his new life: Evie at the center. And he guessed he'd gained a teenage brother, too. His existence had just gotten a hell of a lot more complicated.

A family, the gods help him. With a mate that was part human, part fae—just like Silver. Somewhere in paradise, his sister was laughing her ass off. He let out a breath—and grinned.

Evie nuzzled his jaw. "You're thinking too loud."

"Sorry." But there was more proof; she was picking up his emotions.

She wriggled closer so that she was plastered against his front. He smoothed a hand down her back, heart full.

She smothered a yawn. "Damn, you tired me out."

"Sleep, then." He patted her bottom.

"Mm," she said.

He listened as her breath slowed, deepened. A few minutes later she was asleep.

He could've lain there all day holding her. Maybe even gone back to sleep himself—and there was almost nobody he trusted enough to fall asleep around. And yet last night he'd curled himself around Evie and slept deeply, untroubled by nightmares and more relaxed than he'd been for years.

Wonder filled him. This was what being happy was—this warm, contented feeling.

His cat settled its head on its paws and purred...and Jace dozed.

He was awakened by the buzz of his quartz. He silenced it and, easing out from under Evie, slipped into the hall, closing the door behind him.

It was Adric. "Just wanted to check in. How are things?"

"Okay on this end." He wasn't ready yet to talk about this thing with Evie, even with Adric. "Corban?"

"At least someone had a good night." Adric's tone was amused. Not much got past the alpha—he might not know that Jace planned to mate-claim Evie, but it was clear he'd guessed Jace hadn't slept alone. "Me, I'm on my way back to my den to catch some sleep. I'm sorry, bro—we didn't find Corban. The prick's disappeared into thin air."

Jace's contentment fled. "Fuck."

"He's here in Baltimore—I'm sure of it. But I can't narrow down his location. He's got a new quartz that I can't track him through, and he's smart enough to hide his scent." His friend expelled a breath. "Anyway, I called Beau, and he's on his way back with Suha. She wants to talk to your Evie anyway. Seems she might be a healer."

"Yeah." Jace didn't even argue that Evie wasn't "his." Because she was.

"Beau's under orders to stick with you for the next few days. I don't want you going anywhere alone until we find the bastard —got it?"

"Damn it, Ric, I don't need a fucking babysitter. I took on Corban *and* his little friend, remember?"

"Humor me," his friend drawled. "If nothing else, it's safer for Evie and Kyler."

"Fine." Jace dropped his head back against the wall. "Get some sleep. I'll report in later." He ended the call.

Fear crawled up his spine. Because now that he was wide awake and not stupid from sex, he realized that mating with Evie increased the chance that Corban would go after her. Tyrus, too. Jace's stomach bottomed out at how difficult it would be to keep her safe. That brother of hers as well.

Claws pricked his fingertips. Inside, his animal gave a jaguar-roar, ready to take on the world for its mate.

Evie appeared in the hall, dressed in the striped sleepshirt. It was so old it was practically see-through in places.

The roar faded. A word came through loud and clear. *Mine.*

And he would die to protect her.

"Morning." She gave a stretch that had the shirt riding up until he could see the notch at the top of her thighs. "Is it okay if I take a shower?"

He swallowed hard and for a few seconds, forgot all about Corban and Tyrus.

"Sure," he managed to say. "Towels are on the shelf." He ran a proprietary hand down her hip and tried not to stare at where the threadbare material clung to the hard points of her nipples. "I'll get breakfast started."

"Thanks." She came onto her toes and kissed him.

He watched as she slipped past him. That shirt barely covered her ass. Damn, he wanted to follow her into the bathroom, bend her over the jacuzzi, and—

He heard Kyler moving in his bedroom and pulled himself up short.

Shower. And breakfast.

And that shower was going to have to be alone. He muttered a curse and headed down the hall to the other bathroom.

22

———————

When Evie emerged from the bathroom, the den smelled of breakfast.

A couple of fae lights trailed her to the kitchen. Jace was at the stove, barefoot and shirtless, a pair of shorts hanging low on his hips and a shaft of sunlight illuminating gleaming brown shoulders. Fried ham sizzled in a skillet while he cracked eggs into a bowl. As he beat the eggs into a yellow froth, the muscles under his jaguar tattoo flexed so the cat appeared almost alive.

Heat curled through her. It was insane. She'd just had sex with the man, and already she wanted him again.

Kyler had his back to her, taking plates from the cupboard, and Tigger was supervising from a perch on a kitchen stool. On the counter, an old-fashioned French press was slowly filling with coffee.

Jace poured the eggs into a second skillet. He and Kyler were talking something over in a serious tone. Evie paused, not wanting to interrupt. Jace was good with her brother, treating him like he was an adult, and Kyler was eating it up. She felt a pang of guilt—Kyler needed an adult male in his life.

Not your fault, she told herself. But she ached for her brother.

"You have to step up," Jace said as he added red bell peppers, cheese, and chunks of ham to the skillet. "Your sister needs you. You're not a kid anymore."

Whoa. They were talking about her? She frowned, not sure how she felt about that.

"You think I don't know that?" Kyler set three plates on the sturdy plank table. "I've been working my ass off to get a job, but no one wants to hire a sixteen-year-old."

"Maybe the clan can find you some work."

Kyler's face lit up. "Seriously?"

Jace nodded. "I'll talk to the alpha."

Evie frowned and moved forward. "That's nice of you, Jace, but we're not going to be here that long."

Jace twisted to smile at her. She had a feeling he'd known she was there all along. Guess you couldn't sneak up on a shifter.

"Morning, babe." His gaze moved appreciatively down her body, lingering on the band of skin left exposed by her green cropped tee. "I'm making Western omelets. Sound good?"

"Sounds wonderful. But about finding work for Kyler—"

"Why not?" Her brother rounded on her. "You know I need a job."

"No way you're going to drive to Baltimore every day." *And work for the Baltimore fada.*

Kyler started slamming forks onto the table beside the plates. "Damn it, Evie, when are you going to stop treating me like a five-year-old? People have been working for the Rock Run fada for years and nothing's ever happened to them."

She set her jaw. "We'll talk about it later."

"It's not up to you, Evie. This is my life, my decisions."

Jace laid a hand on Kyler's shoulder. "Apologize to your sister," he said sternly.

Her brother went stiff. "What?"

"You don't swear at your sister and you don't raise your voice to her. She's doing the best she can. She deserves your respect."

Kyler flushed. "Sorry," he mumbled. "I didn't mean anything."

"It's okay," she said.

"No, it's not," Jace replied. To Kyler he said, "I know you didn't. But if you want to be treated like an adult, you need to act like one."

His shoulders slumped. "But I've applied for every frickin' job in Grace Harbor, and no one's hiring. I'm either too young or they already have someone."

Jace squeezed his shoulder and released him. "That's a bitch, and I'm happy to help—but only if it's okay with your sister."

They both turned to her, Jace so clearly deferring to her that she couldn't get mad at him for interfering, Kyler with his jaw set but his eyes pleading.

"Please, Evie? I don't have to take it. Maybe they'll have something I can do in the morning when you don't need the car."

She sighed. She hated being the bad guy all the time. But she wasn't sure they should get in any deeper with the Baltimore fada. Yeah, she was trusting Jace to protect the two of them, but they wouldn't need protecting in the first place if someone wasn't trying to kill him.

Her gaze flicked to the still-healing claw marks on Jace's face. "We'll see," she told her brother.

His face fell. "Which means no."

"It means we'll see," she returned.

But it was Jace's expression that made her flinch. His eyes shuttered and she felt his withdrawal like a physical thing. "Give your sister some time to think it over," he told Kyler. "Pushing her is just going to get you a no for sure."

Evie shoved her hands in her pockets. She'd hurt Jace, and that was the last thing she wanted to do after he'd trusted her enough to share his sister's story. But her brother came first.

"Need any help?" she asked.

"You could make toast." He handed her a loaf of bread and a

knife. "Butter's in the cooling unit." He indicated a steel door set into the stone.

She nodded and set to work.

An awkward silence fell, each of them focused on their task until Jace set a platter of omelets on the table. "Breakfast is served."

"Thank you," Evie and Kyler said at the same time, but before they could take their seats, footsteps pounded down the stairs. The front door banged open and suddenly the kitchen was filled with lean, heavily muscled males.

The newcomers sorted themselves into Sam plus two other men, their faces grim with tiredness. They revived at seeing Jace, though, unashamedly hugging him and asking how he was doing.

When he turned to Evie and Kyler, the shuttered look was gone. "Meet the rest of my den. You already know Sam, and these other two are Horace and Zuri." To his den mates, he said, "This is Evie and her brother Kyler."

"Morning." Sam was already pulling Evie into a hug. "You slept good?"

"Yeah." She couldn't help glancing at Jace. Sam's brow shot up, but he didn't say anything. Instead, he cast a hungry eye at the omelets and all but licked his lips.

Jace waved a hand at the table. "Help yourself. I'll make some more."

"Thanks, man." Sam bumped fists with Kyler and took a seat. A moment later he was tucking into his breakfast.

Next was Horace. He had dreadlocks, deep brown skin and an easy smile, and Evie liked him immediately. "Welcome to the den," he said and gave her a kiss on the lips that had Jace growling.

"Enough already. Give the woman some space."

Horace winked at her, and then shook Kyler's hand. "Hey, bro, wassup?"

"Not much," he replied, and the two of them fell into a conversation while Horace set to work making another pot of coffee.

That left Zuri. As he stuck out his hand, Evie couldn't help widening her eyes. He was gorgeous, the kind of man women went stupid over—tall and broad shouldered with a shaved head, a narrow black mustache and a soul patch beneath his full lower lip.

"So you're Evie."

She gave him her hand. "That's me." Instead of shaking it, he brought it to his lips for a kiss—but the whole time his dark eyes scrutinized her coolly.

"Zuri's one of Adric's lieutenants," Jace said from the stove where he was frying some more ham.

That figured. The man had an edge to him. She gave him a polite smile and resolved to stay out of his way.

"Ric said you couldn't track down Corban," Jace said.

The other lieutenant scowled. "Bastard's gone to ground. We're not even sure he's still in Baltimore."

"Ric thinks he is. Sit down and eat. You need fuel."

Zuri squeezed his nape. "Might as well—the trail's cold for now."

The men helped themselves to the omelets on the table while Evie handed around steaming cups of coffee and Kyler manned the toaster. It was obvious Jace's den mates were tired and upset that they hadn't been able to find Corban. But except for Zuri, they went out of their way to be nice to her and Kyler, acting as if nothing would make them happier than having the two of them as guests for the next month. And even Zuri wasn't rude, just quiet.

Jace took a seat at the head of table with Evie and Kyler on either side and passed her the platter with fresh omelets. Evie took a bite—and closed her eyes in bliss. The man could cook. The omelet was amazing, a perfect blend of flavors.

She opened her eyes to find Jace's gaze on her mouth, his irises a smoldering jade.

She gave a tentative smile. "It's really good."

He leaned closer to murmur, "It's a pleasure to feed you."

Her heart leapt. She'd been afraid she'd ruined things between them, but it seemed he was ready to play again. A glance at the men told her they were focused on their own food, so she slid the fork between her lips—very slowly. When she was done chewing, she licked her tongue up the tines.

Jace's eyes narrowed on her lips. "When I get you back to bed...," he muttered in a voice for her ears only.

Her stomach flexed in anticipation. Their gazes locked, and sound receded as they stared at each other.

Kyler made a gagging sound. "Right here. Trying to eat."

"Shut up, squirt." Evie batted a fae light at him. He slapped it away and there was a blue flash.

"Jesus, Evie." Kyler shook his hand. "That smarts."

Evie gulped. "Sorry—I didn't think it would...what happened, anyway?"

"It felt like I touched a live wire."

All four men were staring at her like she'd grown an extra head. She set down her fork. "What?"

Jace shook his head. "It's just that fae warriors use fae balls as weapons. A light shouldn't flash like that."

Kyler chortled. "Evie Morningstar, fae warrior. I *knew* you were going to try to incinerate me with a fae ball."

She pointed her fork at him, narrow-eyed. "One more word out of you and I will." But she frowned at the fae light, shaken. She could've *hurt* Kyler.

"A fae warrior can conjure his or her own fae balls." Jace squeezed her knee, seemingly reading her mind. "Your Gift seems related to the lights, but unless you can form your own, Kyler's safe."

"We'll just be sure not to make you mad," Horace said straight-faced.

She rolled her eyes, and he winked at her. Evie grinned back. Sam and Horace, at least, had accepted her into their circle. She wasn't sure why she cared since she wasn't going to be here that long—but she did.

Breakfast over, Horace got to his feet and gave a long, bone-cracking stretch. "God's balls, I need a shower. And then I'm going to sleep until afternoon."

"Me too." Sam and Zuri followed him while Evie got up and started to clear the table.

"I'll wash if you dry," she told Jace.

Kyler helped carry the dishes over to the sink, and then tried his phone again. It still didn't work, but he went into the living room to play a game, leaving her alone with Jace.

"Thanks," she said. "For offering to help out Kyler. I'm just not sure..."

"It's okay. I understand. You could always take money from me, you know. As a loan," he added when her spine went rigid. "We don't know how long this is going to go on. I feel responsible for the fact that you can't work."

She unclenched her muscles. Maybe she *was* being too stubborn. If the shoe were on the other foot, she'd want to help him. "All right. But only if it's a loan."

"It's a deal. Of course, you could always pay me back another way." He set down his dish towel and wrapped his arms around her where she stood at the sink, elbow deep in soapy water.

Her heart kicked up. "What do you mean?"

"I think you know." His lips brushed over her neck.

She chuckled and then caught her breath as he nibbled his way to her earlobe. She rinsed the last plate and set in the dish drainer, and then clucked her tongue. "That's bad, paying a man in sex."

"Maybe I like bad girls." One hand squeezed her breast while the other wandered lower to her shorts.

Her nipples prickled. Heat slid over her, thick and sweet as molasses. "In that case, what are your terms?"

"What are you offering?" His cock nudged the small of her back.

"Depends." She twisted her head to kiss his throat and then started in on the silverware. "Pretty much anything is up for negotiation."

"Anything? Oh, angel, you don't know what you're saying."

"No?" Somehow her wet hands were around his neck and his fingers were working their way into her waistband.

"If your brother wasn't in the living room," he muttered against her ear, "you'd be bent over the table right now, taking me."

She gulped. She'd almost forgotten Kyler. She turned her head and gave him an open-mouthed kiss. "And I might even let you."

He slid a finger into her damp panties for a quick, teasing touch. They both heard the front door open. "Anybody home?" Suha called.

23

───────

*E*vie *didn't trust him with her brother*. Jace was still reeling from the blow even as he stepped back from her with a growled, "Later," and turned to smile at Suha.

It clawed at his soul. Didn't she know he'd protect Kyler with his life?

But how could Jace argue Evie was wrong? From what she'd seen of his clan so far, they were dog-eat-dog, like in the Darktime.

His first instinct had been to withdraw. The mate-bond was fragile—a gossamer-thin thread that either of them could still break. It would hurt like hell, at least for him, but it was still possible.

Then his stubborn side asserted itself. Evie was right—and she was wrong. Things had changed under Adric. The clan wasn't like that anymore. Maybe the world didn't know it, but that was because a bad reputation was the best protection as they worked to rebuild themselves.

Damn Tyrus and Corban anyway. A cold anger burned in his stomach. But he refused to let them ruin this for him. Evie was the best thing that had happened to him in a long time, and he wasn't going to give her up without a fight.

He'd just have to be crafty. He was a cat—cunning and patient. Changing Evie's mind would require both, and meanwhile, he had her in his den. What better place to show her the rock-solid bonds that were at the heart of a clan?

Suha took out her quartz to scan Jace. She nodded with satisfaction. "You look good, babe." She gave Evie a sidelong grin. "I'm not going to ask why."

Evie shot Jace a guilty look and then her dimple flashed. He just looked back, straight-faced.

"Nope," Suha said, "don't want to know."

Beau had stopped to say hi to Kyler, but now he shambled into the kitchen. "Hey, girl." He lifted Evie off her feet in a hug.

Suha smacked him on the shoulder. "Take it easy, you ass. She's not used to bears."

But Evie just grinned and hugged him back. "I don't mind."

Beau set her carefully back on her feet. She was flushed and a little mussed and Jace wanted to eat her up.

Suha shook her head and shooed Beau out of the kitchen. "Go do your man-stuff. Evie and I need to talk."

The bear wrapped a huge hand around her nape and nuzzled her ear. "Are you trying to get rid of me, woman?"

"Yeah," she said, but her eyes closed in pleasure.

"All right," he said, and grabbed a mug of coffee before heading back into the living room.

Jace glanced at Evie. "Want me to go too?"

But she shook her head and asked him to stay, so he got the three of them a fresh cup of coffee and pulled up a chair next to hers at the kitchen table.

Suha took the seat across from them. "So," she said, "have you had a chance to think of any questions?"

Evie took a sip of her coffee. "No offense, but I'm not even sure I'm a healer. Like I said last night, I wasn't even able to help my mom."

"Even if you had the Gift of healing, you'd need training. What do you know about the fada?"

"Well," Evie said, "everyone knows you're part animal—and that you're magical in some way. And you earth fada have the quartz"—she nodded at Suha's pendant—"which is important to you in some way."

Suha nodded. "Fada are a mix of animal and human genes, but every fada has at least a few drops of fae blood, too. We don't have the full range of fae Gifts—ours tend to be related to our animals. The most common fada Gifts are hunting and tracking, but we also have a few healers in every generation. Some of us are born protectors—they guard the most vulnerable, like nursing mothers and cubs. Jace is Gifted with crystals. He can do amazing things with quartz."

Jace nodded. "But I had to train under another crystal engineer to fully utilize my Gift. Just like Suha trained as a healer."

Evie blew out a breath. "I wish you were right, but I really don't think I'm a healer."

Suha held out her hand. She had a nasty black-and-blue mark on the back. "Why don't you see if you can make this bruise disappear?"

"Sure, but why didn't you just heal it?"

"Lesson One: Don't waste your Gift. Because every time you call on your Gift, you burn energy. The bruise will heal on its own in a few days. Not that healing it would be a big deal, but what if someone gets hurt bad, and I need every bit of energy? Like Jace when he was stabbed by the night fae—I almost didn't have enough juice to draw the poison from his body. The alpha had to step in and help me. And iron poisoning is a serious thing—he could've died."

Evie's fingers tightened on her mug. "You didn't tell me."

He shrugged. "Things worked out."

"He wouldn't. And not because he's a fada and you're a human." Suha rolled her eyes. "It's because he's a man."

"Guess that's the same with every race," Evie muttered, and the two women exchanged a very female grin.

Suha set her bruised hand on the table. "Give it a try. You can touch the bruise if you want. The key is to picture it healing."

"How do I draw on energy to heal you?"

"You just do. Picture the bruise healing, and the energy will come."

Evie nodded. She stared at the bruise, and Jace could sense her gathering her concentration into herself. Nothing happened that he could see, except a couple of fae lights drifted over to brush across her shoulders.

Evie tried again, this time touching the bruise. Jace felt her whole body go rigid, but still nothing happened.

"Try to picture it whole, unbruised," murmured Suha.

"Okay." Evie's dark brows furrowed.

"Breathe," said Suha. "Slow and easy."

She dragged in a breath and glared at the bruise as if it were an enemy and she an invading arm. When it remained unchanged, her shoulders slumped. "I'm sorry," she said, sitting back. "I can't."

Jace set a hand on her back. "Maybe she's an amplifier," he said to Suha as he massaged her in slow circles.

"A what?"

Suha lifted a brow. "You just might be right. An amplifier works with a healer," she told Evie, "adding their energy to the healer's—but they can't heal on their own."

"Last night," he said, "you were able to add your energy to Suha's."

"And the fae lights?" asked Evie.

"Who knows?" The healer shrugged. "There's something about your energy that draws them, and that enhances your own."

Evie's face fell. "So if this is true—that I'm a—whatever you call it—then I'm not going to be able to heal people on my own."

"Amplifiers are valuable, too," he said.

"Yeah?" She seemed unconvinced. But then, for someone like her it would be a dream come true to have the Gift of healing. Jace hated seeing her so disappointed. He wanted to pull her onto his lap and tell her it was all right, that she was perfect just as she was.

"I'm sorry." Suha squeezed Evie's hand. "To be a healer is an amazing Gift, one I thank the Goddess for every single day. But think about it—you can still help heal people. Any Gifted healer would pay to work with you. We get stretched to our limits, especially when sickness sweeps through the clan, or when we're under attack."

Evie's chin lifted. "I wouldn't charge. I might not have much money, but I'm not going to take payment for helping to heal someone. If you need me, just ask."

"That's good of you," Suha responded, "but it's only fair that you get paid. Look at me—anyone in the clan can come to me for healing, and I'm happy to help however I can. But in return, the alpha pays me a salary. How would I live otherwise? Healing is my calling—but it's my job, too, just like the doctors and nurses in your world. And sometimes, people give me something extra— food, a piece of pottery, a hand-knit sweater. It would be wrong to refuse, don't you think? When they're only trying to thank me."

Evie nodded slowly.

"So if I call on you to help me—and I will—you'll accept payment for it, or else I won't feel right asking. You'll need to be trained, of course. Energy work can burn you up if you don't know what you're doing."

"Leesa," said Jace. The woman was a deer like Suha, and one of the few elders to survive the Darktime. Leron Savonett had simply ignored her—to him, deer were the bottom of the barrel.

Suha nodded. "Leesa is our only amplifier. I'll call her later if you're up for it."

Evie wrapped a hand around her coffee cup. One thumb rubbed the surface. "Thank you," she said without looking at Jace, "but we're probably not going to be here that long."

Suha's brows shot up. "I see. Well, let me know if you change your mind."

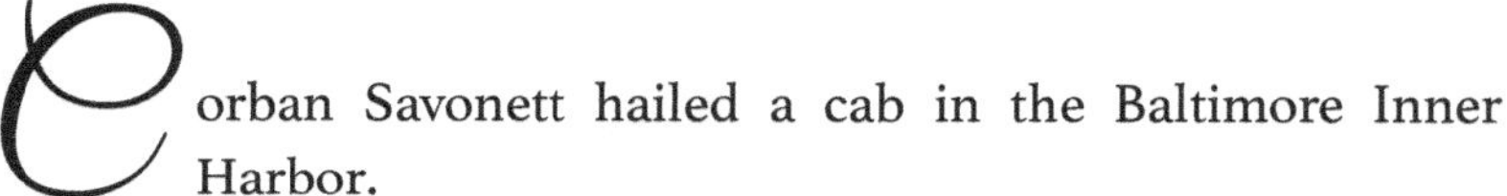

24

Corban Savonett hailed a cab in the Baltimore Inner Harbor.

"Druid Hill Park," he barked.

The cabby was a young male with the black hair and features of a south Asian—Pakistani, perhaps. His gaze went to the bloody gash on Corban's neck, and he opened his mouth to say no.

Corban was already inside. He gazed back steadily.

The cabby shut his mouth. "Yes, sir."

Corban dropped his backpack on the seat and tried not to look as weary as he felt. He'd taken a stolen motorboat to Baltimore and then abandoned it near the aquarium. He'd lost a lot of blood before he'd been able to seal the gash on his neck, and he hadn't had any energy left to deal with the chunk Jace Jones had taken out of his thigh. He was no healer, and his quartz was drained from the demands he'd put on it to track Jace Jones to his human girlfriend's house.

His lip curled. Figured Jones was chasing human tail. The man was weak, just like his sister. Takira could've been a high-ranking sentry, but she'd thrown it all away for her mate and that mixed-blood cub of hers.

The cab bounced over a pothole and pain jolted through Corban. A hiss escaped him and the cabby muttered an apology.

Corban ground his teeth. Damn Jace Jones anyway. The man should be dead by now. It had been two against one, and Corban had always been able to whip his ass.

But the scrawny kid had grown up. Corban should've realized that when the night fae assassin had failed to kill him, but he'd chalked it up to bad luck.

The ride to the park took fifteen minutes. The cabby let him out at an entrance near Jones Falls Expressway. "No charge," he said.

Corban jerked his chin in acknowledgment. He hadn't been planning to pay the guy anyway.

The street was dark and deserted, the nearest streetlight dangling brokenly from its pole. The only sound was the low-grade hum of traffic on the expressway.

The cabby eyed him in the rearview mirror, his scent an acrid mix of fear and perspiration.

Smart man.

Corban toed off his shoes and left them on the floor of the cab. His switchblade was already concealed in his hand. In one swift move, he hooked his left arm around the cabby's throat and at the same time, pressed the blade's catch. It sprang open and he touched the point to the cabby's cheekbone just beneath his eye.

"Don't move or I'll take your eye out."

"Easy, there." The cabby slowly raised his hands. "I don't want any trouble. I didn't even charge you for the ride."

"You're a fucking prince among men. Now give me your shoes."

The man's throat worked. "My shoes?"

Corban pressed the knife deeper. Just enough to nick his cheek. It was a bluff—the last thing he needed was the attention that cutting the cabby would bring—but the man said, "Sure, sure. But you have to let go first. I can't reach them."

"Open your door."

"Okay. Here I go." The man unlocked the door and pushed it open.

"Here's how it's going to go down. I'll let you go, and you toss your shoes out the door."

"That's all? You just want my shoes?"

"That's all."

"Okay, sure. No problem."

Corban released the cabby but stayed close, breathing down his neck.

The man took off his shoes and tossed them out the door as directed. His hands were trembling, and his breath was coming in fearful huffs.

Corban sneered. Humans were so easy to scare.

"There." The cabby met Corban's eyes in the rearview mirror. "My shoes, just like you asked."

Corban shoved open his door without answering. The moment his feet touched the sidewalk, the cabby pulled shut his door, hit the gas and sped off.

Corban swore and jumped back, barely avoiding being side-swiped. The cab kept going down the street, the back door still open.

Corban pushed his feet into the man's leather loafers. They were shiny brown and with that just-bought smell. He wiggled his toes. They fit good, too. He'd got the better of that bargain.

Adric was a legendary tracker. Corban didn't think Adric could follow Corban's scent through his shoes, but he wasn't a hundred percent sure. Better to be safe.

His destination was a quarter mile away near Jones Falls, the large creek that ran through Druid Hill Park. He hobbled toward it as fast as he could, careful not to brush against trees or bushes.

He reached the boulder that covered the entrance and sank down on it, heart pounding with the effort it had taken to get here. But every minute he spent above ground was dangerous. He shoved the boulder aside, uncovering the entrance to a small, hidden den, lowered himself partway down the rickety metal ladder and with his last ounce of energy, set the boulder back in place before descending the last few feet to the floor.

The den was basically a dirt cellar with a water supply and a toilet. Corban had dug it out in secret, so that not even his father had known about it. No lighting, which meant it was pitch black. Corban paused, waiting for his eyes to go night-glow. When he could see again, he limped his way to the two musty wool blankets stacked in a corner. Sinking onto the blankets, he eased off his pants and examined the back of his thigh. The wound had scabbed up, but it needed to be cleaned. With grim determination, he rose back to his feet and went to the sink.

It had been a couple of years since he'd been here. The spigot gave a groan and a pop, and then rusty water gushed out. He let it run until it was clear, and then found a clean T-shirt from his backpack and used it to rinse the dried blood from his neck and thigh.

He was too drained to change to his wolf. He rolled himself up in a blanket and allowed himself a smile. Adric would never find him here.

Then he passed out on the dirt floor.

25

—————

After Suha left, Evie and Jace took a walk to Druid Hill Park along with Kyler and Beau.

"Should be safe enough," Jace said. "The night fae won't be out on a sunny summer day—their skin's too sensitive to light. And Corban's gone to ground."

"And the day Savonett gets past the two of us," growled Beau, "is the day I slit my own throat."

So the four of them headed up to the surface. The way out led through the big shed. Evie had only caught a glimpse of it last night, but now she could see it was filled with motorcycles and a car with most of its insides removed. There was a huge workbench at one end, and a mix of human tools and those which looked like they were quartz-powered.

Kyler's eyes bulged. "Wow," he breathed with a reverence usually reserved only for his favorite games.

"Sam's the mechanic," said Jace, "but we all like to mess with engines."

"Sick." Kyler ran a hand over a cobalt-blue fuel tank. "If you need any help, just yell."

"I will." Jace opened the outside door and inhaled, testing the air. "Seems clear, but wait here a minute." He moved forward. Evie was reminded again that he was part cat. There was something very feline in his walk—loose and easy, each step precise, graceful.

Beau ambled out behind him. He tipped his head back and inhaled deeply. "No sign of Savonett or a night fae," he agreed.

Jace nodded and motioned to Evie and Kyler to join him. Kyler and Beau walked on ahead, leaving her and Jace to follow.

Evie couldn't get it out of her head—she was part fae and she apparently had some kind of Gift. An amplifier, whatever that was supposed to be. But it felt right—she'd felt the heat in her hands and had somehow *known* she was helping to heal Jace.

When Suha had offered to get her training, she'd lit up inside —until she'd realized she couldn't accept. Jace hadn't said anything, but when she'd refused, he'd removed his hand from her back.

But he must know this was only temporary. He'd said himself they didn't mix.

She sighed. What she really wanted was to talk this over with Fane, because if it was true that she was part fae, why hadn't anyone told her?

Jace had said that speaking a fae's name attracted their attention, but it hadn't worked to call Fane in the past, except maybe that time right before her mom died. Still, as they walked down the driveway, she turned to Jace and deliberately said her dad's name aloud.

"Do you think Fane could help me?"

He raised a brow. "Your dad?"

"Yeah. Fane." She repeated it a little louder. "I have some questions—like what kind of fae am I? And why the hell didn't I know?"

Jace slipped an arm around her shoulders. "Maybe he's trying to protect you. If you're mostly human, you don't want to be in the fae world. You'd be at the bottom of the food chain, powerless against the stronger fae. And those pricks eat their young."

Her mouth twisted. "Or maybe he doesn't want to admit he has a mixed-blood daughter."

He tightened his grip but didn't say anything. She winced inwardly, recalling his niece Merry was in a similar situation.

She blew out a breath and set Fane from her mind, because when had he ever come when she needed him? Meanwhile, it was a gorgeous day and a hot-as-hell guy had his arm around her. If she was only going to have these few days with him, then she was going to squeeze every last bit of enjoyment from it.

Jace's neighbors were seated on their marble stoops, chatting to friends and enjoying the morning sun. The houses were small, each on a tiny piece of land, but they were neat and well-kept. Everyone they passed called out a friendly hello to the two fada. Jace and his den mates were clearly well-liked.

A tiny girl in a pink dress with her hair in tight cornrows pelted down the sidewalk, her mother a few yards behind. "Up, Mister Jace." She raised her arms imperiously.

"Chantelle." He released Evie and swung her into his arms. "How's my girl?"

"I los a toof." She pointed to the space where one of her front teeth used to be. "Mama says the toof fairy is gonna bring me a dollar."

Jace smiled at her mother. "Morning, Kari."

"Morning," she returned and then shook her head at her daughter. "Chantelle, don't bother Mister Jace. He's got visitors today." She gave Evie an apologetic smile.

"Oh, I don't mind," Evie said.

"Good," said Jace, "because me and Miss Chantelle are old friends, aren't we?" He dropped a kiss on her small rosebud of a mouth.

Chantelle pursed her lips and kissed him back. "See, Mama. He likes it."

"Hmm," he said with a wink at Kari. "Which little girl I know likes to fly?"

"Me, Mister Jace!" shouted Chantelle. Jace chuckled and tossed her gently into the air. The child erupted in helpless giggles as he caught her with large, sure hands. "Again, Mister Jace! Please."

He tossed her up and down a few more times before shifting her to his hip with the ease of a man used to kids. And right then, a piece of Evie's heart broke off and landed at his feet. He was just so damn adorable, this tough, inked shifter with a tiny girl in a pink dress clinging to him.

Evie gulped and looked away. Jace pulled her close with his free arm and introduced Kyler and her to Kari, before handing Chantelle back to her mom so they could continue on their way.

Evie slid an arm around Jace's waist while the other two walked ahead. He slanted her a sheepish look. "Those are my tenants. Chantelle's dad isn't in the picture, so I help out where I can."

Evie pressed a kiss to his jaw. "You're my hero."

"It's nothing."

"No," she said. "It's something. Trust me, I know."

He squeezed her shoulders. "I'd like to pound some sense into your dad."

She shook her head. "It wouldn't do any good. Some men just aren't meant to be fathers."

"I can't understand it. Cubs are so fucking precious."

"That's what I think." Their eyes met and she looked away, afraid of what he would see in her face.

He's not for you.

Suha had warned Evie away from him in the nicest possible way, pulling her aside to murmur, "Promise me you won't hurt him."

Evie had drawn back, affronted. "I won't."

"Not intentionally, no." Suha's dark gaze was knowing and a

little sad. "But Jace—he's a dominant male, and so you might think he can't be hurt. But he can. You're special to him, Evie. The Darktime left him different. He was always a serious kid, but losing his sister—that ripped him to pieces. He was so dark for a while there that I thought we might lose him. An earth fada can will himself to death. The quartz—we use it to heal ourselves, but it can be used the opposite way. To turn on ourselves."

Evie had swallowed.

"But he came out of it. It helped when they found his niece."

"He told me about her."

"He did?" Suha's delicate black brows had winged upward. "That proves my point right there. He feels something for you. Just—don't hurt him."

Evie had glanced at where Jace was arguing basketball with Kyler and Beau. "I wouldn't," she'd said.

Suha had moved a shoulder. "If you don't want him, say so now. Don't let it go any further."

Now Evie pressed a hand to her breastbone. Because maybe she would hurt him. But if she did, it wasn't going to be one-sided.

Jace glanced at her. "Everything okay?"

She rose on her toes and kissed him. "Yeah."

The rest of the day passed in a happy blur. They walked with Jace and Beau to the park and around Druid Lake, and then headed back to the den, where they sprawled out on the grass drinking iced tea under a big maple. Beau remained standing, one arm propped on the wooden fence that circled the backyard, relaxed but alert, his deep brown eyes continually scanning the area. The men got into a conversation about motorcycles while Evie pillowed her head on her arms and gazed up at the rustling green leaves. It had been a long time since she'd just laid on the grass without anything to do.

Jace traced a finger down her jaw to the hollow of her throat. "Sleepy?"

"Mm."

He nuzzled her ear. "Take a nap if you want. I'll be keeping you up tonight."

Her lips curved. "Is that a promise?"

The answer was a sexy growl that made her abdomen tug.

Sam woke up and wandered outside, yawning. Jace sat up and murmured something to him, and he nodded. Before she knew it, the tiger had his head deep in her car's engine, and when she objected that she couldn't pay, he'd shrugged a big shoulder.

"I'm not asking for money. I need something to do, and I'm sure we have some spare parts in the shed."

"But—"

"Let him," Jace said. "The man's a genius with engines, and he really does like to play with them."

"All right," she said, "but I'm making dinner tonight."

"Works for me," was Sam's reply. "I'll trade a few spark plugs for food anytime."

Kyler joined him, and the two of them spent the rest of the afternoon with their heads under the hood, joined an hour or so later by Horace. There was a lot of shaking of heads and muttering, but by the end of the day Sam literally had the engine purring.

Zuri appeared with Tigger in the curve of one arm. He set the cat down and took over for Beau on guard duty. To Evie's amusement, Tigger stalked around the perimeter of the backyard as if he were on duty too before settling on a branch of the maple. Meanwhile, Horace and Beau went out for groceries, and a short while later Suha, Adric and Marjani showed up with beer and wine.

That night Evie and Jace made fried chicken, biscuits, and sweet corn for everyone. Somehow the whole group fit around the kitchen table. Evie took in the hard-eyed soldiers bantering with one another as they downed her fried chicken, and felt like pinching herself. Two weeks ago, she hadn't even known Jace existed, and now he had his hand on her thigh under the table, his pinky teasing the edge of her shorts—and the Baltimore alpha was seated a few chairs down, grinning at something Kyler had said.

She wanted to gather up the day like the gift it was and hold it close so she'd never forget it.

But the best part was yet to come. This time, Jace didn't even wait for Kyler to go to bed, just stood up as Adric and Marjani left, pulling Evie to her feet along with him.

"Good night, everyone." He nodded to his den mates, who were sprawled around the room, Kyler in their midst, watching the basketball playoffs. Even Tigger was watching, curled up on Suha's lap.

Kyler just gave them a wave before turning back to the game. "Night, you two."

Jace set a hand on the small of Evie's back and steered her down the hall. The moment they were in the bedroom, he backed her up against the door, framed her face with his hands and kissed her, hard and deep.

Evie's head swam. She gripped his waist and hung on as her heart pounded in her ears. He moved his mouth to her neck and nipped the beating pulse, sending a jolt clear to her womb.

"Goddess, I want you." A harsh growl against her skin.

She drew a serrated breath. "Me too."

"Show me."

He didn't need to ask twice. She slid her fingers into his hair and dragged his mouth down to hers. Kissing him with all the hunger in her heart. Sucking his tongue into her mouth. Nipping his lips. Sliding a hand down his back to squeeze one of his firm buttocks.

His breath sped up. His hips moved, pressing into her belly. She could feel his cock, thick and ready.

He removed her arms from his neck and pressed them against the door, her hands on either side of her head. "You're mine,

Evie." His eyes seared into hers, dark gold touched with the green of his cat.

She wet her lips. "You said we don't mix." But a part of her cried, *yes*.

"I'm an ass. Now say it." He nipped her jaw, and pleasure jolted straight to her clit. "I want the words. Just for tonight."

"Or else what?" Her chin jutted. Because that had hurt, what he'd said about the two of them not mixing. She might have her own doubts, but not because he was a fada.

But you agreed, a little voice reminded her.

He lifted a single black brow. "Are you teasing a cat?"

She moistened her lips, but she was damned if she'd back down. "Yes."

"Oh, baby," he crooned in a dark voice that made her inner thighs clench. "Then you better be ready to play." He captured her wrists in one hand and held them above her head, while with his other hand he undid her shorts. "Or else what?" he repeated. "Maybe I'll keep you against the door until you beg to come."

She slid him a look from under her lids. "Maybe I'd like that."

He chuckled and skimmed his fingers under the waistband of her panties. She was wearing her only sexy underwear—black satin with a touch of lace and a bra to match.

His heated gaze took in the black lace against her cream-colored skin. "Did you wear these for me?" When she nodded, he murmured, "Good girl. Now say it, Evie."

But as soon as she opened her mouth, he covered it with his as if afraid to let her speak. Her heart lurched as she realized he didn't expect her to say it. He kissed her as if he were aching as much as she was, his tongue curling over hers, taking her deeper by slow degrees. Meanwhile, his fingers slid deeper into her panties, teasing her sensitized flesh until she was breathless and aching.

She wanted to touch him. Her hands jerked in his grip but he wouldn't let her go. He kept them pressed to the door above her head and continued kissing her until she was dazed, her legs like limp noodles.

He lifted his head, his expression hard and a little wild, and she knew his cat was inside, looking out. He squeezed her bottom. "You're a bad girl to wear these tight little shorts. All day, I kept looking at your ass and picturing what I was going to do to you when we were alone. I swear my cock was hard the whole fucking day. And this shirt…" Long, work-roughened fingers stroked her belly. "The way you keep flashing me. It's enough to drive a man insane."

She laughed up at him, but God, he was making her hot. "I wasn't flashing you. All you could see was my stomach."

"You think that isn't bad?" He released her wrists and jerked up her T-shirt to expose her breasts. "I wanted to taste you, lick you, and then move up your stomach to your hot tits." He pinched her nipples through the black satin…and then his mouth was on her and he was sucking the points to hardness.

She cupped his head, holding him close. His mouth was warm and wet. Each hot suck shot straight to her womb.

She moaned, and he gave a sexy rumble in response. From her breasts, he moved his way lower, trailing a searing line of kisses down her abdomen until he reached her mound.

"Mine," he growled against her panties. He pursed his lips and blew a hot stream of air into the satin right above her clit. "Say it."

She whimpered and pressed her palms against the door, her body straining to him. "God, yes. Please."

He stilled. Slowly his eyes turned up to hers, so that she felt like prey. Sexy, not-even-going-to-try-to-run prey. Then his lips curved in a wicked smile. "But I'm still going to tease you… because we both like it."

He came to his feet and swung her into his arms. The world spun and Evie nipped his shoulder. "I do. Like it, I mean."

His answer was a fierce kiss. When it ended, she was on the bed with him kneeling over her.

The first thing he did was to strip off her clothes. He dropped them next to the bed and sent his own after them. "That's better." His gaze stroked down her body where she lay with one knee bent up, lingering on her nipples, which tingled eagerly, and then continued down to the tuft of dark blond hair between her legs.

"You're darker here." He traced a fingertip through her curls.

"Because I'm a natural blond. This—" she touched the hair on her head—"gets bleached by the sun. That doesn't, unless I sunbathe naked." She slanted him a wicked smile.

"Damn." He pressed her bent leg down and straddled her. "Now I've got a picture in my head of you spread out naked in the sun like a fucking sex goddess." He traced a finger around her nipples and then down her breastbone. "Would you burn?"

"No—I don't burn. I just get a little darker."

"Beautiful," he murmured as he stroked her flank. "This afternoon in the sun, you sparkled like someone sprinkled silver dust on you. I wonder if you have some sun fae in you. You should talk to Queen C about it."

"Sure. I'll just drive up to Rising Sun and knock on her door. If she even has a door..."

"Adric knows her. He could talk to her."

She shook her head. "If the sun fae wanted me, they'd have done something a long time ago."

"Maybe. The fae have their own way of looking at things, though. And time moves more slowly for them. She may be planning on doing something, but by the time she gets around to it, you'll be fifty years old. You should think about it—the sun fae can help you train your Gift, if you don't want to ask Leesa."

"All right—I'll think about it." She trailed a finger down the hard muscles of his abdomen. "But right now, I have better things to do."

"I like how you think, woman." His eyes glinted with his cat: golden brown with shards of green radiating out from the pupils.

She slipped her arms around his neck. "You promised I'd see your jaguar again."

"Mm." His chest rumbled, and she grinned.

"Are you purring?"

"Yeah," he said with a sheepish smile. "The cat likes you."

"So I can see him?"

"Sure." He backed off and crouched on the mattress. Color cascaded over his skin, bright bits of green and gold and copper that reminded her of the inside of a fae light. They spread out until his body glittered, indescribably beautiful.

And then suddenly, his form was more cat than man, and then a black panther stood on the foot of the bed. He was big and brawny, with powerful legs and long, sharp canines. This close, she could see the roseate pattern on his pelt—large, irregular black spots surrounded by a dark walnut that blended in to make him appear all black from a distance.

She drew in a breath, awed and the tiniest bit afraid, even though she *knew* it was Jace.

He settled next to her and nudged her with his head. "You want me to pet you?" He rumbled and nudged her harder, so much like Tigger it was impossible to be afraid. "Okay," she said with a chuckle and smoothed a hand over his head. His fur was velvety soft over the hard bones of his skull. "You're beautiful."

He pushed his head harder into her hand, and then crept even closer so he could rub against her jaw. Marking her with his scent.

She turned her head and their eyes met. His irises were a pure green now, but she saw the man there too, his gaze alive with intelligence.

She stroked a hand over his jaw. This time his purr was loud and clear.

He came up over her, and rubbed his head over her chest. Her already sensitized nipples hardened. Her breasts felt achingly full.

Then he moved down her body and rubbed his head against her mound, too. Her breath sucked in. "*Jace.*"

He gave a badass growl and came on top of her again, a paw on either side of her head. His fur glittered, and she watched as he changed back to man. This time it was a quick shift—less than thirty seconds.

"I want you," he said in a gravelly voice that was half cat, half man. "Now."

"Yes." Her arms were already around him. Her hips rocked off the bed, touching his erection where it hung, hard and heavy.

His fingers speared into her hair, holding her still as he trailed love-bites over her neck. Her insides clenched. Something unexpected in her liked being held down like that—firm and yet gentle at the same time. His to tease however he wished.

His other hand went to her pussy. He dipped a finger into her, and then trailed the moisture around her tender nub. Pleasure swirled through her. "Yes. There."

"That's it, angel. Take it." He continued to play with her, but when her sex tightened, he took his hand away.

She moaned his name, and he said, "You can come when I'm inside you."

"Get on with it then," she said between her teeth.

His cheek creased. "You're so damn cute."

For answer, she reached down and squeezed him. His smile disappeared. She worked her hand up and down him, toying with his balls, learning the feel of him. His cock spurted with pre-cum and she rubbed it over the slick cap, enjoying how his eyes slit with pleasure.

His hips gave an involuntary jerk and she squeezed harder. "Fuck," he muttered. He removed her hand and grabbed a rubber from the night table. He worked it over his erection, and then crawled back on top of her. She reached between their bodies and guided him to her entrance. They both watched as he slowly entered her.

Her breath hissed out. He paused, and she met his eyes. She knew what he wanted.

"Please. I want it. I want you."

He slid in another inch. "That's it, Evie. I love it when you beg me."

"Please," she said again.

He slid deeper, and then withdrew again. He continued moving in and out in tantalizing increments until at last he was fully seated in her.

She rotated her hips in slow circles, pleasuring them both.

His jaw clenched. "That's it. Take me, baby. Tease me."

His hand was in her hair again, the other hand on her ass as he began to move in her, holding her in place for his firm, perfect thrusts. From somewhere far off, she heard herself making sounds of arousal, soft at first, and then louder as her pleasure increased.

It was so good. Her chest constricted. Because she'd found him, but she couldn't keep him.

"Mine," he said, and she nodded, throat tight.

Because she *was* Jace's, for as long as he wanted her. It was crazy, but it felt *right*.

But even if she waited until Kyler was grown up, they were from such different worlds. How did she know it wouldn't just be her mom and Fane all over again?

Sensation stormed through her, searing her nerves. And then she was convulsing around him in an explosive orgasm that both shot her high—and cracked her heart.

26

Corban hurt. His injured leg throbbed, and his head pounded in time.

He'd tried again to heal his thigh, but his quartz had been pushed too hard. He'd have to heal the old-fashioned way, which was too damned slow. Every hour he was incapacitated was another hour that Adric had to track him.

Morning came. He couldn't see the sunrise, but he noted it with a fada's internal clock. He got up to pee and downed several cups of water before curling up in the blankets again. The day passed with agonizing slowness. He was hungry, but all he had to eat were a couple of nutrient bars he'd brought from Iceland. He rationed them out—one in the morning, one that evening—and ignored his hollow stomach.

He considered calling one of his brothers, but he was wary of letting even them know his location. Kane could be trusted, but Nash was Adric's man now. And even if they didn't betray him, they might inadvertently lead someone to his lair.

No, it was safer to remain incommunicado.

Tomorrow. Tomorrow I'll go out hunting. The park had rabbits and other small mammals. His wolf salivated hungrily.

Outside, night fell. He forced himself to move his injured leg. The pain made his chest seize, but it was getting better.

He gritted his teeth and forced himself to exercise the torn hamstring: stretching it, bending the knee.

Midnight came and went. He wrapped himself in a blanket and dozed, tormented by fevered dreams. Nika, furious that he'd left her behind to face the music. His father telling him what a weak excuse for a man he was.

But the worst were the black shadows that slithered out of the walls to wind chill fingers around his limbs. His nostrils twitched. *Metal and decay.*

He jerked awake to find Tyrus staring down at him.

The night fae lord was dressed in black from his overpriced duster to his handmade leather shoes. Tall and thin, he loomed over Corban like an elegant crow, his eyes dark coals in his pale face.

"Get up." He planted his toe in Corban's ribs.

Corban had already thrown off the blanket. He rose to his feet, ignoring the pain that stabbed through his leg. *Never let them see that you're weak.*

Even standing, he had to look up. He was tall for an earth fada, but the night fae had a good six inches on him.

"Jones is still alive." Tyrus's tone was icy with scorn. "And Adric took your woman prisoner. What the fuck am I paying you for?"

"Kill him yourself then," Corban snarled. "Your assassin failed, too."

Tyrus struck. Long white fingers wrapped around Corban's throat, rattlesnake-fast. "You dare argue with me, fada?" He gave Corban a shake.

Corban growled. His claws slid out and he took a swipe at Tyrus, but the night fae grabbed his wrist and shoved him back against the wall.

Stunned, Corban stared at Tyrus. The man must have the Gift

of wayfaring. Only a fae who could move at an inhuman speed could've evaded a fada so easily.

Fear coated his insides.

Tyrus held Corban pinned against the wall. His gaze snagged Corban's. He froze, ensnared by the unholy red flicker in the night fae's pupils.

Energy hummed over Corban's skin—cold and black as the slithering shadows of his nightmare. His bowels iced.

"No," he said, but the sound was swallowed in the darkness.

The energy increased, braiding itself into ropes. One rope twined around his skull, while a second spiraled around his chest and a third licked up his injured leg.

Blackness. Endless as a nightmare. He was small, helpless, cowering before his father.

"Stupid cub." A hand clouted him in the head. His ears rang. A single tear slid down his cheek, and his father hit him again, disgusted.

"Stop your blubbering, you little coward."

Corban tried, but the tears wouldn't dry up. They ran down his cheeks, hot and damning.

The blows fell again and again, until Corban's face was on fire and he was woozy with pain. They didn't stop until Corban forced the tears down into somewhere so deep and tightly guarded, they never escaped again.

The rope around Corban's chest constricted. Panic clawed at him. He was forced to take short, shallow breaths, unable to fill his lungs.

"I own you," Tyrus said, soft and cold. "We have a contract."

Despair washed over Corban. He fought the urge to turn his head and offer submission to the night fae in the way of his wolf.

But he'd been raised by a bastard. Despair and hopelessness were mother's milk to Leron Savonett's son.

Rage rose up in him. All the rage the sniveling little boy had had to hide. It blew away the despair, replacing it with a red-eyed fury. His head pounded, and his vision clouded.

His switchblade practically leapt into his hand. He released the blade with a snick and pressed it into Tyrus's belly. "Get. Your. Hands. Off. Me."

Surprise flashed over the other man's face. He released Corban and took a step back, but his silent assault continued—only now, he was feeding off Corban's anger.

Gods, the man was a sick fuck.

If only Corban had a blade of iron, he'd end this for good. A knife straight to Tyrus's black heart. Because Tyrus's death would serve Corban's purpose almost as well as Jace Jones' death. Prince Langdon would never believe the clan wasn't behind the attack, and he'd be on Adric in a flash.

But without iron, Corban would only make Tyrus madder, and he needed Tyrus to get him to Jones and his pretty little human. Jones was the key to the smartphone tech. Remove him from the equation, and Adric would be back to the beginning. And then Corban would wait until Adric showed up—and kill him as well.

With both Jones and Adric gone, Corban would be the strongest man in the clan. Nothing would stop him from taking over his rightful place as alpha. Some of the lieutenants might squawk, but they'd accept him—or die.

Corban took a fighter's crouch, the knife loose and easy in his right hand. He knew his eyes were pure gold now, his wolf running the show. And with the wolf came calm.

The dark ropes of energy loosened. He sensed Tyrus' confusion.

"Enough," Corban gritted. He might not be able to kill a fae with a steel blade, but he could hurt the man.

The fire in Tyrus's eyes faded. "You're stronger than I believed." He tilted his head, scrutinizing Corban as if he were an interesting problem.

"So this was a fucking test?" Corban remained in the crouch.

"A test?" The night fae lifted a brow. "No. But you've proved you can still be of use to me. Come here." He beckoned with a single long, sharp-nailed finger.

"Why?" he returned without moving.

Tyrus pressed his lips together. "I can heal you. Then I'll take you to the jaguar's lair."

"Jones? He has a *look-away* spell concealing the entrance." Corban knew approximately where Jones lived, but the spell kept him from determining its actual location.

"A child could break that spell. Now come."

Corban stared at him for another moment, and then nodded. What did he have to lose?

He crossed the few steps between them. The night fae set his hand on Corban's chest, and muttered a few words in an arcane fae language.

Corban's entire thigh lit up with an eerie blue flame. Pain seared through him. A shriek escaped his lips. He cursed and shoved Tyrus away, and then fell to the dirt floor where he curled up in agony and waited to die.

And then the blue flame was gone as abruptly as it had appeared.

Corban dragged in a breath. Then another. When his body stopped quivering, he sat up, panting softly. His hand went to the back of his thigh. He froze, and then twisted so that he could see the back of his leg. The ugly gash was gone, the scar rapidly closing over.

Tyrus was already moving up the ladder. "Come. Dawn is only a couple of hours away."

Corban took a cautious step. The pain was completely gone and he could move with ease. He released one last breath and then pulled himself up the ladder after Tyrus. At the surface, Tyrus strode into the woods without looking back, confident Corban would follow.

Corban paused to tap his quartz. It was time to call in the only man he still trusted in Baltimore: his middle brother, Kane.

Born a year apart, he and Kane had formed an alliance against their dad. When their youngest brother Nash came along four years later, they'd protected him as best they could. Maybe that had been a mistake, because Nash had grown up weaker because of it—he was firmly in Adric's camp.

But Kane had stuck by Corban, supporting his bid to be alpha until Adric had won the challenge and forced both brothers to swear allegiance to him or die. It wasn't an easy thing for a fada to break such a vow, but it could be done if you were determined enough.

Still, the effort had made Corban violently ill for a month, especially since he'd smashed his quartz at the same time. But he'd had a new quartz ready and he'd holed up in a cave in the Himalayas until he'd recovered.

"What in Hades is going on?" Kane hissed into the phone now. "The alpha has everyone out looking for you."

"Fuck that. Are you still with me?"

There was a fraught silence, and then his brother expelled a breath. "Of course. But—"

Corban named an intersection near Jace Jones's den. "Meet me there now."

His brother understood immediately. "You have a way to get past the *look-away* spell?"

"Yeah."

"It still won't work. He's got a den full of soldiers."

Corban glanced after Tyrus, who had disappeared in the woods. "I have a night fae with me. Lord T."

"So it's true. You're working with the fae." Kane's tone was gruff with disapproval.

"For now." Sometimes you had to deal with the devil if you wanted to win. "You in?"

Kane bit out a curse. "I'll be there in ten minutes."

27

J ace curled his body around Evie's and played with her breasts. Two nights with the woman, and already he couldn't imagine waking up without her.

She mumbled something in her sleep. Good, she wasn't awake.

He angled his head so he could bite her nape. A light, teasing cat-bite.

Her breath sighed out. He slid his hand down the curve of her rib cage, stroked her stomach. His fingers were inching lower when his quartz buzzed. He swore under his breath but rolled onto his side and answered in a sub-vocal voice so as not to wake her.

The news from Adric chilled him. Luc had reported in from France that he'd finally found Tyrus's lair, but Tyrus had left for Paris soon after.

"And he didn't take a car," Adric said. "He was running. The man's a fucking wayfarer."

"No." Jace's stomach dropped. "But it makes sense—the way he pops out of nowhere..."

Wayfaring was a Gift only the most powerful fae had.

Some—like Queen Cleia of the sun fae—could 'port from place to place. Others could shadow your footsteps so that you never knew you were being followed, and still others could move freakishly fast. Dressed in his customary black, Tyrus would blend into the shadows. If he was a wayfarer, you'd never seen him rushing by. You'd just feel the chill as he passed.

"Luc and Nash are on their way home."

Jace nodded. "You think he's coming to Baltimore?"

"Yep. But why—what the fuck does he want?"

Jace raked a hand over his head. He didn't like this, not at all. "He hasn't tried anything for six years—and Merry's still protected by her father's ward. So what changed? Why go after me now?"

"Hell if I know. But be on guard. Don't let anyone in the den until we know more."

"Got it."

Adric cut the connection and Jace rolled onto his back. His cat was growling lowly, its tail twitching in agitation. Bloodthirsty visions rolled through Jace's mind, the jaguar's way of communication: *Kill. Protect. Mine.*

The cat wanted to stalk and kill Tyrus—but the night fae lord was Prince Langdon's only surviving son. If Jace killed him, Langdon would descend on the clan like a nuclear holocaust. It would be the Darktime all over again.

No, Jace told the cat, and it snarled but retreated further into his mind.

But that wasn't all. Just as he was turning back to Evie, his phone buzzed again. This time it was Merry. Evie was stirring so he slipped out of the room to take the call.

"What's up, babe?"

"Papa Rui wants to talk to you," Merry said.

"Okay, sure." Something was up—Rui almost never asked to speak to him, letting Valeria do most of the communicating.

Do Mar went straight to the point. "You know that female your alpha left on our territory—Nika? She's gone."

"What do you mean, gone?"

"That's what's fucking strange. Dion and I questioned her, but we couldn't get much out of her other than that she's from a Russian clan and that she came with Corban Savonett to Grace Harbor—which I'm sure you already know. Dion told her we'd better never find her making trouble in Rock Run territory again, and then Cleia was going to 'port her back to Russia. But when the guard checked on her an hour ago, she was gone."

Jace scraped his fingers over his hair. "How is that possible? Your wards—" Queen Cleia herself had made sure that Rock Run's wards were practically impregnable.

"I assure you, the queen is looking into it. There's no scent, no sign that anyone was inside. Only a powerful fae could've 'ported in and out of here without anyone knowing."

"Hell. I knew she wasn't all she seemed." He expelled a breath. "I'll inform my alpha. Thanks for letting us know."

"*De nada.* You won't be visiting next weekend." It was a statement, not a question.

"No. Not until we know what's going on."

"I think that's for the best. Here, Merry wants to say goodbye."

Do Mar returned the quartz to Merry, who said, "I heard what Papa said."

"I'm sorry," Jace told her. "I won't be coming to visit, but we'll talk. I promise."

"Is it because of that earth fada lady?"

He hesitated, but Merry wasn't stupid—she'd figure it out for herself. "Yeah. It's for your own safety." Because if he wasn't careful, he could bring this right to her door.

"Okay."

Jace grimaced. Damn, he hated that Merry was so accepting —so fucking adult. She was only thirteen. She should be whining like a normal teenager.

"Love you, sweetheart."

"Love you too." She cut the connection.

Jace remained in the hall, hand wrapped around his quartz, still reeling from the bad news. First Tyrus, and now Nika had escaped. Who the hell was she, really?

And why were his instincts screaming a trap was about to be sprung?

He tapped his quartz. "Adric? There's something you should know." He relayed the news about Nika.

Adric swore under his breath. "Fuck. The fae who can get past Cleia's wards can probably be counted on one hand."

Jace nodded. "The prince," he said, meaning Prince Langdon, "and the ice fae king." Sindre, whose name was coming up too damn often these days. "Those are my best guesses. And possibly my Lord Prick, but if he could teleport, he wouldn't be running to Paris."

"Agreed. Thoughts?"

"That we need to increase security. Corban knows where I live, and if he's working with the night fae, the *look-away* spell won't keep him out of my den." He glanced over his shoulder at the room where Evie was sleeping. Powerful fae or not, they'd have to step over his cold, dead body to get to her.

"I'll put the clan on high alert. No one goes anywhere alone, and the young and the old should be guarded twenty-four/seven. We'll increase our patrols through the city, too. But it's too damn large of an area to protect."

"We could gather the vulnerable in one place, but there's something to be said for keeping the dens scattered around the city."

They'd had this conversation before. On one hand, the small, scattered dens that earth fada preferred made it easier to eliminate them one den at a time. On the other hand, there was strength in remaining spread out. It had saved the clan in the

Darktime—even a crazed alpha like Leron Savonett hadn't been able to wipe out all the pockets of dissent.

"What do you suggest?"

Jace was already running scenarios in his mind. "So far, Corban has focused on me, but it's you he really wants. I'm just a means to get to you."

"So I'll draw him out of hiding."

"No fucking way. That's just what Corban wants. I'll do it."

"No—I'll be damned if I'll cower in my den while that bastard attacks my best people. Besides, Evie and Kyler need you right there."

Jace grimaced. Adric was right. While he trusted that his den mates would guard Evie and her brother with their lives, neither he nor his cat was comfortable with leaving them for any length of time. "Then let Zuri do it."

"It's not your decision," Adric said. "Corban wants me, so let him try to take me. I beat him once."

"He wasn't working with a night fae then," Jace returned.

"It's almost dawn. The night fae will have to go underground. Corban will be forced to deal with me alone."

Jace blew out a breath. "You're the alpha."

Something had been niggling at him ever since yesterday when he, Evie and the others had walked to the park. "Remember when we were teenagers and we tried to track your cousin in Druid Hill Park—but we never could?" Corban would disappear for hours, and he was so good at hiding his scent that even Adric couldn't find him.

"Hell. You think he has a lair in there somewhere?"

"Makes sense."

"We went through the park once already, but it's worth another pass. I'll head up there at noon when that fucking night walker will be sleeping. If Corban's somewhere nearby, just seeing me may draw him out. If not, I'll go over every square foot. If he has a lair, I'll find it."

"Don't go alone."

"I won't. So here's the plan—Horace and Sam are to stick with you, Evie and Kyler. I'll tell Beau to stay with Suha—she's valuable enough that Corban may try to strike at her—and I'll take Zuri and Marjani to the park."

"Marjani? You think that's wise? She's so close to going—"

"Feral? I know. Believe me, I know. But then again, this might be what she needs—someone to protect. She's been better ever since I asked for her help with this whole Corban mess. Maybe I made a mistake, coddling her this long."

Jace rubbed his lower lip. "She needed time to heal. But I agree, maybe it's time to bring her back on duty."

Marjani had been one of the clan's best soldiers. What had happened to her could've broken anyone—male or female—but it must have been a special hell for a woman who'd never taken any shit from anybody. To be violated in such an intimate way, made to feel so helpless. Like Takira. Jace swallowed harshly.

Adric was speaking. "I'll contact Zuri, tell him what's up. You bring Horace and Sam up to date."

"I will. And Ric? Thanks—for Evie and Kyler." Because he was wrapping the protection of the clan around the two humans.

"Hey, you'd do the same for me. Besides, I like your Evie and the kid. They're good people."

"They are." He cut the connection.

A moment later, he heard Zuri speaking to Adric. "On my way," he said. Jace glanced in his room to see the other lieutenant was already up and pulling on jeans and a T-shirt.

"I'm going to spread the word about Corban," Zuri told Jace, "to those who don't have a smartphone, and then I'll head over to Adric's."

Jace nodded. Not everyone could use the new technology—it was one of the glitches they still had to work out. "Watch his back. He thinks he's fucking invincible."

"Don't worry," Zuri replied, "I will."

Jace nodded and continued down the hall to wake up Sam and Horace. He brought them up to date with a few terse sentences, before heading for the shower, his plans for making love to Evie tabled. He didn't even want to get near her in this frame of mind.

He knew Corban had to die, but it still left a bad taste in his mouth. It was so fucking senseless. The Darktime was supposed to be over. He was sick and tired of the infighting, of pointless deaths. He wanted to build things—not kill. To be free to explore this thing with Evie and maybe someday, have a cub of his own with her.

His heart squeezed at the thought of a sassy little girl with Evie's bright hair and dark brows.

And if the clan had a problem with a mixed-blood, well, he'd make his own den with Evie and Kyler and any offspring the gods blessed them with. Adric would support him. Hell, Adric had accepted Merry, the only granddaughter of the night fae prince himself.

But if Corban had his way, it wasn't going to end until Adric and every last one of his lieutenants was dead.

Jace slammed the heel of his hand against the tiled wall. Then he stood under the shower head and turned it to full.

28

——————

It was the fae lights that woke Evie. She'd been on her side with Jace spooned around her, both of them naked. He'd been lazily caressing her, and she had a smile on her lips as she came awake. Then Jace had left the bed, and she'd rolled onto her back and dozed off again.

The next thing she knew, something stung her arm. She swatted it away, but a moment later she felt another sting to her shoulder, and then another to her face. She jolted awake to find the fae lights swarming her—and a tall man dressed all in black staring down at her.

Her heart kicked into high gear. She scrambled up against the headboard, the sheet clutched to her chest.

"Who the fuck are you?" *And how had he gotten in here?* She opened her mouth to scream for Jace.

The man raised a hand. "I wouldn't, if I were you. Your brother..." He cut his eyes at a corner of the room.

She whipped her head around. Kyler was sitting against the wall, knees hugged to his chest, staring unseeingly in front of him.

His face twisted in horror. *"No. No..."*

Her stomach bottomed out. "Kyler! What's wrong?" But he didn't seem to hear her.

Her gaze swung back to the tall man. Dark eyes regarded her from a pale, incredibly beautiful face. *Night fae.*

Kyler moaned again and she launched herself at the intruder. Nobody messed with her brother. "Stop it, damn you." She clawed wildly at his face.

He easily held her off. Those black eyes caught hers and she froze, fingers still curled into claws. The night fae slid a cool finger down her cheek. Fear sliced through her, but she steeled herself to remain calm and bear it. Anything to get his attention off Kyler.

Kyler made an agonized sound. "Evie. I'm sorry. So sorry. I couldn't help it." He came to his knees and looked up at her, his gaze stark.

Help what? But that didn't matter right now. She took a step back and screamed at Kyler, "Run! Get Jace."

Kyler's breath scraped in. But instead of trying to escape, he threw himself at the night fae. "Get away from my sister, you prick."

And ran right past the man. He barely avoided slamming headfirst into the wall. He caught himself with his hands on the stone and glanced around, angry and confused.

Evie blinked. One moment the night fae had been standing in front of her, the next he was gone—and then he reappeared exactly where he'd been, a foot away from her.

Kyler snarled and launched himself at the man again.

"Enough." The night fae's arm lashed out. He grabbed Kyler by the throat and squeezed.

Her brother's eyes bulged. He scrabbled desperately at the man's long white fingers, but the man held on, a slight smile on his lips.

Fury blinded Evie. With an animalistic growl, she grabbed the night fae's wrist and tried to drag him away from Kyler, but the fae shook her off like an annoying insect. When she came right back, he slammed an elbow into her solar plexus.

Pain exploded through her. Her breath left her lungs in a whoosh. She stumbled back, her diaphragm seizing up, and dropped to her knees, opening and shutting her mouth like a hooked fish as she tried to catch her breath.

Kyler's struggles were slacking off. Panic snaked up Evie's spine. Somehow, she found the strength to crawl toward the night fae and wrap her arms around his lower leg.

He glanced down at her and laughed. "By the dark gods," he said in a French accent, "you don't give up."

And then he swung Kyler into the wall like he was a ragdoll. There was a dull thud and her brother slumped to the floor, unmoving.

Evie's breath rushed in as her diaphragm finally unlocked. For a few seconds she couldn't move. She sank onto her forearms, head against the floor, sucking in oxygen.

From the hall came furious shouts and bone-chilling snarls. *Jace and the others. Oh, God, they were in trouble, too.*

Something cool and oily brushed over her back, teased her breasts. Her skin prickled. Suddenly she was aware she was completely naked with a cold-eyed stranger. She pushed herself up on her knees to face him and covered herself as best she could with her hands.

The tall, black-haired fae crouched next to her. Chilly fingers stroked her nape. Fine hairs stood up all over her body. "You know who I am?"

Evie batted his hand away. Kyler moaned and she shot a frantic look at him.

A hand caught her wrist. Squeezed until the bones ground painfully together. "Answer me."

"No," she said between clenched teeth.

"The animals didn't tell you?"

"The animals?"

"The fada. Your lover."

She narrowed her eyes. "He didn't want to draw your attention."

His cruel mouth quirked. "Oh, you have my attention." He drew her to her feet. "I'm Lord Tyrus—and you're part fae."

THE BATHROOM DOOR opened as Jace shut off the shower. "Evie?" he asked.

No response.

His nape tingled. He jerked open the shower door. A huge black wolf stared back at him.

Fuck. Jace started to shift but Corban was already in the air. He slammed Jace into the wall. Lights exploded in his head and he slid to the floor.

His focus lost, Jace couldn't complete the shift. He only just managed to yank himself back to man so he wouldn't be caught in a half-shifted state. It was the devil's choice, because he couldn't fight off Corban's wolf as a man, but the alternative was death as a half-man, half-cat.

He was trapped in the shower with the wolf. Claws dug painfully into his chest, holding him down as Corban's teeth sank into his throat. The metallic scent of blood filled his nostrils.

Jace went clawed and lashed at Corban—slicing at his eyes, his muzzle. The wolf hung on grimly. Black spots swam before Jace's eyes. He shoved his thumbs into the corners of Corban's mouth near his molars and managed to open his jaws enough to pry him off. He threw the wolf against the wall and scrambled to his feet.

He swayed, dizzy from the blow to his head, one thought in his mind: *Evie.*

Corban rose to his feet. Somehow Jace got out of the bathroom ahead of him. He slammed the door shut, trapping the wolf inside.

Where the hell were Sam and Horace?

"Attack," he roared. "We're under attack."

The hall remained ominously silent. He gripped the bathroom doorknob, holding the door closed as Corban slammed repeatedly against it, trying to break out.

Jace's chest heaved. The black spots returned, threatening to blot out his consciousness.

Corban went silent. Then the doorknob jerked. He was trying to turn it with his teeth.

Jace clenched his jaw and willed the black spots away. He was aware of blood running down his chest from the gash in his throat. But he had to hang on long enough to sound the alarm. With Sam and Horace apparently down, he was Evie and Kyler's only hope.

He tapped his quartz and said a brief prayer of thanks when Adric responded immediately. "What's up?"

"My den," Jace rasped. "Under attack. Corban is inside. I'm hurt, and I don't know where Sam and Horace are."

He inhaled—and caught a stench of night fae.

"Fuck." He wasn't sure if he whispered or shouted it. He was sliding down a long, dark tunnel. "Night fae. In my den."

Evie. Kyler.

His knees gave out and he sat on the floor with a thump. He swiped a hand over his eyes, trying to clear his vision. *Was that a black wolf padding down the hall? But how?* Corban was still in the bathroom, clawing at the door. The handle started to turn and Jace realized he'd released it.

"Hang on, bro. We're on our way." Adric's voice.

"Hurry," he mumbled.

The wolf in the hall shifted to man, and Kane Savonett loomed over Jace.

"Bastard," Jace mouthed.

Kane grabbed Jace's quartz and he jolted in pain. But that was nothing compared to how it felt when Kane pulled the quartz off him.

Jace's entire body lit with a tooth-jarring agony, and then everything went black.

The last thing he did was to fall sideways so his body would block Corban when he emerged. Even a few extra seconds might save Evie and her brother.

29

Tyrus raked his gaze over Evie's naked body. "Get dressed."

"Okay, sure." She grabbed some clothes before he could change his mind. Kyler was slumped against the wall near the bed. She shot him a worried glance as she pulled on her cargo pants.

"Come." Tyrus beckoned to her.

She swallowed. "Why?"

Kyler groaned, and the night fae's gaze moved to him. Evie stepped to the left so that she was between the two of them.

"Kyler?" she asked without taking her eyes off Tyrus. "You okay?"

"Think so."

She darted a look at her brother. He was sitting up, rubbing his head. He blinked at the blood on his fingers.

"What happened?" he asked.

"You hit your head against the wall."

He nodded and then winced. "Fuck, that hurts." He glanced at Tyrus, and his face tightened with hatred. "Asshole," he growled.

She moved back and set a staying hand on his shoulder. "Hush. It's okay."

Kyler didn't seem to hear. "I'm sorry, Evie. He got into my dreams somehow—a nightmare. When I woke up, I was at the door, letting him inside." He glared at the night fae. "Why don't you fight fair, you freaking prick?"

She dug her nails into his shoulder. "Kyler. Shut. Up."

"I'm not afraid of him," he returned sullenly, but to her relief, he subsided.

Tyrus ignored their byplay to focus on Evie. "Come, woman."

"No fucking way." Kyler wrapped wiry arms around her legs. "She's not going anywhere with you."

"No?" The fae's black eyes flashed red.

Evie gulped. It was like something out of a horror movie. She slid down the wall until she was crouched next to Kyler, an arm flung out to protect him. Her brother muttered something and dropped his head on her shoulder, and she had the sick feeling he was only half aware of what was going on.

She glared up at Tyrus. "What do you want?"

"Ah...now that's an interesting question." The red faded. Tyrus sat on the mattress and stretched out his long legs, one ankle crossed over the other. The fae lights had clustered around her and Kyler, leaving him in the shadows. Only his face and hands were visible, a pale glimmer like a new moon in a dark sky. The tips of his pointed ears emerged from midnight-black hair.

He was sharp-faced, beautiful—and he made her spine prickle like a thousand spiders creeping up her vertebrae.

"I'm here in Baltimore," he replied, "because I have a dislike of your new friends, especially Jones and his alpha. It wasn't very smart of you to get between me and my prey."

She raised her chin. "So sue me."

He just smiled. "But now that I know about you, Evie, I find I'm interested in you. Very interested. It's been over a week since I last fed—and the fae in you makes your energy special."

The den was still as a morgue now. Where were Jace and the others? If they were all right, surely they'd have burst in by now. Evie's heart twisted. Jace must be hurt bad, because if he could get to her, he would—that much she knew.

The fae lights moved closer to Evie. They were smaller than she'd ever seen, barely the size of a ping-pong ball, but they brushed over her in a warm caress: *Stay strong.* It was almost as if they'd spoken.

She wrapped an arm around Kyler and lifted her chin. "What do you mean, my energy is special?"

"Taking energy from a human like your brother is like drinking beer or a cheap wine. It serves if there's nothing better. But your energy—it is like a fine champagne. I may even invite some of my friends to taste you."

Her stomach lurched. "No," she said fiercely. "I won't let you. I'll stop you like I did before."

"Can you?" Tyrus raised a brow. "So that was you in the kitchen? I thought it was Jones."

"It was me." *At least part of the time.*

"Yes?" He rose to his feet. "Well, do your best, *ma chère.* I don't think you'll win. But it makes the game more amusing."

The bedroom door opened. Evie's heart surged—and then sank. It was a big, dark-skinned man she'd never seen before.

He eyed her coolly. "This is Jace's human?"

"Yes." Tyrus beckoned to Evie, and she found herself releasing Kyler and rising without intending to.

Panic skittered over her nerves. He was controlling her somehow, forcing her to walk the few feet between them.

A finger traced the curve of her jaw, lingered in the hollow of her neck. "I can set you free, but I need your promise that you'll come quietly."

Her chest jolted in and out. She couldn't get enough oxygen in her lungs. Inside, she was screaming, but all she could do was stare at him mutely.

"Evie? Nod your head if you agree."

She jerked her chin in assent, and he released her. Her breath shuddered in.

Tyrus stared down at her from his great height. "Do I have your promise?"

"Not Kyler," she returned tightly. "Only me."

"*No*." Her brother's harsh voice tore through the dark room. He had both hands on the wall, trying to bring himself to his feet.

She took a step toward him. "No, Kyler! Stay there—*please*."

He shook his head and grimly continued, literally crawling up the wall.

"You're bargaining with me, human?" Tyrus narrowed his eyes at her.

She set her shoulders. "Yes. I want your promise—just me, not my brother."

He shrugged. "Done. It's you I want, not him. Now do I have your promise?"

"Yes."

"Say the words."

"I promise to go with you if you leave Kyler here."

"Agreed." Tyrus smiled. A chill, victorious tilt of his lips. "Let's go then." He reached for her.

She took an involuntary step back, unable to help herself.

"Evie?" A soft, deadly question. "You're not breaking your promise, are you?"

She swallowed dryly. Everyone knew you didn't break a promise to a fae. It was the only way to hold them in check. If she broke her promise, who knew what Tyrus would do to Kyler?

"No," she said between numb lips.

He waited, hand out, until she forced herself to step forward again. He swung her into his arms. This close, he was unnaturally cold, and he had the sickly-sweet scent of death. She held herself stiff, her entire being revolting at his touch.

Tyrus rubbed his cheek against hers. "You're strong. I like that. Strong women are so much more fun."

Her fingers curled into claws, but she thought of Kyler and remained quiet. She could endure this if it saved him.

Tyrus followed the large man into the hall. The first thing Evie saw was Jace sprawled unmoving on the floor, a huge wolf the color of midnight standing over him. She made a small, dismayed sound, and the wolf's shaggy head swung toward her. Sharp canines glinted in the dim light.

A fae light wafted over Jace and her breath hitched. What she'd thought were shadows on his face and neck was blood. He was covered in it. She twisted in Tyrus's arms, forgetting everything but the need to save him from the wolf.

The fae's grip tightened. "Remember your promise," he said in silky tones.

She stilled, but narrowed her eyes at the wolf. "Get the fuck away from him," she said, low and mean.

The shifter's burning gold gaze swung to her.

There was a movement behind them, and she glanced over Tyrus's shoulder to see Kyler in the bedroom doorway, hands braced against the frame to hold himself up.

Horror swamped her. She was afraid to speak, but silently begged him with her eyes to stay hidden. When she turned back, the big black wolf had a paw on Jace's chest.

Fury engulfed her. "Damn you!" she spat at Tyrus. "Call the wolf off him. He's hurt—he can't defend himself."

"Quiet." His dark eyes flickered red again.

Evie froze except for the fine-grained trembling of her body. This was how a cornered rabbit must feel. Afraid and hopeless and seething with hatred.

Tyrus jerked his head at Jace. "Bring him," he told the wolf.

The shifter's lip peeled back to reveal sharp white teeth, but Tyrus stared him down. "Bring him. You work for me, remember? And get rid of the boy."

"No!" Evie burst out. "You promised. You said you wouldn't hurt him—that was the deal."

"Actually, I didn't. All I promised was that I wouldn't take him —just you."

Her mouth dropped open. "You...*bastard*." She punched him in the throat without thinking of the consequences, and he staggered back and loosened his grip enough that she dropped to the floor. In an instant, she was back on her feet and flying at him, fingers curved into talons.

She was past caring about herself. She just wanted to hurt him.

Her nails slashed a bloody trail down his cheeks, but he was quick as a rattlesnake. The next thing she knew, her back slammed into the wall, his hands pinning her wrists next to her head. But she was beyond reasoning. She twisted in his grip and aimed a knee at his balls which he barely evaded.

"Fuck," Tyrus said, the earthy curse sounding odd in his cultured voice. He grabbed her chin and snapped, "Stop it right now," and tried to do that mind-control thing on her again, but this time it didn't work, maybe because she was so pissed off she was operating on instinct, not on a conscious level.

"Not until you promise," she snarled back.

"Fine." He jerked his head at the fada. "Don't touch the boy."

The wolf growled, and Tyrus added, "Let me rephrase that. Touch him, and you're dead. Is that clear?"

The wolf curled its lip, but the big man said, "We understand."

Evie halted, chest heaving. "Get inside the bedroom," she told Kyler.

"No." Her brother stared at her, white-faced. "I won't let him take you."

She met his eyes. "Please, Kyler. There's no sense us both going." She mouthed, "Tell Adric."

His throat worked, and then he nodded and obeyed. She saw

the bedroom door shut behind him as Tyrus swept her back into his arms, and then the next second, they were in Jace's shed.

Her jaw slackened. How had Tyrus made it up to the surface so quickly?

To the east, the sun was rising. The night fae cast an assessing eye at the pink haze spreading across the sky and then continued out of the shed. So it was only full sunlight that affected him.

Tigger was returning from a night of tomcatting around. He rounded his back and hissed at the fae, who kicked out at him. The cat yowled and leapt out of the way.

Tyrus took off running at an inhuman speed. The streets passed in a blur. He didn't stop until they reached Druid Hill Park, where he set Evie down, took her wrist in a painful grip and dragged her down an asphalt path at a punishing pace despite the fact she was barefoot.

They'd gone about a half mile when he turned onto a dirt path that led into the trees. A few minutes later they reached a small, hidden clearing. Tyrus stopped by a large rock and moved it aside as if it weighed almost nothing.

She glanced at him and gulped. Already, the cuts she'd made on his cheeks were healing over as if they'd been made yesterday, not ten minutes ago.

Tyrus jerked his chin at her. "Get in."

"Down there?" She glanced over the edge. A rusty metal ladder descended ten feet into a cellar. She felt the color drain from her face at the thought of being trapped in the small, dank space with him.

Her mind screamed *no* but she reminded herself of her promise. If she broke it, it wouldn't rebound just on her. Kyler and Jace would be in danger too.

And besides, running wouldn't do her any good—Tyrus would catch her before she'd gone three steps.

He didn't wait for her to make up her mind. He moved with that preternatural speed, grabbing her by her upper arms and dangling her over the ladder. Her heart leapt into her throat and she instinctively scrabbled for footing. As soon as her foot touched a rung, he released her, and she slipped, dropping a good yard before she grabbed the top rung and halted her fall.

"Keep going." Tyrus set his heel on her left hand, his face alight with a vile enjoyment. "Or I'll break your fingers. It makes no difference to me."

That was when it hit her—he didn't care if he hurt her as long as he could still feed on her energy. In fact, he might even prefer it.

Ice skated down her spine. "All right." She tried to drag her hand out from under his foot, but he ground his heel into the bones before releasing it.

Pain shot through her. She half-climbed, half-fell the rest of the way down the ladder until her feet hit the dirt floor.

Above her, Tyrus slid the rock back over the opening, leaving them in the darkness. He ignored the ladder to drop to the dirt beside her, his duster billowing around him like the wings of a massive black bat.

He turned toward her, his pale face the only thing visible in the pitch-black cellar. "Afraid, *ma chère*?"

She nursed her throbbing hand against her stomach and glared at him without speaking.

His thin mouth quirked. "Good. Fear has its own special taste."

30

———

$\mathcal{A}$dric cursed and met Marjani's eyes across the kitchen table.

She was already on her feet. "Corban attacked Jace's den?"

"Yeah—with a night fae."

Her face darkened. "Tyrus?"

"He didn't say—but who else could it be? And the bastards took his quartz. I can feel it." As alpha, he was connected to most of the clan in a magical way that was like a mate bond, although weaker. His bond to his top people like Jace was even stronger. He'd sensed the minute Jace had gone dark. There was a hollowness where his friend's strong, steady energy had been.

"I'll come," his sister said.

Adric gulped the last of his coffee to give himself time to think, and she made an impatient sound.

"Stop babying me. I'm fine—and you need me."

He gave in, because she was right; he did need her. "Two minutes."

"I'll be ready."

They met at the front door. Marjani had an iron knife in a protective leather holster strapped to her upper arm, and he knew there was a switchblade in her back pocket and a shiv strapped to her thigh. His sister was a magician with knives. You'd think she had a Gift for it, except he'd never heard of such a thing.

He'd brought a switchblade himself, but if things went south, he was going in as his cougar. His teeth literally ached to sink into Corban's carotid.

As they emerged into the early morning light, Zuri arrived on his motorcycle. He looked from Adric to Marjani. "What's wrong?"

"Corban and a night fae attacked your den." Adric slung a leg over his bike while Marjani hopped on behind.

Zuri's jaw set. Without a word, he swung around and took off down the street, Adric right behind.

The outside door to Jace's den was wide open, the *look-away* spell broken. Adric took the lead as they pounded down the steps. The scent of blood was strong—Jace's mainly, but a touch of Corban's as well.

Adric eased open the front door. The living room was intact, except for a thin trail of blood, also Jace's. The bedrooms were dead silent. The three of them moved into the hall on catlike feet.

He inhaled, sorting through the scents: Kyler, Sam, and Horace were all still present, if injured. He set that aside to identify the three that didn't belong. He didn't think they were still in the den, but just in case, he kept his voice too low for anyone but Marjani and Zuri to hear. "It's Corban and Tyrus all right...and Kane Savonett."

The three of them exchanged a glance. Another traitor, this one living and working with the rest of them for the past six years. Even though Adric had never entirely trusted Kane, it was still a blow.

They all saw the pool of blood outside the bathroom. Jace's blood, mixed with a fair amount of Corban's. At least his friend had gone down fighting. But the bathroom was empty.

A faint groan came from Jace's bedroom. *Kyler.*

"Go check the other rooms," he hissed at Marjani and Zuri as he slipped in through the partially open door.

The teenager was seated on the floor, arms around his legs, rocking back and forth and moaning, the back of his head matted with blood.

Adric's jaw tightened, but he kept his voice calm. "Kyler? It's me—Adric."

He started and scuttled away, wild-eyed. "*No...*"

"It's okay." Adric crouched beside him and stretched out a hand. "You're safe now. I'm here to help. Just tell me what happened."

The teen's whole body shuddered.

Adric clasped his shoulder. "Kyler? Snap out of it. I need you to tell me what happened so I can help your sister."

"Evie." Kyler's wide, shocked eyes focused on Adric. "They have Evie."

"Who?"

"A night fae and a wolf and another man. You have to help her."

"Do you know where they took her?"

The kid shook his head. "But you can track them, can't you?"

"Yes. Now come. You can wait in the living room—put some ice on that head." He rose to his feet and held out a hand.

Kyler looked at it for a few seconds and then took it.

"There you go." Adric placed an arm around the kid's bony shoulders and helped him into the hall.

Marjani stepped out of Sam's room to report that he was injured, but that Suha was on her way over with Beau. "They tore him up pretty bad, but he was able to use his quartz to stem the bleeding."

"Good."

Zuri called from Horace's room. "Ric? You'd better come here."

Adric jerked his head at Kyler. "Take the kid," he told Marjani. "His head got banged up, but nothing too much else that I can see. Get some ice on that head of his, will you?"

She nodded and helped Kyler down the hall as Adric strode toward Horace's room.

"That must hurt like a bitch," Adric heard her say.

"They've got my sister," Kyler returned.

Marjani expelled a breath. "We'll get her back. I promise."

Horace was unconscious, his face ashen, his body covered with multiple bite wounds and scratches. But what made Adric's stomach lurch was the wadded-up pillowcase Zuri had pressed to Horace's inside thigh over the femoral artery.

Zuri met Adric's eyes and shook his head.

"It's bad?"

"He's bleeding out."

Adric briefly closed his eyes. Not Horace, the guy who always had a smile, even in the worst of the Darktime. He hesitated, torn. The longer he waited to go after Jace and Evie, the harder it would be to track them, but he couldn't just leave Horace to die.

"They sliced him with a fucking iron knife," Zuri said grimly. "I can scent it."

A muscle jumped in Adric's jaw. "Salt water," he barked. "And hurry. I'll take over here."

He pressed the heel of his hand to the pillowcase over the wound, bearing down hard. When Zuri returned, he stopped the pressure so Zuri could thoroughly rinse the wound. The artery was spurting blood, but if they didn't neutralize the iron, Horace was going to die anyway.

When Zuri was done, Adric sent a pulse of energy into the wound to try and stop the bleeding, but the wound was too deep for him to heal. Suha was Horace's only hope. Thank the gods she lived close by.

Zuri was waiting with a clean pillowcase. He pressed it to Horace's thigh above the artery.

A minute ticked past, then another. Adric washed the blood off his hands and checked on Sam. When the burly redhead heard how bad Horace was injured, he tried to get out of bed.

"Stay." Adric pressed him back to the mattress. "There's nothing you can do, and we need you to focus on your own healing."

Sam muttered but subsided.

Adric left him to return to Horace's room. The cougar was still unconscious. His scent had taken on a distinctive iron scent, more like a human's than a fada. Adric sent another pulse of healing into him, but the iron resisted his attempts to close the wound.

Zuri ground his teeth. "Where in Hades is Suha?"

"It's only been five minutes," Adric said. But he was beginning to wonder, too. He scraped a hand over his hair. "I've got to go. You and Marjani hold down the fort."

"No fucking way. That's just what they want. I'll go."

"Then I'll have to outthink them." Because Adric was the best tracker in the clan and they both knew it.

But as he turned to leave, he heard Suha's low voice accompanied by Beau's deep rumble. A moment later the healer's light steps came rapidly down the hall, followed by Beau's heavier tread.

"What happened?" she asked as she removed her quartz from her neck.

"Iron poisoning," Adric replied. "The bastards made sure to hit an artery, too." The iron would spread through Horace's blood even faster. Even now, it might be reaching his heart and brain.

"You cleaned it out?"

"Yes, but it had at least fifteen minutes to spread through his bloodstream before we got here—maybe more."

Suha muttered something dark and held her quartz over Horace's thigh.

"I have to go," Adric said. "They have Evie and Jace."

"Okay," she said without taking her eyes from her patient. "I've got this."

Adric squeezed her shoulder. "I'm counting on you."

She snorted. "So what's new?" She blew out a breath. "I'll do my best, Ric, but you know how tricky iron poisoning is." She smoothed Horace's dreadlocks away from his face.

Adric nodded grimly—and then sprang into action. "You stay with Suha," he told Beau, who was staring down at Horace, jaw tight. "Zuri—you're with me."

In the living room, Kyler was on the couch holding an ice pack to his head, while Marjani was pacing restlessly to and fro. Her head snapped around as Adric entered.

"Tell me he's going to be all right."

"Suha's doing everything she can."

It was a non-answer and they both knew it. Marjani slapped her palm against the wall. A sudden, sharp sound that made Kyler jerk.

"What I want to know," she ground out, "is how the fuck they got past Jace's security?"

Kyler made a choked sound. "That was me."

Zuri had stopped to wash the blood off his hands. He entered the living room in time to hear Kyler. All three of them gaped at the young human.

"*What?*" asked Marjani.

"I'm so sorry. I didn't mean to, I swear I didn't. I couldn't stop myself. He—the night fae—made things so fucking bad." Kyler dropped the ice pack to press his fists into his stomach. "So dark. Nightmares—and the only way to stop it was to let him in." Shame reeked from him. "He said it would be all right if only I let him in—but it wasn't. He took Evie, and the earth fada took Jace."

Marjani's glare softened. "We'll find her. I promise."

He shot an accusing look at Adric. "You said we'd be safe here. But we weren't."

His stomach twisted. "You're right, and I'm sorry. All I can say is that I'll get your sister back."

Two young soldiers pounded down the stairs, Ryder and Jamila. Adric ordered them to lock the door after them. "No one else gets in without my say-so—got it? Zuri and Marjani, you're with me."

He squeezed Kyler's shoulder. "I have to go find Evie. Meanwhile, you're on duty with Ryder and Jamila. A soldier-in-training. Help them however you can. Okay?"

The kid swiped a stray tear from his cheek. "Yeah, of course."

Adric headed up the stairs, Zuri and Marjani at his heels. Behind him, he heard Kyler asking, "Is my sister going to be all right?" The heavy front door closed, cutting off the response.

"Don't." Marjani elbowed Adric as they reached the surface. "This isn't on you."

"Like hell it isn't. He's right—I'm alpha, and I promised they'd be safe."

"Doesn't mean you're responsible for every fuck-up in the clan. This is Corban's fault, not yours."

Adric rounded on her. "I'm the one who let the prick go last year—remember?"

His sister scowled back. "You did the best you could with the available evidence."

"Tell that to Evie and Kyler." He shook his head. "One thing I know—this time, Corban's gone too far. I finally have the proof I need to take him down."

Marjani's eyes met his in cool agreement.

"Not even his supporters can argue he wasn't behind this," Zuri added. "His scent is all the fuck over our den."

"Damn right." Adric bared his teeth. "Far as I'm concerned, Corban Savonett is dead." He strode toward his bike. "Evie first. It's what Jace would want."

He knew he was right, but by the gods, it wrecked him to say it—because if Corban had Jace, they had only a small window of time before his friend was dead.

31

*J*ace fought his way back to consciousness. He was in motion, being jolted around inside an enclosed space. He opened his eyes to find he was in the trunk of a car speeding down a pot-holed street. He braced his hands and feet against the inside of the trunk and tried to think.

His body was one big ache, but worse, there was a huge, echoing silence where his quartz should be. The bastards had taken it.

Hell. He couldn't even shift. Even if he were completely well, the shift would be slow and laborious without his quartz to draw on. But injured as he was, there was only a small chance he'd make it through.

And Tyrus had Evie. He'd been unable to open his eyes, but he'd been aware enough to realize Tyrus had taken her. Gods, he'd been guilty of a huge miscalculation. Trusting his defenses to keep the night fae out. But he'd never thought Tyrus would go for Evie instead of him.

At least Kyler was safe. He'd heard the bargain she'd made. A mama bear didn't have anything on Evie Morningstar. His chest clenched. *I should've told her I love her.*

He pushed that thought aside to take inventory. He had various assorted bruises and cuts from his fight with Corban, but the worst was the gash on his throat. When he touched it, his hand came away bloody.

Somewhere nearby, his quartz murmured. He also scented Kane, and to a lesser extent, Corban. So this was probably Kane's car, and Corban had Jace's quartz because there was no way he'd let his younger brother take charge of it.

The car stopped and he heard the brothers quarreling. "Why the hell would you sign a contract with a night fae?" Kane demanded.

"Tyrus wants Jones—and I want him gone. Adric has sunk every penny the clan has into the new smartphones. Take Jones out, and Adric's back to the beginning. It will prove once and for all that that I'm the stronger."

Jace shook his head. Corban would never understand that people didn't follow Adric just because he was strong. They followed him because he was a natural leader, one who always put the clan first. Not a weak prick who would use a night fae against his own people.

Kane growled. "You're going to get us both killed."

Hope sparked in Jace. So Kane wasn't a hundred percent in?

But Corban snarled and the younger man said, "It's your funeral," and shut up.

Car doors opened and slammed. Jace tensed, preparing to fight.

The trunk popped open and Corban stared down at him, Jace's quartz in his fist. It was the first good look Jace had had of him in over a year. He was leaner, his face lined with exhaustion as if the months away had been hard on him.

"Get out," he snarled. "We're taking you to your woman."

"My woman?" Jace froze in the act of launching himself at Corban.

"That human-fae mixed-blood—your scent is all over her.

Now get out." Corban squeezed Jace's quartz, and pain slammed through him as if Corban had reached into his chest to grab his heart.

Jace set his teeth and obeyed. There was no sense in resisting if it would get him to Evie, but he was weak from loss of blood. He only made it a few steps before he stumbled and dropped to one knee. His body wanted to stay folded in on itself, but he forced himself back upright. They were in a parking lot in Druid Hill Park. To the south he could see downtown Baltimore, the skyscrapers hazy in the simmering heat, the humidity already on the rise. On a nearby path, an early morning runner loped past, earbuds in place, oblivious to their tense little tableau—or pretending to be.

Evie was nowhere in sight. "Where is she?" Jace demanded.

"That way." Corban motioned at Kane, who started down the path after the runner.

Jace nodded and focused on putting one foot in front of the other. Corban fell in beside him.

Jace shot him a look. "Tell the night fae to let her go—she has nothing to do with this. You know what perverted bastards they are."

The wolf shrugged. "I have a contract."

"On me, yes. But what did she ever do to you?"

"Nothing, but Tyrus wants her. And he wants you gone because you're one more thing standing between him and Merry." Corban's lip curled. "And because he's a night fae, and if he can't get at Merry, he wants to make her suffer."

Jace stared at him, chilled despite the heat. It made sense. Tyrus couldn't kill Merry because of the ward, but he was a night fae. He'd enjoy making her suffer, and what better way than to kill off the people she loved? Which could mean that Valeria and the babies were in danger, too. He didn't count Rui—it would take a hell of a lot to take down the shark assassin.

Jace had to contact Rui, warn him his family might be a target.

He raised a hand to his quartz before he recalled that Corban had it. His fingers curled into his palm.

"*Move*." Corban gave Jace's quartz a warning squeeze.

Jace sucked in a breath and obeyed. The trek was less than a mile, but it seemed like hours, each step an agony, as if he were pushing through quicksand. The only thing that kept him going was a grim determination to reach Evie.

At last they stopped in a clearing. Jace scented both Evie and Tyrus. The wound on his throat was bleeding in earnest now. He licked dry lips and blinked woozily in the rising heat as Kane uncovered the entrance to an underground den.

Corban pushed Jace toward the ladder. "Down there."

"Jace?" Evie peered up at him, her eyes huge.

"Coming, angel." Jace started down the ladder, but his hands and feet felt like they belonged to some other man. His foot slipped off the rung and he tumbled the rest of the way down, banging his head against the side of the ladder before hitting the earth floor with a jarring thud.

He wavered for a moment and then crumpled to the ground.

The next thing he knew, Evie was running her hands over him, her breath coming in jagged sobs. He wanted to reassure her, but he couldn't speak or even open his eyes, his whole being focused on simply breathing.

"Oh, God." Evie patted his face. "Please don't be dead. Please don't be dead."

Behind his eyes, the darkness shifted. He slit his lids. Evie was crouched next to him, her scent filling his head and bringing a measure of calm. On the other side of the small space, Tyrus and Corban were speaking in undertones, and he could hear Kane on the surface pacing agitatedly back and forth near the entrance.

The cat peeled its lip. *Attack. Kill.* Claws scored Jace from the inside.

Not yet, he told it.

The jaguar subsided, tail twitching angrily. It hadn't given up, and Jace agreed. To save Evie, he'd shift even if it killed him, but first he needed more intel.

"Jace?" Cool fingers touched his cheek. "You okay?"

"Yeah." He moistened dry lips. "You?"

A jerky nod. "I'm fine. And you're going to be okay. Just hang on, got it?"

He forced his lids to open more fully. "Okay."

Evie's shoulders slumped in relief. She dragged off her T-shirt, leaving her clad only in a bra and pants, and dabbed at the blood on his throat and chest. Tyrus loomed behind her, watching them with avid eyes. Sick bastard.

Fresh blood welled from the wound on Jace's throat; the fall must have ripped it open even further. Evie wadded up the shirt and pressed it to the wound. "Heal yourself, damn you."

He pointed at his chest where his quartz should be. "Can't."

"They took it?" Evie twisted to glare up at Corban. Her eyes lit on the quartz and she lunged for it, but he jerked it away and backhanded her across the face. She stumbled and made a hurt sound that was like a blade to Jace's heart, but came right back up.

Jace grabbed her arm. "It's okay."

"No, it's not." She pressed a hand to her cheek and he realized she was holding the other hand to her stomach, favoring it. It was red and swollen.

Fury blazed through Jace. He shook with the need to take down both men. That they *dared* hurt his mate. But on its heels came a cold-eyed determination. He would bide his time, and wait for his chance—and then all three men would die.

"It's okay," he told Evie again and mouthed, "Trust me."

She removed her hand from her face and gave a short nod.

Corban turned back to Tyrus. "Give me the diamonds. I'm outta here."

The night fae's gaze raked over Jace. "He's damaged. I'll be fortunate if he lasts the day."

Evie snarled and Jace tightened his grip on her.

"Nothing in the contract said how long you get to play with him," returned Corban. "He's here, and my part is done. You've got his woman, anyway—that will make it even sweeter. Now, my payment?"

Tyrus tossed a small black pouch at Corban. He snatched it in mid-air and checked the contents. He frowned. "There's one extra." He removed a glittering stone from the bag and thrust it at Tyrus. "Don't play your fucking fae games with me. You'll pay what we agreed—no more and no less."

The night fae regarded him coolly. "Consider it an advance."

"For what?"

"I want you to lay down a false trail. I don't want your alpha finding us."

"Adric's not my fucking alpha."

"Pardon." Tyrus inclined his head mockingly. "Lay down a false trail for the Baltimore alpha. I'll leave at dusk—but I don't want to be disturbed before then. I don't care how you do it."

"Or," Corban returned with a smirk, "I could lead Adric here and let him drag you into the sunlight. How long would you last, I wonder?"

Tyrus struck. One moment he was eyeing Corban coldly, the next he had Corban up against the wall, a knife to his throat. Jace felt the dark hum of Tyrus's energy, sucking at Corban. The whole thing was done in a creepy silence.

"What the fuck?" Kane started down the ladder, but Tyrus bared his teeth at him, and the other man froze.

The night fae turned his gaze back to Corban. "Do we have a deal?"

Corban glared back, hate in his eyes, but growled an assent.

Tyrus released him and stepped back, but kept the knife out.

Corban shoved a few things into a backpack and headed for the ladder.

"You forgot something." The night fae held out a hand. "The quartz?"

Corban shrugged, and then to Jace's horror, tossed his quartz to Tyrus. The night fae's cold fingers wrapped around it, and Jace felt an answering chill clear to his soul. Terror touched him, black and stark. Anyone who held his quartz could hurt him—but a fae who knew the secret could *control* him. It was the earth fada's Achilles' heel, the price exacted by the fae who'd created them. Those fae had feared the water fada's independence and had ensured Jace's people would have both greater power, and a greater weakness.

"You fucking S.O.B." Jace struggled up on his forearms to glare at Corban. "You...give our secrets to a fae? This is the kind of alpha you'd be?"

Corban's jaw worked. "Shut the fuck up."

Kane was crouched at the surface, mouth slack with dismay. "Corban. Think about this, man. You'll have every earth fada in the world gunning for you."

Corban swung on him. "Only if they find out."

Kane shook his head. "I don't like this."

"You don't have to like it."

Kane's throat worked, but he nodded and backed away from the opening.

A shadow fell over Jace. Corban stared down at him, his face dark with loathing. "You're just like your sister. Bringing mixed-bloods into the clan."

"At least I didn't betray my alpha and sell secrets to a fae."

Corban's heavy black brows snapped together. "Make sure you kill him for good this time," he told Tyrus as he aimed a kick at Jace's stomach. "I swear the fucking cat has nine lives."

Evie threw herself forward to block the kick, but she was too late. It landed squarely on his still healing knife wounds. Jace grunted and fought to remain conscious as Corban swarmed up the ladder.

The rock dropped back over the entrance. He and Evie were alone with Tyrus.

---

32

*A*dric spent a precious few minutes tracking Tyrus. The night fae's noxious scent covered Evie's but he caught a hint of her as well.

"He's headed north," he told Marjani and Zuri.

The three of them jumped on the bikes, Marjani still behind Adric, and accelerated down the quiet street. He deliberately didn't call any backup. Any more men and they'd risk spooking Tyrus, and then they'd never find Evie. The same applied to Corban and Jace.

As alpha, Adric could use Jace's quartz to pinpoint his location to within a hundred yards. However, with the quartz removed, that ability was gone. Still, he had the sense the quartz —and possible Jace—were moving in the same general direction as Tyrus.

He refused to think about the fact that his friend had been bleeding right up until they'd apparently put him into a car. The only good thing was that if he was still leaving a trail of blood, Adric could follow the scent.

But Evie first.

"Faster," Marjani said in his ear. "If he takes her out of the city, we'll never find her."

He shook his head. "Sun's too high. He'll have to go to ground until tonight."

"You hope," his sister returned.

Zuri zoomed up beside them, and they wove through the early morning traffic, ignoring red lights and stop signs. The trail led into Druid Hill Park.

They pulled into the nearest parking lot. Zuri inhaled. "Jace is here, too."

Adric's heart leapt. Maybe when they found Evie, they'd find Jace, too. "He said something to me early this morning about Corban having a lair in the park. Let's spread out to search."

The three of them loped into the woods to shift. They needed their animals' heightened senses to track Evie and Jace.

Adric completed the shift first. He took off north without waiting for the other two, his Gift for tracking on hyperalert. It was like a sixth sense that let him know if he was on the right or wrong path, and it also sharpened his regular senses.

Behind him, he heard the other two finish their shifts and spread out to the east and west.

He crossed an asphalt path and scented the night fae. A few yards later, a drop of blood. *Jace.*

He changed back to man so he could alert Marjani and Zuri through his quartz, and then back again to his cougar to continue following the scent. When the trail left the path to go into the trees again, he overran it for few seconds, but his Gift soon alerted him.

Wrong.

He doubled back and met Marjani and Zuri arriving different directions. He jerked his head to the right and they all darted into the trees. Zuri had his nose to the ground, but Adric and Marjani were using their cougars' sharp vision as much as their noses.

They were on the right track. There were multiple signs that men had come through these woods, and recently: a broken twig, a partial shoeprint, a short blue thread caught on a wild rosebush's thorn.

He scented Jace's blood and a hint of sweat—the acrid odor of a man pushed to his limits.

Where the fuck are you?

He drew on his quartz and frowned. The connection he had to Jace's quartz was fainter, as if a barrier had been thrown up between the two of them. Then the connection broke.

Adric's heart punched. *Damn you, you're not dead. You're not.*

He halted. His cougar couldn't communicate in words, but he yowled a warning: *Danger.*

The scent trails split, with Tyrus's going in one direction and Corban, Kane and Jace's going in the other. Adric didn't hesitate —the important thing was to find Tyrus, and hopefully, Evie. He loped after Tyrus.

Something was balled up on the ground. Adric's breath caught, but it was just a bloody T-shirt covered with Jace's scent. When he investigated more closely, he realized it wasn't even Jace's T-shirt.

He snarled. Corban was messing with him—trying to confuse the trail.

But that didn't mean Jace wasn't close. Adric slowed down, slipping from tree to tree, eyes peeled and ears pricked.

The woods went silent. The fur on his nape bristled. Zuri and Marjani sidled up to stand on either side of him.

A black wolf burst out of the trees. Corban.

Go! Adric hissed at the other two. He could hold off Corban while they rescued Jace and Evie.

Marjani tore off. Zuri hesitated, torn between obeying his alpha and protecting him.

Adric had never demanded unquestioning obedience from his lieutenants—he wanted men who could think for themselves

—but now he put all the force of his dominance behind his growl. "*Go—now.*"

Even then, Zuri might have stayed, but protect the vulnerable had been their creed since they were cubs, and Jace and Evie needed him more than Adric did. He turned and sprinted after Marjani.

Adric planted his paws and snarled at his cousin. *Bring it on.*

And then Kane slunk out of the shadows.

33

———

*E*vie crouched over Jace, instinctively trying to protect him as the tall, hard-eyed shifter—Corban—closed them into the darkness with Tyrus again.

Jace groaned. She ran her hands over him, furious tears pricking her eyes. What kind of coward kicked a man when he was down?

And what did Tyrus mean, Jace might not last the day? Icy shards pierced her chest.

No fucking way. She was *not* going to let Jace die.

She squeezed his hand. "You're going to be all right—I promise."

He muttered something unintelligible.

"Jace? Can you hear me?"

This time he didn't even answer. Her fear spiked.

To her left, Tyrus rustled and she guessed he was sitting down. All she could see were his eyes, a strange blue-black glow in the gloom. Better than that terrifying red, but not much.

Gradually, her eyes grew accustomed to the dark and she could make out Tyrus's outline. He'd settled onto his coat, his back against the wall. Jace's quartz was suspended from his fingers, a weak green light at its heart.

If Jace had his quartz, he could heal himself. She had to get it back.

Black tendrils teased at her arms and face, but Tyrus seemed tired. The sun was fully up now—this must be when he slept. She slapped at them, but her hands went right through them. Then the tendrils brushed over her breasts.

Oh, no. Hell, no.

She sat on the floor with a thump and crossed her arms over her chest. "No sex," she rasped. "That's not part of the deal."

"No? Not even if I tell you I can heal the fada?"

"What do you mean?"

"I'm a healer in my clan."

Her mouth dropped open. "You're kidding."

"A fae can't lie, Evie." A cold smile curled his mouth. "Of course, a healer knows precisely the right places to cause pain, too."

The tendrils snaked past her. Jace jerked and then whined, the sound of a hurt animal.

Evie's heart clenched. "Stop it!" She lunged at Tyrus, only to realize too that that was what he'd wanted.

Strong hands clamped on her arms, forcing her to her knees between Tyrus's thighs. She tried to strike at him, but he simply tightened his grip.

Her fingers curled helplessly at her sides, but she raised her chin and snapped, "Get your fucking hands off me."

He trailed cool fingers down her throat, teasing her breasts above the bra. She shuddered and jerked back.

"Should I hurt him again?" A soft, malevolent murmur.

She briefly closed her eyes—and surrendered. "You heal him first," she gritted. "Or I'll—I'll—" She stuttered to a halt, because she hadn't a clue of what to threaten him with.

"Or you'll what?" Tyrus nuzzled her ear. "Fight me, Evie."

Her spine went rigid. *Run*, her brain screamed, but he had her trapped.

The darkness latched onto her like a many-armed octopus. Sucking at her...feeding on the fear and anger, and it *hurt*. Like no pain in the world. Icy-hot agony that slithered over her skin, drank from her soul, caressed her most secret parts—rape without the physical act.

"Fight me." A dark breath against her throat.

She bared her teeth at him and he chuckled. She shouldn't fight him, she knew she shouldn't, but she couldn't help it. It was instinct, a trapped butterfly battering its wings against the glass.

Her hands came to Tyrus's chest. She dug her nails into him through the silky material of his shirt and his head dropped back, eyes slit with enjoyment.

Her stomach bottomed out. Whatever she did, she was fucked. Hopelessness swamped her. Her only consolation was that he'd forgotten Jace to focus on her.

Block him.

But she couldn't. It wasn't like in the kitchen when she'd had Kyler to help her, and Jace had been intermittently shielding them as well. This time Tyrus was totally focused on her, and he was strong, relentless. All she could do was endure.

He fed on her for what felt like an eternity but was probably only a few minutes, and then released her. He sat back, replete.

She slumped on the dirt floor, breath scraping in and out of her lungs.

A bone-chilling growl filled the small space. "Let. Her. Go."

She lifted her head to see Jace's eyes glowing green with fury. He was struggling to sit up.

"It's okay," she whispered.

He didn't seem to hear her. The growls continued, his cat pushed to its limit.

Evie forced herself to crawl the few feet to him. She felt old, wrung out, each movement of her arms and legs an effort. The whole time, she felt Tyrus's gaze on her, but he said nothing.

When she reached Jace, she set her cheek against his, still on her hands and knees. Her breath shuddered out. She was shaking, her fingers and toes like ice. She inhaled and tried to calm herself.

"Don't try to get up—please. It's okay."

His gaze swung to her. His jaguar stared out of his eyes. She touched his face. "I'm okay."

His head tilted and he rubbed his cheek over hers, catlike. The prickles of his night-beard were comforting—a welcome antidote to the smooth, cold tentacles.

"Come. Here." Guttural tones that she had to strain to understand.

She lay next to him, careful not to jar his injuries. He slid an arm under her, and she nestled her head into his shoulder. Seeking safety, even though she knew it was just an illusion. Tyrus wasn't going to let them go.

Gradually, she grew warmer and she realized how cold Tyrus had left her. Her shivers ceased, and she sensed Jace calming.

When he spoke again, his voice was that of a human. "Kyler?"

"Back at your den. I made Tyrus leave him behind."

He exhaled. "Thank the gods."

She nodded, although she wasn't sure how much control Tyrus had over the black wolf, who must've been Corban. And on top of that, Tyrus had fed on Kyler, too. She swallowed and burrowed closer to Jace.

Kyler's okay. He has *to be.* If they got out of this alive, she'd never bitch at him again.

Jace set his mouth to her ear. "Hang on," he said in a faint voice, each word clearly an effort. "I got word...to Adric before... they took us. He'll come...save you. And I'll keep that...prick away from you...until then."

"*No,*" she returned in an urgent, equally low tone. "Don't try anything. He can't hurt me. Not really." Not like Jace, who was rapidly growing weaker. She knew he had to be hurt bad—he hadn't even been able to get off the floor to help her when Tyrus was feeding on her.

Jace's only reply was a grunt.

She drew in a breath. "I can get your quartz."

"No." His grip on her tightened. "I don't want you...anywhere near...him."

She didn't reply, but she'd made up her mind. Jace needed his quartz to heal himself. They couldn't count on Adric finding them in time.

Tyrus shifted position. She sat back up so she could keep an eye on him, but Tyrus was only settling back against the wall. Why the hell didn't he go to sleep? But he seemed wide awake, although relaxed, sated from his meal.

Tyrus spoke. "You and the fada—you love him?" He sounded curious, but she didn't trust his reasons for asking—and she was damned if she'd tell him before she'd told Jace himself.

She moved a shoulder. "I haven't known him that long."

Jace tugged on her hand. When she leaned closer, he murmured, "I love *you*," the words a warm tickle in her ear.

She blinked. Heat crept into her chest, chasing away the last of the chill. "I—" She halted and shook her head.

"You feel it." Jace brought her hand to his heart. "My mate," he mouthed.

"You're telling me this now?" she whispered back.

He gave her a crooked grin. "Didn't know myself...until a few hours ago." He sobered. "Wanted you to know...in case..."

She shot a glance at Tyrus, but he was holding Jace's quartz by the cord and examining it.

"You are *not* going to die," she told Jace.

He pressed a kiss to her hand and then released it. He opened his mouth and tried to speak, but couldn't.

She squeezed his fingers. "You're not going to die. I won't let you."

"Mate bond," he said at last. "Not complete. But might help. The two of us...together...stronger."

She nodded. She did feel calmer, and she could swear there was a fine thread connecting her to Jace. Her heart filled with wonder. Could this be the mate bond? She touched a hand to her sternum, right where she felt the connection, and Jace nodded as if he'd heard her question.

Tyrus closed his fingers around Jace's quartz. He touched it to the hollow of his throat and muttered something in a language Evie didn't recognize. "Sit up."

His dark eyes focused on Jace—and Jace jerked upright. He snarled, and Tyrus said, "Quiet," and Jace's mouth clamped shut as if a switch had been flipped.

Evie started. *What the fuck?*

Tyrus's mouth curved. "The possibilities are so interesting. I could order you to do anything. Kill that niece of yours, even."

Fine hairs raised all along Evie's spine. "You wouldn't."

Jace's throat worked. His expression was murderous, but whatever Tyrus was using to control him wouldn't allow him to speak.

"No?" the night fae said. "I can't kill her myself—she's protected by a ward. Anyone who touches her dies himself. But if Jones does it for me..." Tyrus released the quartz and let it swing from his fingers.

Whatever had been holding Jace upright released. He flopped forward like a marionette with its strings cut, but came right back up with a snarl. He lurched at Tyrus, but the night fae touched the quartz to his throat again.

"Stay where you are."

Evie had worked out what Tyrus meant. Her stomach dropped. "He would die, too."

"Exactly. It would kill two birds with one stone, yes?"

Jace strained against the invisible bonds, the cords of his neck quivering with tension. But it was no use, and he was dangerously weak. All too soon his shoulders slumped. He sent Evie an anguished look and leaned back against the wall.

Evie took his hand and racked her brain for ideas. But she kept circling back to the one sure thing: *Steal back Jace's quartz.*

Tyrus's eyes drifted shut, but she'd bet her last dollar he wasn't sleeping. Still, if they were going to fight back, it had to be now, before the night came again. Daytime was when a night fae was weakest.

Beside her, she sensed Jace gathering his energy. She felt that spark of amazement again. So this was the mate bond? This deep *knowing* of another person? Even as faint and new as the bond was between them, she felt connected to him in a way she never had to any man.

Then her heart sank. Jace was going to attack, weak as he was—and even though he believed he couldn't win. She could *feel* his uncertainty—and his determination.

She gripped his hand. "Not yet," she whispered.

"Can't." He subsided, his expression bleak. "Can't...shift."

"That's bad, right?"

He grimaced in assent.

She glanced at Tyrus. How the hell was she going to steal back the quartz? If only she had a weapon... But even if she did, she wasn't sure she could hurt Tyrus. He moved so freaking fast—and he was fae, practically unkillable.

Jace had gone silent again, his breath coming in shallow pants. Then his lips moved. "I'm sorry," he said in a nearly inaudible voice. "For dragging you...and Kyler into this. If I hadn't...come to your door...Tyrus would never have..." He trailed off.

"Stop it," she hissed back. "This is *not* your fault."

His throat worked. "Shouldn't have...brought you to Balti-more. But seemed...like the right thing to do."

"Oh, Jace. Don't do this to yourself—I agreed to come, didn't I? They would've gotten to us even easier if we stayed in Grace Harbor."

His eyes flicked to Tyrus, his expression stark. "But when I make a mistake, people die."

Her heart contracted. She knew he was thinking of his sister. "No one's going to die," she said fiercely. "Now stop talking. Rest."

His lips quirked. "And think happy thoughts, right?"

Her cheeks heated. "You heard that?"

"Yeah."

"It worked, didn't it?"

"You." He reached for her hand and brought it to his chest. "I'm thinking about you. You make me happy."

Emotion welled up in her. She brushed a kiss over his lips, too full to speak, and then settled next to him, cross-legged, a hand on his thigh. "Rest. I'll watch Tyrus."

He nodded and shut his eyes.

Silence fell. Tyrus's eyes had closed and his breathing changed. She was almost sure he'd fallen asleep. He'd set Jace's quartz on the coat beside him. The fae were so arrogant and sure of their superiority, it probably didn't even occur to him that Evie might try to steal it back.

She rubbed her palms over her upper arms. When Jace had sat up, the T-shirt she'd pressed to his throat had fallen to the floor. When she'd kissed him just now, her hand had touched the wadded-up material. The shirt was soaked with blood.

There was no more time. Jace needed his quartz—now.

She forced herself to wait another five minutes to allow Tyrus to fall more deeply asleep. That was when she realized something was digging into her ass.

She slipped a hand into her left pocket and caught her breath. A fae light had somehow shrunk to the size of a marble and hitched a ride. She rolled it between her fingers. It was soft and warm, and made her hand tingle. Nice, but probably not any help.

She left the tiny light hidden in her pocket. No point in letting Tyrus know about it. And knowing it was there comforted her, made the dark seem less threatening.

Let's go, Evie. She crept across the floor. If Tyrus woke up, she'd say she was getting a drink of water. It wasn't a lie; she was dry-mouthed with fear.

The quartz had stopped glowing. She brushed her hand over the dirt where she'd last seen it, keeping a chary eye on Tyrus.

When she couldn't find it, she inched closer. Tyrus's darkness reached out for her, but a quick glance told her he was still asleep. Heart in her throat, she scrabbled around in the dirt until her fingers touched a smooth, oblong shape. She snatched up the quartz and slipped it into her bra before rising to her feet and continuing to the sink. She gripped the edge, waiting for her galloping heart to settle.

Behind her, Tyrus stirred. She shot him a look. His eyes gleamed at her in the darkness but he didn't say anything. Hands shaking, she took a metal cup from a hook and filled it with water. She drank deeply, then refilled the cup and returned to Jace, aware of Tyrus's gaze on her the whole time.

Kneeling next to him, she slid an arm under his shoulders and lifted him so he could drink. He drank greedily and she realized with a pang that she should've gotten him water sooner. He'd lost so much blood.

But at least she'd retrieved his quartz. She turned her body so that Tyrus couldn't see and slipped it into his palm.

Jace stilled, and then his fingers closed on it.

Her neck crawled. Tyrus was still watching her. Any minute he'd figured out she'd stolen back the quartz. "Hurry," she whispered to Jace.

His chin moved in a slight nod. He didn't move or show in any way that he was drawing on the quartz, but she saw the glow brighten between his fingers. She set her hand over his to cover it.

A minute passed, then another. When she flicked a glance at Tyrus, his eyes were closed again.

Jace's breath altered. It was deeper, more powerful. He nudged her hip. "Help me," he mouthed.

Of course. She mentally smacked her forehead. She was an amplifier; she could help Jace heal himself.

Tyrus might have weakened her, but nobody got the best of Evie Morningstar. She set her hand on Jace's stomach and focused with everything she had.

34

Jace hurt in every bone of his body. But that was nothing to the pain and fury he felt when the night fae went for Evie, and he was too fucking weak to help her.

He ached to get her out of here. If he thought it would do any good, he'd humble himself, plead with Tyrus to let her go. But he knew Tyrus would refuse. It must be a rare treat for the prick to be able to feed on another fae's energy, even a part-human like Evie.

At least Jace had had the chance to tell her he loved her, that she was his mate. The bond had sprung into being. He had to believe that was a good thing, that together, they were stronger than either was alone.

Evie moaned, and Jace cursed Tyrus, dark and vicious. The wound on his neck spurted blood, and he blacked out. He came back to consciousness to find he was trying to sit up, attempting to get to Evie.

Another harrowing minute ticked past before the night fae released her. She crawled back to Jace and huddled next to him, her body trembling.

He might have gone for Tyrus anyway but the fucking fae had his quartz. The pendant wasn't alive. It didn't know it was being used to control Jace. It just called mindlessly to him and he was forced to obey.

Fury condensed in Jace, cold and grim. Tyrus's plotting made sense now, but he'd miscalculated one thing.

Jace would never harm Merry. He'd kill himself first.

But first, he had to save Evie. He tucked her close to his body, comforting her the only way he could. Tyrus dozed off and Jace forced himself to relax and conserve his energy. He must have drifted off again, because he didn't realize Evie had left his side until she was lifting his head, urging him to drink.

He eagerly gulped the water. It was cool and good, soothing his parched throat. "Thank you," he rasped.

Then she slipped the quartz into his hand. He went rigid with shock—and admiration. How the hell had she managed to steal it back?

Hope surged. Maybe they had a chance after all.

He gripped the quartz and drew on its energy with everything he had. The crystals' song was high-pitched, agitated. Drawing on the quartz so hard was dicey—he risked blowing it out— but he had no choice.

The first thing he did was close the wound on his throat. Replacing the blood loss would take hours, but he could stem the flow. Next, he pushed energy into his body—a quick-and-dirty fix. It would take the place of the blood he'd lost, but only for a short time. But he only needed a few minutes to take Tyrus down.

And he *would* take Tyrus down. Failure wasn't an option.

Sweat beaded on Jace's temples. He drew harder—and hit a brick wall. He hated to ask Evie for help—she was already drained from Tyrus—but he might only have a few minutes. Night fae usually slept in the day, but Tyrus was running high from feeding on them.

"Help me," he whispered, and Evie gamely added her own energy to his. Pride filled him. His mate had a spine of pure steel.

Tyrus started awake. His eyes gleamed red in the darkness. "You stole from me." His tone was surprised—and cold as only a fae's could be.

Jace swore under his breath. "That's enough," he told Evie. It would have to be.

"You're...okay?" She collapsed onto the floor without waiting for an answer, her chest working.

Jace's heart lurched. He lifted her onto his lap. "I love you," he said. "So fucking much." Her mouth curved but she didn't speak. He rubbed her back, terrified that between him and Tyrus, they'd drained her too deeply.

But Tyrus didn't care.

Dark energy slipped over the two of them. Soft at first, like the damp brush of fog, then they were enveloped in chilly tendrils. Jace burned with guilt and shame.

He'd failed his sister.

He'd failed Merry.

And now he was going to fail Evie.

The tendrils multiplied like a ball of squirming maggots, enveloping Jace in a slimy darkness. He had the urge to flail at them wildly, but that would only play into Tyrus's hands. The more negative energy Jace put out, the more Tyrus had to feed on.

Evie wrapped her arms around his waist. "We can beat him," she whispered fiercely against his neck. "Happy thoughts, right?"

He buried his face in her hair. He didn't know about happy thoughts, but he knew one thing—this woman was his heart. Warmth flared in his chest. He brought her hand to his mouth and kissed the palm.

A trembling smile bloomed on her lips. She curled her fingers as if capturing his kiss for safe-keeping. "Love you."

Their eyes met. The blackness receded, but hovered nearby. Testing for weaknesses.

Jace gathered himself for a fight.

The tendrils returned, insidious, relentless. This time they burrowed deeper, sucking at their energy. Evie shuddered and Jace snapped.

Enough.

"Run if you can," he told her and set her on the floor behind him.

"No," she said, but he was focused on Tyrus now.

He crouched on all fours, man and jaguar united. "You fucking S.O.B. Can't you see it's too much for her? Feed on me, damn you."

Tyrus's eyes bored into him. Icy claws of dread clamped on his nape, but he ignored it to prowl closer.

Something black and sharp bored into his heart. Tyrus was feeding in earnest now, but a feeding night fae did nothing to relieve the pain. Instead, he somehow made it double and then redouble, so that Jace was lashed with regret: so many people dead...so many ways he'd fucked up, let down those he loved.

"*No.*" He hunched his shoulders as if the lash were a physical whip, and grimly bore it.

Beside him, Evie swallowed audibly. "Jace..."

She was curled up on the floor, gasping for breath. Tyrus hadn't let up on her. She was being sucked into the darkness with him.

Fuck that.

His growl was low and primal. He had enough energy now to shift. One chance to save Evie. He'd have to make it count.

The cat was a hundred percent with him. *Kill. Save the female.*

Jace dropped the quartz pendant over his neck and set his mouth. The shift was agony. His skin burned, and his bones popped and cracked, twisted beyond their capacity. An involuntary groan tore from his lips.

"*Jace.*" Behind him, Evie gasped and pushed herself up on her hands and knees. "What are you doing?"

He ignored her to focus on drawing enough energy to fuel the shift. Lights exploded behind his eyes. A fireball of pain scorched through him until it was all he could do not to scream.

He folded his fingers around his quartz and squeezed, sucking every bit of energy he could. *Now.* He wrenched his form from man to cat—and then collapsed on the ground, weak as a kitten.

Evie sobbed out his name. "Jace."

He pushed himself to stand on wobbly legs, and snarled at the night fae.

Tyrus stalked toward him—and Jace struck.

A jaguar's bite was twice as strong as a lion's. He could kill an animal by sinking his teeth into its skull. Jace went for Tyrus's spinal cord, determined to end this.

But the night fae was incredibly fast. In the blink of an eye, he was on the other side of the small room. Still, Jace had him on the run. The dark feeding stopped as the other man focused on surviving.

Evie scuttled into a corner, smart enough to get out of the way. Something glowed in her hand—a fae light. She held it up, casting a light over their battle.

Tyrus raised a hand and muttered a phrase in an ancient fae language. The air gathered into a sharp point and flew at Jace. It would've taken out his eye if he hadn't flung himself to the side, but instead, it sliced open his cheek.

He leapt for Tyrus and again, the fae evaded him. Jace's jaguar rumbled angrily. They circled each other, breathing hard.

Tyrus raised his hand and muttered another spell. This time, the air formed itself into a rope that wrapped around Jace's throat like a noose. He clawed furiously at it, but it was some magical material that repelled his attempts to dislodge it. The noose tightened. His vision darkened at the edges. He made one last, desperate attempt to sink his teeth into Tyrus but the other man easily pushed him off.

"No!" Evie dashed between them, the fae light in her hand, and shoved it into Tyrus's face.

The room seemed to explode. Tyrus's body lit up with an eerie blue fire that danced up and down his limbs, burning through his clothes. The scent of scorched flesh filled the air. He shrieked and stumbled backward.

Jace blinked, temporarily blinded, but he could hear Tyrus moaning to his left. He growled and moved toward him, the cat in ascendance. The fae was slumped against the wall, hands to his face.

Jace pounced, slapping his paws on Tyrus's chest and ripping open his throat. The sickening taste of metal and decay filled his mouth. He gave Tyrus a hard shake, and the body flopped lifelessly in his grip. He let Tyrus fall to the dirt floor and stood over him, still partially blinded. He was quiet, but was he dead? He cocked an ear and heard the faint beating of the fae's black heart.

Evie was moaning. "Ohmigod. Ohmigod."

The rock over the entrance shifted, and shadows moved down the ladder. Jace growled, still unable to see clearly, until he recognized the scents as Marjani and Zuri.

Tyrus's breath rattled in.

"He's not dead," Evie breathed. "Oh, God."

Jace's vision cleared enough to see Marjani thrust an iron blade beneath Tyrus's rib cage. A single expert stab to the heart, one of the only sure ways to kill a fae.

Tyrus grunted and then went limp.

"Now he is," Marjani said.

35

Adric ignored Kane to focus on Corban. He and his oldest cousin were evenly matched, his cougar as large as Corban's wolf. He'd beat Corban once before in a fair fight—the duel for alpha, with the clan's lieutenants and top soldiers as witnesses.

This time, it wouldn't be fair, and his animal was coldly pleased. Fuck the rules. Corban needed to die.

Adric crouched low, ears back, and bared his teeth. Kane circled uneasily, his gaze darting between Corban and Adric.

Adric's tail twitched. *Traitor.*

Kane's eyes cut to his brother. Corban growled, and Kane whined. Then he made up his mind and ranged himself next to Corban.

So be it. Adric would take them both on.

Corban's muscles bunched, preparing to attack. Adric struck first, darting in and sinking his teeth into Corban's ruff. The wolf's blood filled his mouth, hot and salty.

Corban shook him off and snapped at Adric's leg. Adric danced away. Kane sidled closer for a sneak attack, and Adric snapped, tearing a gash in Kane's muzzle.

The battle started in earnest then. The two wolves came at Adric from either side, but he twisted and leapt straight up, and they crashed into each other.

He came down and ripped into the nearest nape with his teeth. It was Kane. He gripped his vertebrae and gave him a vicious shake. There was the sound of snapping bones, and the wolf grunted and went limp, his head at an odd angle.

Regret twanged through Adric. He'd grown up with Kane, the other shifter just two years older than him. But there was no time to mourn.

He released him and turned toward Corban, but the bastard had run, leaving his brother to distract Adric while he escaped. Corban was already disappearing into the trees.

Adric shot after him, but the wolf had a good head start, and Adric was bleeding from wounds he hadn't known he had.

His cougar's blood was up. It urged him to give chase, but the man knew it could be a trap. And even if it wasn't, Corban was leading him out of the park and away from Evie and Jace. He slowed, but his cousin did, too. Then the air around Corban shimmered and twisted.

Adric halted and watched from a safe distance as the wolf disappeared. A fae had 'ported the bastard out.

Adric let out a furious snarl. And he scented silver, not a night fae's unpleasant scent, which was one more layer of mysterious to this whole hellacious business.

He shifted to man and started limping back toward Kane. The wolves must have chomped on his leg, too. He had to pause a minute to pulse some healing energy into it. He couldn't afford to be at less than full strength.

That done, he contacted Beau, bringing him up to speed with a few terse sentences. "Put out a call to the nearest soldiers," he finished. "Corban's gone rogue. Their orders are to kill him on sight."

"If he's still in Baltimore," the bear replied. "A powerful fae could 'port him anywhere in the world."

"I know." Adric gripped his quartz and willed his pounding anger to subside. "Meanwhile, get a healer to Druid Hill Park ASAP. Jace is hurt and Kane is dying."

"Evie?"

Adric expelled a breath. "I don't know, but I'm hoping she's with Jace."

"I'll tell Kyler."

Adric gave Beau his current coordinates and returned to where Kane lay on the ground, breathing shallowly. Adric knelt beside him. "Shift." It was his cousin's only chance at healing.

Kane closed his eyes and changed to his man. He remained motionless, his head at that odd angle, his narrow face ashen. His lips twisted. "Can't feel...my legs or arms."

"Fuck." Adric sat back on his heels, his chest tight with a mixture of pity and anger.

Kane moistened his lips. "Sorry...I—he's my brother."

"Fuck that. I'm alpha. You swore an oath to me." *And we were family.*

Kane's gaze slid from his. "I know." To break an oath was a terrible thing. It must have torn his cousin up inside. Probably he hadn't even used his full strength against Adric—his wolf wouldn't have allowed it.

Kane's eyes closed, his only movement the shallow rise and fall of his chest.

Adric glanced around. "Where in Hades is that healer?" But he knew it was already too late.

His cousin did too. "There's something...you should know. Our dad...Leron...he let the night fae in. The Darktime."

"*What?*"

"He knew...he couldn't win alpha...in a fair fight. So he invited the night fae. They were happy...to feed on our misery. To make it worse."

"God's balls." Adric scraped his hands over his face. But it made sense; he'd seen it himself. Too often, the night fae had been conveniently near at the clan's worst moments, ready to feed off their anger and despair.

Blackness filled his head. The guilt of assassinating his own uncle was a weight he carried with him. Always. But at that moment, he would've gladly stuck a knife into Leron's black heart all over again. So many men and women dead or hurt to feed that prick's ambition...and the young, innocents who'd never even had a chance to live.

And now he'd killed his own cousin.

Tipping back his head, he let out an anguished growl that iced the blood of every animal within hearing range.

Kane's mouth quirked in an ironic smile. "You're better... alpha. Leron would...have hated that." His breath sighed out and his eyes blanked.

"Damn you," Adric bit out. But he closed his cousin's eyes before rising to his feet. Then he called Beau, telling him to send a couple of soldiers to remove Kane's body from the park before some human stumbled upon him.

The chase through the park had led him close to where they'd left their clothes. He dressed and grabbed Marjani and Zuri's clothes as well and started off at a trot to Zuri's coordinates.

It was only then that he realized he could no longer sense Jace's quartz.

EVIE'S STOMACH ROILED. She pressed a hand to her mouth and tried not to lose her supper on the dirt floor. She was not some girly-girl, damn it. She didn't fall apart at the sight of blood. But she could smell Tyrus's scorched flesh, and he was sprawled like a broken doll just ten feet away.

She wrapped her arms around herself. Jace paced toward her,

his mouth stained with blood. She shrank against the wall. His stride checked and she *felt* his hurt.

Her heart constricted. She unpeeled her fingers from where they were digging into her upper arms. "I'm sorry." She stretched out her hands to him. "It's okay. I know you had to do it." She was babbling. She clamped her mouth shut.

He remained where he was and her stomach sank. Sparkles danced over his fur and she realized he was trying to shift. The sparkles brightened, and then dimmed, and she realized he was having trouble.

"No," she whispered, knowing he was forcing the shift for her. "Don't…"

But then the bits of colors intensified and cascaded over his body. She squeezed her eyes shut against the brightness, and when she opened them again, he was a man and the blood was gone.

"Evie?" He opened his arms to her, eyes wary. Powerful, naked, and *hers*.

She stepped forward and his face lightened. They met in the middle, hugging and kissing each other. Jace framed her face in his hands. "You're all right?" He kissed her eyes, her mouth, ran his hands over her back.

"Yes, yes. But what about you?" She pulled back to examine his throat and chest. His original wounds had closed up, but there was a bloody slice across his cheek and he had a nasty rope burn around his neck. She touched it with her fingertips and felt all over again the icy fear that had gripped her as Jace had struggled against the magical noose. "I thought you were going to die."

"Cat, remember?" He shrugged a big shoulder. "Nine lives, although I may be down to four or five at this point."

She made a sound that was half-laugh, half-sob. "Oh, God." She laid her head against his chest, and for a long moment, they just held each other, forgetting everyone and everything else. His heart thumped loudly against her cheek and she realized he was as affected as her.

"What the fuck did you do with that fae light, anyway?" he asked.

"I don't know. I just wanted to distract him." She was shaking. He squeezed her tight.

The cellar was filling with people—Marjani, Zuri, and a couple shifters Evie didn't know.

"A healer's on the way," Zuri told Jace. "Can you get to the surface?"

Jace nodded and guided Evie to the ladder. She stared at it, not sure her legs could carry her to the top. The adrenaline that had fueled her desperate attempt to save Jace had dissipated, leaving her feeling like a wrung-out dishcloth.

Jace swung her into his arms. "Hang on, angel."

"Y-you c-can't!" she protested through chattering teeth, but he stopped her mouth with a kiss and carried her one-handed up the ladder while she clung to his neck.

A lean blond man lifted her from Jace's arms and set her on the ground beneath a large oak. Jace sank down beside her, his back against the oak.

"I'm Tommy," the blond said. "A healer."

She nodded. "Evie."

"Good to meet you. I've been hearing all sorts of good things about you and Jace." While he talked, he ran his quartz over Evie. He frowned. "You're dangerously weak."

"The night fae fed on her," said Jace, "and then I took more energy to heal myself. It was the only way."

"I'm fine," she said between chattering teeth. "Jace is...the one...who's hurt."

Jace shook his head. "Evie first."

"You're outvoted," Tommy told her. He gently pressed her shoulder, encouraging her to lean against the oak trunk next to

Jace. "You won't feel yourself for a few days," he said as he set his quartz over her heart, "but I can give you an energy boost."

She nodded and gave in, letting her eyes drift shut as her chest warmed with a healing glow that spread throughout her body. She soaked it up like rain on parched earth.

Tommy moved the quartz to her bruised left hand. She'd almost forgotten it in all the excitement, but now that the adrenaline was fading, it hurt like a bitch. But within a few minutes, the bruises disappeared.

"That should do it." Tommy smiled at her. "But take it easy for the next few days."

She tentatively moved her fingers, amazed to find it barely hurt. "I will," she replied, "and thank you."

He nodded and turned to Jace.

Evie rested her head against the trunk and watched, tired to her very toes. She was aware of people coming and going, and intense, low-voiced conversations, but it seemed to be happening far away.

Adric appeared and dragged off his own T-shirt so that she had something covering her. He'd been in a fight himself—his face and chest had been clawed—but his wounds were already closing up. He crouched next to her, bronze eyes concerned. "You okay, love?"

She nodded jerkily. "Kyler? He's...all right?"

"Yeah. A little shook up, but he's fine. Suha and Beau are with him, along with two soldiers."

Relief flooded her. "Thank you," she rasped.

He squeezed her shoulder. "No thanks necessary. I'm just sorry the two of you got caught up in this."

"At least it's over."

"I hope so," the alpha muttered.

Jace roused himself enough to ask about Corban and Kane.

Adric shook his head. "Kane's dead. Corban took off like the rat he is—left his own brother to take the fall."

"No surprise there," Jace said.

"We'll get him," Adric returned grimly. "He's a dead man." He lifted a brow at Evie. "That was you who took Tyrus out with a fae ball?"

"I guess." As if sensing their interest, the fae light wafted onto her lap and glowed a little more brightly. She stroked it, not sure herself exactly what had happened. "I don't know anything about a fae ball—I just used this light. He—the night fae—was hurting Jace. He was fighting with magic, strangling Jace with some kind of magical rope."

She swallowed, recalling her horror as Jace had clawed desperately at his neck, unable to stop the rope from constricting. "I couldn't just stand by and do nothing. I thought about how night fae can be burned by the sun, and—" She spread her hands. "I only wanted to distract him. I never thought it would set him on fire."

Jace's mouth curved. "She was fucking awesome."

Adric squeezed her shoulder again. "Whatever you did, good work." He turned to answer a question from one of his soldiers, and Tommy sat back.

"That should get you home," he told Jace. "But both of you need rest. Go back to your den and stay in bed the rest of the day. Healer's orders."

Jace stood up and gave a bone-cracking stretch. "Sounds like a plan." He bent down and before Evie knew what he was doing, swung her into his arms. To Adric he said, "She's had enough. You have any more questions, you can ask them later."

The alpha inclined his head.

"I can walk," she said, but Jace fixed her with a glare.

"Let me take care of you, okay?"

Evie blinked. She couldn't recall any man ever saying those words to her. She opened her mouth to argue—she could take care of herself, damn it. But although Jace's expression was stern, she saw the worry way back in his eyes.

"Okay," she said and rested her head against his shoulder. Because she *was* a little shaky, and if it made him happy, why not?

Jace headed into the woods with a ground-eating stride. She had the feeling he would've walked all the way back to his den butt-naked, but someone must have called for backup because a jeep pulled up as they emerged from the trees at the park's south end.

A pretty black-haired woman rolled down the window. "Need a ride?"

"Dina," said Jace. "Right on time."

"Anything for you, boss." She gave Evie a friendly smile and hopped out to open the back door.

Jace helped Evie into the jeep and then donned the shorts Dina tossed him. Sitting next to Evie, he pulled her onto his lap. She snuggled against his chest and heaved a sigh.

"That's it." He stroked her nape. "It's over."

She nodded against his shoulder and burrowed closer. He smelled sweaty and a little earthy, and all male. She tongued the ridge of his collarbone, tasting the salt.

His eyes creased in the smile she thought of as all her own. "What was that for?"

"Just because." *I love you.*

"I like it." He dropped a kiss on the top of her head. "Do it whenever you want."

Jace said they were mates, but she knew from Suha it wasn't a done deal. The woman had to accept the bond.

Her chest constricted. Because it wasn't just her—she had Kyler to consider, too.

36

____

$\mathcal{A}$dric stared down at Tyrus's badly burned body. Marjani was explaining what had happened, including the fact that it was Evie who had somehow fried Tyrus with a fae ball.

Adric didn't give a flying fuck that the man was dead, but —"The prince can't know we did this."

Tyrus had been Langdon's last living son. The night fae prince was going to be out for blood, and if he found out the Baltimore clan was involved, the Darktime would look like a warm-up compared to what he'd bring down on them.

"Agreed," said Marjani.

He eyed her. He didn't need anyone to tell him that she'd struck the final blow. The knife work had her signature. "You okay?"

She stared back with chocolate-colored eyes shot with the chill blue of her cougar. "Yeah."

"Good," he said, although he wasn't so sure she *was* okay. But what was done was done, and she'd only done what she'd had to. "We've got to make him disappear—completely. Call the engineers and tell them to bring explosives." Marjani needed something to do, something human to keep her cougar at bay.

While she started making the calls, Zuri organized the soldiers to bury Tyrus in the soil beneath Corban's lair and clear the surrounding area of any trace of him. No one could know he'd been here.

Adric climbed the ladder to check on Jace and Evie. Tommy, a young male who was training with Suha, was working over Jace. Jace's wounds were partly healed, but his quartz was blown out, explaining why he'd gone dead to Adric. He'd have to find a new one.

Evie sat close by, dressed only in a bra and bloodied pants. Her face was smudged with dirt, her gaze hollow. Adric knew that expression; it was that of someone who'd been pushed to her limit.

He stripped off his T-shirt. "Here. Put this on."

She nodded and lifted her arms like a child. He dropped it over her head. He wasn't a big man, but she was swamped by the gray cotton. A delicate blond fairy, all the glow stripped from her.

He muttered something dark.

Jace curled his fingers over hers and the thousand-yard stare left her eyes. She glanced at Jace. The look that passed between them made something deep and unacknowledged in Adric constrict. So his best friend had found his mate.

He was happy for Jace, of course, but a part of him cried out, *Why not me?* And then he thought of Rosana and clenched his right hand.

While the healer worked on Jace, Zuri walked over to ask about Corban and Kane.

"Kane's dead," Adric told him. "Corban got away. The bastard sacrificed his own brother to save his hide."

Marjani had come up in time to hear that last part. She shook her head. "He's gone rogue."

Adric nodded grimly. "I've got a kill order out on him."

"It's worse than you think. He didn't just help Tyrus kidnap Jace. He sold Jace's quartz to him."

Adric's gut tightened. "He gave him the secret?" He glanced down at Jace, who nodded.

"Fuck." Even knowing Corban as he did, Adric found it hard to believe. Earth fada swore to guard the secret of the quartz with their lives. As it was, most fae treated the fada as their pet mercenaries and errand boys. If the secret of the earth fada's quartz became general knowledge, they could turn the earth clans into slaves.

"I'll let the other earth alphas know." This was no longer simply a battle for supremacy between Adric and Corban; it was a full-out war. Every earth fada in the world would be on the lookout for Corban now, with orders to execute him on sight.

Adric glanced at the dank cellar where Tyrus's body lay. "Thank the gods the man's dead, or I'd have to kill him myself."

"But did he tell anyone else?" Marjani spoke before he could. "His father?"

Adric grimaced. He was still reeling from the information that Leron had invited the night fae into Baltimore. The idea of Prince Langdon having that kind of power over the clan made his stomach churn. *What did the prince know?*

An hour later, it was done. Tyrus was in a shallow grave beneath the dirt floor, and every trace of his scent was removed from the area.

Just to make sure, one of their explosive experts—a woman barely out of her teens—set off a charge after everyone was out. The rest of them watched from a safe distance as the earth rumbled and shook, and then collapsed inward.

Adric didn't kid himself that this was the end of it. Langdon would eventually track down his son's remains, and he might even suspect the earth fada—but he wouldn't have proof.

And if he went after the clan anyway, well, Adric would cross that bridge when he came to it.

37

*T*wo grim-faced fada were guarding Jace's entrance. Jace stopped to talk to them, but Evie pushed past them to run down the steps to the den.

Beau opened the door for her. She barely noticed him saying hello, her gaze searching the room for Kyler.

His face lit up. "Evie!" He bounded off the couch toward her and then halted. "You're okay?" He rubbed his hands nervously over his shorts.

She gathered him into a hug. "I'm fine." Her vision blurred, and for a few moments, she just held him tight. Then she swiped a hand over her eyes and pulled back to look him over. "What about you? You're okay? The wolves—they didn't hurt you?"

"Nah." Kyler knuckled a tear from his cheek and she pretended not to notice. "They left right after you. But you...that prick didn't—"

"I'm fine," she repeated, because he didn't need to know how close Tyrus had come to breaking her. "Jace was with me." She nodded at Jace, who had come up behind her.

"Thank you." Kyler stuck out a hand to the earth fada.

Jace ignored his hand to pull him into a hug. "Hey, it was a team effort. Your sister smacked the bastard with a fae light."

"You did?" Kyler's gaze swung to her. "Seriously?"

"Yeah. Don't ask me how."

Kyler looked back at Jace. "He's dead? You're sure?"

"Yes."

"Good," Kyler said, low and vicious. "Because I was the one who let him in. I'm sorry, but I couldn't help it. I—"

"You did?" Evie knit her brow. "But why?"

"He got to me." His Adam's apple worked. "He—showed me things. Of you, dead—all of you. And—and—" He pressed his knuckles into his eyes. "I'm sorry. So sorry."

"Oh, Kyler. It's okay—you don't have to talk about it." She took a step toward him, but Beau was there first, dropping a massive arm around his shoulders.

"You have nothing to be sorry about. The man was a fucking fae lord—one of the strongest night fae around. It could've happened to anyone."

"But it didn't." Kyler's eyes were stark in his narrow face. "It was me he got to. Me who let him in—and not just him, but the wolves. And Horace—he's hurt bad. Suha's still with him. Sam's hurt, too, but not as bad."

"Horace is hurt?" Evie's stomach tightened. She met Jace's eyes.

"Fuck," he said, and strode toward the bedrooms.

Her brother hung his head. "If he dies, I'll never forgive myself."

Evie's heart hurt for him. It could've easily been her—she knew all too well how strong Tyrus was. "It's not your fault. I know. He tried that crap on me, and I...I couldn't break away."

"Really?" Kyler shot her a hopeful look. Then he shook his head. "But at least no one got hurt because of you. I'm the fucking weak human."

Evie swallowed and tried to think of something to say, but

Beau just gave him a shake. "Enough with the self-pity," he growled.

Kyler flushed. "Sorry," he mumbled.

Beau gave him a squeeze and then released him and headed for the kitchen. "I could use your help here," he said over his shoulder. "Suha's going to be starving when she gets done with Horace, and your sister and Jace could use some food, too."

"Kyler," Evie said. "Horace is going to be okay. Suha's good at what she does."

He nodded, and then gave a little shrug. "I'd better help Beau. You don't want to mess with a bear."

"Yeah." She watched, bemused, as he hurried after Beau. *What had just happened?* But that rough male compassion seemed to be exactly what her brother needed.

She left the two of them debating whether to make breakfast or lunch and headed after Jace.

Horace was on his back, the cover drawn up to his waist. Evie sucked in a breath. He was so still, his cheekbones tinted a fevered red. Suha hovered over him like a benevolent witch in a lime green tunic, her quartz glowing. On the other side of the bed, Jace had pulled up a chair and had Horace's hand clasped between his two palms. His jaw was set. He looked like he was trying to heal his friend through sheer willpower.

Evie touched Suha's shoulder. "Can I help?"

The healer shook her head. "Almost done," she muttered.

Evie set her hands on Suha's back anyway and concentrated on sending her energy.

The healer visibly perked up. A minute later she sat back. "There," she said with satisfaction. She put a hand to her sacrum, massaging it. Her pretty face was drawn, but she winked at Evie. "Thanks for the boost. He's going to be all right."

Tears stung Evie's eyes. She met Jace's eyes across the bed. The relief on his face made her heart twist. "Good," she said. "That's good."

Horace's eyes opened and he glanced from Jace to Evie. "You're all right," he murmured. "I thought—"

"No fucking traitor is going to take me out. Or a fae, either."

"Yeah." Horace's mouth curled in a shadow of his usual smile. His gaze moved to Evie. "Sorry, love. Tried...to stop them."

She touched his hand. "I know."

"Don't talk, you ass," Jace said tenderly. "Save your breath to get better. We're fine, and that motherfucking fae is dead. Here." He slid an arm under Horace's shoulders and held a glass of water to his lips.

The other man drank thirstily before sinking back onto the pillows. Then his eyes popped open, and he clutched Jace's wrist. "What about...Corban and Kane?"

"Kane's dead," Jace assured him. "But Corban got away. Adric said a fae 'ported him out."

"Lord Prick?"

"Nah. We're not even sure it was a night fae."

"Well. Two...out of three...ain't bad.'

"Horace needs to rest," Suha inserted. "You, too," she told Jace and Evie. "The two of you look like you're running on fumes. If a night fae fed on you, you need to recharge. That's the alpha's order, by the way."

But they waited until Horace's eyes closed before slipping out of the room.

"Shower first," she said. "I can still smell that night fae on me." Residual fear rippled up her spine. She had a feeling she was going to have nightmares about Tyrus for a long time.

Jace's fingers spread across the small of her back, large and warm. "It's over, angel."

"Yeah. And the good guys won, didn't they?" She gave him a crooked smile.

"You go ahead," he told her. "I have to call Rock Run."

"I'll wait."

She listened as Jace patched into the Rock Run Clan's landline and asked for Rui do Mar. "You didn't hear this from me," Jace told him, "but Tyrus is dead."

He wrapped an arm around Evie's shoulder and she leaned close, nuzzling his neck. She couldn't hear Rui's side of the conversation, but she could guess the river fada was relieved.

"Yeah," said Jace. "I think he planned to go after your family next."

Rui's growl came through the phone. Jace held it away from his ear.

The other man spoke and Jace nodded. "You're welcome. Tell Merry I love her and I'll be up to see her in a couple of days." He ended the call and brushed his lips over Evie's. "How about that shower?"

He nudged her into the bathroom, locking the door behind them and stripping off his shorts. She had time to remove her shirt, and then he pushed her up against the stone wall. Hot and aroused, and yet his fingers on her face were so gentle, fresh tears welled up.

She blinked them back. "I don't know why I keep crying."

"Reaction. It hits everyone a little different. Me, I'd like to rip Corban's head off. We'll find him, I promise you."

"I know." Because these men weren't going to let a threat like Corban walk around alive for long.

Jace set his forehead against hers. Concern poured off him. "Don't ever do that to me again—go off with a fucking night fae. My heart can't stand it."

She was tired and hungry, but at his touch, a slow burn started in her belly. Her fingers slid into his hair. "It's not like he gave me a choice."

"I don't care." He brushed away her tears with his thumbs. "Promise me anyway." He didn't wait for an answer, just slanted his mouth over hers. His tongue swept inside, tasting her deeply. She sucked on it, and he groaned, a primal sound that made her insides tingle.

His mouth moved to the turn of her shoulder, his night beard an erotic scrape against her skin. He bit her—a sharp nip that made her nipples pebble. "I'm mate-claiming you."

Yes, shouted her heart. But practical Evie said, "What does that mean?"

His gaze bored into hers. "That you're mine—forever. Any objections?"

"I—" He was moving at the speed of light. She felt like she was on a carnival ride, whipping dizzily through space. Her fingers dug into his shoulders, seeking equilibrium.

But he seemed to want her dizzy. Green fire flashed in his irises. "Mine." The word was intensely possessive—but his hands moved over her as if she were the greatest treasure on Earth. Tracing the line of her collar bone...cupping her breasts...teasing her nipples through the satin bra until her knees turned to jelly. She would've slid down the wall if he wasn't holding her up.

Kisses seared her throat, the tender skin of her cleavage. Need washed through her, rich and intoxicating.

Her head fell back against the wall. If it were only her, she'd take the chance—jump on the ride with Jace and see where it led. But it wasn't only her.

She caught his wrists, stopping those clever fingers as they started down her abdomen. "I want to say yes—you know I do—but I have Kyler to think about."

Jace didn't hesitate. "He's mine, too. I always wanted a kid brother."

God, she loved this man.

"But—"

He lifted his head. "What are you afraid of, Evie? Because I'm not sure this is only about Kyler."

"What do you mean? Of course, it is."

"Is it? Or are you afraid that someday I'll leave you—that it's just for a few years like your mom and dad?"

She opened her mouth to say no, and then swallowed. "How do you know it isn't?"

"Because we're mates. I'd cut off my hand before I'd leave you. Say yes, and you'll see."

"Jace—" She shook her head, unable to bring herself to say the word.

He blew out a breath. "There are no good choices here, Evie. I hate like hell that I dragged you into this, but you're a part of it now. And your being part fae means you might not be able to hide in the human world, either. If another night fae finds you…"

She felt her face drain of color.

"I'm sorry, Evie. But I'd die for you and Kyler."

"I don't want you to die for us!"

"I know." He smoothed his fingers over the short hairs at her temples. "But I would, and that's part of it. We brought Tyrus down together, and even then, we needed Marjani to finish it. That's what being a clan means."

She chewed her lower lip. "I can't go back, can I?"

"Afraid not, angel."

"And Kyler will be a member of your clan?"

"Adric will make sure of it. Kyler wants this, Evie. You know he does. He needs something to be a part of."

She stared at him, and then it struck her. This man would have her back until she was old and gray. It would not be her mom and Fane all over again because Jace was committing himself to her, body and soul.

And more, he was right about Kyler. Her brother wanted this —no, he needed this. They both did.

She cupped his hard, beautiful face. "Kiss me."

His eyes flickered green and gold—and then the corners creased in a smile that wrenched her heart. His kiss this time was lazy and sweet. The kiss of a man who knew what he was doing. And when he was done, she felt thoroughly claimed.

She pulled back to scrutinize him. "And you? It works both ways, right? You're mine, too."

"You have to ask?"

She shook her head. Because her heart knew the answer.

His hands went to work again, stroking her to madness. He nipped her lower lip, and then sucked on the small hurt. "Say yes, angel. The woman has to accept the claim."

She nodded. "Suha told me."

"Ah…" His mouth edged up against hers. "I can see you two are going to be a force to be reckoned with."

Her dimple flashed. "Yeah, I guess we are."

His breath caught. Love poured into her. She basked in it like a flower in the sun, and returned it with equal passion.

It was too fast; he was a fada and she was some bizarre human-fae mix. She had Kyler to think about, and how the two of them would fit into Jace's world.

But it felt *right*. One thing she knew was that this man would never leave. As for the rest, they'd make it work.

Teeth closed on her earlobe. "Say yes, Evie."

She wound her arms around his neck. "Yes."

JACE SHUT his eyes in gratitude. *Thanks all the gods.*

He should sit Evie down, make sure she understood what it meant to mate with a dominant fada male. The commitment was deep, intense, unbreakable. He'd be possessive and maybe a little overprotective, but he trusted that she'd let him know when he went too far. Nobody pushed his Evie around.

She *knew*. At some basic level, she knew. She was his, and he was hers—until death and maybe even beyond. The mate bond wouldn't have come to life otherwise.

With her *yes*, it took form in a way that was impossible to put into words. It just *was*—a magical ribbon running between him and Evie. Insubstantial and yet as real and bright as the three fae lights dancing gleefully about their heads.

Emotion swamped him. Love...desire...need. He rested his forehead against hers. "You won't regret it. I'll take care of you and Kyler. Anything you want, it's yours. You just have to ask—"

"Jace." Evie stopped his words with her fingertips. "All I want is you. Yeah, I could use help with Kyler, but only because he could use a man in his life. I'm not looking for anything else. We're in this together."

"Together. Right." He nodded while secretly resolving to help her however he could. But for now, he had a mate-claim to christen. He sucked her middle finger into his mouth, enjoying how her sable eyes darkened to near-black. "Now, about that shower..."

He helped Evie out of her pants and they stepped into the shower. He was still more than a little shaky. He'd have to find a temporary quartz to tide him over while he searched for a permanent replacement.

Evie wasn't much better. As he turned the handle to hot, she yawned and pinched the bridge of her nose. "I could sleep for a week."

He traced a finger down her straight nose, over the slope of her cheek. There were shadows under her eyes. His heart fisted. She might seem tough, but she was much more fragile than he.

No sex, then. Just loving care.

"I'll wash you." He encircled her waist with his arm and nabbed a bar of soap. "You don't have to do anything but relax."

"Mm." She leaned against him, her firm ass up against his groin. His cock sprang to attention, but he gritted his teeth and ignored it to concentrate on Evie. He rubbed the soap over her body in slow strokes, massaging her breasts, running his hand down her abdomen, then turning her around and giving the same careful attention to her back. He knelt to wash her legs and feet, and then stood back up. Squeezing some shampoo into his hand, he worked it into her short blond locks, massaging her scalp for good measure before continuing down to rub her neck and shoulders as well.

Her head lolled back against his chest. Water spilled over her face and her dimple flashed. "That feels so good."

He pressed a kiss to her cheek at the place where her dimple hid. It felt like a secret only he was privileged to know. "I love you."

"Love you too." She turned her head to kiss him.

She rinsed off and then picked up the soap. "My turn."

"You don't have to," he said, but she ignored him to slide the soap over his chest and abdomen. Then she soaped up her fingers and slid them down to where his erection jutted out, washing him with an excruciating care that had him groaning. "You're too tired," he made himself say.

The answer was a very Evie grin. "I'm reviving fast," she said, and gave him a good squeeze.

Heat shot through him, but he grinned back. Loving how nothing kept her down for long. Loving how she could always make him smile. Loving *her*.

He took the soap from her and set it on the ledge. Taking her by the shoulders, he backed her up against the wall and kissed her, slow and deep. She was still smiling; the curve of her lips imprinted itself on his.

Water streamed down his back. Evie twined a leg around his hip and pressed against his front, her nipples pebbled against his chest.

He gulped. "No," he said, although he was having a tough time recalling why not.

She tilted her head and gave him a wide-eyed look that made his breath snag. "Please?"

"You're a witch." He slid the broad head of his cock over her soft, welcoming folds.

Her breath hissed out. "Jesus."

"Is this what you want?" His jaguar rose up, the two of them intent on one thing: claiming their mate. He pinched one tightly furled nipple, and her eyes slit with enjoyment.

"Yes. That's... perfect." She undulated against him, sending a jolt of electricity to his balls.

She was wet and hot and so ready for him. "God's cat," he muttered as he rocked his hips against her, "you're so fucking sexy."

She squeezed his ass. "And you're so...hard." She nipped the sensitive skin beneath his jaw and the jaguar rumbled in approval.

"You like that?"

"Hell, yeah. Mark me."

She nipped him again, harder, sucking and biting at his skin until he knew he'd bear the print of her teeth. When she lifted her head, he held her against the wall and left his own mark at the turn of her neck. Everyone in the den would know he'd claimed her.

Both man and cat felt a primitive satisfaction at that.

He slid his hand down to toy with her clit. She made a murmur of pleasure and he slid his fingers into her folds. She was hot and slick and ready.

He kissed her again while his fingers kept up their slow dance: in and out of her passage, around her tight, swollen bud. Soft, teasing touches until she was writhing in his arms, her breath jerking in and out.

His muscles locked under the strain of holding back. But he kept it up until she said, "Jace," and started chanting "please" over and over.

"Take it," he growled against her ear. "Now." He dragged his fingers over her clit.

Her back bowed as she cried out his name. He kept up a steady, circling pressure until she went limp. "Oh. My. God."

He chuckled and gave her a soft kiss. "Be right back." Exiting the shower, he grabbed a rubber from a basket under the sink, worked it over his erection and returned.

Evie was slumped against the black tile wall, her creamy skin slick, her dark lashes spiked with water. Her nipples were a dusky rose that made his mouth water. She held her hand out to him with a secret little smile that shot straight to his groin.

He stalked toward her and lifted her up against the tiles so he could suck each nipple in turn. She moaned and gripped his nape. Sharp nails dug into his skin, stoking his arousal higher.

His cat purred. It liked a mate with claws.

He set his tip at her entrance and rocked his hips, small nudges until he was full seated. He expelled a harsh breath. She was so tight. So perfect.

Then she squeezed herself around him and his vision blurred.

He wrapped one arm around her shoulders, the other holding her hips to protect her from the hard tiles, and thrust into her. Harder this time.

Pleasure slammed up his spine. She tightened her legs around him and met him thrust for thrust. Her wet body was cool against his, but inside she was a silky hot glove.

On his chest, his quartz warmed, and a distant corner of his mind felt surprise. So it had some life in it after all.

He bent his knees and thrust straight up, hitting a spot deep inside Evie's womb that made her eyes roll back in her head. She gasped and clenched on him, rhythmic tightening that set up an answering pulse in his balls. It was too much. He buried his head in the side of her neck, tonguing the mark he'd made on her, and then joined with her, hard and fast until he came with a muttered curse.

He held himself deep inside, letting the hot, wet pleasure of her sweep over him. Wringing him out, and then filling him again to his very essence.

His breath scraped in and out of his lungs. He let her legs

slide down to touch the floor again as he said a prayer of thanks to the gods that had brought him to her door. He'd been only half-alive, his only focus work and Merry. Scarred and bitter from the Darktime, even more than he'd known.

Evie had saved him in more ways than one.

"Mine," he said one last time.

Her arms tightened on him without speaking. But he heard her answer loud and clear through their bond: *Yours.*

38

Beau and Kyler had settled on brunch. Evie and Jace emerged from the shower to find everyone in the kitchen, including Suha and the two hard-eyed soldiers, who were introduced as Ryder and Jamila.

Beau and Kyler were busy putting together breakfast burritos. A pitcher of orange juice and a bowl of ripe strawberries sat next to fresh salsa, and Suha handed Evie a mug of hot coffee as she entered the kitchen.

Jace fussed over Evie, having her sit and then filling a plate for her. When she started to protest, he stopped her with a kiss. "You'll find I take good care of my mate," he murmured against her lips.

"So do I." She tugged him down next to her. "Now eat." She made him a plate and set it before him. Then she noticed the open mouths. Everyone at the table was staring at them.

Suha recovered first. "You're mates—congratulations!" She jumped up and hugged Evie, and then frowned at Jace. "Does she know what that means?"

He wrapped a possessive hand around Evie's nape. "Of course."

Suha set a hand on her hip. "You know it's not binding unless the woman accepts. And she has to know exactly what she's getting into."

"Too late. She's already accepted the claim."

Suha opened her mouth to argue further, but Evie said, "It's okay—I know what it means, and I want it. I can feel him—here." She touched her chest. "The rest we can work out," she said with a smile at Jace, "as long as you all are okay with it. And Kyler, of course." She slid him a cautious look. She hadn't planned on making the announcement in front of five other people; she'd intended to talk to him privately after they ate. "But you seem to like everyone, and—"

"Hey," he said, "of course I'm okay with it."

Suha's face split into a grin. "I guess you do know. And of course we're okay with it. Welcome to the clan." She gave Evie another hug, and then the men were on their feet and hugging her, too.

"Guess we're all one big happy family, now," Kyler quipped as they took their seats again, but the look he shot Jace was wary.

Jace had taken a seat at the end of the table with Evie on one side and Kyler on the other. He dragged Kyler into a one-armed hug. "Yep. You're mine too, bro."

Kyler's shoulders relaxed. He squeezed Jace back and reached for more bacon. "Does this mean I get one of those quartz phones?"

Jace shook his head. "Sorry, they only work for fada or fae. You have to have some magic in your blood."

Her brother's face fell. "Not humans?"

"Not yet. But if we figure out the technology, you'll be first on the list."

Kyler brightened. "That's lit. I can be a test subject."

"It does mean we've always got your back," Beau rumbled.

"Even after what I did?"

Beau's bushy black brows lowered. "Hey, what did I say about that?"

"Sorry," Kyler muttered. "And I'll have yours, for what it's worth."

"Don't worry, we'll whip you into shape." Beau slapped Kyler on the back, nearly knocking him into his plate. Her brother just grinned and started eating again.

Adric, Marjani and Zuri arrived along with a man named Luc, a tall, rangy lieutenant with skin the color of teak who was Jace's fifth den mate. The three of them were somber when they arrived, but as soon as they heard the news, it turned into a celebration.

Adric pulled Evie out of her chair for a bear hug. "Welcome to the family, love. We'll make it official with a mate ceremony, but I'm claiming you and Kyler for the Baltimore clan." He kissed her on both cheeks, ignoring Jace's growled, "Get your own damn woman."

Then it was Zuri's turn. To her surprise, his dark eyes were smiling. "Welcome," he told her. "Jace is a lucky man."

For a moment Evie gaped at him. Then she recovered enough to shoot back, "Thanks. I think so, too."

Jace chuckled. Zuri grinned and gave her a hug that lifted her off her toes.

When she sat back down, Jace squeezed her knee. "They like you," he mouthed.

The noise level increased. Suha toasted Evie and Jace with orange juice, and Marjani brought Luc up to date on everything that had happened. It seemed he'd been in France tracking Tyrus, and was disgusted that he'd gotten back too late to help take the night fae down.

Jace informed Evie that Luc was a wolf, and seeing his cool amber eyes and lean, intelligent face, she could believe it. His expression only softened when he looked at Marjani, but she appeared not to notice.

After brunch, Adric and Marjani left along with the extra

soldiers. Jace changed the security code on the outside lock, and then they all took naps, even Kyler.

Jace spooned his hard body around Evie. "God's cat, I'm tired."

"Me too."

But when she closed her eyes, she saw Tyrus's beautiful face and those malevolent red eyes. An involuntary shiver traced up her spine. She opened her eyes and tucked Jace's arm closer around her.

He's dead. He can't hurt you now.

But then she saw his charred, lifeless body and that was almost worse. Because even though she knew it had been him or them, Tyrus might not be dead if not for her. Her chest tightened.

Jace pressed a kiss to her nape. "Want to talk about it?"

"Tyrus. I—"

He squeezed her waist. "You're safe, angel. I promise."

"I know, but—that was my first dead body. Well, except for my mom, and that was different."

"He needed to die."

"I know."

He stroked her abdomen. "Is it what he did before? When I was passed out?"

"That's part of it." She swallowed over the rock lodged in her throat. "I felt so violated. Why the fuck does it bother me that I helped kill him?"

Jace blew out a breath and said, "Because you're a good person. Nobody but a psychopath finds killing easy. Even when you have no choice, it haunts you."

"Yeah?"

"Yeah."

They were silent then, but his hand continued to move over her abdomen in slow, easy caresses. The constriction in her chest eased.

And this time, when her eyes drifted shut, she saw nothing.

39

---

*E*vie pulled her car onto the concrete pad. The lavender had bloomed; several fat bees were buzzing around the fuzzy purple spikes. Other than that, the house was unchanged, its gray Formstone exterior practically indestructible. Was it only Tuesday? It felt like they'd been gone a month.

She nudged Kyler, who was hunched over his phone playing a game. "We're home."

He pocketed the phone. "Looks like everything's still in one piece."

"Yeah." She couldn't help but smile; it was what their mom had always said.

Jace pulled his motorcycle to a stop behind them. Adric was sure Corban had left the country, but Jace wasn't letting Evie out of his sight. "There's still the night fae," he'd said. "We don't know what Tyrus told his lair."

If Jace wanted to stay close, that was fine with Evie—she wasn't an idiot. Besides, why would she want to be separated from her mate?

She watched in the rearview mirror as he removed his helmet

and glanced around, a badass fada in sunglasses and a worn leather jacket. Her womb clenched. She still couldn't believe he was hers.

She jerked her chin at the mirror. "You sure you're okay with this?" she asked Kyler. "Me and Jace?"

"Sure. I mean, how many guys have a shifter as a brother-in-law?"

"There is that." They exchanged a grin. "But seriously—we may have to move to Baltimore. I haven't talked to Jace, but I don't think he wants to live up here."

"I can adapt." Kyler reached into the backseat for their backpacks. "Don't forget, I'm not always going to be living with you. This way, I don't have to worry about you."

"Worry about me?" she repeated faintly.

"Yeah," he said as they got out of the car. "It goes both ways, you know."

She met his eyes over the car roof. "Yeah," she said. "I guess it does."

Mrs. Linney was on her stoop, heart-shaped sunglasses perched on her nose and a pink visor on her steel-gray curls. She waved her cigarette in their direction. "Hey, Evie. Kyler."

They waved back. "Morning, Mrs. Linney."

Jace set a hand on the small of Evie's back. She smiled up at him and turned to Mrs. Linney. "I want you to meet my friend—"

"Jace Jones. I remember. How are you, son?"

"Good," he returned politely. "And you?"

"Not bad." She dragged on her cigarette. To Evie she said, "I wondered where you were. I was fixing to call the police."

She grimaced. "Sorry about that. I would've told you but it was kind of sudden."

"Um-hmm." Mrs. Linney eyed Jace. "Well, as long as you're all right."

"We're fine. Thanks for keeping an eye on the house."

They headed up the gravel path. As Kyler unlocked the door, Evie's nape prickled and she was hit by a sense of déjà vu. This was how it had started, except instead of being dark and rainy, it was a sunny morning.

"Inside—both of you." Jace pushed her into the kitchen and turned to face the alley.

A tall man with white-blond hair sauntered into the yard. Jace tensed, but Evie set a hand on his arm. "It's okay. It's my dad." Trust Fane to show up when the danger was past.

"Evie, love." He held out his arms.

She slipped around Jace and down the steps. He was her dad, after all.

Long arms wrapped around her. "I hear you had a spot of trouble."

"You could say that." She rested her head against his shoulder. He smelled of the outdoors, a familiar grassy scent that made her eyes sting. "How did you know?" she asked as she released him and stepped back.

He moved a shoulder. "Word gets around. I came as soon as I could."

Jace came up beside her. "We handled it."

"Did you now?" Fane asked mildly.

Mrs. Linney wasn't even pretending not to eavesdrop. Fane nodded at her. "How are you, Betty?"

She beamed back. "Can't complain. And yourself?"

They exchanged a few words and then Fane set his arm around Evie's shoulders and headed with her toward the house. "Why don't we take this inside?" He quirked a brow at Jace, who was blocking the way. "Do you have something to say, fada?"

Jace shook his head and stepped aside. "Not here," he muttered.

In the kitchen, Evie got beers for Jace and Fane, and sodas for her and Kyler. They sat at the table, Evie and Kyler on one side, her dad across from them. Jace took a stance behind Evie, arms folded over his chest.

Fane studied them with clear blue eyes that somehow didn't give away a thing. As usual, his sharp-boned, handsome face hadn't aged a day. Pretty soon people were going to think he was her brother, not her father. He wore his usual loose linen shirt over skinny black jeans, and his pale hair was tied back with a leather cord so that you could see his ears. With a jolt, she saw they came to a point at the top. Why had she never noticed? But then, she hadn't been looking for proof her dad was part fae.

"Now what's this I'm hearing about you and a night fae?" Fane asked. "And why does this earth fada think he has a claim on you?"

Jace placed his hands on Evie's shoulders. "I'm her mate."

His dark brows shot up. "Are you now?"

"Yes." Jace's tone was that of a man who wasn't going to give an inch.

"This is true?" Fane asked her.

She touched Jace's hand. "Yes."

"Well," he drawled, "that's a complication I didn't expect."

"Why?" she asked.

Fane jerked his head at Kyler. "Why don't you leave us? There are some things it's best a human not know."

Kyler bristled, but before he could object, Evie said, "He stays. I'm not keeping secrets from my own brother."

Her dad's eyes narrowed but Evie simply stared back. Fane rubbed his lower lip and then inclined his head. "You'll promise to guard her secret, then," he said to Kyler. "It's for her safety as much as yours."

"Of course." Kyler folded his arms. "I'm not the problem here —you are."

Fane shrugged and turned back to Evie with a rueful smile, the one that could always get around her mom.

Evie stared back stonily. "I'm waiting."

"So I see." He took a sip of beer. "Where do I start?"

"How about with what kind of fae you are? And why you never told me? And why you left me and my mom—"

"Slow down, love." Fane held up a hand. "The first question's simple—ice fae."

"Ice fae?" Evie blinked.

"Not sun fae?" Jace inserted.

Her dad shook his head. "My father was half ice fae. I was born and raised in Canada. As for your other questions, well, let me tell you a little something about myself first."

Kyler moved restlessly. "Is this going to be one of your stories?"

Fane's blue eyes glittered. "Fae don't lie."

"But you're not pure fae, are you?"

"No, but the fae blood makes it hard for me to tell lies, and it hurts like a bitch if I do." He sat back, one arm on the chairback, long legs stretched out before him. "Do you want to hear this or not?"

"We do." Evie elbowed Kyler and he subsided.

"I'm not that old, as fae go," Fane said, "and I won't live as long as a pureblood. But I was born in the early 1900s. My father was an ice fae, and my mother was a human. They were mates, and he was faithful to her until she died. But I didn't grow up with the ice fae—they don't have much use for half-bloods. My father was stationed in Newfoundland by the ice fae king. He pays the half-bloods to keep an eye on things for him in various territories around the world."

"To spy for him," Jace said. "Just so we're clear."

Fane moved a shoulder. "The king likes to stay informed."

"Is he still alive?" Evie asked. "My...grandfather?"

"He is."

"But—didn't he ever want to meet me?"

"No." Fane's eyes slid away from hers. "I figured it was better that way—your world is the human world. Why complicate things by letting you know you have a bit of fae in you?"

"I see." Her tongue felt thick. This was a fresh hurt. It was bad enough to have a father who could go for years without seeming to recall her, but she hadn't even known her grandfather was alive —and worse, that he wanted it that way.

"I haven't seen him for years myself," Fane said. "My mother lived into her eighties. After she died, my father went a little crazy. It's hard on the fae, losing a mate. They say you feel like your heart is ripped out."

Behind her, Jace murmured agreement and squeezed Evie's shoulders. Love pulsed to her through their bond. Warmed, she sent a pulse back, still awed at this intimate connection they shared. A connection that told her Jace loved her no matter who or what her father was.

The hurt faded. Because she had Jace at her back, caressing her shoulders, and Kyler at her side, glaring at Fane.

"We lost touch," Fane continued, "but last I heard Father was in Patagonia for some damn reason. As for me, I'm one of the king's envoys."

"An envoy? You're some kind of messenger?"

He nodded. "Turns out I have the fae Gift of wayfaring, which is rare in a quarter fae."

"That's what Jace said the night fae was," Evie said.

"Lord Tyrus? Word is he's dead." Fane glanced from her to Jace.

Evie's chest tightened. Jace gripped her shoulders, asking her to let him handle this. "Is he?"

Fane recognized evasion when he saw it. "The son of the night fae prince," he confirmed. "As you know damn well—and that's why I'm here."

"What d'you mean?" Jace asked.

"I'll get to that in a minute."

Jace rumbled irritably, but Fane just lifted a brow. "You don't scare me, fada."

"Then you're a fool," he shot back.

"No. Just a man who's smart enough to know you won't attack your own mate's father."

That silenced Jace. He gave a terse nod. "Go on."

"You're right that Tyrus was a wayfarer," Fane told Evie, "but his Gift was to move very fast. Mine is different—I blend into my surroundings. Even if you know I'm there, your gaze slips right past me. You never see me unless I want you to."

"So you sneak up on people?" Kyler inserted.

"You could put it that way." Fane gave him a cool, dangerous smile, and Evie instinctively jumped in to draw his attention back to her.

"And you work for the ice fae king?"

Fane inclined his head. "I'm part messenger, part negotiator. The king can send his own messages, but for some things, he needs an envoy who can carry a message back, or cut a deal if need be. Or simply observe and report back."

Evie's hands balled on her lap. "You should never have married my mom."

"I didn't. We weren't married, and we weren't mates."

"Oh." She swallowed. "I didn't know that."

Sorrow flickered across Fane's fine-boned face. "I know I hurt her, and I'm sorry for that. I wouldn't have done that for the world."

"But you did."

"She wasn't supposed to have a child. Usually only mates can conceive." Fane passed a hand over his face. "Hell. That sounds as if I didn't want you, love, but I did. I was so happy when your mother told me about you. Believe that if nothing else. As for why I never told you?" He moved a shoulder. "I intended to get around to it someday. You don't have a fae Gift, so it didn't seem urgent."

Evie scraped a hand over her hair. She'd sort through this later. "So what about me and the fae lights?"

"What do you mean?"

She opened her backpack and lobbed one at him. Fane threw up a hand and it smacked against his palm. They all heard the sizzle.

"Holy mother." Fane swatted the glowing orb away. "Did you make that yourself?"

"No. I brought it from Jace's den." Actually, a fae light had split itself in two, and one half had floated into her backpack while the other half remained back in Baltimore.

"So it's a fae light?"

"Yes," said Jace. "But she used it against the night fae. Not that it killed him, you understand. But it did burn him—bad."

"How about that?" Fane rubbed his chin. "Your great-grandfather is one of Sindre's top warriors. He can make fae balls from the energy in oxygen. If you hit someone hard enough, it's like tossing a grenade at them—and poof." He opened his fingers. "They're gone."

Evie's mouth dropped open. "So you're saying I'm a fae warrior?"

"You're freaking kidding me." That was Kyler. He'd straightened and was eyeing Evie with shock.

"Not unless you can make a fae ball yourself," her dad replied.

She shook her head. "I can't."

"Have you tried?"

"No. It didn't even occur to me."

"If you have the Gift for it, you simply visualize one into being." Fane nodded at her. "Go ahead—give it a try."

Evie looked at Jace, who gave her an encouraging squeeze.

"Try it, Evie." That was Kyler.

With a shrug, she opened her hand and visualized a fae ball shimmering in it. But it was like when she'd tried to heal Suha's bruise—nothing happened, except the fae light drifted across the table to settle into her palm. With a flick of her fingers, she sent it spinning into the air and tried again, jaw set, but still nothing happened.

"Take a deep breath," Fane suggested. "Imagine it forming in your hand."

Evie dragged in a breath and obeyed, but again, nothing happened. She didn't even feel her hand warm like when she'd added her energy to Suha's.

She shrugged. "So much for my career as a fae warrior."

Fane's long fingers touched hers. "Don't be disappointed."

"I'm not, really. I want to be a healer, not a warrior." She thought of the burns on Tyrus and stifled a shudder. She never wanted to do that to anyone again.

"But," said Fane, "maybe you inherited enough of your grand-father's ability to use a fae light in a similar way."

"She's an amplifier," Jace said. "She helped heal me."

"Ah." Her dad looked impressed. "That's a Gift indeed."

Jace released Evie to set both hands on the table. "You won't tell the ice fae about her," he said in a hard voice.

"Do you think they don't already know? I reported her birth to the king. But I won't tell him about her Gift, no."

"Good. Because if anyone comes after my mate, I'll rip your head off your body, Evie's father or not."

"Stop it, Jace!" Evie grabbed his arm and tried to give him a shake, but it was like trying to move a stone wall.

The two men ignored her. "I don't want that any more than you do," her father said. "She's my daughter, after all."

"Then swear it. I want your word that no one will learn of Evie's Gift from you."

"You have it."

"The words," Jace said between his teeth.

Fane inclined his head. "I vow before all three of you that no one will learn of Evie's Gift from me."

The tension went out of Jace. "Good." He came upright again.

"But why would the ice fae come after me?" Evie asked. "It's not like they've cared about me up until now."

"It's not just healers that can use an amplifier," Fane said. "A warrior could use you to make more powerful fae balls, for instance."

"And the night fae would just keep you to feed on," said Jace.

Goosebumps popped up on Evie's arms. She rubbed her hands over them, and instantly, Jace was behind her again, caressing her shoulders.

"That's what Tyrus told me," she said. "That he liked to feed on other fae."

"He didn't realize you were an amplifier?" Fane asked sharply.

"No."

"Thank the gods. Whatever happens, the night fae can't know. They won't hesitate to feed from a mixed-blood. They lump us with the humans and fada," he added with a twist of his lips.

"They'd have to get past me first," Jace growled.

Her father nodded. "Perhaps it's not a bad thing you two mated, then."

Jace folded his arms over his chest. "I take care of the ones I love, fae. Can you say the same?"

"It's fair that you ask, which brings me to the reason I'm here." Fane produced a silver-and-gold pendant suspended from a leather cord and handed it to Evie.

She turned it over in her hands. It was clearly fae made—an intricately crafted cutout of a gold sun cupped by a silver half-moon.

"Fire and ice," her dad murmured. "Sun and moon. A protection charm made by one of the best spellcasters I know. Together, the sun and moon will reflect into the eyes of anyone who might come looking for you, blinding them to your fae nature. Put it on."

Evie's vision blurred. "Thank you." She swallowed over the lump in her throat and slipped it over her head.

Fane shrugged. "I'm a terrible father, but I'll be damned if one of those night fae bastards comes after my only daughter again."

Evie touched the pendant. It was so light she could barely feel it, and yet it hummed with power. "It's beautiful. Thank you."

"Think of me when you wear it—and if I were you, I'd wear it everywhere, even to bed."

She nodded. "I will."

Fane rose to his feet and extended a hand to Jace. "Peace to you and yours, Jace Jones."

Jace's eyes flashed a predatory green, and Evie knew he was wondering how Fane knew his full name. But he shook the proffered hand. "Peace to you and yours...and thanks for the charm."

Evie stood up as well. "You don't have to run off. I can make you lunch. I—"

"Thank you, but I should go. I'm not supposed to be here as it is."

She felt a hint of the old hurt, but it was muted. She rose on her toes to kiss Fane's cheek. "You're welcome anytime."

"I know." He squeezed her shoulders. "You'll be moving to Baltimore?"

"I'm not sure," she said with a glance at Jace, who said, "For the summer at least." He gave Fane the address.

Her father gave her a last hug and then nodded at Jace. "You'll keep her safe." It wasn't a question.

"Like you care," Kyler muttered, but Jace slung an arm around Evie's shoulder.

"She's my mate," he said simply.

Fane nodded. "As for you—" He turned to Kyler, who raised his chin.

"What?"

"That mouth of yours is going to get you in trouble someday.

But you're loyal. Evie's lucky to have you." He tossed something glittery into the air.

Kyler snatched it and then stared down at it, mouth ajar. "It's another fucking diamond." He held it up and it caught the morning sun, and for an instant, Evie was blinded. The back door opened and shut, and when she could see again, her dad was gone.

"Ice fae, huh?" Kyler touched Evie's arm, his expression mock-serious. "You don't feel cold."

She knocked his hand away, and then burst out laughing. "Go soak your head, squirt."

40

———

Merry jiggled Jace's arm. "Where is she? It's after seven o'clock."

"Calm down. She'll be here." He smiled down at his niece, but inside he was almost as jittery. Not because he was afraid Evie wouldn't show, but because he was as excited as Merry. But then, a man had a right to be excited at his own mate ritual.

They were in his backyard. It was mid-July, more than a month since Tyrus's death. The evening sun cast long shadows across the lawn, but the fae balls had blossomed into life, illuminating the crowd. People stood on the back porch and spilled down the driveway, members of the clan rubbing elbows with Jace's neighbors. Some of the cougars and jaguars were perched on the roof.

There was even a family of river fada—Valeria and Rui do Mar, along with their two young children—invited at Evie's request, because Merry wanted them there. Jace had always liked Rui's dark-haired Portuguese mate, but it was a revelation to see the strong, silent shark with a toddler on one shoulder, tugging on his ear, and another pint-sized person wrapped like a vine around his leg.

Jace kissed the top of Merry's head. "You look beautiful, by the way. Your mom—Takira—would've been so proud of you."

"Really?" She shot him a pleased look and smoothed her hands down the skirt of the flirty red dress she'd somehow talked Valeria into.

"Absolutely. I like that crown-thing you did with your hair."

"My friend Rosana did it." Merry touched the braids wrapped around her head. "Thanks for inviting me to be part of your mate ceremony."

"It was both our ideas. Evie likes you."

"I like her, too. And Kyler."

Jace smothered a smile. Kyler had taken Merry under his wing. He was loving the chance to be a big brother—and Merry hung on his every word. It was good for Kyler. The kid was still beating himself up for letting Tyrus in. He'd asked Marjani to teach him how to handle a knife, and to everyone's surprise, she'd agreed.

"You look good, too," Merry told him. "I've never seen you in a suit before."

He looked down at the slim gray suit and white button-up shirt he'd donned for the ceremony. "I wanted to look nice for Evie."

Merry adjusted the white rose pinned to his lapel. "She's going to love it."

Suha appeared from his den and held up five fingers. "Five minutes," she mouthed.

Jace nodded at Zuri, who began clearing a path from the shed to the flower-entwined arch under which he and Merry stood. Meanwhile, Adric started through the crowd to take his place for the ceremony.

Merry fingered her quartz. "I wish I could remember my first mom. I can remember Silver a little. He did magic tricks and bought me that clown." Jace nodded. Merry's clown was the only thing she had from her old life, since Tyrus's men had torched her house as she escaped with Rui. "But I don't even know what Takira looked like."

Jace's heart squeezed. "She looked a lot like you, sweetheart. You both take after my mom—your grandmother. You have Takira's hair, her eyes. But inside, that's where you're most like her." He tapped Merry's narrow chest. "You have a jaguar's heart. Forget that bullshit you hear about lions—they only rule in Africa. In the rainforest, jaguars are the biggest, baddest cats around."

Adric arrived in time to hear that last part. He snorted. "As long as they don't run into a cougar."

Merry giggled at the two of them, but her shoulders straightened.

Then Jace forgot everything else as Evie stepped into the yard on Kyler's arm. He'd always thought she glowed, but now she shone as bright as the sun. All the air left his lungs in a whoosh.

She wore a simple cream dress with broad straps that left her toned arms bare. Jace had drilled a hole in the rose quartz he'd given her, and it hung around her neck next to her dad's charm. Her only other ornaments were the glittering silver star in her short blond hair and the matching stars on her strappy sandals. Her mouth was painted a bright red, and her eyes were dark and a little mysterious.

She strolled toward him, his beautiful, edgy, sexy-as-hell angel, and he wondered how the fuck he'd gotten so lucky as to get stabbed practically on her doorstep.

Then her fingers wrapped around his arm, and together, they turned toward Adric, waiting to bless their mating. Three fae lights wafted closer, casting a soft gold and pink light over the proceedings.

Adric was smirking as if he'd arranged the whole thing. "Welcome," he said in a carrying voice to the assembled throng. "We are gathered today to celebrate the mating of Jace and Evie. Peace to you and yours."

"Peace," the crowd returned.

Adric spoke a few more words, and then nodded to Jace. The alpha might introduce and bless a mating, but the words were spoken by the couple themselves.

Jace took Evie's hands. Her dimple flashed at him, and he stared back unsmiling, emotion clogging his throat. He cleared it and said, "I take you, Evie Morningstar, as my mate. My light. My heart. You bring out the best in me, and I will love you for all of my days."

They'd chosen a bracelet to mark their mate-day. He slipped it on her. The jeweler had created a striking design of silver vines entwined around a translucent green chalcedony quartz.

Evie bit her lower lip. She firmed her chin and then met his eyes. "I take you, Jace Jones, as my mate. My lover. My panther. My soul. I wasn't looking for you, but somehow you found me, and I will always be grateful. I love you."

Jace removed his quartz pendant and undid the clasp, and she slipped a tiny rose quartz in the shape of a heart onto the cord. The heart had belonged to his mom, an anniversary gift from his dad. It settled next to Jace's quartz with a click, and he could've sworn he felt a jolt of love.

Adric spoke the words of blessing and then formally welcomed Evie and Kyler into the clan. He finished by pulling Evie into a big hug. "Thanks for taking him on." He gave her a smacking kiss on the mouth.

Evie grinned as Jace retrieved her and tucked her firmly up against his side. "He doesn't scare me." She nipped Jace's neck, and then let out a chuckle that ended in a gasp as he bent her backward over his arm for a kiss.

He took his time, exploring her mouth, mate-claiming her in front of his entire clan. When he released her, her eyes were smoky, and he'd almost forgotten their audience. "Later," he murmured with a slow wink as behind them, his pumped-up clan hooted and clapped.

The street had been blocked off for the evening. Sam and Horace, both almost completely recovered, were supervising two huge barbecue grills, and Zuri had cracked open a keg of beer and was handing out mugs as fast as he could fill them.

Jace wrapped an arm around Evie and turned to face the crowd. "Who wants to party?"

EPILOGUE

"No," Marjani growled. "He's trying to get you to follow him. It's a trap."

Adric put his fork down. They were in the kitchen eating scrambled eggs and ham. Marjani had surprised him by having breakfast ready when he'd walked in the door that morning—and then she'd told him Corban had sent a message.

See you in Reykjavik.

It was a fucking dare.

"Do you really think Corban's stronger than me?" he asked. It had been six weeks since his cousin had disappeared. Adric had alerted the other earth alphas about Corban's treachery, but it was as if his cousin had dropped off the face of the earth. But if he was in Iceland, that explained why they couldn't find him; King Sindre didn't allow any fada clans that close to home.

Marjani blew out a breath. "Of course not. But he's not working alone. Maybe Tyrus is dead, but that doesn't mean Corban's not working with another night fae. And then there's the ice fae, too."

Adric took a gulp of coffee. Hot as Hades and liberally dosed with cream, it washed away the bitter taste that filled his mouth every time he recalled that Leron had invited the night fae into Baltimore, and then stood by while they manipulated things to get darker and darker, just so they could fucking feed. Like there wasn't enough darkness in the world for them to draw on already.

Holy mother, if Adric ever grew that power-hungry, he hoped his lieutenants would put him down like a rabid dog.

"I need to find out who in the ice fae is helping him—and why. Is it that ice fae woman I sent him to capture last year? Or the king himself? And how does Nika fit into this?"

"Not the ice fae woman. If it was her, Corban wouldn't try to get you to Reykjavik. That's the heart of Sindre's territory."

He shook his head. "Whoever's working with him, I have to go. He's my responsibility." He'd promised the other alphas that he'd take care of Corban, once and for all.

"No—I'll go. The clan needs you right now."

He scraped a hand over his hair. His sister was the one with a Gift for strategy. When she spoke, a wise alpha listened. And she was right—people were still reeling from the recent attacks by Tyrus and Corban, and Kane's death hadn't helped. There were whispers that Adric intended to wipe out that entire branch of the Savonett family, even though Nash himself said that Corban was the one at fault.

The clan was seething. Mistrust. Fear. Anger. Everything Adric had worked so hard to put behind them.

And then there was Prince Langdon. The night fae ruler had been seen in Baltimore twice in the last six weeks, when he normally came to the city only once every five years, if that much.

But damn it, sending Marjani to Iceland wasn't an option. "Absolutely not," he told her. "You're too—" He halted as her shoulders hunched.

"Weak," she finished for him.

His stomach hollowed. "Fuck, I'm sorry. I don't really think that. But I—"

She lifted her chin. "Maybe you're right. But I need to know, and that's never going to happen if I stay here in Baltimore. Everyone treats me like I'm made of frigging eggshells."

"What about Luc?" The lieutenant had loved Marjani for years. He'd waited patiently for her to heal, and these past few weeks, it had seemed Marjani was finally responding. She'd even danced with Luc last week at Jace and Evie's mating.

She arched a delicate brow. "What about him?"

Adric swallowed. He didn't hesitate to meddle in his clan members' lives if he thought it would do some good, but when his sister went all soft and curious, he'd learned to tread with care. "I thought maybe you and him—"

"No. We're friends, and that's all we'll ever be. And while we're on the subject, what's up with you and Rosana do Rio? Do you think I don't know you slip off to Grace Harbor just on the chance you'll run into her?"

Adric's chest tightened. Rosana was his guilty secret, even if he rarely got close enough to talk to her, let alone kiss her again like that night by the river. "Leave it," he growled.

Marjani's jaw set. "Only if you leave off me and Luc."

"Fine." He returned his attention to his breakfast.

They ate in silence until Marjani said, "There's something I'd like to know—why didn't the prince stop Tyrus? He had to know Tyrus was targeting Jace and the clan. You're not going to tell me a man like that doesn't know what his only son is up to."

"Think about it. Jace is one of the last people left who knows he had a half-blood son. Yeah, the prince kept Merry a secret for her own safety—but it benefits him, too. How long would he rule the night fae if they knew he had a child with a human? And worse, that his half-human son then mated with an earth fada— which means he's got a granddaughter who's part animal. You know how purebloods think."

Feral blue streaked his sister's eyes. "He'll protect Merry. She's family, and even a night fae feels that bond. But not Jace. It would be better for him if Jace was dead."

"And me," Adric returned with ruthless practicality. "If he knows anything about fada, he knows Jace wouldn't keep a secret like that from his alpha."

"Hell." Marjani scraped a hand over her cropped black hair. "I had to kill Tyrus. He wouldn't have stopped until Jace and Evie were both dead."

He touched her hand. "You did right. He was going to use Jace's quartz to force him to kill Merry—and then the protective spell would've killed Jace. You saved both their lives, and probably Evie's too."

"But the clan. I put all of you in danger. When the prince finds out—"

"He won't," Adric stated. "I obliterated every trace of Tyrus. And if he does, we'll just have to deal with it. I'll track him to his lair and take him out myself if I have to."

She nodded, and he thought that was the end of it.

But in the morning she was gone. Her smartphone was turned off, but the link between them told Adric she was on her way north. To Iceland.

And he literally shook with the need to follow.

But he couldn't, because Marjani was right, the clan needed him in Baltimore, especially with Langdon sniffing around. So he sent Luc instead—and prayed to all the gods that he'd made the right decision.

Charming Marjani: **The Darktime Trilogy continues...**

He's rich, sexy...and part-fae.
But she's a shifter assassin on a mission. She can't let herself be charmed...

Marjani Savonett is the strong, silent second-in-command to

her brother Adric, alpha of the Baltimore Earth Fada. She's seen too much death, lived through too much loss. Now her cat threatens to take over, leaving her a cougar in a human body. But before it does, she undertakes one last mission to Iceland.

Fane Morningstar holds a prestigious position as one of the ice fae king's envoys. But the fae never let him forget he's not a pureblood. Then he meets Marjani and everything he ever thought he wanted gets turned on its head. He'd sell his soul for a night with her.

Unfortunately, he just might have to...

Charming Marjani (#5, Fada Shapeshifters)
Get it now at your favorite store.

MARJANI'S SKIN PRICKLED. She sipped her ale and glanced around.

A tall, rangy man with shoulder-length blond hair slouched at a nearby table, drinking a beer. He met her eyes, not bothering to hide that he was checking her out.

Her breath snagged.

Holy singing crystals, he was beautiful, with slanted cheekbones and sky-blue eyes framed by dark eyelashes. His straight nose had a small bump on the bridge, a tiny imperfection that only heightened his appeal, and his black ribbed sweater stretched across a hard chest.

His cheek creased in a smile—and fear wrapped icy fingers around her lungs.

She jerked her gaze back to her sandwich, her stomach tight, heart thudding in her ears.

Fuck, she hated this. A couple of years ago, she might have smiled back, seen where this led. But not anymore. No one touched her. She didn't even let members of the clan get too close.

A shadow fell across the table.

She snarled, her cougar rising to meet the threat. She forced it down. Shifting in the middle of a human pub could be fatal. The fada and humans had treaties about those things. A fada shifting in a pub for no reason would be automatically targeted by the authorities as feral.

She could be shot on sight—or slapped into a cage.

And she'd have to admit Adric was right after all—she was too broken, too close to going feral, to be out on her own.

The tall blond smiled down at her. Spoke.

Still fighting the cougar, she had to concentrate to make sense of his words.

"I said, mind if I join you?" A surprisingly deep voice, gravel wrapped in silk.

She gave a shake of her head. "Yes."

He lifted a single dark brow. "No, you don't mind, or yes, you do?"

"Yeah, I mind. I don't want company."

His gaze went to the slight lump her quartz made beneath her sweater. "Your accent is American, which means you're from one of two clans."

Fine hairs rose all over her body. He was correct; the only earth fada clans in North America were her own clan in Baltimore and the Navajo clan in Arizona.

But how the hell had he made her as an earth fada so fast?

Her nostrils flared, subtly testing the air. Human—he smelled of salt and iron—but with a trace of silver. The man had fae blood, although it might be so faint he didn't know it himself. Overlaying it was a pleasant grassy scent, as if he spent a lot of time outdoors.

Her cat liked his smell, but the human part of her didn't like that hint of fae. Not on top of the fact that he knew a little too much about earth fada.

Easing the switchblade from her pocket, she released the catch.

"You don't want to use that." He set his plate and glass on her table and took the chair across from her.

"No?"

He leaned back in his chair and rested an arm on the back as if she were an old friend instead of a pissed-off shifter with a sharp blade aimed at his privates. "Too messy."

Read a longer excerpt on my website
(rebeccarivard.com/shapeshifters).
Or, get it now at your favorite store.

ALSO BY REBECCA RIVARD

The Fada Shapeshifter Series

The Rock Run River Fada

Stealing Ula: A Fada Shapeshifter Prequel (Nisio & Ula, set in Ireland)

The Rock Run River Fada

Seducing the Sun Fae (Dion & Cleia)

Claiming Valeria (Rui & Valeria)

Tempting the Dryad (Tiago & Alesia)

Sea Dragon's Hunger (Cassidy & Nic)

The Baltimore Earth Fada (The Darktime Trilogy)

Saving Jace (Jace & Evie)

Charming Marjani (Marjani & Fane)

Adric's Heart (Adric & Rosana)

Fada Shapeshifter Short Reads

Lir's Lady (#3.5—Lir & Isleen)

Shifter's Valentine (#3.6—Jenny & Chico)

To find out more, go to: https://rebeccarivard.com/shapeshifters/

The Vampire Syndicate Romances

Pursued (Gabriel)

Craved (Rafael)

Taken (Zaquiel)

The Vampire Blood Courtesans

Ensnared: Star

Compelled: Cerise

To find out more, go to: https://rebeccarivard.com/vampires/

Join ***Rebecca Rivard's newsletter*** to stay informed and be eligible for giveaways and sneak peeks. As a thank you, Rebecca will gift you with "Lir's Lady," a steamy short story!

Sign up at rebeccarivard.com or go to this link: Rebecca's newsletter

ABOUT THE AUTHOR

Rebecca Rivard read way too many romances as a teenager, little realizing she was actually preparing for a career. She now spends her days with dark shifters, sexy fae, vampires and other magical creatures—which has to be the best job ever. When she's not writing, she walks, bikes and kayaks in the Chesapeake Bay area with her guitar-playing, storytelling husband.

Five of her novels have been awarded the coveted Crowned Heart Review from *InD'Tale Magazine* and the FADA SHAPESHIFTER SERIES was voted Best Shifter Series in the Paranormal Romance Guild Reviewer's Choice Awards.

Her books have also won the prestigious PRISM Award (*Charming Marjani)* and the PRG Reviewer's Choice Award (*Saving Jace*), and have finaled in both the RONE and the HOLT Medallion.

www.ingramcontent.com/pod-product-compliance
Lightning Source LLC
Chambersburg PA
CBHW021758110726
47902CB00006B/1565